The Good The Bad and the Uncanny

TALES OF A VERY WEIRD WEST

Edited by Jonathan Maberry

THE GOOD, THE BAD, AND THE UNCANNY:
TALES OF A VERY WEIRD WEST

Published by Outland Entertainment LLC
3119 Gillham Road
Kansas City, MO 64109

Founder/Creative Director: Jeremy D. Mohler
Editor-in-Chief: Alana Joli Abbott
Senior Editor: Scott Colby
Project Director: Anton Kromoff

ISBN: 978-1-954255-68-5 (print), 978-1-954255-69-2 (ebook)

Worldwide Rights

Created in the United States of America

Editor: Jonathan Maberry
Copy editors: Alana Joli Abbott, Scott Colby, and Em Palladino
Proofreader: Ariel Kromoff
Cover Illustration: Chris Yarbrough
Cover Design: Jeremy D. Mohler
Interior Layout: Jeremy D. Mohler

Visit outlandentertainment.com to see more, or follow us on our Facebook Page facebook.com/outlandentertainment/

ACKNOWLEDGEMENTS

A posse of folks—each gunslingers in their own way—rode out with me on this one and I wanted to thank them. In no special order...thanks to my literary agent, Sara Crowe; my amazing assistant, Dana Fredsti; Chuck Sellner for roping me in on this; and the folks at Outland with whom I passed through some rough country.

DEDICATION

This one is for friend, fellow writer, martial arts colleague, and all-around good guy, Joe R. Lansdale. I was a fan before we were friends, and my appreciation for your work in more genres than I can count deepens with each new book or story. Best to you and yours, Joe.

And, as always...for Sara Jo.

CONTENTS

EDITOR'S FOREWORD: RIDING ALONG DARK TRAILS

JONATHAN MABERRY

I love westerns.

Always have.

I grew up in the era of *Gunsmoke, Bonanza, High Chaparral, Maverick, The Big Valley, Branded, Have Gun Will Travel, Wagon Train, Laredo, The Monroes, Rawhide, The Rifleman,* and god help me, *F Troop.*

I watched every movie John Wayne ever made. And I saw all the others featuring Glenn Ford, James Stewart, Roy Rogers, Charles Bronson, Clint Eastwood, Lee Van Cleef, Gary Cooper, Steve McQueen, Robert Mitchum, Burt Lancaster, and the rest.

And, sure, I have my favorites among what you might call the "standard" westerns. *Rio Bravo, Winchester 73, Valdez is Coming, The Magnificent Seven, Red River, My Darling Clementine, Tombstone, Stagecoach, Cat Ballou, The Wild Bunch, The Man Who Shot Liberty Valance, High Noon, Shane,* and *She Wore a Yellow Ribbon.*

But I'm a bit odd (ask anyone), and my favorites are, and will always be, a pair of TV shows that set a certain tone for me. One was relatively recent and—sadly—didn't last long: The

Adventures of Brisco County Junior, starring the wonderful Bruce Campbell. The other...well, if you're reading this and are of a certain age you can probably guess.

The Wild, Wild West.

Yeah. That one. The TV series with Robert Conrad and Ross Martin. It ran for four seasons, from 1965 to '69. I was seven when it launched, and I watched all 104 episodes. First when they aired, and then many, many times on reruns, VHS, DVD, and now streaming.

Without a doubt it was one of the most foundational elements of what would—decades later—become my career as a best-selling author known for jumping genres and combining them. Along with the Hammer Horror films, the Bantam reprints of the Doc Savage pulps, reprints of *Weird Tales Magazine*, and Richard Matheson's immortal novel, *I Am Legend*, that TV show made me who I am. It informed my tastes and stoked the fires of my creativity. It was the blend of western action, mystery, weird science—both real and entirely fantastical, romance, and quirky humor. That is my happy place. For fans of my Joe Ledger thrillers, you'll understand right away.

The genre was not called weird west back then. That moniker wouldn't be hung on it until DC Comics launched *Weird Western Tales* in 1972. And even then "weird west" was an informal nickname given to TV shows, books, comics, movies, and games that had western elements as a framework for tales that involved everything from robots to vampires. Few people can even agree on what constitutes weird westerns because they overlap with so many other genres, including Gothic Westerns (*High Plains Drifter*), Fantasy Westerns (Stephen King's *The Dark Tower*), Literary Gothic Westerns (*Blood Meridian* by Cormac McCarthy), Horror Westerns (*The Burrowers, Billy the Kid vs Dracula*), Dark Western Thrillers (*Bone Tomahawk, Ravenous*), Science Fiction Westerns (*Cowboys & Aliens*), and some that defy descriptions (*El Topo, Hex, Valley of Gwangi*).

The point is that the Old West was a blank canvas on which all kinds of stories can be told.

Over the last few decades Steampunk has put its mark on the genre, with Victorian-era science fiction technology blending with tropes of the western adventure. This last genre is one I know very well. I've read a hell of a lot of it—*The Half-made World* by Felix Gilman, *Dead Iron* by Devon Monk, *Iron Council* by China Miéville, *The Doctor and the Kid* by Mike Resnick, *Mistborn: The Alloy of Law* by Brandon Sanderson, *Six-Gun Tarot* by R.S. Belcher, *A Master of Djinn* by P. Djèlí Clark, *Buffalo Soldier* by Maurice Broaddus, *The Builders* by Daniel Polansky, and many others.

I added my own contribution to the genre when I was asked to write an original novel based on the *Deadlands* role-playing game created by Shane Hensley. My novel, *Ghostwalkers*, was followed by two more Deadlands books written by very good friends. They are *Boneyard* by Seanan McGuire, and *Thunder Moon Rising* by Jeffrey J. Mariotte.

The fun thing about writing a story set in a very weird west is that there are few creative limitations. My *Ghostwalkers* can best be described as an alt-history, steampunk, supernatural western with an uncredited appearance by a sandworm from *Dune* and zombie dinosaurs. Why did I add those last things? The better question is why wouldn't I? Weird west not only allows that kind of wildness bit *invites* it.

Which brings us to this book.

The Good, the Bad, and the Uncanny lives up to its subtitle of "Tales of a Very Weird West." Every one of these stories—some written by writers I've already mentioned—are unusual in every important way. They're fun. They're dark. Some are brutal, others have a wicked sense of fun. But all of them are weird.

Very, very weird.

I'm a novelist by trade. I edit *Weird Tales Magazine*. I write comics, and I edit anthologies. I love my job. Editing a book like this, with stories like these, written by writers whose work I read and love...well, that's just too much damn fun.

I have no doubt you'll have fun, too.

So saddle up, make sure your six-gun is loaded with those *special* rounds, and let's ride!

—Jonathan Maberry

San Diego, 2023

The Disobedient Devil Dust-Up at Copper Junction

CULLEN BUNN

The wagon thundered along the winding road, down the steep hill, and toward a horizon painted red by the rising sun. Metal-reinforced wheels bounced over jagged rocks in the dirt. Black vapor puffed from the mouth of a shuddering stovepipe. Water and steam spat from between riveted seams of the boiler. Beneath the weathered bonnet, wooden crates filled with scrap metal, gizmos in various stages of completion, and bottles of combustible liquids clanked and rattled. Heavy barrels packed tight with gunpowder rolled across the wagon bed. The explosive kegs cracked against the stolen coffin, and the contents of the pine box thumped and clunked in what should have been a final resting place.

From the jockey box, Professor Dimitri Daedalus swore an old German curse and gripped the wheel, fighting with all his might to maintain control of the wagon as it careened along the narrow dirt track.

Yiska clung to the sideboard, the bare muscles of his arms bulging and spasming as he swung his tomahawk at the small, hideous creatures scurrying and leaping across the wagon. The nasty beasts tested their claws and teeth. They scratched at Yiska. Bit at him. Ripped at his leather vest. They laughed with a cruel, screeching joy.

"This," Yiska yelled as he chopped through one of the horrid creatures as it jumped at him, "was a bad idea!"

"There are no bad ideas!" the Professor replied from his driver's seat. "Only poor execution!"

"This was *poor execution*, then!"

"Noted!"

A spindly green creature hopped onto the wagon's steering apparatus. Even as the Professor struggled to guide the vehicle, the beast antagonized his efforts. It yanked at wooden pins with wiry fingers and tugged at nails with needle sharp teeth. A second beast crawled up from under the seat to aid in the task of sabotage. A third bounced onto the Professor's feather-adorned derby hat, smashing it down over the man's eyes.

"Tarnation!"

The Professor yanked the hat from his sweaty, balding noggin. The monster, about the size of an organ grinder's monkey, held on and hooted with glee. The Professor flapped the hat, once, twice, three times, trying without success to shake the beast free, then gave up and flung the derby—and the creature—to the floor. The little beast grinned, savoring the taste of salting a wound, and then cruelly tossed the hat out across the rocky badlands.

Too bad. Daedalus had liked that hat, worn out and thread-bare though it was. It had been a gift from Marybelle, his sweetheart from his youth, a reminder of the halcyon days long since passed and never to return.

The stovepipe howled, spewing a geyser of steam, and a half-dozen twisted little monsters were blasted, tumbling, into the air. They swarmed every square inch of the wagon. They squeezed into the nooks and crannies. They clung to the axles.

They rode, chittering with terrible delight, upon the pistons and gears. They clung to the wheels, spinning wildly as they yanked at the spokes.

The wheels struck a cluster of large stones, and the wagon bounced.

With one hand, Yiska gripped his tomahawk. With the other, he held onto the wagon's frame. From under the canvas covering stretched across the rear of the wagon, one of the beasts emerged, sneering, hissing, hurling bottles of colorful liquids at Yiska. Glass shattered, and volatile concoctions splattered against the Navajo.

The contents burned his skin.

Up ahead, the world simply dropped away.

The wagon rocketed toward a cliff.

A vast gorge full of jagged spires of stone awaited.

Tiny green beasts ran riot all around.

They cackled with destructive joy.

Holding on for dear life, Yiska yelled.

"I hate gremlins!"

Not even twelve hours earlier, Professor Daedalus's Marvelous, Magical Steam-Carriage, laden with inventions and free of gremlins, had arrived in the town of Copper Junction, Utah.

"An odd name for a town," the Professor mused as the collection of clapboard buildings came into view. "At least, odd for this town. 'Junction' would imply an intersection or crossing, yes? My word, but I barely see even a *road!*"

Yiska, sitting next to the Professor, glanced over the side of the jockey box, and took note of the faintest of rock-covered tracks below. He raised an eyebrow and nodded, to himself more than anyone, taking some small comfort in the idea that the road *was* there, even though it looked like time and the elements had done their best to wipe it away.

So, too, did he relish the notion that this town did not lie at a crossroads.

He found such places—and the weird spirits that often lurked there—to be bothersome and dangerous.

Professor Daedalus had traveled to many small, dusty communities along many nearly forgotten roads. He roamed from place to place, showing off his latest inventions, peddling his potions. "Step up, step up, one and all! Come along on a journey of wonder and imagination! Explore fantastic flights of scientific vision!" The Professor was, in his heart, as much a showman as a scientist. He mused, when he was in his cups, that he had once dreamed of performing Shakespeare when he was a young man who had not yet discovered his skill with invention.

This trip, though, was not one of stagecraft and commerce. A letter, even now tucked into the Professor's vest pocket, had summoned them. The hastily written note had been simple in its request.

"Your assistance is needed on a matter of dire importance. An amazing discovery awaits. You are the only scientist I trust with such findings. Make haste to Copper Junction, Utah."

It had been signed by Dr. Lincoln Praetorius, the Professor's longtime friend and mentor.

"He would not send such a missive," Daedalus had said, "unless he truly needed help. He was not a man who asked lightly for aid. Nor did he often need it."

And, so, they had set off, casting aside preexisting plans

and making steam for Copper Junction. Along the way, the Professor told his Navajo companion tales of his exploits as apprentice to Dr. Praetorius, a fearless man of science, one who pushed the very boundaries of possibility with his astounding creations.

"I, of course, was young," Daedalus said, "thinking I had learned all I could from Praetorius. I set off on my own, hoping to make a name for myself. Feh! I was such a brash, pig-headed young fool!"

"Sooner or later," said Yiska, "we all leave the nest."

"True, and some of us fall from tall branches to be pulped in the dirt."

"You are too hard on yourself, my friend." Yiska waved toward the wagon. He was no stranger to the Professor's bouts of sadness and self-loathing. He knew how to lure his friend back from the brink. "Do not forget, it was *your* pioneering mind that created the Marvelous, Magical Steam-Carriage."

The Professor nodded in appreciation of his companion's words. "That's kind of you to say, but..."

His voice trailed off as he noticed Yiska's smirk.

Daedalus coughed out a chuckle. "Aw, you're just funning me, aren't you?"

As if in response, the wagon's stovepipe belched and shuddered.

The Marvelous, Magical Steam-Carriage rattled toward Copper Junction as the sun began to set.

Corpses loomed in the shadows.

Not the corpses of men.

But of *machines*.

In the alley between the mercantile and the barber, the assembly and massive cylinder of what must've been an advanced printing press lay abandoned and forgotten.

In the next narrow lane, the wheels and pipes and ruined conveyor belts of a piece of farming equipment rose out of the dirt like the weathered bones of some ancient creature.

A barrel placed along the plank sidewalk was filled with shooting irons of sophisticated design, as well as the weaponry of less civilized folks. Each of the firearms was in a state of disassembly and disarray.

A sewing machine, smashed to bits, lay in the street.

A telegraph transmitter and receiver, mired in a tangled spool of ripped-down wire, had been kicked across the road and left to rust.

Parked nearby was a steam-driven wagon, not too different from the Marvelous, Magical Steam-Carriage. It had been stripped down to the frame. Disassembled and discarded components littered the ground around the ruined vehicle in a metallic halo.

The dirt street was strewn with bolts and gears and bits of metal, glinting in the moonlight.

"What happened here?" Yiska asked.

"Can't be sure," said the Professor, but there was uneasiness in his voice, and he reached under his jacket to place his hand upon the grip of his gatling pistol. He had not invented the weapon himself. He *had*, however, concocted the hellish ammunition with which it was loaded.

Yiska's own hand fell to his tomahawk, and while that weapon was not enhanced by the Professor's ingenuity, it possessed fearsome blessings of its own.

"It is almost as if," Daedalus said, "an *inquisition* has happened here, a purging of technology. Tarnation and damnation! What a grim notion!"

"Perhaps this is why your friend needed help," Yiska said.

"It is a possibility. But Dr. Praetorius mentioned a great discovery. That, in and of itself, should not be overlooked. He has uncovered a great many grand and wonderous revelations. I was at his side for many. For him to reach out now, to summon me forthwith, a true marvel must await."

The carriage rumbled to a stop outside a saloon—the Lucky Lady. Light shone from within. Voices could be heard. There was no laughter, though, and certainly no music, as one might expect. A couple of horses, tied to the hitching post out front, neighed and stomped nervously.

The Professor pulled the handbrake and hopped down from his seat.

He kept his pistol within easy reach.

All eyes turned toward Yiska and the Professor as they stepped through batwing doors into the saloon. Steely, cold stares from rugged men who had spent all day digging in the earth. Surprised, gawking stares from saloon girls who were not expecting out-of-towners. Curious stares from cowpunchers and gamblers fidgeting with the edges of dog-eared playing cards.

Certainly, the pair stood out. Professor Daedalus, lean and spry in his suit, feathered hat, and round-rimmed spectacles. Yiska, tall and strong, dressed in his leathers, tomahawk strapped to his side. Most folks might not expect such traveling companions, let alone friends and blood brothers.

Another barrel filled with broken pistols sat next to the entry. No one in the Lucky Lady went heeled, though a couple of men sported empty holsters at their hips.

A pianist sat next to a piano, but he played no music. He tapped absently, longingly, at some of the keys, but no sound was produced.

"Good evening, friends. Good evening." The Professor removed his hat as he strode through the saloon. He spoke confidently. Loudly. Like he was on stage peddling his inventions and potions. "My name is Professor Dimitri Daedalus. My colleague is Yiska. We've come to wash the grit of the world from our throats, if the barkeep might be so kind to oblige."

"We got beer and whiskey." The bartender, a thin man dressed in clothing that might have been dapper in ages past, was already grabbing a bottle. "Wouldn't suggest the beer, though, unless you like the taste of skunk. The whiskey ain't bad. At least it's not watered down."

"I think, perhaps, we'll take your suggestion under advisement." Smiling, the Professor approached the bar. He pulled a coin from his vest pocket. "A bottle, if you please, and two glasses."

The bartender poured two drinks, left the bottle on the counter, and eagerly slid the payment into his own pocket. Yiska and the Professor kicked the glasses back. The whiskey burned like a brushfire going down, but neither man flinched or grimaced. After years of mixing, brewing, and testing his own concoctions, Daedalus was accustomed to stringent drinks. And Yiska's stoicism wouldn't allow for such reactions. Another two shots were poured.

Turning to the other patrons, the Professor raised his glass in salute, first to Yiska, then to the other patrons.

"Here's to all of you, my fine friends!"

A few of the townsfolk tossed a smattering of mistrusting grumbles the Professor's way.

Undeterred, the Professor drank.

A thin, dirty cowboy stood at the batwing doors, looking out at the street.

"That your contraption out there?" he asked.

"It is indeed!" Daedalus smiled. "That, my friend, is the Marvelous, Magical Steam-Carriage! A wonder on wheels! An apparatus of my own design, of course!"

The cowboy snorted, shook his head, and wandered away from the door.

Behind him, the door hinge broke, and the left side of the batwing fell loose, cracking against the floor.

The cowboy paid it no mind — as if such minor calamity was commonplace.

"I wonder," the Professor said, addressing the patrons of the Lucky Lady once more, "if one of you might be able to tell me where to find my colleague and mentor, Dr. Lincoln Praetorius. He's been spending some time in your fair town, I believe. I've come a long way to assist him on a remarkable discovery, the illumination of which, I'm sure, will be a boon to..."

"Copper Junction," Yiska said without turning away from the bar.

"To Copper Junction," Daedalus said, "of course."

Across the saloon, a sea of cold and uncaring eyes stared back at the Professor.

Someone chuckled humorously.

A grizzled old man spat, intentionally missing a nearby spittoon by an inch or two.

The pianist tapped out a silent, doom-filled tune on the busted piano.

Otherwise, no one responded.

Yiska moved to the Professor's side. "It doesn't seem like they are in a helpful mood," he said, his voice low.

"So I see," the Professor said.

"I don't like this place," Yiska said.

"We're quite all right," the Professor said. "Quite safe."

"Being safe has nothing to do with it. This place is full of unease. I taste it with every breath."

The Professor glanced toward the barkeep.

"If nothing else," he said, "might this fine establishment have a couple of beds a pair of weary wanderers might lease for the evening?"

The bartender chewed at the inside of his mouth for a second, then shrugged.

"It'll cost you a dollar."

"A fair price," the Professor said. "Well thought out."

He paid the man.

The bartender eyed one of the saloon girls, a pale, bewildered-looking child in a faded blue dress. "Sally over there will show you the way."

Sally, keeping her eyes down, headed for the stairs. A set of keys jangled in her pale fingers. She motioned for the Professor and Yiska to follow.

Every patron in the saloon stopped what they were doing—which, admittedly, wasn't much—to watch the two newcomers.

At the top of the stairs, Sally unlocked the door to a small, dreary room.

"Much obliged, my dear," the Professor said, tipping his hat.

Handing the Professor the key, the girl said, "You say you're here looking for Doc Lincoln."

"That's right, my dear." An excited smile spread across the Professor's face. "He is a dear old friend."

"He was always good to me," Sally said. "Kind. I feel terrible bad about everything that happened to him."

The Professor's smile slipped away.

"What do you mean?"

"I shouldn't say."

"He invited me here to help him." The Professor pulled his letter from his pocket. "If you could point me in the right direction, it would be most appreciated."

Sally looked to the floor.

"I can tell you where to find him," she said, "but you ain't gonna like it."

————————————————————

"Dead." The Professor sat on the edge of his sagging bed and hung his head low. His jacket, his hat, and his gatling pistol were scattered on the mattress. "I can barely believe it."

"We know death is coming for each and every one of us." Yiska stood at the window, looking out at the darkened streets of Copper Junction. "And yet we are always surprised when it arrives."

"Yes, yes. I know. I suppose I've always seen Praetorius as somehow beyond the traditional concepts of life. *Immortal* in a way."

"You admired him."

"He was a genius. Fearless. Always searching for new discoveries, always pulling at the very threads of understanding and reality."

"Interesting how a *genius* and a *fool* breathe the same air."

"There's no need to be so damned callous."

"You're right. I'm sorry." Yiska turned his head to look at Daedalus. "And I'm sorry for the loss of your friend."

Daedalus scoffed. "You would have *hated* him."

"How can you be sure?"

"Even I must admit Praetorius could be a bit high-and-mighty from time to time. He had frequent brushes with *sanctimoniousness*. More so than me. And there are times, my friend, that I believe you can barely stand to be in my presence."

"When you use words like 'sanctimoniousness' it is particularly difficult."

Yiska smirked.

Daedalus returned the expression.

"That's one of the reasons I turned away from him, I suppose. I saw opportunity. I saw potential. I dreamed of bringing our inventions, our formulas, to the masses. And he saw only—"

"A snake oil salesman," Yiska said.

The Professor, confronted as he was with a term he never did appreciate, let his shoulders droop as he nodded.

Yiska looked out the window once more and gazed out at the moonlit street.

"Perhaps this will take your mind off your grief," he said.

"What's that?" the Professor asked.

"The townsfolk."

"What about them?"

"They're ripping the Marvelous, Magical Steam-Carriage apart."

"What is the meaning of this?" the Professor's voice boomed as he strode onto the street. He kept his gatling pistol hidden behind his back. He gripped the handle with bloodless knuckles.

A group of a dozen townsfolk surrounded the Marvelous, Magical Steam-Carriage. They were searching it, throwing items out the back and into the dirt. Here was an autonomous bear trap, created when Daedalus and Yiska had been hired to stalk a wendigo. There was a half-finished acid-thrower, which might have worked wonders against prairie ticks if the Professor had ever figured out how to keep the tanks from melting. Here was the now-fried remains of the Professor's telepathy gun, a strange, helmet-like contraption intended to read and control thoughts. There was the harness and tattered wings of the Professor's one-man ornithopter, which could fly, but not well enough for the inventor to trust a test flight.

His life's work, scattered into the dirt.

"Step away from my carriage at once," Daedalus said.

The voice of a showman was gone.

Now his words were stern, commanding.

Yiska towered behind the Professor, arms crossed, tomahawk in hand.

The townsfolk—among them the bartender, the skinny cowboy, and several others who had been in attendance at the Lucky Lady—glowered at the Professor and Yiska.

"You shouldn't have come here," said someone.

"Just makes things worse," said another.

"We don't want you here."

"You rile up the demons."

The crowd took a step toward the Professor.

"That's quite far enough."

Now, the Professor aimed his gatling pistol. His finger teased the trigger. The barrels started to whirl. If he tensed his finger, he would unleash Armageddon.

The crowd took another collective step.

"I'm quite serious," the Professor warned. "I do not want to resort to violence, but I will."

He trained the pistol on the skinny cowboy.

The crowd moved closer.

"You'll leave me no choice."

The crowd surged closer still.

Before the Professor could issue another warning, his gun fell apart. Screws came loose. Brackets shifted out of their mountings. The trigger guard dropped to the dirt. Barrels tumbled, clattering, to the ground. The Professor was left holding nothing but the grip of his trusty weapon.

The crowd moved closer.

Yiska stepped between the Professor and the townsfolk. He raised his tomahawk above his head. Where there had once been a clear, star-filled sky, dark, churning clouds suddenly rolled in. Lightning danced in the clouds. Thunder rumbled. A ragged bolt of lightning sizzled across the sky, tiny, licking jolts strafing across the head of the tomahawk. A metallic, burning smell clung to the charged air.

The crowd paused.

And they were right to do so. If Yiska had wanted to, he could've called down the maelstrom to blast each and every one of the townsfolk into oblivion with burning electricity.

The Professor straightened his collar, pulling at the lapels of his jacket.

"Now," he said, "will someone kindly tell me what is happening here?"

"It's a curse," one of the cowed townsfolk said.

"That's right," said another, "and it gets worse whenever any kind of mechanical contraption is brought into Copper Junction."

"It was that friend of yours— Praetorius —who brought the curse with him."

"He's up there, in the Orchard of Bones."

"On the hill."

The Professor and Yiska looked toward a jagged outcropping of rock. A circle of leafless old trees stood sentinel around gravestones. The flickering lightning in the clouds overhead shed light upon the scene.

The hill.

Boot Hill.

"That's where you'll find him." A tall scarecrow of a man in a black suit stepped forward. "I put him there. Him and all them others, too."

"The others?" the Professor asked.

"Them like you. Scientists."

Yiska looked toward the cemetery.

"We'll have a look."

He glared at the undertaker.

Flickers of electricity danced across the tomahawk.

"And you're coming with us."

Loose rocks crunched under the wheels of the Marvelous, Magical Steam-Carriage as it ascended the hill toward the Orchard of Bones. The undertaker—his name was Sasser—sat between the Professor and Yiska. The hooded lantern hanging next to the driver's box swung back and forth, casting an eerie glow across the rocks and twisted scrub lining the trail.

A foulness clung to the air.

The stench of decay.

From his vest pocket, the Professor pulled a lace handkerchief—another gift from his long-lost and beloved Marybelle—and placed it over his nose to block the smell.

"Dear Lord," he said.

Even before he stopped the wagon, he could see several

coffins were scattered around the tree-lined cemetery. Most of them were uncovered, standing upright, a decaying corpse on display within. The Professor and Yiska had encountered similar displays, usually lining the walkways in rough-and tumble towns, criminals presented for all to see as a novelty and warning. In the center of the graveyard was another casket, this one lying down and sealed shut.

A puff of steam rose from the stovepipe as the wagon came to a stop.

The Professor, Yiska, and Sasser hopped down and walked among the unburied dead.

Handkerchief over his nose and mouth, the Professor approached one of the caskets. The body within was pale and rotting. From under the dead man's vest, a scrap of yellowed paper peeked out. More than a scrap, really. The Professor gingerly withdrew a folded letter from the dead man's vest. The handwriting was familiar, as was the message.

> *Your assistance is needed on a matter of dire importance. An amazing discovery awaits. You are the only scientist I trust with such findings. Make haste to Copper Junction, Utah.*
>
> *Signed, Dr. Lincoln Praetorius*

The Professor's breath hitched in his chest.

"There are more letters." Yiska nodded toward another corpse. A folded letter could be seen sticking out of the breast pocket. Another one of the dead—a woman—squeezed a crumpled letter and envelope in a rigid grip.

"His students," the Professor said. "These were all his students."

"He brought them here," Yiska said, "summoned them, one by one."

The undertaker nodded solemnly.

"He offered them up as sacrifice."

"Sacrifice?" the Professor asked.

"Indeed. To the spirits that hounded him. And you were meant to be next, it would seem."

"We tried to bury them," the undertaker said. "Seemed only right, especially after what we done to them. But the shovels kept breaking."

He kicked at the rusty head of a shovel that lay in the dirt.

"So, we just left them where you see them, where the spirits can feed on them til they rot."

"What you did," Yiska said.

"What's that?" Sasser asked.

"You said you did something to them."

"It's not like we had much choice," Sasser said. "We killed them, each and every one of them. We thought Doc Praetorius might have been the end of it. We thought maybe if he was dead, the evil spirits would just sort of dry up and go away. For a bit, that's how it seemed, but not for long. As soon another one of you scientists showed up, it just got so much worse."

"So, you killed them?"

"Is it any worse than the demonic curse Praetorius inflicted upon them? He meant to sacrifice them anyhow. I like to think we spared them some suffering."

The Professor did not answer. He glanced around the boneyard, letting his gaze linger on each of the caskets.

"And the center coffin?" Daedalus asked.

"Your friend." Sasser fidgeted nervously. "That's him in there."

Daedalus looked at his mentor's casket.

He strode to the pine box. He put his boot on the lid.

"I wouldn't do that," the undertaker said.

The Professor kicked the coffin open.

The body was withered and grey, the lips peeled back in a gruesome grin, the nose and eyes disintegrated to gaping holes. The monocle Dr. Practorius had always worn still clung to one of the eye sockets. The corpse's long grey hair was spread out all around the head. The hands, like skin-covered sticks, were clutched together.

"You bastard," Daedalus whispered. "Did any of us mean a damn thing to you?"

As if in response, the corpse twitched.

It shifted in the casket.

Its chest rose and fell.

"He's still alive," Daedalus said. "He—"

But Praetorius wasn't taking a breath. Rather, something moved beneath his clothing, beneath skin dry as onion husk. Something crawled. Buttons popped. The dead man's interlaced fingers peeled away from one another. The shirt opened, and a hideous face peered out.

At first, the Professor thought it might have been some sort of hairless possum, sharp-toothed and hissing, its own flesh gone greenish from disease. But as it wriggled free, it used tiny, human-like arms and legs. Sharp black claws protruded from its fingertips. Its eyes were round and red. Its nose was little more than bat-like slits. Its ears were long and tattered and twitching.

Another emerged from the body.

And another.

While some seemed to slither out of the dead scientist's clothes, others were now slowly materializing into view all around, flesh and blood coalescing like vapor where that had been only air seconds earlier. Dozens of the creatures crouched on the casket. In the tangled branches of the surrounding trees, even more manifested, perched and ready to pounce. Several more clambered on each of the caskets.

The Professor took a step back.

Yiska knew these creatures. He had known other men of science who had been driven to madness and death by their exuberant wickedness.

"Gremlins," he said.

The citizens of Copper Junction were right. Dr. Praetorius had been stricken by foul spirits. They were not, however, demons. They were altogether different. To men and women of science, they might have been much, much worse. Gremlins were mischief-makers. Born out of mankind's collective distrust of science and progress, they existed only to corrupt and destroy technological advances, to spread fear and mistrust and madness.

They had done their job well in Copper Junction.

And, so, they propagated.

"He never flinched in the face of the unknown," the Professor said, almost eulogizing his dead mentor as he backed away from the growing number of gremlins. "And that was his undoing. Somewhere along the way, he must have attracted the attention of these…gremlins. They latched onto him. Infested him."

The gathering of gremlins…

…the *mischievousness* of gremlins…

…howled with laughter at their mention in the Professor's tale.

"They drove him beyond the brink of insanity. He wanted to rid himself of the beasts. He wanted to pass them on to someone else. So, he brought his students—all of his students—here to serve them up."

"Sanctimoniousness," Yiska said.

A flash of metal caught the Professor's eye, and he jerked his head out of the way just as the undertaker slashed at him with a straight razor. The Professor staggered back, and the undertaker followed, moving the razor back and forth.

"I'm sorry!" the undertaker said. "But you riled them up when you came here! They won't rest, not now! They'll torment us! They won't give us a moment's peace! Not until you're—"

Yiska kicked the man squarely in the chest. Stomped him, really. The undertaker dropped the blade, and he went flying across the graveyard. He landed hard, rolling in the cemetery dust.

A gremlin jumped down, grabbed up the straight razor, and used its flicking, serpentine tongue to remove the tiny screw that held the blade to the handle. The instrument dismantled, the gremlin tossed the pieces to the ground and hopped away.

The Professor glanced toward the Marvelous, Magical Steam-Carriage .

"They ain't gonna let you leave," the undertaker said. He sat on the ground, wheezing, grabbing feebly at his chest.

"I have no intention of leaving this place," the Professor said. "At least, not without Praetorius."

Yiska raised an eyebrow.

"He's the source. He brought this curse to Copper Junction. It's my duty as his student to put an end to his mistake."

The Professor grunted as he hefted the long wooden lid and slammed it back on top of the casket.

Gremlins hissed and cackled and scurried all around.

Daedalus looked at Yiska.

"Help me load him up."

The wagon thundered along the winding road and down the steep hill, toward a horizon painted red by the rising sun, toward a yawning and hungry canyon.

Dozens of laughing, hooting gremlins crawled and jumped and scuttled all over the wagon. Some had taken physical form. Others faded in and out of the material realm. Still others, one could only assume, lingered just beyond the veil of sight and sound and touch. They were there, though, waiting for their moment to sow insanity and misery.

Professor Daedalus had been right. The gremlins were bound to the corpse of his friend and mentor. When they had put the casket into the Marvelous, Magical Steam-Carriage , the gremlins followed. Now, they used the wagon as a playground of chaos and destruction.

Gremlins leaped at the Professor. They slashed at his hands

as he grabbed at the controls. They worked to dismantle the steering apparatus, the handbrake.

They snapped with nasty teeth at Yiska's face. They worked at his fingers, trying to pry his grip free so he would tumble into the dirt. They hurled bottles of the Professor's strange concoctions, smashing them against Yiska's back.

"Just a little farther!" Daedalus called. "Hold on!"

"They're pelting me with potions!" Yiska yelled.

"You'll be all right!" Daedalus hurled a nagging gremlin to the floor and stomped it. "Most of the elixirs are harmless! Just watch out for anything blue! Those are the potentially lethal tinctures!"

A gremlin emerged from the back of the wagon, its arms loaded with bottles of blue liquid.

In Navajo, Yiska cursed the Professor's big mouth.

The wagon bounced again, and the gremlin toppled backward. Still clutching so many bottles of blue elixir, it fell to the earth. The bottles shattered. The liquid inside, coming into contact with open air, exploded into a fireball of blue flame. It consumed the gremlin. A wave of heat washed across the Marvelous, Magical Steam-Carriage, nearly lifting it completely off the ground.

"Get ready!" the Professor cried, his voice almost completely muffled by the dozens of gremlins tackling him.

The canyon drew ever closer.

Without benefit of a working braking mechanism, the wagon sped toward the precipice.

"Now, Yiska!" the Professor called. "Now! Leap clear!"

Yiska threw himself into the dirt and rocks, rolling, tearing clothing, stripping skin from his arms and face.

The wagon was mere yard from the cliff's edge.

Professor Daedalus shrugged himself free of the gremlins and made to leap clear.

A withered, grey hand grasped his wrist.

"Tarnation!"

From the rear of the wagon, the corpse of Doc Praetorius emerged. His motions were herky-jerky. His head lolled dreadfully to the side. The dead scientist grabbed at Daedalus, holding him tight.

The Professor's mind reeled.

It took several seconds for his perceptions to clear.

Doc Praetorius, the man who had lured him to Copper Junction, had not returned from the dead. Instead, a half-dozen gremlins, some conjured wholly into the world, others still half-ethereal, worked the corpse like a puppet. They cackled at their own horrible joke.

The Professor punched the corpse squarely in the face. The head rocked back, almost coming loose from the neckbone. A gremlin went tumbling.

It felt good.

Daedalus punched his dead mentor again and again.

On the third punch, the body fell backward. The arms tore free at the elbows. The hand still clutched at the Professor.

Daedalus jumped just as the Marvelous, Magical Steam-Carriage took flight over the canyon's edge. He slammed painfully to the ground, felt his teeth rattle in his skull, and rolled in the dirt. He sprang shakily to his feet and cast aside the near-skeletal hands that still grasped at him.

"Now, Yiska! Now!"

The wagon, covered in gremlins, sailed through the air, plummeting toward the jagged rocks below.

Yiska held his tomahawk to the sky.

He called down a tumultuous blast of lightning to strike the falling wagon.

The carriage exploded in a multi-colored blast of flame and smoke. Dozens of gremlins, caught in the conflagration, were roasted alive, shrieking in ghastly pain. The wagon smashed to the rocks, and a second explosion erupted, incinerating the vehicle and turning the tiny green beasts to ash.

Daedalus staggered to the edge of the canyon. He clutched at his arm, fairly certain it had snapped in more than one place during his fall. Yiska, bleeding from dozens of cuts and scrapes, joined him.

Below, the Marvelous, Magical Steam-Carriage burned. Smoke rose blackly from the gorge. Strange shapes churned in the soot-fog. A metallic, oily stink clung to the air.

"What now?" Yiska asked. "Your wagon, your life's work, has been destroyed."

"And with it—" Daedalus nodded. "—every last one of those malignant little creatures."

"How can you be sure?" Yiska asked.

A dusty derby hat adorned with a feather rolled like a tumbleweed across the ground.

The Professor smiled as he picked up his hat.

"Faith, my friend, is not the sole province of the devout."

THE DEVIL'S SNARE

R.S. BELCHER

(Note: This story takes place after The Six-Gun Tarot novel and prior to The Shotgun Arcana novel- R.S.B.)

February 1870

She sat waiting at the edge of oblivion, at the edge of the 40-Mile Desert. The 40-Mile was one of the paths to the mythical West. The West was a promise, a hope, a place to start again, after the blood and chaos of the war. It was a place you could lose yourself, forget who you had been and what you had done, or reinvent yourself from whole cloth. It was a realm of milk and honey, where you could pluck gold from the very air, find your fortune, or change it. Anything was possible, just a little further out west.

But first there was the ordeal, the rite, the passage. She waited at the ragged edge of forty dead, dry, unforgiving miles of Nevada desert for all of them—the blessed and the damned. She welcomed them all with open arms. Her name was Golgotha, and she was Clay Turlough's home.

Clay was a vulture of a man, gaunt, with a ragged halo of wild hair circling his liver-spotted pate. He wore thick, brown-stained bandages on the side of his face, his upper chest, and the backs of his hands, covering recent and horrific burns. Clay had never been very pretty, but the burns he had suffered last fall, rushing into Shultz's General Store as it was devoured by flames, had sealed the deal. Clay didn't pay his looks much mind.

He owned a livery at the edge of Duffer Road and was also Golgotha's only taxidermist. Most folks knew he was obsessed with death, but since the fire, Clay had become even more reclusive than normal, having his ranch hands keep up the stables for him while he stayed in his workshop, working. Today it was chemistry.

He carefully poured an exact amount of black liquid from the contents of an alkalimeter into a wide glass tank full of clear liquid. The liquid in the tank bubbled vigorously, agitated courtesy of a pair of vulcanized rubber tubes pumping air into the mixture, connected to a gear and spring mechanism that Clay maintained. He cursed silently that he could not be more precise in his administering of the agent into the tank. A part of his mind was already puzzling over a more efficient and accurate means of dispensing liquids than Monsieur Descroizilles' alkalimeter—a puzzle for another day. The black liquid swirled and diffused in the bubbling tank, like a dab of ink in water.

Floating in the glass tank was a woman's severed head, almost mummified, the wrinkled skin stretched too tight over the skull, tufts of singed and blackened hair drifting like clumps of seaweed. The eyelids of the skull were closed and concave, as if no eyeballs remained within the orbits behind the shriveled lids. Her name had been Gerta Shultz—Gertie—and Clay loved her, had always loved her, since the first time they had met.

He loved her so much that when she died, he could not, would not, allow such a sweet light to pass from this world. He had maintained her head, her seat of consciousnesses, in a tank much like this one, filled with a nutrient solution of his devising that also stimulated and maintained her electro-chemical conductivity. He gave her back life, or a twilight semblance of it, anyway. He didn't lose her, and that's all that mattered. Then there had been the fire and she was boiling in the tank, dying, again. He couldn't bear it. He had saved her and all it cost him was a little skin, a cost he was more than willing to pay. Now, he was going to make it all better, for her, for him…this time.

There was a knock at the workshop door. Clay knew it wasn't his ranch hands—they had been given strict instructions that he was not to be disturbed. The knock came again, this time much more insistent, a powerful pounding. "Ach! Clayton! Open up!"

Auggie, it was Auggie. Clay muttered a curse and draped a cloth over Gerta's tank and wound the compressor springs to maintain the flow of formula around her shriveled head. He unbolted the door and opened it enough to peer outside.

Augustus Shultz was a bear of a man. He stood in the bright daylight holding a picnic basket. Auggie was around Clay's age, broad, heavy, and tall. He sported a rust-colored handlebar mustache. The fringe of hair that covered his sun-freckled head was the same color. Auggie regarded Clay with eyes bright as morning sunlight but clouded with worry. "What are you doing in there?" His voice was thick with the accent of his native Germany.

"Trying to work, you big dumb mule," Clay snapped. "But it seems I can't get a decent day's labor in without someone coming by to fret at me."

"Hm, don't you kick at me, you old coot! I know for a fact you have been cooped up in that barn for far too long."

"It's my workshop—"

"It's a barn! No one has seen you in months, Clay. Gillian and I have been worried sick about you." Augie thrust the basket toward Clay, "Here! She made you some vittles."

Clay sniffed the basket and liked what he smelled. He opened the door a bit wider and reached for it. Auggie pushed past him into the workshop, handing off the basket as he did.

"Hey! Now you wait one gol-danged minute," Clay shouted. "I didn't tell you you could come in!"

"What *are* you doing in here, Clay?" Auggie looked about. There were slate boards with chalk calculations mounted everywhere. Huge sheets of brown butcher paper were nailed to the walls, each covered with scribbled handwriting, formulas, and technical sketches of various devices, all of which were alien to Auggie. He turned to his oldest friend and regarded him as if for the first time. "Is it…the burns? Is that why you have been keeping yourself away?"

Clay sighed. He shut the door and locked it and wandered over to one of his wooden worktables, littered with wires, scraps of wood and scattered tools. He sat the picnic basket on a clear spot. "I don't think it's proper to inflict how I look on folk, but no…I'm…I'm just…powerful busy, Auggie. That's all."

"Is it about Gertie?"

Clay was silent. He rummaged through the basket.

"Are you angry that I didn't bring her out of the burning store?"

"No, you said she wanted to die, and I believe you," Auggie said.

Auggie and Gerta had come to America over twenty years ago and had put down roots in Golgotha, back when it was little more than a mining camp. They owned Shultz's General Store and Butcher Shop, on Main Street. Auggie had lost Gerta about three years ago to influenza and it had gutted him. Clay had been there, mourning with him, suffering as well, but Clay would not let it stand. He had resurrected Gertie, animated her head and kept her brain intact. He did it as much for himself as he did for Auggie. The truth was, he loved Gerta, always had.

It all came—no pun intended—to a head, last year when Auggie fell in love with a living, breathing woman, Gillian Proctor. In one horrible night Clay's feeling for Gerta had been revealed and Gerta was lost to Clay again in a fire at Auggie's store. Auggie had said in her last moments, Gertie asked to be freed of her demi-existence and Augie left her to pass, but again, Clay simply couldn't let her just fade into nothingness. He'd risked his own life, and the burns he now carried to save her from the fire. He'd hidden that he had retrieved her from Auggie. He just couldn't let such a beautiful light in this dark world end.

Clay's rational mind respected and understood Gert's choice. But it was his damn, uncooperative, incomprehensible emotions that drove him to rush into the burning building to recover her remains. The mechanics of the universe were beautiful, and they made perfect sense to Clay, but human emotions were a puzzle, one he had never been very good at solving.

He had spent his every waking moment since that night trying to bring Gert back. He knew it was selfish, realized if Auggie knew he would be furious, but if he could spit in death's eye and return her to a full, complete corporeal existence, it would change the world. He kept telling himself that was why he was doing it, and not the ragged bullet hole in his life that Gertie had filled.

Clay lifted a small loaf of warm bread out of the basket. He tore off a hunk and ate it.

"There's butter and preserves too," Auggie said. Clay grunted in appreciation and rooted about in the basket, searching. "Clay, this is not good, you staying cooped up in here."

"I'm good. You tell Gillian I'm much obliged for the grub—"

"Ah! Clay, there is a little boy, he's very ill. He needs your help," Auggie blurted out.

"What? Who?" Clay sat the food down, his full attention on Auggie now.

"You remember James Walsh?"

"I do, vaguely. He was a wheelwright over at the stagecoach depot, right?"

"Ja. Nice young man. Came here a few years back with his wife and son from Ireland. Gerta and I met them through church."

"What did he end up dying from?"

"Fever. I hear that came on sudden. His widow's been working as a seamstress since he passed. His little boy, Daniel, is sick now too, Clay. Very sick. He needs your help."

"Auggie, I'm not a doctor! Go fetch Tumblety."

"Mrs. Walsh—Aisling, tried already. The 'doctor' refused to treat the boy."

"What? Dang it! That old quack!"

"Clayton, everyone knows you have forgot more about medicine than Tumblety's ever known. Please, he's seven years old."

Clay stood for a moment, his hands on his hips, eyes unfocused. Auggie had seen his old friend this way many times and knew that Clay was churning thoughts over in his vast mind. Finally, he blinked and looked around the workshop.

"Let me fetch my bag, and a few things I might need. You got your wagon with you?"

Auggie nodded. "Thank you, Clay."

"I know this is just some hooey to get me out," the old inventor grumbled. "I'll take a peek, but then I have serious work to get back to. Boy's probably just got the sniffles."

"I'm going to kill you, all of you!" Daniel Walsh snarled, trying to pull free from the twisted sheets tying him to his bed. "Get away from me! Leave me alone!" The seven-year-old boy thrashed with considerable strength. Clay, Auggie, and Daniel's mother, Aisling stood at the bedside. Aisling had light strawberry blonde hair, like her son, and was clearly exhausted, at the end of her physical and emotional rope. Dark circles were evident under her tear-reddened eyes. She was a strikingly beautiful woman, but she looked brittle and frail in the dimness of the bedroom. Auggie put a reassuring hand on her small shoulder. He crossed himself. The boy's demeanor shocked and horrified even the burly shopkeep. The boy roared in anger and tried to launch himself up at his mother and the two men, his face a pale mask of rage.

"No spittle," Clay said mildly over Daniel's raving.

"What?" Auggie asked.

"No saliva. The boy's mouth is as dry as a ditch out in the 40-Mile." Clay glanced over to Mrs. Walsh and at a dark lantern on a table beside the door. "May I?"

"Of course, Mr. Turlough," Aisling said. "I keep it dark. The light hurts him."

"Hmm," Clay muttered. He lit the lantern and raised the shroud on it, bringing it close to Daniel's face. The boy lurched back in the bed, screaming in pain. Clay pressed on, even as the boy shook his head violently and squeezed his eyes shut.

"Cutting me! You're cutting me! You old devil!"

Clay was undaunted. He took the boy's head with one hand and pried one eye open with his thumb and forefinger. The boy howled in pain and began to blurt out obscenities. Aisling started to pull Clay off her son, but Auggie's strong, gentle hands stopped her.

"It is all right, Clay will not hurt the boy. I told you, he's here to help."

Aisling stopped her struggles. "If you trust him, Mr. Schultz, then I will. It's just…hard to see your child like this.

Clay peered closely into Daniel's eye, "Mydriasis," he

muttered. He released the boy's eyelid and closed the hood on the lamp. Daniel settled in the darkness. The cursing and screaming stopped but the boy moaned quietly. Clay looked at the child and gently rumpled his hair. He stepped away from the bed. "I need to talk to you outside," he said to the Widow Walsh.

Aisling's house was small but cozy. Clay and Auggie sat at the table that was the center of the main room. Aisling prepared tea. Dean Freed, Golgotha's resident barber and dentist, helped her. It was clear Freed was sweet on the widow and was trying to help her as best he could. It was also clear that Aisling was quite used to taking care of herself, but Dean kept trying. Auggie smiled at that.

"So, Mr. Turlough, what do you think is going on with Daniel?" Father Thorne of St. Cypians church asked from across the table. Thorne, a stern, white-haired man in his 40s, had been sitting vigil with Aisling and Dean for several days now. There were only a handful of Catholics in Golgotha, maybe sixty all told, with all of the newcomers since the Argent Mine had reopened.

Thorn was the sole priest in the town, though numerous scholars of the Holy Mother Church often visited Golgotha to review the sealed archives stored at St. Cypians, said to rival the occult library of the Vatican itself.

"I've got some suspicions," Clay said. "But those symptoms are pretty broad. Mrs. Walsh, I wanted to ask, does your boy normally act up that way when he's feeling peaked?"

"Goodness, no!" Aisling said as she set a tea service on the table and poured each man a cup. "Daniel has always been a very good boy, never a mean bone in this body, never cussed like that! I don't even know where he'd have heard such words!"

"That is concerning," Thorne said. "Has he spoken in any other languages? Languages he would have no way of knowing?"

"I...I'm not sure," Aisling said, as she poured the tea, her hands shaking. "A lot of what he says sounds like gibberish. What do they call it?"

"Glossolalia," Clay said absently, "speaking in tongues." Clay bent over and rummaged in an old leather bag at his feet.

"Wait, what?" Auggie said, shaking his head. "Father, why are you asking about all that?

"Possession, Augustus," Thorne said. "Inhabitation by an alien spirit, usually demonic."

"Oh, sweet Mother," Aisling crossed herself and Dean placed his hands on her shoulders.

"I'm sure it's nothing like that, dear," Dean said.

"I hope you are correct, Mr. Freed," Thorn said, sipping his tea. "However, given the, um, odd proclivities of our town..." The priest let the implication hang in the air.

Everyone who lived in Golgotha knew the place was filled with strange occurrences. From talking animals to vengeful spirits, from lunatic killers to monsters straight out of the most fevered of imaginations. Anyone who lived in the town for any length of time knew this was the case. They just pretended it wasn't so, grasping at any rational explanation to ignore the strange voices carried on the desert winds at night, so they could sleep...with one eye open.

"We've had to petition the Holy See three times in the last year for an exorcist to come to Golgotha," he continued. "All three cases were found to have merit and the ritual was performed. It even cost one of the priests his sanity, poor man."

Aisling covered her mouth, clearly trying to remain calm.

"Father, forgive, but do we have the time to seek out aid from Rome?" Auggie asked. "The boy is very weak, ja? I have heard that Professor Mephisto, the man who owns the theater, has some experience in such matters."

Father Thorne frowned. "Mephisto, yes, I've heard that as well. Curious chap. I'm sorry Auggie, but I'm afraid I can't condone bringing in some soothsayer to minister to the boy."

There was a sound under the table like an asthmatic goose with a head cold honking as it flew south for the winter. Auggie recognized it as Clay's rare laugh.

Clay popped back up from his search, an odd, six-inch-long glass wand with a metal tip in his bandaged hands. He was still chortling a little.

"Something amusing to you, Clay?" Thorne asked, frowning.

"Just struck me funny a fellow in your line of work making a fuss about calling in a soothsayer."

"I take it you have no use for the rituals of the Holy Mother Church, Turlough?"

"Oh, they're all well and good, I suppose," Clay said. "If you put stock in that sort of thing. I prefer things I can quantify, thank you all the same." Clay turned to Aisling, "Mrs. Walsh, has the boy made water excessively since he fell ill?"

Aisling blushed and Father Thorne got very interested in his cup of tea at the question. Clay didn't notice. "You got any cookies?"

Auggie harrumphed. "Clay why on earth would you ask such an embarrassing—"

"What? About the cookies? I like cookies with my tea. Well, ma'am?"

"Um, no," she said, recovering her composure. "He drinks a lot of water but he's hardly, uh, piddled, at all, Mr. Turlough."

"Interesting," Clay said. "I'm going to need to see the boy again."

"What is that gadget you got there?" Thorne asked, nodding toward the glass wand.

"Clinical thermometer," Clay said. "I fashioned it from the descriptions provided by its inventor, Sir Thomas Clifford Allbutt. This device can accurately measure the temperature of the human body within five minutes of application."

"I've heard of those," Dean said. "Pretty newfangled, Clay. You think Daniel is running a fever?"

"With all his agitation, I couldn't tell by skin contact," Clay said, rising, "but this will do the trick."

"You won't hurt him, will you?" Aisling asked. Clay shook his head.

"No ma'am, Just gonna put it right under his armpit. Lad won't feel a thing. However, I also need to draw a sample of his blood, unless Doctor Tumblety did any of that already."

Aisling lowered her head. "No. The doctor refused, I'm afraid."

"Auggie mentioned he refused to treat the boy, but not even to see him? Well, we'll see about that!"

"Thank you so much, Mr. Turlough," she said. She tried to hug Clay but he stiffened awkwardly at the attempt. Auggie smiled.

"Most folks just call me Clay," he said. "We'll get your short britches up and running again in no time. Now, about those cookies…"

After taking Daniel's temperature and collecting a sample of the boy's blood, Clay and Auggie excused themselves, promising the exhausted widow they'd return soon. It was dark outside the little house. Freed followed them out into the cold night.

"Clay, if I can be of any help to you at all, please let me know," Dean said. "My chemistry is pretty rusty, I have to acknowledge the corn. These days I do more shaves and tooth-pulling than anything else."

"Much obliged, Dean," Clay said. "Say, do you know anything about what happened to Mr. Walsh?"

Dean looked back to the house to make sure the door was shut behind him before replying. "James? Why you ask? You don't think the same thing is happening to Daniel?"

"Don't know enough to say."

"Well, what I heard was it was some kind of fever with delirium. He dehydrated pretty fast too. Nothing seemed to make it better. He got weaker and weaker. He kept seeing things, and then he just gave up the ghost. I heard a few folks said James had crossed some of the Indians…that one of their medicine men put a hex on him, if you believe in that kind of thing."

"Witchcraft?" Auggie said, frowning.

"Hmm. What did our esteemed Doctor Tumblety think it was?" Clay asked.

"Doc wouldn't see him or treat him," Freed said.

"Ah, again!" Auggie said. "Why not?" Dean looked sheepishly at the ground. "Dean?"

"Because they're Irish…and Catholic," Freed said.

Auggie pounded on the door to Doctor Francis Tumblety's small cottage, tucked away by itself near Absalom and Rose

Roads. There was light in the small window off to the right of the front door. After a moment the door came violently open and Tumblety appeared, regarding the hulking shopkeeper and the cadaverous Clay.

Doctor Tumblety was a compact man, wiry and of no great height. He had short, side-parted hair and a long, drooping walrus mustache, both the color of dirt. At this hour, the doctor sported a maroon smoking jacket. "Ah, Shultz, Turlough." Tumblety reeked of whiskey. "This is most unorthodox and untoward. My hours of appointment are clearly posted upon my shingle. I assume at least one of you is capable of reading English, yes?"

"I don't give a spit what time it is," Clay said. "You have a very sick little boy down there in town. Why in Sam Hill haven't you treated him? Why did you let his father die?"

"Ah, you mean the Walsh clan, I assume." Tumblety slurred a little.

"*Ja!*" Auggie said, taking a step toward the much smaller man. "That family has done you no harm, Doctor, yet you let them suffer and die! I did not think doctors did such things!"

"You see here now, Shultz!" Tumblety was getting red-faced in the sallow light of the lantern he had on a table beside the door. "Who I choose as a patient is my business and certainly none of yours or this...footman's business. Goodnight to you!"

Tumblety began to slam the door, but Clay placed a burned hand and a wiry forearm against it, holding it open. Clay's forearm was cabled with taut muscles. If the burns were paining him, it was impossible for Auggie to tell. He placed his own hand on the door to support his injured friend.

Clay's eyes narrowed, staring accusingly into the doctor's florid face. "Why? I want to hear it from that privy you call a mouth, doc. Say it, hell, I know you're proud of it."

"They are like roaches," Tumblety hissed, his face in partial eclipse from the sick light of the lantern and the dingy shadows, his eyes wide and almost fevered in their glassiness. A froth of spit clung to the edges of the man's lips. "They live and rut and breed in squalor and filth. They are brutes, drunken beasts, who only heed their unholy masters who serve the Whore of Babylon, herself."

Auggie winced at the defamation of his beloved church.

Tumblety spit on Clay's boot.

"You...took an oath," Clay was angrier than Auggie had ever seen him, but his voice was low and even. "You're no healer, you're a quack and a charlatan."

"I shall summon the sheriff!" Tumblety roared. "I'll have both of you thrown into the clink for such audacity, such slander! Get out! Out, I say!"

Auggie took Clay's arm and as gently as possible pulled him away from the door. "Ah! Come on Clayton, we should go now." Clay reluctantly released the door at his friend's urging and walked away.

As they retreated, Tumblety shouted out, "I hope the little Irish bastard dies, just like his supposed father! One less mackerel snapper to pollute our fine American town!" Auggie was on Tumblety in a flash, grabbing the doctor by the lapels and lifting him off the ground. Tumblety gasped at the speed and strength of the usually placid shopkeeper.

"You...shut your mouth...*böser ding*, before I break your jaw!" Now it was Clay pulling Auggie away.

"Come on now, pard. He ain't worth it. Gentle down now, leave it. Let's go."

Auggie blinked and released Tumblety. The doctor sputtered and slammed the door and the two men found themselves wrapped in darkness. They trudged silently down the hill, back towards the few feeble lights of town.

"That man is infuriating," Auggie said, pacing back and forth in Clay's workshop. "And he has the nerve to call himself a doctor."

"He's a jackass to be sure," Clay said absently. He was scanning various pages from the stack of books he had gathered in front of him. "But getting riled up over him ain't going to help Daniel Walsh none."

"What do you think it is?" Auggie asked.

"I'm pondering that," Clay said, closing one book and opening another.

"That child is not getting better, Clayton, and that poor woman can't lose someone else, *ja*?"

"I know…"

"Loss can eat at you in ways you never fully recover from. Enough loss and you just…fade away, like a ghost. Living, but not." Auggie looked up to see Clay staring at him, an odd look in his eyes.

"I'm…happy you found Gillian, Auggie. I never wanted you to be a ghost. I know how much Gertie meant to you. She'd want you happy."

"You know, Clay, Gerta would have never wanted you to be a ghost either. She thought the world of you." Auggie looked around the workshop. "Please don't haunt this place. The town needs you, and…I do as well."

Clay closed his book. "Well, I'm not quite done in yet. Come on, hitch up your wagon. We got a trip to take."

"What, where?"

"We're going to get one last piece in this puzzle. Pack some supplies, we might be gone a few days."

"A few days? Ah! Clay, that boy doesn't have that much time!"

"He's strong, he'll hang on. He has to."

"Why must we do this? Where are we going?"

"To see a man about a hex."

The Washoe camp was near the town of Hazen. It wasn't much more than half-dozen of the cone-shaped dwellings the Indians used in winter, called *galais dungal*. The dwellings were covered in branches and then reinforced with animal hides to keep out the desert's bitter, winter nights. Dogs barked as Auggie's wagon approached. They chased the buckboard and were soon joined by a gaggle of young boys who shouted out as the two white men approached.

As they got closer, Auggie noticed a group of women and girls sitting together in the communal area at the center of the cluster of dwellings. They were weaving with branches and strips of wood, forming beautiful and intricately patterned baskets.

"I still think we should have asked Deputy Mutt to go with us," Auggie said, his voice low.

"Why? Because he's an Indian?" Auggie asked in his normal voice.

"Ur…well, yes."

"Mutt was chased out from his people, and besides, he's off with Deputy Jim hunting that thing that's been stealing folk's faces. It did in poor Andrew Beal a few days back. We'll do fine." A group of men, summoned by the boys' calls, approached the wagon. Several of them carried rifles.

"Ah, I hope so, ja?" Auggie pulled the wagon to a stop ahead of the approaching crowd and waved.

"What do you want?" a broad man with a craggy face asked in English. He kept his rifle low and beside his leg.

"I'm from over by Golgotha," Clay began. "There's a sick child there, and I was hoping I could ask a few questions of your healer, if you got one." Several members of the group muttered among themselves.

"Golgotha," the apparent leader frowned. "Bad place, bad medicine there."

"So you've met our doctor, I see," Clay said.

"What if the child gets sicker?" asked a younger man in the crowd. By now, most of the women and girls in the weaving circle had joined the men. Most of the village were surrounding them. Auggie looked nervous, Clay didn't seem to even notice. "You'll blame it on us!"

"White men will come!" one of the women called out. "No! We don't need any trouble!"

"A white fella has already said one of your medicine men put a hex on the boy and his father," Clay said over the growing din. "I don't believe that. I'm here to learn and try to help the boy survive."

"Please." Auggie stood up off the bench on the buckboard. "I know why you are concerned, why you fear to help, *ja*? You may not believe it, but I'm feared and hated too, because of where I come from, because of how I worship God. Please, this boy hates no one! He's done nothing wrong." He pointed to one of the women, holding her son, "This child is about the same age as your boy. Please!"

The crowd buzzed with conversation. After several moments, the craggy-faced leader gestured for Clay and Auggie to dismount from the wagon. Slowly, the two men did. "I will take you to talk to our eldest," he said. "Perhaps they can help you."

"Thank you," Auggie said.

"We're not quite so bitter yet that we would wish ill upon a child," the man said.

"Datura Stramonium," Clay said. They were assembled in Aisling Walsh's cabin. "It goes by quite a few names: Ditch Weed, Stink Weed, Devil's Snare—but not quite the devil or the snare you suspected, Father." Father Thorne stood alongside Aisling, Dean Freed, Auggie and Sheriff Jon Highfather, who had arrived with Clay and Auggie. "Some of the native tribes hereabouts call it thornapple, or moonflower. Most folk know it as jimson weed."

"What is it?" Aisling asked.

"Well, it's related to nightshade," Clay said. "An alkaloid poison, nasty one too. The boy's symptoms got me thinking it was some kind of poison, but I couldn't be sure, not until I talked with the Washoe medicine men. You see, they use jimsonweed in some of their rituals, peyote too. They cook up a tea that lets them have visions and such. It's a very careful process. Too much of the stuff and you can end up dead, not just visiting. If you do get too much you don't just hallucinate, you also get real ornery."

"Oh my god," Dean said, "so the Indians did put some kind of a spell on Daniel, using this stuff."

"I didn't say that," Clay said. "No magic, at least not this time in Golgotha, just good old-fashioned murder."

"What are you saying, Clay?" Thorne asked, "and how can you be so sure that it's this jimson weed?"

"Fair question, Padre," Clay said. He reached into his bag and removed two corked glass flasks. Both were full of an orange-red liquid. "This here is a formula called Dragendorff's Reagent. I'll spare you the chemical breakdown, but it was invented a few years back by a German chemist to detect the presence of alkaloids. I dropped some seeds from a jimson weed plant the Indians gave me in this one, and the swatch of cloth I took with Daniel's blood in the other. They both test positive for alkaloids."

"Oh, sweet Mother!" Aisling said.

Dean pulled her to him. "It will be all right, dear," he whispered, "won't it, Clay?"

"Mrs. Walsh, is there anything your late husband and your son ate or drank that you didn't particularly care for?"

Aisling stepped away from Dean's embrace. She wiped her red eyes and sniffed. "Nothing comes to mind, Mr. Turlough. Are you saying this is what killed my sweet James too?"

"I think so," Clay said. "We'd need to dig up the body and have me run some tests on the remaining fatty issue to be sure, but I can't rule it out."

"Perhaps the boy just picked some up outside," Thorne suggested. "Does it grow wild?"

"It does," Clay said, "but at this concentration, it would be nearly impossible for it to have been some kind of an accident. No, someone gave it to the boy– and most likely the father too– at lethal dosages."

"The tea!" Aisling exclaimed. "Peppermint tea! I can't abide it, but James loved it, especially when he was feeling a bit under the weather, and Daniel, well, he loved whatever his Da loved. They both drank Peppermint tea."

"Would you fetch it, please, ma'am?" Clay asked.

"Clay, who would have any knowledge of all this business?" Sheriff Highfather asked.

"The Indians, clearly," Dean said. "I heard tell, James had a run-in with some of them a while before he got sick."

"I don't think so," Clay said.

"Tumblety?" Thorne posed. "The man hates Catholics, to be sure."

"I doubt Tumblety would know jimson weed from willow bark," Clay said. "That man could only poison someone through incompetence, and he never came near either victim."

Aisling set the ceramic tea urn on the table. Clay lifted the lid. He produced another flask of clear liquid and uncorked it. Pouring a scoop of the tea into the flask, he resealed it and shook it vigorously. The liquid turned the same sunset orange-red as the other two samples. Aisling crossed herself. "Sweet Lord Jesus, no! I killed my beloved and my son!"

"No," Clay said. "You didn't. Where did you get your tea from?"

"Mr. Shultz," she said with wet, red eyes.

"All right," Clay said. "No offense, Auggie, but you don't know enough about chemistry to do this, and you got no reason to. So, who's had access to your home?"

"Just the Father and…"

Everyone's eyes fixed on Dean.

"Dean, you know enough chemistry…and you're the one that's been going on about this story of the Indians being angry with Mr. Walsh," Clay said. "And—" He glanced over at Aisling. "You'd have a reason to want the lady's attention focused on you."

"Oh my god, Dean… How could you," Aisling looked at Freed in horror.

Dean lowered his head. The sheriff stepped to him and took him by the bicep. "I… I just wanted to take care of you," Dean said, pleading, to her. "I wanted us to be together. Alone…no distractions. I love you, Aisling."

"Okay, Dean," Highfather said, "enough of that. Let's go."

Aisling hugged Clay and again he stiffened at the embrace. "Oh thank God for you, Mr. Turlough! Can you save my boy?"

"I can try," Clay said, untangling himself from the hug. "But he ain't going to like it." Father Thorne looked at Clay and shook his head. "What, Padre?"

"The Lord works through some strange angels," the priest said.

"Don't he just," Auggie replied.

"Soot," Auggie said, "You cured the boy by feeding him soot."

"Charcoal," Clay said. "Once I knew what kind of poison he'd ingested, it was easier to find a cure. He'll live." Auggie brought the wagon to a stop inside Clay's compound.

"So, you saved a child's life, and you brought a murderer to justice. Aren't you glad you ventured out from your barn for a few days?"

"Workshop," Clay corrected as he climbed down. He walked to the workshop door and unlocked it.

"Clayton?"

"Yeah?"

"See you tomorrow?"

Clay stared at him for a long moment. "You bet."

"Good!" Auggie winked and drove away. Clay watched him go.

Stars were spilling out across the vast indigo sea of the western sky. Most folks would be thinking of supper, then bed, sleeping next to the person they loved. He thought of Dean Freed sitting in a cell, awaiting the hangman's rope, his mad love for Aisling Walsh keeping him warm, still giving him delusional hope. A devil's snare. He pitied the madman. Clay swung the door open and stepped into the barn, prepared for another night's work on Gertie's mummified head. Maybe tonight he'd tell her why he'd been away.

BAD

JOSH MALERMAN

Back in years nobody would call better, in the counties of Ucatanani and Miskaloosa, there ran a profound tract of dangerous land known simply as The Trail. Framed by evergreens in every season, a forest as dense as the men and women who threaded it, the path was uneven, uncared for, and at times, too slim for even one carriage to pass. Outlaws paced this land, hitmen hired in one town to carry out grotesqueries in another, and it was these men and these towns that rotted into legend, so that the names Portsoothe, Abberstown, and Griggsville were spoken far from the fabled Trail.

The southernmost town was a quiet one, a place where ruffians retired, lived far from one another, and much further from the rancor of the road. Mackatoon, known best for once hosting James Moxie, a man who proved duel-victorious without drawing his pistol, was a two-day ride, at best, from the very tip of The Trail—that is, the town of Harrows, the wealthiest and therefore most protected of all places.

It is the town of Harrows that concerns us now. As this is where two young hatchet-men, too new to know, attempted to rob the bank.

Jacob Feller and D. Allen Watson first heard of the bank while jailed in Juniper. Neither man had a horse, nor, at the time, their freedom. Still, familiar with the routine of the law and the lawless, they were bright enough to understand they couldn't be held forever. While behind bars, they found little to do but listen to the Sheriff and the guards as the law swapped news of The Trail, that news not only including but highlighted by the building of a bank up north in Harrows. Feller and Watson were the sort of naïve that wasn't aware of its own current state of affairs, its present lot, and therefore they didn't imagine two like themselves might stand out in a town like that. They believed in a great number of things they shouldn't have, but believing themselves to be modern men was perhaps most dangerous of all.

Sheriff Dickens of Juniper spoke freely in earshot of the two, likely unconcerned with any probability Feller or Watson would make heads nor tails of the information, let alone come up with a plan. They were young in body, yes, but even younger in mind. That is, they'd been jailed for attempting to unhitch a horse, unaware its owner sat flush upon it, watching them as they worked. But sometimes a blade of grass grows in the mud of a particularly barren cavity in the Trail, and so Feller and Watson were blessed with a sudden intention.

Both had learned enough about banks to understand the root concepts: men and women placed their money in the care of the bank and the bank charged them a little bit for doing so. This way, all the money of any particular Trail-town would receive the most protection, and citizens north and south could cease worrying about hitmen breaking into their homes after dark. What they didn't know was much more. For example, Watson was right stunned to hear a teller wouldn't simply hand over someone's money if you told them you'd come on their behalf. And Feller, put involuntarily in the place of being the more knowledgeable, hadn't ever heard the word "vault" till it was used by Dickens himself, the Sheriff's back to the two temporary inmates, his dusty Trail boots on the dusty office desk. Still, it wasn't until one of the deputies mentioned the new bank in Harrows wouldn't allow guns within a fifty-yard radius that Jacob Feller was struck with what some might dub inspiration, others dark folly.

They would need to appear as a customer, of course, dress as one, a specific one, disguise themselves so entirely the teller would, after all, hand over the money without being forced to do so at gunpoint. This way, by the time the true customer learned of the trick, Feller or Watson would be out of the building, the pair long gone south again, perhaps to Kellytown, where men such as themselves were known to hide in the woods until their deeds had quieted down. This plan they whispered to one another, even as the men of Juniper continued with their Trail gossip, Feller and Watson growing more excited by the minute. They had devised, after all, a non-violent plan, and therefore couldn't be held accountable to the law. Why, if someone hands you money, surely you can't be jailed for accepting it? But foolish as this thinking was, it paled beside the inanity of the root belief they held. For, there was nothing more hazardous on The Trail than to assume a situation to be violence-free, even with the cleanest intentions.

This story, in which Jacob Feller and D. Allen Watson attempted to rob the brand-new Harrows Bank, would end in a violence neither man had envisioned prior, a bloodshed so lurid it bespoke of impossibilities, pockets of inhumanity from which even two cocksure triggermen would have abstained.

If only they had thought to do so.

They crossed the Ossiwak River by way of the C.C. Bridge at Portsoothe because they'd decided to "play it orderly" (Watson's phrase) rather than being spotted wading the waters, the way most outlaws traversed. They stole no horses and begot no brawls. Neither man looked West Franklinville's way as they put boot to Trail, heads and hats down, comporting themselves the way they'd seen civilized people go about it. At the entrances to both Abberstown and Kellytown, Watson spoke briefly about how nice it'd be to snatch a quick plate of chicken and Feller snapped at him, running hotter than he normally would, as the dream of robbing the new bank in Harrows had begun to consume him. The farther north they walked, the greater they detailed their communal fantasy, so that by the time they reached Albert's Port at nightfall, both had already been wed, their wives borne children, their neighbors requested financial assistance, their photos celebrated upon saloon walls, and the bridges in and out of each town named for them. Tired legs and weary eyes indeed, they'd been propelled by triumphant visions, their hearts pumping enthusiastic blood to their brains.

Watson learned early not to ask Feller the plan unless he wanted a cursing out. They weren't to speak of such things on The Trail; The Trail had ears, a thing Watson ought to well know by now, as both men had found deep trouble before, flummoxed as to how trouble had known they were coming. They would whisper, Feller said, once they were in for the night, and even then, it depended on what walls would hold them. In the end, the end of that first day's walk, they slept within no walls, opting for the evergreens behind a grand hotel on Howard Street in Albert's Port. The two were encouraged by the lack of distrust shown by the deputy who'd asked them their business when they arrived in town. It only erroneously bolstered their delusion of fitting in to the finer towns of The Trail. But Albert's Port was no Harrows.

That night Feller slept fitfully, waking with ideas, parting his hair on the opposite side of his head, attempting to quietly voice another man's voice, even rising to a standing once to try out a different man's walk. He'd never acted before, but he'd attended the theater in Griggsville and believed he knew what a performer did. Watson slept soundly, despite wanting badly to talk things out, to speak freely about their design. Turned out walking The Trail all day had him beat. And often, to a tired man, the fruits of curing that day's exhaustion outweighed any preparations for the next one.

In two days, he'd wished he hadn't weighed it that way.

They passed Samhattan at noon, unafraid to show their faces to passing carriages and riders. Feller even tipped his hat to a lady, who closed the purple drapes of the small square window in turn. Samhattan, both had heard, fancied itself a sister town to Harrows, the latter citizenry constantly attempting to rationalize the ways in which it wasn't. Neither man had traveled this far north before. Neither had cause to. Anything you could find in cold, business-as-usual Samhattan could be found in West Franklinville, even Mackatoon. And these northern towns had nothing on Griggsville in the way of libation. Both men smiled toothily at fellow Trail-travelers, and somewhere just south of Harrows, Feller thought to scold Watson for perhaps overdoing the kindliness. Then he recalled himself, up in the woods the night before, playacting the parts of numerous men he'd seen in his thus far limited time in this world. Watson, he guessed, was doing something of the same. Performing. Or learning to. And besides, they wouldn't look like themselves when they entered that bank, no matter how short they fell in mastering the art of portrayal.

The sign welcoming them to Harrows galvanized something in Feller that had been brewing these past thirty-something hours. He couldn't rightly *not* think about the bank, about disguising himself, about asking a man for money and receiving it in turn. He'd grown obstinate since waking, obsessed with these partials, these bits of the greater fantasy. It had all become a necessary precursor to the life he and Watson would next lead. But the sun, mostly blocked by the height of the evergreens reaching across the Trail like tall children playing pattycake, broke through and illuminated the town's sign in such singular fashion, Feller had no choice but to take it as a signal of Fate, pure existence letting him know he and Watson were doing the right thing.

He felt relief then for the first time since Juniper. And so he spoke, too. A whisper to Watson, as they entered the town of their fancy. Yes, at perhaps the precise moment he should've kept most quiet, he couldn't. He spoke of staking out the bank, of what type of man they ought to be looking for, of how it could all be done. But while Watson seemed to relish in this dulcet conversation, Feller didn't speak his whole mind. For, the obsession had grown as uneven as The Trail, and simply dressing the part no longer felt adequate. No.

As the roofs of the homes of Harrows came into view, as the establishments on Main Street could be seen peeking above these finer abodes, Feller and Watson paused by the evergreens' edge, confabulating once more, designating themselves for assignment. And they still didn't see themselves as outsiders, even as they entered the town proper, they didn't consider the fact someone might describe them, and do it well, even if they succeeded in their program and were long south again after, reaping their spoils in Griggsville. Watson, for his part, might be forgiven for such an oversight, as it had been established long ago Feller would be the brains of most operations. But Feller's reason didn't go quite as deep, no, as his ignorance floated on the surface of the pool of all thought. It floated in the form of a face. A face not his own. A face taken.

When Watson asked Feller what he meant by "taking a face," Feller expressed some surprise at having spoken that part out loud.

But what of it? And there was nothing to be done about revealing it, as such revelations must come to light in a partnership. Yes, he told Watson, as they approached homes the likes of which neither had ever seen, gardens as gorgeous as the paintings that only hung in the saloons of the southern sticks, yes, he believed they needed the face of the man they would imitate, the face and the hair, so that anything they lacked in performative quality would be made up for in the authenticity of the real.

The new bank of Harrows was not difficult to find, as it was more heavily guarded than the jail. Three armed men stood sentry at the far northern end of Main Street, the edifice a long fifty yards behind them, built upon an open expanse clearly rid of once verdant trees. Stumps dotted the distance beyond the bank, giving a sense of scale, and it stood to reason another armed man would be standing out back, obscured from traditional viewing angles. Feller and Watson observed from across the wide, dusty road. Main Street's boardwalk ended before the bank's lot began, and the pair decided it best to be seen here, a part of the town, rather than be spotted in the evergreens beyond the businesses. Here, on the wood planks, they could be ordinary citizens, two men upon a bench outside the furrier.

They'd already stepped inside and perused the goods, unaware the proprietor, a woman of short stature, had trained her fiery eyes upon them, recognizing them as trouble from The Trail and certainly not part and parcel of this place. They asked her questions that only supported this conclusion, and when they exited and took to the bench outside, she opted to count her blessings rather than make a fuss. They had left her store, after all, and that was most important in the end.

Feller and Watson watched as men and women approached the armed guards with head nods and tips of their hats. These people were dressed fine, in vests and long skirts, umbrellas to reduce the sun. They walked with purpose and tapped their shoes against a single brown brick before entering; that way showing the bank some respect. Feller nudged Watson at the sight of a lean man in a pale blue three-piece suit. He was perhaps a trifle smaller than either of the outlaws, but his mustache and low derby obscured him, making him a natural mark. Like the other men, this one removed his hat before entering, showcasing brown curls that positively reflected the sun, and Feller imagined himself with that same full head of hair, that same face.

He didn't need to tell Watson this was their man. Watson sat so his butt was on the very edge of the bench until the man exited the new bank, at which point Feller took hold of Watson's wrist, stopping him from rising to a standing. They waited that way, unafraid to watch the man as he passed the guards, crossed the lot, and stepped upon the boardwalk across directly across from the furrier.

Feller now stood, allowing Watson to do the same.

They went in tandem with the man, smiling and nodding to the men and women they passed, those they made room for, and those they paused to allow passage. They kept their eyes on the man in the pale blue suit and thought nothing of the sour expressions they brought to the faces of the citizens of Harrows. There was only one face they were fixed on. And that face was kept below the rim of said derby, behind the flush of a full mustache, floating above the fine collar and vest of a suit nobody south of here could afford. When the man took an elegant right turn onto a side street overflowing with purple rhododendrons, Feller and Watson followed. They crossed the street, at pace, careful not to rush, and were content no law was on their rudder. For Feller, the fact the man walked all the way to the end of the long street before making for the steps of a wide dwelling was as serendipitous as the sun shining on the town's welcome sign. Fate, it felt, was with them. Fewer neighbors at the end of the street, any street. And in a town like this, the homes were so far distanced from one another; you could've fit three Abberstown homes between them. And a schoolhouse.

Feller and Watson did not wait outside the man's home after he opened and then closed the door. They simply kept pace, as if they, too, lived there. As if they, too, were returning from the bank. And so they, too, climbed the single limestone step to the same door and then opened and closed it, too.

The man, having not yet made it down the long hall to whatever room lay beyond it, turned at the sound they made. He eyed them with justifiable suspicion and did not ask what business they had with him. It was clear, whatever it was, he should run. And so run he did, toward that back room where Feller and Watson would later find the gun he was hoping to reach. The gun he'd left at home for two reasons. The first was that crime was rare in the town of Harrows. It was the main glory of paying such large fees to call it home. The second was that the new bank insisted nobody carry as they came.

But the man did not achieve his aim, as the triggermen moved swifter, having lived years in the belly of The Trail. Feller got his shoulders and Watson slid across the wood floor to take hold of the ankles of his pale blue pants. Together they dropped him, so that his head cracked against a limestone shelf, his body falling half into the room revealed to be a parlor. No smoke rose from the fireplace. No dog barked at the intruders.

Feller knelt and checked the man to make sure he was out, then rose and took the hall back to a fine kitchen they had passed on the short chase. There, as predicted, he located a small, keen knife. He eyed the dining space before leaving, imagining himself eating in something like it soon. When he returned, Watson had the man on his back. There was some apprehension in his partner's eyes, but Feller only saw the expression of the man, like he was sleeping, still out.

He knelt again and brought the blade to the soft chin. The blood came fast and pooled near the collar and Feller put his hand there to stave it. The outlaws discussed things fast then. Feller told Watson they need to remove the suit and shirt. They couldn't rightly enter the bank painted red. Watson said he thought the point here was to commit a crime without violence, therefore rendering the action legal. Feller paused to consider this. The man began writhing between them. Feller said the plan hadn't changed; the *crime* in the bank would remain *legal* because there would be no crime *in the bank*. This was good enough for Watson. Feller admitted he hadn't expected so much blood. The man started to groan. The outlaws removed his jacket, his vest, his shirt. They set all neatly on a wicker chair by the fireplace. Watson held the man down as Feller began again where he'd left off. The chin, then up the left cheek. The man screamed. Feller held one hand over his mouth, careful not to thereby ruin the mustache he would soon wear. Blood came fast. It was all over Feller's hands. Too much, he thought. He wouldn't be able to get it all out unless he got it out now.

He rose again. Told Watson to finish the job. The face *and* the hair. The face *and* the hair. Then he took to the hall again and returned to the kitchen and found there a bucket of clean water. He dunked both hands, scrubbing the fresh red from his fingers. The man stopped yelling in the other room, and he knew well why.

His hands as clean as he'd get them, he returned to find Watson holding what looked like an animal cursed by Fate, trampled by a carriage on The Trail. Feller removed his own shirt and coat. Set his hat on the limestone mantel. On the floor, a shirtless, faceless, hairless thing. A bucket of red paint with two white pearls at its surface. Watson removed the man's boots and pants. Feller put on the man's shirt and vest. All too snug, he couldn't button the vest. With the coat, it didn't matter.

He put on the pale blue pants and stepped into his own boots again, knowing now the man's would be too small. He held out his hand for the face and hair. Watson, his own palms as bloodied as the body, gave it all to him. Feller stepped back, into the doorjamb of this the parlor, and brought the headless face to his own. He started with the hair, donning it like someone would a wig, allowing the man's former face to fall, like carriage drapes, upon his own features. Watson was up then; he handed Feller the derby and just as Feller put it on, just as he looked to his partner through the eyeholes, asking silently if it looked the part, if they were going to pull this off, the home's from door opened and a woman's voice came calling. And a child's, a son's, too.

Feller, in the pale suit and black derby, the emancipated face and dark curly hair, turned to see the pair just inside the front door. And they saw him. The woman called him Tim. Feller took this as a good sign. Even as their expressions changed from uninformed to educated.

The woman grabbed the child and turned for the door, but it was too late for them.

Watson was already tearing up the hall, knife in hand, set to convey more violence.

And more violence he conveyed.

After all, it wasn't violence in the bank.

The outlaws spent the night in that same parlor, the three bodies stacked in what they determined to be the master bedroom. Neither had slept in a home with so many rooms before. They burned wood in the fireplace and rationalized how the smoke from the chimney would give the guise of normality. There they practiced. Feller stood in full costume by the mantel, the hat on, the hat off, nodding, frowning, and speaking. They made adjustments to the mouth so he'd have more freedom to inform the teller he'd been accosted, and therefore wished to remove all his money, as he was now moving south to Mackatoon. This, they surmised, would explain the blood and bruises upon his face. And if prior to this evening the pair had deluded themselves into believing they didn't stand out in a town like Harrows, they positively lied to themselves now. The chin hung like drool. The mustache covered most of Feller's mouth, no matter how fastidious they got with it. And still, they envisioned themselves in another Trail-town, feasting off the rewards of their hard work.

They spoke of their plan freely. Watson would stage just enough of a distraction. He would pocket the man Tim's gun and approach the bank with its handle clearly seen. Then, as he argued the rules of the new bank of Harrows with its three guardsmen, Feller would approach at a safe distance, safely beneath the derby, and nod the way those familiar with the bank would do.

To two men caught stealing a horse by the very man who sat upon it, this plan felt armored. The distraction, the nod, the canard about being beaten and bruised in his own hometown. Surely, the bank would empathize. Surely, in a town so civilized, they would quietly hand Feller the money, asking him to accept their apologies for having played any part in the illusion of a safe society.

Still, neither slept much. Watson found some in the wicker chair by the fire, but Feller mostly remained standing, pacing the length of the parlor, then the length of the hall, passing the very bedroom in which lay the man whose face he now wore.

He didn't take it off for many hours. Until he convinced himself rest was worthy. Then, feeling as though he would be as inconspicuous as the man Tim himself, Feller slept on a white lounge, the face and hair in a small pile beside him. Later, the likeness of that face would be discovered in the fabric of the lounge. And the deputy who discovered it would simply say, they slept in here.

On August 15th of a year nobody would say was better than

this one, Jacob Feller and D. Allen Watson left Timothy and Amelia Holbrook's Harrows home later than they expected to. They both woke with starts, anxious to get the money they could almost feel already in their pockets. As for Feller, those pockets belonged to another man, as he'd slept in the pale blue suit, thereby waking in it. Once ready, Watson took the gun, and Feller found a small satchel in the kitchen, used for carrying onions from the grocer to home. There he placed the face and hair, not having the intuition to guess the mask would then smell of onions when he put it on. They didn't want to come up behind the bank for fear of being spotted by any backdoor guard, and so they took a long route back to the end of the boardwalk, to where the furrier's store stood. There, in the shadows of this the last shop on Main Street, Feller adorned Timothy Holbrook's face and hair. He put it on as he had practiced the night before. Hair first, face hanging, then, with fingers clean of blood, he tightened and tucked where he believed he should. It felt looser today. But before he could ask his partner's opinion, Watson stepped out of the shadows and onto the boardwalk, where he pretended to ponder a moment to give the illusion of having come from the town bustle and not the woods beyond it. Feller, his view somewhat obscured by the eye holes of the drooping face, remained standing in those shadows and watched Watson cross the wide road and approach the armed men at the head of the lot. It felt as though Fate had touched him again, as first one, then two, then all three guards got into conversation with Watson, demanding he leave his firearm with them before stepping any closer to the bank.

The plan was working.

So, on August 15th, at roughly nine fifty-one a.m., Jacob Feller stepped out of the shadows of the Harrows furrier's shop in another man's suit, wearing another man's derby, face, and hair. He tried to walk as the man Timothy had, upright and swift, confident there was no crime in this town. But Feller recalled the plan, and Timothy was supposed to have been accosted by ruffians, and so wouldn't he walk with some diffidence, some doubt, some slouch? He did so, adjusting his walk so suddenly that Jane Marion, the furrier herself, would later say it caught her attention, and, after spotting the man D. Allen Watson arguing with the bank defenders, she felt it prudent to notify Sheriff Opal. Jacob Feller was nodding to the third and still closest of the armed men as Jane Marion walked the planked boardwalk to the station. Watson made a fuss as the third gun eyed Feller with suspicion. Then Watson made a louder fuss and Feller was free of the gaze. He crossed the lot, unsure how to walk. He mumbled as he went, attempting to find the voice he'd practiced by the fire last night. He couldn't find it. At the bank's door, he removed his hat. The sun felt too hot. Too much heat inside the other man's face.

Still on August 15th, at close to nine fifty-five a.m., Jacob Feller entered the new bank of Harrows wearing Timothy Holbrook's face and hair. The door swung closed behind him, cutting off the day's light, and for a fearful second he believed the mask had slipped too low. He couldn't see. As he adjusted the face, his eyes adjusted, and the aghast expressions of three bank employees came into focus.

Wearing his own boots still, Feller crossed the bank's wood floor. He started speaking before he reached the window. He told of being abused. Ambushed in his own home. He spoke of blood and beatings. He brought his hands to the sides of his face and held it there, adjusting it as he spoke in a voice with numerous inflections, Feller unable to zero in on the most appropriate one. Beneath the face and hair, Feller was sweating. Even as he spoke of his wife and son. Even as he demanded all his money in the name of leaving this unsafe town, this town that was no better than any other on The Trail. Half-blinded by the now uneven eye holes, he stepped up against the counter, hard enough for the face to come free of his own, before he caught it in time, the hair of the mustache curling between his trembling fingers.

Nobody moved. Nobody made to get the money. One teller, a man older than any Jacob Feller knew, told him he had come in the day before to ask for a loan. You have no money, the old man said. But the other tellers quieted him. That isn't Holbrook, one said. Stay away from him, Wes.

The bank's door opened then, and heavy boots clomped onto

the wood floor. Feller turned to partially see a heavyset man in uniform brandishing a silver gun.

"You have two choices in death," Sheriff Opal said. "You can either hang as you will or come at me now and be shot for doing so."

Feller stood still. Incredibly, he thought the mask should still work.

"I haven't done anything illegal in here," he said.

"Everything you've done since you did what you did has been illegal, son."

"What did I do? I was beaten. Bruised. I want to leave town now. I am Tim."

"You're no more Timothy Holbrook than I am James Moxie. But I'd recognize that suit and 'stache combination from the other end of Main. You coming at me or not? Hangman's got to know."

Outside, a single gunshot, followed by three others. Feller heard Watson crying out in injury. No; in death.

Not thinking to remove the mask, not thinking it might be to his advantage having all faculties as he did what he did next, Feller ran toward Sheriff Opal and was shot not two steps from the counter. The tellers remained silent. Even as the smoke from Opal's gun reached the high ceiling. Even as Jacob Feller fell upon the floor, Timothy Holbrook's face-first.

Opal then opened the door a slit and peeked outside. He holstered his gun and came walking to the heap of pale blue and blood on the new bank's floor.

"Hell's heaven," he said. He knelt beside it. "The only thing equal to the evil that ran inside this pair is how thick they were." Then, "But I s'pose it's something to get used to." He looked to the counter, to the celling, to the tellers. "Where there's a bank," he said, "there is bad."

BIGFOOT GORGE

GREG COX

We reached the abandoned mining camp well before dark. The claim was hidden away in a remote valley high in the Cascade Mountains, not far below the snowline, where frothing white water had carved a cleft between two steep, thickly wooded slopes. A crude log cabin nestled at the foot of the eastern slope, a prudent distance from the surging rapids. After days of hard riding, I was relieved to discover that the camp was not just a pipe dream after all.

"You see!" Cameron Pierce crowed from atop his horse. Ostensibly the leader of our party, the erstwhile saloon bouncer beamed at the reportedly deserted camp. He was a heavyset bruiser with a ruddy complexion, who liked to throw his weight around. "Just where that miserable rummy said it was. Our fortunes are made!"

"Assuming he was telling the truth about the rich lode he left behind," I cautioned from my own mount. A dime-novelist would likely describe my leaner frame as "rangy." My fringed buckskin jacket kept out the chill. "And that this claim really is abandoned."

"Trust me, Larson," Claudette Pierce said. Cam's sister was the actual brains of the operation from what I could tell. Curly saffron tresses escaped a wide-brimmed felt hat, although she'd traded her dancehall finery for more practical attire, including a pair of sturdy brown trousers. "I've worked enough saloons to know when a man is blowing smoke and when he's spilling his guts. There's a bonanza in gold here, just waiting to be mined." She fingered the lustrous yellow nugget she wore as a pendant. "If you don't believe that, why come all this way with us?"

"Didn't say I didn't believe. Just saying we ought not get ahead of ourselves."

Our joint venture had begun in Seattle, where, according to Claudette, a down-and-out prospector named Grady, deep in his cups, had told her of a fabulously abundant vein of gold he'd been forced to abandon when "mountain devils" had attacked the camp and slaughtered his partners. His nerves shattered, Grady wanted nothing more to do with the claim and had been all too easily persuaded to draw Claudette a map to the camp in exchange for free drinks and a smile, or so she said. She was a mite cagier about what became of him afterwards, insisting only that we shouldn't worry about Grady sharing the secret with anyone else.

"Well, what are we waiting for then?" Tommy Miller, a green-horn kid still wet behind his ears, spurred his weary mare to one last burst to speed, galloping out in front of us. "Last one there's a prairie dog!"

I almost called him back, in case the camp wasn't as empty as it appeared, but figured I'd be wasting my breath. On top of his youthful exuberance, Tommy was in a hurry to strike it rich so he could marry some farmer's daughter he was sweet on. Lord knows he'd talked about little else the whole way here.

Anyway, there was no indication of danger ahead. My senses alert, I sniffed the brisk mountain air and detected nothing alarming. No campfires, sweaty human bodies, tobacco, or gunpowder. Just perhaps the faintest trace of a rank animal odor wafting from somewhere deep in the evergreen hills overlooking the gorge.

"That young buck needs to learn some patience." Ezra Shanks shook his head. The seasoned old 49er, who was hoping for one last jackpot to retire on, completed our party, not counting our horses and his beloved mule, Beatrice, the last of whom was stoically carrying the bulk of our gear. Ezra scratched a voluminous gray beard that looked as though it hadn't been trimmed since Lincoln was president. Weathered features attested to years spent digging in the outdoors. "Not like that paydirt's going anywhere. No need to rush in like a goshdarned jackrabbit."

"Give the boy his head," Claudette said. "Just as long he can swing a pick and lift a shovel."

Or fire a rifle, I added silently, should we need to defend the claim from "mountain devils" or anyone else. The Pierce siblings hadn't enlisted the rest of us because they were eager to share their hoped-for bounty with others; they'd known they would need some extra muscle, one way or another, plus whatever else we brought to the table. For Tommy, that was youthful vigor and stamina. For Ezra, that was plenty of hard-earned experience in mining. And for me? Well, Cam knew from a barfight or two that I could hold my own in a free-for-all. He also knew I was flat-out broke. One-fifth of a jackpot would go a long way toward improving my finances—and paying for my "medicine."

Not for the first time, I checked to make sure a certain pewter hip flask was still safely tucked in my vest pocket. It wouldn't do to lose it before nightfall.

We caught up with Tommy at the cabin, where grisly evidence supported Grady's tale of being the sole survivor of a massacre. Human bones, long since stripped of flesh, were strewn in and about the empty lodging. Shattered skulls, ribs, vertebrae, and other skeletal remains spoke of brutal ends. Dust, cobwebs, and animal droppings, along with smashed and overturned furnishings, confirmed that the cabin had been uninhabited for some time. The door was torn off its hinges.

And then there was the footprint.

Dried blood, soaked into the floorboards, held the imprint of a bare, gargantuan foot easily twice the size of an ordinary man's. The telltale print proved what I'd already suspected regarding Grady's fearsome "mountain devils."

"That cinches it. This is sasquatch territory."

"B-but I still don't understand, Mister Larson." Tommy swallowed hard, his high spirits visibly shaken. "I always heard the bigfoots were peaceable sorts, just wanting to be left alone."

"Mostly perhaps," I said, "but not always. Word is they can sometimes be considerably testy when it comes to humans encroaching on their stomping grounds, no pun intended. Not sure anybody quite knows what sets them off on such occasions."

"Makes no difference to me." Cam brandished his Remington. "I'll be damned if I let some half-human apes get between me and that gold."

"Just the same, we should stay on our guard." I looked over the cabin's desecrated interior. "Seems this claim's indeed up for grabs for a reason. Bigfoots are nothing to take lightly."

"You've got that right, Larson," Ezra agreed. "Why, I could tell you stories—"

"Later." Claudette turned her back on the gruesome wreckage. "Time's wasting, and I, for one, prefer to find out just what we're risking our hides for."

Turned out Grady hadn't been exaggerating about the gold either. A toppled wheelbarrow had spilled a full load of excavated rocks and dirt onto the bank of the stream. Mixed in with worthless rubble were shining yellow nuggets, some no more than pebbles but one or two as large as a fist. I'd be lying if I didn't admit that all that precious paydirt, and the promise of more to come, served to offset the pall cast by our ghastly discovery at the cabin. Claudette's eyes fairly gleamed, and the rest of us eyed it greedily as well.

"Ye Gods!" Tommy whooped. "That's the real thing, ain't it?"

"Sure looks like it."

Just to be certain, I stooped to pick up a crumb-sized sample, worn smooth on all sides by the rushing stream, and placed it atop an ordinary stone. Then I picked up another rock, a good and solid one, and hammered the tiny nugget with it. Sure enough, instead of shattering like fool's gold, the nugget merely flattened beneath my blow, proving as soft and ductile as the purest gold. I hammered it again and again just for the satisfaction of seeing our hopes pan out.

But was it just my imagination, or could I also hear, over the pounding, indignant yowls emanating from high in the hills above us? As though protesting the commotion?

"Look at that!" Cam rubbed his hands together, seemingly deaf to what I thought I might be hearing. "That's the genuine article all right." He smirked at me. "Satisfied, Larson?"

"Reckon so."

I lifted my gaze to the looming slopes but saw only pines and brush and shadows. Perhaps I *had* simply imagined those echoing yowls?

I kept my rifle close at hand anyway.

The mineworks were in a sorry state. From the looks of it, the doomed prospectors had dammed up the stream, diverting the current through a deep trench dug into a bend in the shore, to expose a stretch of damp riverbed to be mined. Unfortunately for us, the manmade logjam had been demolished (possibly by non-human hands?) and the trench caved in, so the stream had resumed its accustomed course, drowning what we presumed to be the richest part of the claim beneath surging, frigid water. A wooden sluice, once meant to harness the diverted current to capture gold from shovelfuls of wet earth, had been reduced to splinters. Me and the other men got to work repairing the dam, while Claudette busied herself making the cabin habitable again. I kept watch over the woods as we labored, something that did not escape Tommy's notice.

"Maybe the bigfoots have moved on," he said, more for his peace of mind than mine, I suspected. "Headed higher up into the mountains, away from here."

"Maybe," I replied without conviction. "Figure we'll find out soon enough."

The sun was already dipping by the time we called it a day and retired to the cabin. We'd made good progress restoring the dam, although we still had to re-dig the trench and construct a new sluice. We'd also been unable to resist collecting all the loose chunks of gold that had spilled from the dead miners' wheelbarrow. It occurred to me that Grady must have fled the site in a panic to have left those valuable nuggets behind. Then again, he *did* survive, so maybe he'd made the right call.....

The one-room cabin, now cleared of bones, cobwebs, and vermin, boasted a rehung front door, two pairs of bunkbeds, a few salvageable chairs and stools, and a cast-iron stove to cook our supper on. An unfurled bedroll, destined for whoever didn't get a bunk, concealed the bloody footprint. Missing chinks in the log walls let in drafts as well as what remained of the daylight, but we'd been too intent on getting the mineworks up and running again to bother filling in the narrow gaps between the logs with sticks or rocks or mud. Peering out through one of the gaps, I glimpsed a gibbous moon rising in the twilight. Fog was rolling in.

Time for my medicine.

Uncapping my flask, I took just a sip, the better to conserve my supply. The elixir came from a back-alley alchemist in Tacoma whom I still owed money to. That powdered gold was one of its primary ingredients had made the Pierces' offer all the more enticing.

Mountain devils or not.

The siege started just after nightfall.

A chorus of bestial yowls clamored all around us. Rocks pelted the cabin from every direction, some even crashing against the roof's timber shingles. Jolted to our feet by the sudden uproar, we grabbed our assorted firearms and retreated instinctively to the center of the cabin, away from the walls. The rank odor of the sasquatches, much stronger and closer than before, invaded my nose and throat. Our horses, fenced up behind the cabin, whinnied in terror. A crude wooden spear, sharpened to a point at one end, jabbed through a missing chink. Tommy, spooked, fired back with his Colt revolver, but only succeeded in splintering part of a log. The sharp report of his gun competed with the bellowing pandemonium outside.

"Steady!" I said. "Don't waste bullets on our walls."

The cabin's single door was bolted from the inside, but I darted over and wedged a chair against it, for whatever good that would do. Stony missiles pounded against the door, threatening to shake it from its hinges once more. I thanked Providence that, by all reports, sasquatches hadn't mastered fire. At least they couldn't burn us out.

"Goddamn it!" Cam snarled. "I'll give those apes something to scream about!"

Clutching his rifle, he started toward the door, but I rushed to block him. "Don't be a fool, Pierce. Who knows how many of those things are out there in the dark? We're better off in here, where we've got walls, lanterns, even torches if we need them."

"Like those poor bastards whose bones we buried?" Cam shot back. In our haste to get down to mining, we had given the slaughtered prospectors only the barest semblance of a proper burial, shoving their mixed and mangled remains into a single shallow grave topped off with a few shovelfuls of dirt. "Out of my way, Larson!"

We were roughly the same height, but his beefy physique had several pounds over mine, much of it muscle. I didn't back down, however.

"We'll fight them off if we have to, but let's not charge headlong into their clutches."

"Listen to him, Cam." Claudette gripped her own revolver. "We're here to get rich, not to throw our lives away. Use your head for once."

Her words carried more weight than mine, at least where her brother was concerned. Huffing indignantly, he turned away from me. "I'll tell you this, first ape through that door gets a face full of lead!"

"No argument," I said. "If and when it comes to that."

The pounding and yowling went on for hours, all but eliminating any possibility of sleep, but, to our surprise and relief, the sasquatches had yet to storm the cabin. Perhaps they were hoping to scare us off so they wouldn't have to brave our gunfire?

Unless we didn't get the message.

"Ain't they ever going to let up?" Tommy put down his own rifle to clasp his hands over his ears, then reconsidered and snatched up his weapon again. "What the devil's got them so riled up? We ain't hurt them none!"

"Why don't you go ask them?" Ezra chortled, enjoying a laugh at the scared youngster's expense. He was stretched out in a bunk, trying to get forty winks despite the hellacious racket. "Who knows? Maybe a frisky she-'squatch will take a fancy to a strapping young feller like yourself."

Tommy turned pale at the thought.

For myself, I couldn't help wondering if my presence in particular was agitating the creatures. But, no, chances were they were almost surely just objecting to human beings invading their territory in general—or maybe this gorge specifically? I pondered what possible significance the site might have to the sasquatches for them to defend it so fiercely. A burial ground? The birthplace of some legendary bigfoot leader? The site of an historic battle against a rival tribe of ape-men? For all we knew, wc were desecrating the bigfoot version of Gettysburg.

Or maybe it was just damming the river that had gotten their dander up. Hell if I knew what exactly had provoked them. I just hoped we'd survive to live with the mystery.

―――――――――――――――――――――――――――

Sunlight revealed sabotage. The dam we'd sweated so hard to restore had been torn apart again, undoing all our back-breaking labor. The fences corralling the horses had been demolished as well, allowing our mounts to bolt during the night. Only Beatrice remained, much to Ezra's relief, wandering back into camp shortly after dawn, none the worse for wear.

Unlike our nerves.

"Blue blazes!" Cam kicked angrily at a toppled fence post. Lack of sleep had hardly improved his temper. "Goddamn trespassing apes! You should have let me shoot them last night, Larson. You see what they got up to!"

He and I were reinspecting the damage while the rest of our party tried to catch a few hours of shuteye before tackling the day. The wind shifted and I stiffened, catching a whiff of a now-familiar odor. The hairs on the back of my neck rose again.

"Head's up," I warned Cam in a low tone. "We've got eyes on us."

I snuck a peek up the hill to confirm what my nose already told me.

"To our left, about ten yards up the slope, crouching behind some brush. Don't make any sudden—"

In hindsight, I should've thought twice about alerting Cam to the sasquatch's proximity, but I wasn't at my sharpest after last night's harrowing ordeal, so I was caught by surprise when Cam abruptly drew his Colt and fired up at the lurking bigfoot, emptying his revolver. An agonized yelp issued from the brush and a large, shaggy body tumbled down the slope, landing practically at our feet. The smell of freshly spilled blood overpowered even the rank stench of the bigfoot.

"Damnation, Pierce!" I drew my own gun, in anticipation of immediate retaliation from any other unseen sasquatches. "What the hell did you just do?"

"Showed these jumped-up monkeys who they're dealing with, that's what!"

The gunshot bigfoot was only seven feet tall, his simian frame thickly carpeted in lustrous black fur without a trace of silver. An anthropoid countenance, such as might belong to the fabled Missing Link, appeared unlined by age. A young male, possibly, whose curiosity got the better of him? Blood, as brightly crimson as any man's, spilled and spurted from mortal wounds to his hairy torso. Fear and anguish showed in his unsettlingly human-looking eyes before the light went out of them. One last strangled breath wheezed from his chest.

I gazed down at the lifeless creature. "Not sure that was a good idea, Pierce."

"That so? I didn't see you protecting our claim."

He gloated over the sasquatch's bleeding remains, then drew a hunting knife from his belt. A vicious smile told me I wasn't going to like what came next.

"What's the blade for, Pierce?"

He knelt beside the corpse. "I'm not done teaching these apes a lesson…and don't you even think of stopping me."

Cam nailed the skinned hide of the sasquatch to a wooden post, turning it into a grotesque scarecrow. A crossbar supported its outstretched arms, giving it the look of a simian crucifixion. The bigfoot's flayed carcass was left as a feast for scavengers; it said something about the disturbingly semi-human nature of our foes that nobody even suggested cooking the dead creature for supper.

"There, that should do it!" Cam stepped back to admire his work, so bedecked in blood that he looked and smelled like a walking slaughterhouse. "Get it through their thick skulls that this is *our* territory now."

The rest of us looked on with various shades of dismay and revulsion. Cam's gunfire had drawn our dozing partners to the scene, where his fierce glares had discouraged anyone from interfering with his relentless butchery.

"It's our own skulls I'm worried about," I grumbled. "Hope we haven't just upped the ante here."

"Because the bigfoots were ever so hospitable before?" Claudette turned toward her brother, her nose wrinkling in disgust. "Don't you even think of setting foot in our cabin, Cam, until you've washed all that beastly gore off you. And spare me any complaints about how cold the stream is."

Cam wiped off his bloody blade. "Okay, sis. Whatever you say."

"And as for the rest of you," she added, "what are you standing around for? That gold is not going to mine itself."

"Please, no more," Tommy whimpered. "I can't take another night of this."

As I feared, the gruesome scarecrow only goaded the vengeful sasquatches to even greater ferocity. As the moon rose again, waxing brighter and fuller than before, I needed an extra dose of my medicine to keep a cool head as the bigfoots resumed their siege, their bestial yowls growing ever louder and more frenzied. Boulders, not just mere stones, slammed into the walls and roof, hurled down at the cabin from above. Rafters shook beneath the barrage. Spears assailed our stronghold, a few passing through the gaps between the logs and forcing us to crouch and duck for safety. I cursed myself for not chinking those gaps during the day instead of laboring on the mineworks; greed had trumped bolstering our defenses. Beatrice brayed in fright outside, upsetting Ezra, who had wanted the mule to bunk with us indoors, instead of remaining roped up in the corral. The rest of us had overruled him, not wanting to share our cramped quarters with livestock. Ezra had been sulking ever since.

"Goddamn brainless baboons!" Cam's face flushed with anger. "What's it going to take to show them who's boss? Do I have to skin their whole goddamn troop?"

"Sounds like they got the message all right." I braced myself for a frontal assault on the cabin, such as the original miners must have ultimately faced. "Just not the one you intended."

"B-but they're only trying to scare us off their lands, right?" Tommy looked like he'd rather be anywhere else just now. Ashen, he was shaking like a rattler's tail. "Like they were last night?"

"Not sure we can count on that," I said. "Sorry to say."

"Then we'd best get ready to—" Claudette began, only to be interrupted by a boulder crashing through the roof and slamming into the floor only a few paces away from where she'd been crouching. Alarmed, she jumped back against the nearest wall, where a huge, hairy hand forced its way through a gap and grabbed onto her hair, yanking her head back into the battered logs between her and the belligerent sasquatch. Her gun went off, blasting a hole in the floor, even as she screamed in terror. We swung our own firearms toward her but held our fire for fear of shooting her instead of the bigfoot. The gleaming pendant around her throat caught the light from our lanterns.

"Claudette!" Cam brandished his Remington uselessly.

I tossed my own rifle aside. Acting more on instinct than deliberation, I snatched the iron poker by the stove and brought it down hard on the bigfoot's gorilla-sized hand, taking what care I could not to shatter Claudette's skull instead. Bones crunched and, bellowing in pain, the sasquatch let go of her hair and yanked its injured paw back through the gap between the logs. Claudette threw herself forward, away from the wall, gasping at her close brush with the bigfoot. Cam rushed over to embrace her.

"Oh, Lord, are you all right, sis? Did that monster hurt you?"

She needed a few moments to regain her composure, during which time I kept one eye on the newly breached roof. I fired a warning shot through the gaping hole to discourage any bigfoots who might also be contemplating it. Whether that would deter them was anybody's guess.

"I'm fine, Cam." She gingerly massaged the back of her head, where it had slammed into the wall. "Just the start of a goose egg is all." She glanced over at me. "Thanks, Larson. Knew you'd come in handy eventually."

"Just glad it's only your hair it snatched. A few more moments and—"

The braying of the panicked mule suddenly changed in a way impossible to mistake. It was screaming in agony now, not fear.

"Beatrice!" Ezra raced for the door. "They're attacking her, those devils!"

"Wait, Mister Shanks!" Tommy hollered. "Don't be crazy!"

He tried to restrain the frantic prospector and was rewarded with a rifle butt to his head. Ezra barreled past him and, before anyone else could stop him, unbolted the door and charged out of the cabin.

"Hold on, girl! I'm coming for you!"

Gunshots rang out in the night. Moaning on the floor, Tony clutched his head as he stared aghast at the open doorway through which Ezra had vanished. Within moments, more screams came from outside.

Human screams.

"Ain't anybody going to help him?" Tommy asked.

I shook my head and hastily re-bolted the door. In the moonlight, I had already spied large, hairy figures cautiously converging on the exposed entrance.

"Keep watching the roof," I said, "and stay clear of the walls."

In the morning we found Ezra, along with his beloved mule, strewn about the campsite in pieces. Unlike the skeletal debris we'd discovered upon our arrival, nature had yet to strip the pulverized bones clean, although at times it was difficult to tell which mangled, dripping gobbet of flesh had belonged to the man and which to his equine companion. Ezra's head, on the other hand, was all too easy to identify. We found it stuck atop the post that had held Cam's shaggy scarecrow, the sasquatches having claimed their dead brother's hide in the night. The young bigfoot's skinned body had been spirited away as well.

"I've had enough," Tommy announced, after vomiting his guts out. "No jackpot is worth this. I'm going before I end up... like Mister Shanks."

"So you're going to let a bunch of bloodthirsty apes chase you off the richest claim any of us are likely to see in our lifetimes?"

Cam sneered at Tommy. "Don't be an idiot. Act like a man, not a scared little boy!"

"He's got a point, Pierce," I said. "The bigfoots aren't going to let up. If anything, they're getting more and more hostile by the night. Maybe we ought to cut our losses and pull up stakes."

Without our mounts, it was going to be a long hike back to civilization, but if we got started soon enough, we could probably put plenty of distance between ourselves and the gorge before nightfall. And, if we were lucky, the bigfoots would leave us alone once we left their territory.

"You too, Larson?" Claudette regarded me with scorn. "Never figured you for a quitter."

"Sorry to disappoint, but we can still split the gold we salvaged from the shore." Four ways, not five, now that Ezra was gone, although I wasn't crass enough to point that out. "So it won't be a total loss."

"Chicken feed!" Cam spat at the ground. "You truly intend to walk away from a king's ransom with only a pocketful of paydirt?"

"And what's that girl of yours going to think, Tommy?" Claudette asked. "When you tell her you tossed away your prospects because you were too chicken to stand up to some subhuman primates? I thought you wanted to make something of yourself, for her, or was I mistaken?"

"Sorry, Miz Claudette. I stay here, I'll likely never my Jennie again."

"Goddamn yellow-bellied cowards!" Cam erupted, spittle spraying from his mouth. "This is our claim. No goddamn ape can take it from me!"

"Suit yourself," I said with a shrug. The Pierces were past reasoning with, but I figured Tommy needed company if he was to make it back to Seattle alive. I was going to have to find another way to pay for my medicine. Gambling, perhaps, or bounty-hunting. "C'mon, kid. Let's claim our shares and get packing."

Starting back toward the cabin, I turned my back on our former partners. The cocking of their guns instantly told me I'd made a big mistake.

"Can't let you do that, boys," Claudette said. "Hands away from your guns."

"You heard her," Cam added. "Don't think we're bluffing."

Swearing under my breath, I turned around slowly to find Cam's rifle and Claudette's revolver aimed at me and Tommy, respectively.

"Mister Pierce?" Tommy gaped at them in confusion. "Miz Claudette?"

I was taken aback, too, but shouldn't have been. Gold fever could burn hot as Perdition, consuming souls and sanity. Ordinary avarice was tepid by comparison.

"Look," I said. "This doesn't have to go sour. You can have our shares and the whole damn claim. Just let us go our way."

"So you can tell the whole world about our bonanza?" Cam shook his head. "Don't make me laugh."

My darker suspicions about what had become of Grady grew stronger, not that it would be politic to voice them at the moment. I'd have bet good money, though, that the unlucky prospector was no longer drawing breath.

"We won't tell anyone!" Tommy pleaded. "Swear to God!"

"Can't take that chance, I'm afraid." Claudette fondled her

pendant, her repeated caresses rubbing it ever smoother. A smirk lifted her lips. "Besides, who else is going to mine that paydirt for us?"

"You've got that right, sis." Cam glared at us down the barrel of his rifle. Dark circles, testifying to lack of sleep, shadowed his bloodshot eyes. "Drop your weapons and get to work."

We labored at gunpoint all day, first patching the hole in the roof, then digging out the trench to divert the stream. The Pierces took turns bossing us before finally marching us back into the cabin around dusk. Ezra's remains were still scattered around the camp; Cam and Claudette had decided that giving the man a decent burial was a waste of daylight. I wondered how they expected to keep us under their thumb all night long, even while attempting to sleep, until Cam produced a length of rope and ordered me to tie Tommy to a chair.

"Are you completely insane?" I protested. "You may need us if the bigfoots storm the cabin tonight."

"Least I won't have to worry about you not having my back," Cam snarled. "Get to it."

Tommy fought back sobs as I reluctantly complied. "Please, I just want to see Jennie again. I don't want to die."

"You don't stop being such a crybaby, it won't be the apes that kill you." Cam approached me with another rope while Claudette kept her Colt aimed at my heart, which was already beating faster in anticipation of another hellish, moonlit night in the gorge. He indicated an empty chair. "All right. Now your turn, Larson."

"Just a moment," I said, reaching for my medicine.

"Not so fast!" Cam swatted my hand away from my vest pocket. With his sister still having the drop on me, he confiscated the flask. "You want this, you're going to have to work for it from now on."

"Damnation, Pierce! You don't want to do this!"

"Is that so? You'd best think twice about telling me what I want to do, considering." He handed the flask to Claudette and roped me to the chair, over my strenuous objections. She uncapped the flask to sniff its contents. Her face curdled in disgust.

"My, that's vile. Still, I suppose we all have our vices..."

"Give it back!" I demanded. "You're making a big mistake!"

But it was already too late. All at once, the night brought bedlam. Yowling like demons, the sasquatches attacked the cabin in full force, battering the door and walls, even as the full moon pulled on my sanity and the Change came over me. Bound to his chair, only a few feet away from me, Tommy started shrieking hysterically, as though he was the one losing his mind, not me. He fought frantically against the rope binding him, his fear-crazed exertions threatening to topple the chair. Panicked eyes bulged from their sockets. Jennie would never find out what became of him.

"Sorry, kid," I managed. "Wish it hadn't gone like this."

A growl devoured my words. Teeth sharpened into fangs. Bristling gray fur, more lupine than simian, sprouted from my skin as, foaming at the mouth, I tore loose from my bonds and sprang at the Pierces, who pretty much froze in horror at my lycanthropic transformation, only getting a few shots off from their guns before I ripped into them, snapping and slashing. Hot lead stung, but barely slowed me down. There was a reason I'd opted to prospect for gold instead of silver.

And then the door burst off its hinges, knocking a spare chair aside, and the sasquatches charged in, feral and savage and out for blood.

Snarling, I met them in kind.

Sunlight found me lying naked by the stream, bruised and scratched and splattered with blood, with bits of raw meat stuck between my teeth. I vomited into the flowing water; turns out bigfoots *did* taste all too human.

As I was cursed to know.

Despite being hungover from the Change, I sensed the sasquatches lurking in the misty evergreen hills. Since I was still alive, I assumed I'd held my own against them last night, giving as good as I got. Perhaps now they'd give me a wide berth, at least for the time being.

Not that I intended to stick around.

"You win!" I shouted hoarsely into the wilderness, my throat raw from howling and growling the night before. "You can have this godforsaken place! I don't belong here!"

Or anywhere else, truly.

I staggered back to the cabin to get my things, some fresh clothes, and as much gold as I could carry all the way back to Seattle. Carnage greeted me, including a trio of flayed human bodies, all missing their skins.

Three new scarecrows, crudely fashioned from the torn and shredded hides of my former partners, now guarded the campsite, pegged to wooden posts wrested from the corral. Horribly, I could still make out who was who. Claudette's saffron hair marked her pale epidermis as surely as the delicate chain and pendant twisted around the now-empty skin of her neck. Cam's size and build was evident even without his body. And Tommy...?

He deserved better.

I took the time to bury him and Ezra. The other two scarecrows I left as a warning to any other avaricious souls who might be enticed by the treasure buried in the gorge. Some jackpots, it seemed, were better left undisturbed.

As were the sasquatches.

I wondered how much elixir a few of the larger nuggets would buy me.

The Story of the Century

MARIE AMBROSE

(As passed down to C. Edward Sellner)

Call it women's intuition or simply good fortune, but I'd always had a nose for news, one which often put me in the right place at the right time. I had been there for the signing of the new Texas State Constitution on February 15th, 1876, and just happened to be local when our horrid State Capital building burned to the ground on November 9th, 1881. I had covered the major Texas range wars from Colfax and Mason counties, as well as the San Elizario Salt War. I'd also covered my fair share of the more regular sort of stories you come across out here: new gold and silver strikes, new towns and mining camps springing up around them, unsavory politics, and whole rosters of cattle rustlers, thieves, and killers. I'd done work for the belated *Telegraph, Dallas Daily Herald, Galveston Daily News*, and others, filing stories during my travels.

All that to say, I'd spent a good number of years being a journalist of some renown in some of the most untamed territories of the West. I'd seen many things that would give most decent folks nightmares for the rest of their lives.

But, by God in Heaven, I'd never seen anything like what I set eyes upon that December 20th evening of 1882 in the town of Hope Falls, Texas.

It all started that morning as I was taking my breakfast at my hotel in Junction City. Runny eggs and hash but surprisingly good coffee was the order of the day. I'd come to town to connect with Mr. Elias Wilson, the editor of Kimble County's first newspaper, *West Texas*.

While eating, I noticed a man who stood out among the others. The breakfast room was full of businessmen, miners, and cowboys, all sluggish. Some from having just awoken to prepare for the day, others just coming in off the range, filling their bellies before getting much-needed sleep in an actual bed. But this man was alert, glancing around constantly as if expecting trouble and looking more than ready to deal with it. He had a firm jaw, a heavily lined and darkened face from the sun, and was dressed like a lawman or bounty hunter more than a herdsman, including a long, worn duster and the typical Texas-brimmed hat. He wore two heavy colt pistols in his holsters and moved with surprising grace for his size and appearance.

He noticed me watching, and I quickly turned away. But when I glanced back, he was still watching, and for that moment, it felt as if a bird of prey had alighted near me, sizing me up for the taking.

I then studiously ignored him as I finished my breakfast.

At least until Benjamin Williams crashed in through the doors in apparent shock.

"The shopkeeper, Mr. Kimble! I think he's dead. There ain't nothin' but ashes!"

This, of course, caused quite a stir among everyone in the room. Most just shook their heads and mumbled. A few seemed genuinely shocked. My stranger, on the other hand, didn't hesitate and headed straight for Benjamin. "Take me to him."

Well, I did say I had a nose for news, didn't I? Surely there was a story in this. I took a final sip of my coffee and headed after them as they left the hotel. I was running to catch up as they moved fairly fast down Main Street to get to the shop Kimble owned, the stranger obviously moving slower than he wished in order to let Ben, who was quite a mess, lead him. Ben was what folks called simple in those days. His mind and body didn't work as well as most folks, but he was a pleasant enough fellow, if a bit childlike.

"Come on, man! Can't you move any faster?" He must have heard me following because those dark eyes then turned back to me and narrowed. Clearly not what he expected. "What do you think you're doing?"

"I am a reporter, and this sounds like a story for the *West Texas News*," I shot back as I was huffing and catching up.

The stranger took one long look, once more sizing me up, and surely thought it ridiculous that a mere woman in a lace dress and high heels would be racing to a murder scene. "We're likely to see something you ain't gonna want to see."

"I assure you, sir, I've seen plenty." I hefted and swished the hem of my dress. "This is not my usual attire. I have a formal interview today." I then shook my head, wondering why I needed to justify myself to this man. "My name is Marie Ambrose, and you are?"

He glanced back once more, then shook his head. "Jacob Whately."

"And what is your interest in this affair?"

Before he could reply, Benjamin reached the storefront and stumbled up the walk through the doors, with Whately following him.

"Back there, in the storage room, that's where Mr. Kimble sleeps nights."

Whately pushed past and was in the room in an instant.

I took a moment to stop as an aside to poor Benjamin. "You don't need to go back there again if you don't want to." He nodded, and I then followed Whately.

He was already crouching near Kimble's bunk, carefully eyeing the rather large pile of what did indeed look like ashes spread upon it, draped by the now loose clothing of dear old Mr. Kimble. "Heaven above! How could this happen?"

As I approached, Whately reached out to the pile to pinch a sample, rubbing it between his fingers. "He coulda fallen asleep with a cigar and whiskey, and it got the better of him."

I looked brazenly at Mr. Whately. "Oh, really? Do you think so?"

"Or it coulda been a case of, what do you call it, spontaneous combustion."

I crossed my arms and stared ice-cold at him. "I'm not sure whether to be more insulted by you lying to me or by the lack of credit you give my intelligence."

"I don't get your meaning, lady."

"Well, first, I hardly believe in the so-called spontaneous combustion theory, as that has yet to be a proven phenomenon. But beyond that, while I will say these remains appear as ash, there is no pungent ashen smell. And how did his body burn so thoroughly and yet not leave the barest mark on his clothes, the mattress, bed, or wall it sits against? Any actual fire would have spread by all rights, and one hot enough to do this would have taken the building down with it."

Whately smiled slightly as he seemed to improve his disposition toward me. "Ain't you a smart and sassy one." He stood and walked briskly past me back to the front. I took one last glance and followed him.

"What's your name?" he asked Ben as he entered the front of the shop.

I cut in. "It's Benjamin. Ben, we just want to ask you some questions. It's alright. Mr. Whately here is quite friendly, I'm sure." I glanced harshly at him as he gave a quick sneer.

"What all did you see?" Whately asked with a bit more friendly tone to his voice.

"I didn't see anything," Ben said, "I just came in to work this morning. Mr. Kimble is always up and bustling about getting ready for the day. When he weren't, I went back to check on him and found him like that."

"When were you here last afore that?"

"Last night, 'round ten o'clock or so. We were cleaning up. He was fine then."

"Was there anything else? Did anything unusual happen?" I chimed in, earning another side glance from Whately.

Ben scratched his chin, shaking his head, but then something sparked as he started nodding. "Yes, yes, there was this man who came in after we was closed. He seemed pretty determined to do business even after Mr. Kimble asked him to leave. When he wouldn't, Mr. Kimble told me to go on home; he'd take care of it."

"Was this man pale and thin, with wispy white hair?" Whately shot back.

"Why, yeah, he was. How'd you know?"

But Whately's only response was, "Goddammit!"

I then asked, "Benjamin, did you see this man leave?"

Benjamin shook his head. "Nah, I listened to Mr. Kimble and went on home."

With that, Whately, clearly realizing he'd gotten everything he was going to get from Benjamin, stormed out. I nodded curtly and touched Benjamin's arm as I passed. "Benjamin, I want you to go find the sheriff and tell him about all this. Then you should go back home for now. We will figure this all out, I promise."

"I trust you, Ms. Ambrose. You've been nice to me every time you come in. But I don't much like that other feller."

I smiled, "Oh, I don't either." I then found myself once more chasing after the long-legged Whately, who was now moving back to the hotel at top pace.

I finally caught up to him as he was entering his room.

"You still here?"

I huffed and put my hands on my hips. "Something happened back there that defies logic, and you know something more about it and know the man you believe did it, so yes. Wherever you're going or whatever you're doing, I'm coming."

He seemed to weigh my words and the consternation behind them, then opened the door and half-stepped through before he turned back to me. "Not like that, you ain't."

"Give me ten minutes, and I will meet you in the lobby. Promise?"

He nodded, and I had the strange feeling that was the same as a solemn oath for him. I then raced to my room and switched into my traveling clothes: pants, a thicker cloth blouse and sweater, a broad-brimmed hat, and worn boots—a knife slipped into a sheath inside each one.

I was in the lobby in seven minutes and told the barkeep to give the *West Texas* Publisher my apologies if I wasn't back in time for my meeting but to assure him he'd be delighted to see me when I came back. That was when I glanced out the window and, to my dismay, saw Mr. Whately riding away.

"Confound that man," I hissed as I flew out of the building.

Right outside was Riley Miller, a local cattle owner, about to tie his horse up to the hotel hitching post. Mr. Miller and his wife thoroughly enjoyed my work and had been thrilled when I came to town. Time to leverage that.

"Why, good morning to you, Ms. Ambrose," he said with his normal geniality.

"Do you need your horse today?"

He was clearly taken aback. "Well, I was going for a ride after I break my fast."

"It appears Mr. Kimble has been murdered in a most unusual way during the night, and that man—" I pointed to the dwindling figure riding out of town "—is going after who did it. I aim to follow him."

"Well, um, I'm sure I can go out tomorrow...."

I climbed gracefully up in the saddle, thankful for the lack of a long skirt, and took up the reins, virtually pulling them from the man's hand. "It might be longer than that," I said as apologetically as I could while practically stealing his horse out from under him. "Thank you!" And then I pulled to the right and gave the reins a fair snap, and we took off after Whately.

I hit a full gallop to keep him in sight. Fortunately, he was heading off into open plains, so there was nothing he could disappear behind any time soon. After a few minutes, he glanced back with those hawk eyes again, and when he saw me, he spurred his horse onto a full gallop.

"Why, you insufferable bas—!" I stopped myself from finishing. Even I wasn't that unladylike. I drove my horse even harder, determined not to be dismissed so quickly, and slowly closed the distance between us.

Finally, he saw losing me as fruitless and stopped to rest his horse. I closed the distance and slowed to a trot as I approached. "Well, here we are," I said, somewhat snappish as I pulled up alongside. "I thought you promised to wait."

"Didn't promise nothing. I nodded."

"I had the distinct feeling that was enough from you, but I suppose I was wrong."

He looked at me differently then, his eyes not so narrow, less grimace to his face, perhaps even a hint of what you might call a smile, lacking anything better to compare it to. "Normally does. Look, lady, this is bad business, it's dangerous business, and it ain't no place for a woman."

"Oh, shove it, Mr. Whately. I've seen things that would make even you step back."

"Doubt it."

We both then set off at a more leisurely pace so as not to tire the horses too soon. "So, since you seem to have finally accepted my company, are you going to tell me what this is about and who this thin, pale man is?"

"I don't think you're ready for the full truth yet, but if you stick with me, as determined as you are, you're likely to learn all about it."

"I expect I will, and I expect it will make quite a fine story when I do." I smiled.

Whately just glanced at me and shrugged. "Maybe, maybe not."

As we continued to ride briskly and the sun climbed higher in the sky, I thought to learn what I could. "So, if I'm not ready for the whole truth, how much of the truth can you at least share now while we have the time?"

He didn't turn to me as he began to speak, but his voice

was deep and even. "I know the man who did this. I've been hunting him for...well, let's just say a long time now. I also know where he's going because I've been tracking him in a nearly straight line, heading for Hope Falls, Texas. It's a place he called home. Once."

"Does he have a name?"

"He's used many names, but I knew him best as Magnus."

"So you were associated with him at some point?"

"You could say that."

"But you're not telling me how or when? Or how he killed Mr. Kimble, if indeed he did."

"Oh, he did. I know it don't make no sense how he did it, but Kimble wasn't his first victim."

I started to ask about those other victims but paused. I had almost begun to think Kimble's "body" was some trick; perhaps he'd been kidnapped instead, and the supposed ashes were left to mislead. But I now dismissed that theory. The room had felt of death, and Mr. Whately did not seem the sort to jump to conclusions as wild as he was claiming without knowing the truth of them.

We'd passed a while in silence when he finally drew up rein and turned to me with a genuine look of concern. "Look, Miss Ambrose, I'm sorry for being so dismissive earlier, and I get that you are fairly determined to see this through, even though you have no idea what you're getting into. But I owe it to you to give you one last warning. If you follow me from here, it will most likely mean your death."

"I beg your pardon?" I said, a bit astonished.

"I simply mean the...thing...we're pursuing ain't a normal man, and he's left plenty of dead in his wake. I can look out for myself, but you...?"

"I can handle myself quite well, thank you very much, Mr. Whately." I started my horse moving forward once again. "But I may have some reservations about you."

"What the hell does that mean?"

I smiled, hearing the astonishment in *his* voice for a change. "After all, you know the murderer. You've been chasing him a long time by your own admission and yet obviously not been very successful in catching him. So, I would hope this time you might prove capable enough of actually doing the job with my help."

I was not expecting the outburst of laughter that seemed strange issuing from his throat. "Well, don't that beat all. Come on, then. We're almost there." He spurred his horse back to a gallop, and I followed suit.

It was nearing dusk when a small town came into view, which turned out to be Hope Falls. He slowed, and I matched his speed as we approached.

"I don't suppose you'd be inclined to at least let me ride in first to check things out?"

"Given your prior antics, I should say not."

"I figured."

As the town came into view, there seemed nothing out of the ordinary at first. People were still out in the streets, and smoke was rising from the chimneys...but then the silence hit me. I had gotten used to it riding through the open plains, but this close to a town that size? We should've been hearing horses neighing, wagons making their way down the dirt streets, people talking and laughing, the clang of the blacksmith's hammer, the hustle, and bustle...but there was nothing.

I then looked closer and realized something startling. The people I saw in the streets, the horses, even a stray dog, none of them were moving. At all. It was as if they'd all been frozen in a moment of time.

"Stay behind me," Whately whispered as he moved in front. I felt a chill so cold race down my spine that I offered no argument.

We slowly entered the confines of the town, and I got close enough to take a better look at the people nearby. Every one of them was frozen in place like a statue. Their clothing was untouched, but now I could see all their faces were blackened, with tiny cracks running through what had been skin, their eyes gray and dead in their sockets, staring into the abyss. Every one of them—men, women, children…even the horses… all of them…I then noticed piles of ashen remains with jumbled clothing mixed in where others had just… crumbled.

"My God in Heaven!" I cried out.

"God had nothing to do with this."

I heartily agreed with him on that. "These people are all dead?"

Instead of answering, he got off his horse and walked into the saloon, and I followed again. As I entered, a fresh chill ran down my spine, just as bad as the last. Every patron, including the bartender, was in the same state. A few loose piles lay where others had fallen. A lady was near the door; her arm had broken and fallen to shatter on the floor where her purse lay next to her, as if it was more weight than her ashen arm could bear. I reached out to touch her face, and with the slightest touch, she collapsed into a pile of ash at my feet.

I screamed. Admittedly, this was more than I had expected.

"Don't touch none of the rest of them, you hear me? You're lucky she'd been gone long enough it was done with her."

I heard his voice distantly even though I was quite in shock at the moment. It was bad enough to see these poor souls in their deathly effigies, quite another to know your touch robbed them of that last shred of humanity, reducing them to scrapings from a fireplace.

Whately turned to exit the abattoir that was once a saloon. "These are fresh. He's got to still be here."

At that moment, I collected myself and turned on Mr. Whately. "What in Hell is going on here? Who did this, and how? And I was lucky that *what* was done with her? Are these..." I fumbled for words, "Are they dangerous?"

"They can be."

I then found myself doing something I'd never done before. I knew I sounded like I was pleading, but I suppose I was. "Jacob, please? What is going on?"

He turned with sorrow and compassion on his face and looked as if he was about to speak when—

"You found me, Legionnaire!" The strong voice came from outside at some distance, and Whately jumped at the sound before racing out. Yet again, I was reduced to following.

Whately no sooner stepped through the doors when the crack of a rifle shot sounded from the roof across the way. Whately whirled, almost falling back inside, but then braced himself against the doorjamb, blood flowing out of his right upper arm. He pulled both his pistols and was looking to spot his shooter.

"You're injured."

"Ain't nothing."

"Is that Magnus?"

"Seems so."

"What did he call you? A legionnaire? You both seem a bit far from France."

"Further than you know."

At that point, I decided it was time to be a little better prepared. So I stepped next to another ashen corpse and gently pulled the six-gun from the holster about its waist.

"What d'you think you're doing?"

"I think I'm arming myself if this is going to be a gunfight."

"You know what to do with that thing?"

I clicked open the cylinder, spun it to check it was free moving and full, then set it back in place and felt the hammer click. "I can manage," I said.

"I expect you can." He finally turned from the door to look toward the back. "Let's see if there's another way out so we can circle around."

There was. We stayed silent as we made our way past a few buildings, hoping to get out of the line of sight of our quarry. I knew just then that our silence was necessary so as not to give away our location. Magnus, however, obviously did not feel the same need.

"I'm surprised at you, Justus. Is that a woman with you? You brought her here to this, our final Coliseum? You've fallen a long way, Legionnaire."

We finally made our way through a narrow alley between a livery and tailor shop back to the main thruway. Jacob, guns at the ready, stopped at the leading corner of the one building and glanced back the way we had come toward the man he was hunting.

"It seems you've forgotten the rules of the arena."

"What is he going on about?" I whispered somewhat hoarsely.

"He's out of his head. The thing inside him…he's losing control."

"I have so many questions right now."

"Now? You want to do this *now*?"

I shook my head. "No, now I want to know what you plan to do."

"I've got to get across."

"How? You step out there, he's sure to see you, and he's bound to suspect by now we're no longer in the saloon."

"Which means he'll suspect we're doing exactly what we're doing, and he'll be aiming right this way."

"Indeed."

"Which means I'll need some cover." He looked down at the ground, then bent to pick up a good-sized stone from the dirt. Then, he went back to looking at the street. There was a small wagon, its driver half crumbled in the front, and two horses still intact in their tackle.

"You should stay here," he whispered as he threw the stone with all his might. It plunged through the dark horses, smashing them into oblivion as clouds of dust from their remains exploded outward, filling the street, and their tackle dropped free to the ground. He then ran right through the thick of it, using it to obscure Magnus's view.

Well, I'd be damned if I was going to wait there. So I steeled myself, held my breath, pinched my nose, and followed, trying very hard not to think about what it was I was running through.

A couple more rifle shots sounded off before we both made it across, but it was clear Magnus couldn't get a fix on us in the dust cloud. Once we reached the other side, I saw Whately had ducked under the overhang of one of the shops, hugging the side of the building, making it impossible for Magnus to draw a bead on him. I joined him, and it was the first he noticed I had followed.

"Do you ever listen, woman?"

"No, not really."

"I'm startin' to like you."

"Well, let's hope this is the beginning of a long-lasting friendship."

"As in, we don't get killed?"

"Exactly."

He genuinely smiled at that and turned back to Magnus. "We got us a stalemate now, Magnus! Neither of us can get to the other from where we are."

"I beg to differ, Justus." The voice came from behind us, and we both whirled.

Magnus already had the rifle raised and fired, hitting Whately square in the chest and punching him back against the wall to slide down, leaving a slick trail of blood, and no doubt dead before hitting the ground.

He then looked at me with eyes all white with black threads weaving through them. "You should leave."

"I am getting very tired of men telling me what to do," I said, setting my jaw and whipping up the gun from my side, pulling the trigger in one smooth motion like my Daddy taught me.

He wasn't expecting me to be armed, of course.

The bullet caught his right eye, blowing out the side of his head. He whirled, screaming in agony. But the blood? The blood was black. And it didn't fall. Instead, long streamers of it writhed in the air about his head like snakes. He turned back briefly to me, then gigantic black legs like those of a spider ripped out of his back. Those legs lifted him when they touched the ground, and the monstrosity that had been a man a moment ago skittered down the dirt street and quickly climbed atop another building.

I stood there, frozen, my brain stunned by the sheer impossibility of what I'd just seen.

"Nice shot."

"*Ahhhh*! What in Hell?"

With a gaping, bleeding hole in his chest, Jacob Whately was now rising. I turned on him, aiming the gun straight at his head. "You can't be…not with that?" I gestured to his bleeding wound.

"It can be. I can explain."

"And if I shoot you in the head right now?"

"Then it'd hurt like hell and piss me off, and it might be a while, but I'd get up again. In the meantime, you'd be left alone with Magnus."

I thought for a second, and slowly reason once more came to me amid the nightmare. "Good point." I lowered the gun. "So, now what?"

"I need to finish healing. He's going to take a while to collect himself as well, so we need to find a secure place to hold up."

I reached out and he took my hand, draping his arm over my shoulder as I helped him struggle to his feet and walk toward the back of the row of buildings. Lucky for us, we were alongside a market, with an underground cellar behind. I quietly pulled open the metal doors and helped Whately down the stone steps. Fortunately, a lantern was lit in the otherwise pitch-dark pit stocked with goods. I steadied Whately against the wall, then pulled the doors closed behind us and latched them. I then got him to a far corner with an open view of the cellar door and the steps leading down from the shop above.

He was already moving better, and the hole in him was definitely closing up. On the other hand, I felt lightheaded after everything and slumped to the floor next to him.

"I think it's high time you tell me the whole truth."

He sighed heavily. "I asked you not to come."

"What's done is done, but I think I just saved both our lives. Well, at least mine, since you apparently don't die."

"Nope, you saved my bacon too. He can kill me, just like all of them people in the street. What he does, there ain't no healing from."

"Well, dandy then, both lives it is, so you owe me."

"Magnus and I aren't all human."

"I noticed."

He sighed, clearly not wanting to say what he knew he had to say. "I'm a Nephilim. Magnus is a Shedim."

"Nephilim? Like in the Bible? Like the giant David fought?"

"Coulda been. But we're not all giants. We come in all shapes, sizes, and colors, like normal folk. Hell, our parents and our siblings often are normal folk. I don't know how it works. It's just in rare cases that someone is born…different."

"Weren't the Nephilim supposed to be the children of angels and human women?"

He nodded, sitting up a little straighter. "Those were the First Ones. Us later versions aren't like them, but we do have gifts."

I then flashed my mind back over Magnus's ramblings. "You weren't in the French Foreign Legion, were you?"

"No."

"Rome? Do you mean to tell me you've been alive since the times of the Roman Empire?"

He nodded again.

"Magnus, that's a Roman name. He wasn't calling you 'Justice,' but by your Roman name, wasn't he? The two of you fought in the arena, and you were part of the Roman legion over a thousand years ago?"

"Yep."

"And you said he's a Shedim? What is that? Wait, if your ancestors were angels, are you saying his were...?" I couldn't say the word; it seemed so preposterous.

"Demons, yes. Nephilim often pass for normal; we're mostly all immortal, and our gifts work for us without cost. Shedim are also usually immortal but can't always pass for human because their abilities are more a curse than a gift, sometimes warping their bodies and minds, sometimes completely consuming them—like what's happening to Magnus."

"What exactly *is* happening to Magnus?"

"His curse is that dark force inside of him. It's some kind of living thing that, I don't know, seems to be waking up after all these centuries."

"What does that mean?"

"When it first manifested in him, he could kill a man with a single touch, just like he did to Kimble. But he had to focus on making it happen like I do with my light. Then it got to where he had to focus to *not* let it happen. Now he loses control and vents it out in waves that kill everything around him. But not by his choice."

"But how could he kill all these people at once?"

"I don't think you understand. That thing inside him? It comes through him from somewhere else. It seems limitless. I saw him lose control once; it exploded out of him like a shockwave, and every living thing within a hundred yards of him was just like those folks. Happened in an eyeblink."

"Then this whole town? All these people from one end to the other? Just dead?"

"Most likely."

"And your warning? About touching them?"

"The thing kills instantly. But it invades its victims, consuming the life out of their bodies from the outside in. It takes a while to finish, and while it's still feeding, it will reach out to anyone else coming too close. Then it dies inside them once their bodies are fully consumed, leaving this ashen dust behind."

I was speechless. This was all too much. "What about this town? You said he called it home?'

"Forty years ago, he lived here with a woman, someone he loved very much. The first time he lost control, he lay sleeping next to her in their bed. It broke him. He ain't been the same since."

I bowed my head in pity. I couldn't imagine. "How is it no one knows of you, of your kind? His kind?"

"Well, folks know more about us than you might think. Remember your myths? Legends? All the ghost and monster tales? Well, our kind makes up a good bit of those. We've always kept to the shadows, keeping our existence secret. Most of us just want to live normal lives, even if we have to pack everything up and move every twenty years or so. That's for both. Nephilim ain't all good, and Shedim ain't all evil. We just are."

"And you?"

"Mostly, I'm the enforcer for both sides of the treaty between his kind and mine. Anyone that seems a threat, intentionally or otherwise, of exposing us or worse, well, the leaders of both pass judgment, and I carry it out."

"Then more an executioner?"

"Not always." He climbed to his feet, still a little shaken, but when I looked, that hole in him had closed entirely.

"You do realize what telling me all this means?"

He smirked. "The story of the century?"

"Something like that."

That was when the cellar doors were ripped off as if by a tornado, and Magnus descended the steps. His eyes were pitch black, and oily slime followed him, coating the floor, walls, and ceiling as he moved downward. It lapped in waves at his feet and slithered along the walls.

I pulled my gun, but Whately pushed my arm aside. "That won't do it."

The black tendrils were oozing and creeping along the walls, quickly closing in on and surrounding us. "Tell me something will?"

"Me," he said, and with that, he held up his hands, and sheer light flashed from them, filling the room. An unearthly scream cut through me to the very core of my soul, such that I wasn't sure if I was hearing it with my ears or my mind. I recovered, looked around, and saw the slick mass trembling, like a thousand pebbles dropped into stormy waters, rippling out, swirling, whipping—but pulling back. The light was driving away the darkness, and Magnus himself was now bent over in agony.

Whately started walking toward him, his hands still flooding the cellar with light, the thing from Hell fled back to its source, hiding itself in Magnus, who then collapsed to his knees and looked up. Whately drew closer, holding those blazing white hands before him.

Then, oddly enough, Magnus grew docile, calmed, breathing heavily as if exhausted but not in pain. Finally, he looked up, and his black eyes had returned to normal. He then smiled and chuckled. "I knew you could control it, Justus. Ever the light in my darkness."

"I think it's time, Magnus. We knew this would come."

Magnus nodded, chuckling once more. "I haven't been in control for a while now. All this...this was the thing inside me. It knew I was losing to it, and it brought me here, to the last place I thought of as home, to make it my grave." Magnus looked around, eyed me with genuine sorrow, and turned back to Whately. "You'll have to—"

"I know."

"It's already coming back. I can feel it, like before. Do it. Do it *now*!"

Jacob's hands flared even brighter as he grabbed Magnus by his head. Magnus now screamed in agony, sounding all too human. I drew back, not sure what I was witnessing. The light pierced through the frail body, now on its knees and desperately grasping at Whately's arms. Then he began gagging, choking as black bile spilled from his lips but burned away at the touch of the light. Then Magnus stopped struggling, his skin turning ashen gray.

Whately saw it happening and cried out, "No, Magnus, no!"

"Don't stop. You have to end this, Justus. For me, end my pain."

A final flare drove back the bile and seemed to swallow Magnus's body. Then, as the light faded, Magnus's now ashen corpse collapsed into a pile of dust at Whately's feet.

Whately nearly fell himself from the effort but leaned heavily against a support post, and I could swear I saw tears in his eyes. "You didn't intend to kill him, did you?"

He shook his head. "My light cleanses Shedim, can burn the curse out of them, making them mortal."

"But then why?"

"That thing had been feeding on Magnus for centuries. Even with his Shedim strength and healing, he…he was just swallowed up by it."

Given the circumstances, it seemed evident to me this was less a man hunting a killer and more a man having to sacrifice a brother. "I'm truly sorry," I said as gently as possible.

"So am I." He pulled his revolver and aimed it straight at me.

I flinched back, losing every shred of pity for the man before me. "You sonnuvabitch. You have to keep your secret no matter what, don't you?"

"You understand what would happen to us if people knew we existed? In the past, we've been burned at stakes, shot with silver, stakes driven through our hearts, crucified, tortured, and locked away in dark tombs where we can neither live nor truly die." He then looked at me sadly. "I tried to warn you." And he pulled the trigger.

When I woke, it was completely dark outside, with only a lantern still burning in the corner. Whately and Magnus's body were both gone. I then remembered what he'd done and desperately looked down to my chest, where he had shot me directly in the heart. A note was pinned to my sweater. I pulled it loose and unfolded it.

"The first time for us Nephilim always takes the longest. Our fate is now yours," was scrawled on it. I began laughing, fearing I'd lost my mind in that cellar, but then it all clicked. It all made sense, why he'd been unsure but finally let me come, trying to protect me from the truth but finally realizing I needed to know. And somehow, he knew I was one of his kind. Maybe that explained why I was drawn to him back at the hotel and him to me. Maybe that dread I sensed wasn't just a dread of death, but me sensing Magnus.

I rushed out of the cellar into the streets that were now clear. Hope Falls was now nothing but a ghost town, completely empty of life and with no trace of the ashen remains. I could see the headline now, "Town residents go missing," another mystery for the history books.

And, for me, at least, a story.

The Stacked Deck

AARON ROSENBERG

The grizzled old coot glared as he rose from the card table. He was shorter than Barry, and skinnier, but there was that tough-as-nails quality about him that old-timers sometimes got. "Gimme back my money, you dirty cheat." His volume had dropped along with his tone, and the demand came out low and gravelly.

"Now, you know that ain't right," Barry "Bull Rush" Joseph argued, hefting the messenger bag he'd just scooped his winnings into. "I won fair and square. Don't be a sore loser, friend." He turned away but the fella angled in front of him, hand dropping to the gun holstered at his side.

"I ain't asking." Those eyes were cold, and Barry read his death in them. He sighed and, ignoring his own pistol, reached for the table instead, grabbing the hand he'd left there.

Time seemed to slow around him as he let his mind roam and his senses expand. The world took on brighter colors, objects and people limned with a strange halo that sparked and flared. Power arced everywhere, touching everything.

Barry pulled in some of that energy, focusing it through himself and into the cards.

He felt the change, felt the previously inert squares of stiff paper take on a charge, staticky against his fingers. There were more of them, too, two new cards manifesting with no paper at their core, only that energy. He glanced at them quickly, and the three of spades and the three of clubs winked back. A pair, if a mighty low one. Still, it would have to do.

The world slipped back to normal, and Barry sighed again. "Best move, old-timer. I'm in a hurry." And he dipped his shoulder into the other man to wedge him aside.

He saw the hand lift, saw the gun clear its leather, saw the blued barrel rise and angle toward him. Watched the hammer drop back, then slam forward with a click.

And nothing happened.

The man gaped at him, but by then Barry was already past, weaving among other saloon patrons, putting bodies between him and the risk of being shot in the back. After all, he wasn't sure how long his weak hex would stop that gun from firing. Or even if—

Something went off behind him, less a gunshot than a small explosion, and someone yelped in pain. Yeah. That. Barry winced but didn't look back. He did drop the spent cards on the floor just before he ducked outside, however. The phantom cards had already vanished.

He felt a little bad for the old fella. The hex wasn't supposed to do that, of course. But, well, accuracy wasn't Barry's strong suit. All power and no finesse—it was why they called him "Bull Rush."

Still, he'd warned the man. And he had won fair and square. Not his fault the fella'd fallen for his bluff!

Anyhow, that was all behind him now. Literally. Ahead lay the docks, and waiting at the end of one was his destination, a grand, gleaming spectacle—the *Lazy Ace*. Barry whistled as he stomped down the wooden pier, falling in behind a few others making for the same steamboat. A pair of gentlemen in long dusters stood before the gangplank, both well-heeled and hefting rifles to boot, flanking a smaller man in shirtsleeves and a string tie, round glasses perched atop his nose as he peered at a heavy ledger.

"Tickets?" The clerk asked each person as they approached, then checked the printed slips against his ledger before adding a checkmark next to the name and nodding them on. But when Barry got to the front, what he handed over wasn't a regular ticket. It was a small, slightly weathered envelope, with the name "Austin Appleby" written tidily across the front.

"Ah. Mr. Appleby?" The eyes that studied Barry from behind those lenses were skeptical. "I seem to recall hearing that he was an older gentleman, with silvered hair and a limp?" Barry himself, of course, still looked like the farm boy he'd been less than a decade ago.

"Oh, that was him, all right," he agreed easily. "I took that from him in a card game." He grinned. "Figured, given its nature, Mr. Abernathy wouldn't object."

He held his breath, but after barely a pause the clerk nodded. "Indeed, you are correct," he said briskly. "The tournament is reserved for those adjudged the finest players in the country, and if you beat one of those originally selected, that confirms your place among their number." He found a line in his ledger, crossed out the name there, and treated Barry to a small smile. "Name?"

"Barry Joseph." He watched as the man wrote it in.

"Welcome aboard the *Lazy Ace*, Mr. Joseph," the clerk told him once that was done. "You're in cabin 11. Enjoy your stay, and good luck."

With that the two armed men stepped aside, and Barry resisted the urge to whoop and holler as he stalked up the gangplank, the wood swaying under him as he crossed to the ship. He'd done it! He was in!

His cabin was a fancy affair, finer than many hotels he'd seen, with a brass four-poster bed, a private wash basin, and a pair of windows looking out across the promenade to the water. After dropping his bags there—and secreting the bulk of his money under the sink, behind towels and blocks of soap—Barry set out to get the lay of the land. He'd been on boats a few times before, but only in steerage, so traveling first-class was a new experience and one he aimed to enjoy.

Not that the purpose of this particular excursion was mere sightseeing, of course.

When he'd first heard about the *Lazy Ace* and its upcoming poker tournament, Barry had barely believed it. Will "Wild Card" Abernathy was a legend, a gambler so skilled they said he could cheat the Devil himself at cards and never get caught. Abernathy had vanished years ago, and most had assumed he was either dead in a ditch somewhere, having finally tricked the wrong victim, or living it up on some private island. To turn up out of the blue, the owner of his own riverboat, announcing an invite-only tournament with a four-hundred-thousand-dollar cash prize— well, that was certainly spectacular in the old Abernathy fashion!

Barry was determined to be in that tournament. Winning it would be grand, of course, but he was still new to all this, relatively speaking. Simply taking part would cement his place, however. People would know his name. That was useful—when you wanted it to be.

There were only two problems. The first was the entry fee of five thousand dollars. He hadn't been too worried there, and indeed that last game had delivered with room to spare. The second, and far trickier, was the invite. Eighty gamblers had been invited to participate, from all over the country and maybe beyond. Barry hadn't been one of them. That had meant finding someone who was and luring them into a game rich enough to make them toss their invite into the pot.

Fortunately, Austin Appleby had obliged.

Now here Barry was in his place. And what a place! The whole ship gleamed like gold and shone like a museum, fancy as a palace with its white columns and polished floors and brass rails. The maids and bursars and sailors he saw hustling past were all in spotless white uniforms, making Barry feel grubby in his denims, chambray shirt, and sheepskin coat, and he saw plenty of passengers in fine frills and brocade and silk. Others were dressed more like him, though, and Barry told himself it didn't matter. No one was here to see his clothes, just how he handled himself at the table.

The promenade ran all the way around the upper deck—the boiler deck, or saloon deck—and after strolling it a bit Barry settled in along a stretch of rail to watch the opposite shore and the broad expanse of the Mississippi between them. A call had gone out for final boarding, and overhead the chimneys spouted great billows of steam as the ship prepared to get underway.

"Hello." The voice was soft and sweet, with a hint of Southern drawl, and Barry twisted his head—and straightened, pushing his hat back as he felt his face flush. The young lady before him was a vision, though he knew the more discerning might balk at his use of the word "lady." But her gingham dress, while slightly faded, was clean and fitted nicely to her lithe figure, and her blond curls were tugged back from her face, their golden luster adding a bewitching counterpoint to her fine blue eyes and shy smile.

"Howdy." He tipped his hat, breaking into an answering smile. "I'm Barry. Barry Joseph."

Hers widened, and she dipped into a simple country curtsey. "Addie Fitzpatrick. Nice to meet you." Her gaze slipped past him as, with a loud whistle, the riverboat chugged away from the dock and began its journey downriver. "Ain't it grand?" She stepped up to the rail at his side, though not so close as to be improper. "I've never been on a steamboat before. It's just so exciting!"

"It is," he agreed, half watching the water slide past and half eyeing his pretty new companion. "Where you headed?"

"Oh, all the way to New Orleans." She spared him a warm glance. "You?"

"Same." She clearly didn't have a lot of money, not with that dress, yet she was on the upper deck, which was reserved for first class. The large bag at her side was assembled from a patchwork of different fabrics and looked sturdy but handmade rather than store-bought. "You here for the tournament?"

This time her smile was dazzling. "I am! You too?" She laughed at his expression. "Well, aren't we a pair? Won our way into a first-class trip, and some time at the tables besides!"

Barry couldn't help laughing at her clear delight. "Yeah, it's a treat, all right. I'm looking forward to dinner—I hear these boats serve a top-notch meal, better than most fancy restaurants. And it's all included in the ticket—or the invite, in our case."

"I'm curious to see the truth of that tale myself," Addie confided, a twinkle in her eye. "For now, I'm going to explore a bit. Save me a seat?" And, with a quick grin, she spun away from the rail and danced down the deck, leaving Barry staring after her.

"I will!" he called, and she waved to show she'd heard, but didn't glance back. He watched her a bit longer before finally returning his attention to the river.

This trip had just got a whole lot more interesting!

––––––––––––––––––––––

Dinner was indeed sumptuous, and Addie's company—for she made good on her promise and claimed the seat Barry had fiercely guarded to his right—delightful. Barry couldn't remember having had a finer night. Still, all that faded to fond memory the next morning when a porter knocked to inform him that "the tournament will begin promptly at ten."

Twenty minutes later, having dunked his head in the basin and then put on a fresher shirt, Barry was back at the main cabin, which also served as the ship's saloon. It was a grand space, long and wide and high-ceilinged, with white columns marching down either side and crystal chandeliers overhead down the center. Fine rugs covered the floor, and the tables that last night had been decked out in white linen tablecloths now were bare, revealing their green felt tops. The same trio who'd examined boarders on the dock were stationed just inside the saloon doors, and when Barry reached them and gave his name, he was checked off the same list as before.

"Entry fee?" the clerk asked next, and Barry handed over the wad of cash he'd collected over recent weeks. The money was counted, not meanly but efficiently, and then he was presented with a silver cuff in return. It was a broad, thick band, curved at the ends where it would fit around a wrist, and was incised with strange symbols he almost recognized.

"What's this?" he asked, taking the cool metal wristlet.

"That's your ticket to play," one of the guards told him brusquely. "Lose it and you're out of the game."

Seeing that it would do no good to argue, Barry squeezed it onto his arm and immediately felt a strange shock, as if he'd plunged his hand into ice water. The sensation spread rapidly, then faded, leaving him with only a last shiver. The clerk was already focusing on the next person in line, so Barry allowed himself to be shepherded into the saloon, where a porter guided him to one of the many tables.

Each table had four chairs, and he quickly counted twenty such stations. That would be all eighty, then. He was pleased to see Addie, and just as happy they were at different tables. He liked her, and nothing could be worse for courting than to drum her out of the contest. That might come eventually, but for now he honestly wished her luck.

Everyone had found their seats when a loud voice declared, "Well, then!" Barry turned with the rest to stare at the rail-thin gentleman framed in the doorway, his goatee snow white but his long hair still a mix of silver and black. His dark suit was handsomely cut, and his bolo tie's clasp was a silver playing card, a joker in particular. This, then, was "Wild Card" Abernathy.

"Welcome, one and all, to my first-ever annual poker tournament!" their host declared, confirming his identity. "You may have noticed the item on your wrist." Here he held up his arm to display a matching cuff there, gracing them with a smile Barry found slightly predatory. "Consider them protection as well as confirmation. Now, let's play!" And he made his way across the room to the farthest table, where a seat still stood empty for him.

The dealers followed behind, and as one joined his table Barry forced himself to focus. He'd consider Abernathy's eccentric performance later. For now, as the man had said, it was time to play.

The thing about an event like this, where you'd either been invited or won your invite off someone who had, was that there were no amateurs here, and no fools. Everyone at these tables knew their way around a deck of cards. But that didn't mean they all had equal skill. The first player struck from Barry's table overplayed his hand, calling when he should have folded and bluffing to cover it. Another quickly followed, a solid player who lacked the guts to stand against even a moderate push and whose few small wins were quickly reversed by much larger losses. That left Barry and one other, and the stranger's top-notch clothes and expensive cufflinks marked him as a man of wealth, likely to be careless with his money and cavalier with his bets. Barry, who'd had to earn every penny he'd ever had, played tighter and fiercer, and it was not yet four o'clock when he cleaned that gentleman out as well.

"Congratulations, sir," the dealer told him as the man rose, bowed, and left the room, pausing at the door to relinquish his cuff. "You've advanced to the next round, which will be held up in the Texas tomorrow. Don't worry about your chips, I'll see them set at your place."

"Thank you." Barry stood and, since he knew the amounts

had to match, pulled a dollar from his pocket to tip the man instead. Then he turned his attention to the other tables.

He recognized several of the players, either by sight or by reputation. There was Earl "King Flush" Two Moons, a massive gentleman who played the role of "strong, silent Indian" to a tee but who Barry'd once heard reciting poetry to a young barmaid. Over at another table was Dandy Dan Sinclair, black as night and slick as oil, dressed to kill and with a killer smile. One over from him was Pappy, who looked like every pig farmer Barry'd ever met, being old as sin and poor as dirt with a beard as long as the Mississippi and twice as bedraggled. His counterpoint was Philip Murtaugh, known as the Numerologist, small and tidy as a pin, everything in its place and not a lick of emotion on his scrubbed face.

Addie was still in the game, Barry was pleased to see. Nor was she the only woman here, or the only one left. Madam LeTour presided over a table to one side, tall, sultry, and slinky—she could make a man blush just by laying down her cards. And over there was Evelyn Hunt, who could've been the Numerologist's twin, while at a different spot sat Betsy Rhodes, a prospector as dirty as Pappy but a lot more friendly. Barry had played her once before, and she'd lost with a smile and bought a round for the table afterward, with a pouch of gold flake she'd panned herself.

Of course, Abernathy was making short work of his own opponents, but Barry's eyes were drawn elsewhere, to a slim man with good but unremarkable clothes, a pleasant but forgettable face—and a gold tooth that winked when he smiled. Even as Barry watched, the man beat his last rival, nodded at him in a friendly manner, and stood to stretch. Then he spotted Barry in turn, and that smile widened, as did his eyes.

"Barry?" Marcus "Aurelius" Palmer crossed the distance in an instant, shaking Barry's hand and clasping his arm at the same time. "How the hell are you, lad? And what the devil are you doing here?" His gaze drifted down to Barry's wrist, as if to confirm he had a right to be in the room.

"Austin Appleby," Barry explained to his former mentor, grinning. "Turns out he couldn't resist betting on the flush. Too bad I had a boat."

Marcus laughed. "Yeah, that'd do it. Well, I'm glad to see you, and no mistake. But stay out of my way, hear? You know I won't hesitate to take you down."

"Nor I you," Barry replied, and they both nodded, no animosity present. That was just the game. Marcus had taught him well, and it'd be a disservice to those same lessons to not give the game his all, even if that meant beating his own teacher.

The glance at the bracelet had reminded him, though, and now he lifted that same wrist between himself and his old mentor. "Any idea what this fancy bauble is? I can tell it ain't just jewelry."

The look he received was a familiar one, half amused and two thirds exasperated. "You never did study enough, boy. Don't you see those symbols? It's been hexed, and powerfully so. All protections, though. Strong enough to block anything I could throw at it, that's sure. The cards, too."

Ah. Abernathy was either a spellslinger himself or knew enough to be wary of them, so he'd provided charms to block anyone from hexing their rivals. Including him. That was smart.

Barry let his hand fall as Addie skipped over to join him. "I won, can you believe it?" she said, beaming. "Oh, hello!"

"Addie Fitzpatrick, this is Marcus Palmer," Barry introduced them.

"Charmed, I'm sure." Marcus bent over her hand, then quirked a brow. "Fitzpatrick? Not the Sailor's girl? Seamus Fitzpatrick?"

She nodded, clearly pleased. "That's Pa, all right. He wasn't up to making the trip, so I came in his stead." Ah, that explained it. She'd been bequeathed her invite, and no doubt had learned the game from her father. Barry remembered hearing about the Sailor from Marcus.

The three of them chatted a bit, but half of Barry's attention was on the other remaining players. They were his competition, after all, and he wasn't about to miss this opportunity to study them. Poker was only half about the cards. The rest was reading your opponent. The more tells he could pick up now, the better off he'd be tomorrow.

That night, however, Barry was awakened by a terrible scream. Leaping to his feet, he grabbed his gun from the bedside table and bolted for the door, wearing only his denims. There were folks already gathered at the railing, and he joined them. "What happened?"

A woman turned to him with a shudder. "Man overboard," she explained, voice trembling and eyes bright with tears. "Gator got him."

"It was King Flush," someone else offered. "I saw him in the water, but it was too late. That gator was bigger'n a dugout canoe, and faster than a rattlesnake."

Barry shook his head, lowering the pistol to his side. There was no danger here, only in the silvered waters sliding past below. But what had possessed the big Indian to go swimming at this hour, and in such a place? Or had he tripped and fallen somehow? With a small tremor, Barry moved away from the railing, just to be safe.

He was returning to his room when he spotted Addie, curled in on herself in one of the deck chairs. "You okay?" he asked, stepping over to her. He kept the pistol pressed against his leg, hopefully unnoticed.

"I—no, not really," she admitted, her voice small and quivering. "How awful! I just met him today. He hugged me when he learned my name and told me to send my father his regards.

And now he's dead?" Her eyes were bright and her cheeks wet as she gazed up at Barry. "How did that happen?"

"I don't know," he answered, perching carefully on the corner of her chair, far enough away to give her space but near enough to converse. "Wet deck, a slip of the foot, something like that?" She nodded woodenly. "Do you want me to escort you back to your room?"

That earned him a tremulous smile. "Thank you. That would be… I'd appreciate it."

Rising, he did his best to ignore the chill breeze off the water, and the fact that he was bare-chested. So did she, it seemed, as she kept her eyes resolutely ahead or on his face as she led the way back to her own room, which was on the far side. They were nearly there when they heard a muffled pounding sound. It was coming from the room two doors from Addie's.

"Hello?" Barry asked, moving to the door. "Do you need help?" He tried the handle, but it was locked. Or worse, perhaps—it didn't budge at all. And the pounding was becoming more frantic. "Hang on!" he reversed his gun and bashed its butt against the handle, but without effect. That left only one option. "See if you can find something to batter it down," he told Addie, who nodded and hurried away. As soon as she'd gone, Barry closed his eyes and summoned his strength. Then he dealt himself a hand.

Luck was with him this time, as the glowing cards materialized in his fingers—six, seven, eight, nine, ten. A straight. That would certainly do the trick. Focusing, he flexed his wrist and then hurled the cards at the door. They struck with a loud pop, disappearing in a flash, but the door burst open as if it had been kicked from the inside.

And a slim figure tumbled out—Evelyn Hunt.

"Oh!" Addie had returned, and rushed to Evelyn's side. But the other woman was blue in the face, strands of her hair having escaped their tight bun to fall across her face, and her eyes beneath them were glazed. It was too late.

"What happened to her?" Addie demanded, and Barry shook his head. Edging around the dead woman, he peered into her cabin but didn't see anything amiss. An empty glass rested upon the nightstand, however. Had she taken a drink and choked on it? She must have. A tragic accident.

Still, two of them in a single hour? That struck Barry as odd indeed. As he helped Addie up and to her own cabin, he resolved to sleep lightly that night, pistol in hand, just in case.

The next morning, Barry headed up the stairs to the Texas, which was the top deck save only the glass-walled pilothouse itself. He'd thought the saloon was grand, but the Texas had it all beat to hell, with its fine wood paneling, arched roof, thick gilt-trimmed columns, and heavy upholstered chairs. Only five tables were arranged down the center of the smaller, cozier room, and the same clerk checked Barry's name against the list before allowing him in and directing him to his spot. Addie was already there at the next table over, and though she looked a trifle pale, her smile hello seemed genuine.

As people filed in, Barry noticed a few empty spaces. He'd known there would be two, since both 'King Flush' and Evelyn Hunt had won their games yesterday, but where was everyone else? One absence in particular concerned him, as the time to start drew closer and he did not see his mentor anywhere.

"Excuse me," he finally said, catching a passing porter's sleeve. "Where's Marcus Palmer?"

Betsy Rhodes was at his table, and she leaned forward, her usual smile absent. "You didn't hear? Sorry, kid. He died in the night. Literally drank himself to death."

"Drank...what?" Barry stared at her. Marcus, dead? How was that even possible? And drank himself to death? The man hadn't touched a drop of booze in over a decade, not since his wife had passed. What was going on around here?

Abernathy was the last to arrive again, and once he'd taken his own seat play began, forcing Barry to put aside such questions. He'd think about that after he'd won today's match.

Of course, his three opponents were all excellent. Betsy he already knew, but he'd never faced the Numerologist before, and their final tablemate was a complete stranger, a big, loud man named Sergeant Barnes who still wore his cavalry uniform, complete with sword. Fortunately, Barnes played like he talked, rough and crude, and kept betting high in the hopes of buying the pot. The other three ate away at his chips, and he was the first one out.

Betsy was next, going all in on a flush and losing to Murtaugh's small boat. At least she left with a smile and a pat on Barry's shoulder, unlike Barnes who'd stormed out cursing and kicking furniture.

That just left him and the Numerologist. The man was a machine, but Barry saw where that could be a weakness. Murtaugh relied too much on logic, and in poker that only took you so far. You had to be able to read people, and sometimes you just had to go with your gut. Barry won three hands in a row, none of them big, but he could practically see his opponent's thoughts—surely the odds would not allow four? So Barry played into that, showing some hesitancy about his next hand, and sure enough his rival pounced—and then stared as Barry revealed his four nines. "That makes no sense!" Murtaugh exclaimed. "The odds…"

Barry just shrugged. "Sometimes, you gotta buck the odds."

He stretched and looked around. The next table was already empty, and he was sorry to see that Addie had left the room, while Dandy Dan Sinclair lingered. She was out, then. In a way, it was a relief—they wouldn't have to play each other. Still, he felt bad for her.

At the third table, Madam LeTour had just laid down her hand with a seductive smirk. And, across from her, a gentleman Barry didn't know, short and heavyset with thick whiskers, pushed back from the table and jerked to his feet in a way everyone knew to back away from.

"You cheating whore!" the man bellowed, reaching not for his gun but his cards. He fanned them in his hand, and Barry caught the flash as two more formed on the end. Before he could even consider stepping in, the stranger hurled those glowing new cards directly at Madam LeTour—

—and they vanished in a flicker, as her cuff briefly glowed brighter than a lantern.

Marcus had been right. The charms did work.

But that made Barry think of his mentor, evidently dead in a way that made no sense. Had someone killed him and then poured booze over him to make it look like suicide? Maybe the same someone who'd tossed King Flush into the river, and drowned Evelyn Hunt?

Someone was bumping off contestants, he was sure of it.

And if they were only going after the competition, Barry had just made himself a target by winning through to the final round.

———————————

That night, Barry shunned all company, even Addie's. He collected some food from the saloon—making sure he saw others eat from the same dishes first, just in case—and then took it back to his room, where he barricaded himself in, pistol close at hand, and stared at the door and the windows, forcing himself to stay awake.

He wasn't taking any chances.

———————————

The next morning—the last of trip and tournament both—found Barry bleary and exhausted, but still alive. He presented himself at the Texas with ten minutes to spare and found the clerk and the riflemen in their usual places, guarding a room that now stood empty save a single table at its center. Two men were there already, and both nodded as Barry walked in and took a seat.

"We haven't had the pleasure yet, son," the slick gambler said. "Dandy Dan Sinclair."

"Barry Joseph," Barry replied, shaking hands. The dealer just shuffled the cards.

"Hear about Madam LeTour?" Dan asked. He shook his head and seemed genuinely sad. "Took her own life, the porters said. With a straight razor. Damn shame."

Barry didn't believe it for a second.

Will Abernathy sauntered in at the stroke of ten, and the clerk shut the door behind him. "Just us three today," the riverboat's owner stated as he joined them. "Seems Pappy had himself an accident, got wound up in his bedsheets and wrapped 'em round his neck. Horrible. But the game must go on." He smiled, and something about it sent a shiver down Barry's spine.

Then the dealer started tossing cards, and he concentrated on the game.

There was the usual back and forth, some wins and some losses, some calls and some raises and a few bluffs, but slowly Abernathy pulled ahead. Barry did his best to moderate his usual style of play, shooting for more caution and less foolhardiness, and more often than not he folded and let the two more experienced players battle it out. And almost every time that happened, Dandy Dan came up just short.

"Dang it!" the man declared after one such bout, his nines over jacks losing to their host's tens over queens. "Lady Luck is teasing me today!"

That was surely true, but a bit too often for Barry's liking. He watched the dealer closely on the next game, cards still on the table beneath his hand, but could see no cheating there.

Then he felt something shift beneath his palm, and a quick flicker of heat.

What?

Raising the cards, Barry saw that he had a low pair and nothing more. But something felt wrong, their surfaces slick and warm. That faded so quickly he wondered if he'd imagined it. But Dandy Dan was frowning at his own hand, and not simply like a man displeased with what he saw.

More like a man trying to reconcile sight with memory.

Abernathy's lips twitched, a hint of a smile slipping through, and suddenly Barry understood.

The man was a spellslinger. And he was changing the cards.

But they were warded, Marcus had said. Heavily so. How was he getting past that?

He glanced up just in time to catch his host's eye—and saw a flicker of red there, deep within. The sight sent chills through him, because now it all made sense.

Barry and Dandy Dan weren't playing Will Abernathy right now. There was a devil wearing his skin. And the hellspawn had power to spare. More than enough to force its way past those wards.

Barry folded, but Dan just grinned and pushed what was left of his money to the center. "All in," he stated. "Boat again, and this time it's tens over kings."

Abernathy—or the creature possessing him—stared at that a second. "All I got is two pair," he stated. Then he grinned. "Fours and fours."

He slapped the cards down, and Dan howled in frustration—but the sound turned to a true wail of pain a second later, as steam began rising from his skin. Barry stared in horror as the fancy gambler began thrashing about, the smell of cooked flesh making him gag. He could do nothing as Dandy Dan Sinclair seemingly roasted on the spot, finally collapsing in a heap of seared flesh and cracked teeth.

"And then," Abernathy stated, "it was just you and me."

Barry glared at him. "This your plan all along?" he demanded. "Win the tournament yourself, any way necessary?"

That made his host roar with laughter, a horrible, grating noise. "The tournament? I don't care about such things, boy! That's this body's fancy. I'm in it for darker, tastier game." He licked his lips. "The fear—and the souls. Play against me and lose, I get your soul." He glanced at poor dead Dan, then at the dealer, who somehow seemed oblivious. "Now deal."

Barry thought fast. He couldn't overcome a demon, and couldn't harm it anyway, not with that cuff on. But what'd Marcus said? "All protections. Strong ones." Not strong enough.

But what Barry himself lacked in skill, or subtlety, he more than made up for in sheer force.

Calming himself, he shut his eyes and summoned his will. Then he dealt himself cards from the deck of his magic. Four kings. A strong hand indeed. Blinking, he leaned back—and hurled the cards at his opponent, who reflexively raised an arm to block the attack.

The cards struck true, however, hitting the cuff itself full on. There was a mighty burst of light, and the cuff glowed brighter than the noonday sun, that nimbus spreading around the entire man.

And Abernathy screamed as the demon was forced out of him, a dark shadow that spun round and round the table but could not regain its former home, the cuff's protections now increased tenfold.

"Now," Barry said, eyeing Abernathy, "it really is just you and me." He pushed his cards back toward the dealer. "New deck, new deal."

The man nodded—he seemed dazed, perhaps charmed to keep from reacting to the horrors around him?—and set aside the used deck, taking a fresh one and cracking its seal. He dealt, and Barry lifted each card as it came to him, ensuring that they could not be altered unnoticed. Two sixes, two sevens, and the ace of diamonds. Not a winning hand, but with several ways out. So, play it safe and trade the ace, hoping for a boat? But a small one, if that. Keep the diamonds and try for the flush? Toss one pair and hope for four?

Or go for broke.

Abernathy took two, and grinned, his previous swagger restored. "I'm gonna put you all in, lad," he warned, shoving all his chips forward.

"Fine by me." Barry slid both pairs back across the table. "I'll take four." And he flipped over his remaining card, proving he had an ace.

The dealer nodded, but as he started to deal the first one Barry stopped him. "Face up," he instructed, and the man did as he was told, tossing the five of diamonds out beside Barry's ace. The three followed—no chance of boats or quads now. But it was another diamond. Next came the two, also a diamond. And finally, the four. Of diamonds. A straight flush.

Abernathy stared, then slapped down his own cards. Four eights. A strong hand. But not strong enough.

"I can't lose," he whispered, and it was fear Barry heard, rather than pride. "I can't!" His gaze was desperate. "You don't understand!"

"Oh, I think I do," Barry replied, pushing back his chair and standing. "You really did bet the Devil, and the devil won, didn't he? Claimed your soul—unless you offered him others in return. But you could only give him ones you'd won. And now you've lost, he's gonna claim his due." He looked at the cuff on the other man's wrist. "Soon as that charm wears off, that shadow'll suck you dry. Just like you did poor Dandy Dan. And maybe Marcus, and Evelyn, and the others." He scowled down at the former legend, now slumped with tears streaming down his lined cheeks. "Well, you bought that hand yourself. Time to pay up."

Turning away, Barry strode to the door. The clerk answered at his banging, and—after glancing inside and getting a nod from the dealer—handed Barry a large, heavy satchel. "Congratulations, sir," the man told him.

"Thank you." Barry hefted the bag. Up above, the steam whistle sounded, notifying them that they were pulling into New Orleans. Along the upper promenade, whispers sprang up from the former players gathered there, upon seeing him emerge victorious—and one smile shone from the pack, as Addie pushed her way forward.

And behind him, Will Abernathy cowered, a dark shadow circling him like a hungry dog, snapping at his fingers and nipping at his nose.

But the weather was fine, there was a pretty girl waiting, and he had a whole bundle of money and a major win to his credit, so Barry Joseph found himself smiling as he walked away into the bright, beautiful afternoon. For once, the deck was stacked in his favor.

ᗪESERT JUDGMENT

MAURICE BROADDUS

Augustus Villard cradled the postcard in his hands like it was a treasure he was afraid to let go of, despite how much it burned him. Staring at the sepia-toned image left nothing but the taste of ash in his mouth. When the gnawing emptiness threatened to consume him, he slipped the postcard back into his vest.

The oak-hickory forest fingered its way across the Oklahoma Territory. The thick tree cover obscured most of the night sky, the outline of branches swaying against the inky backdrop. Soon dawn would crest the horizon, but Augustus had a day or so worth of travel left if he were going to reach the edge of the city of Langston or, more precisely, the desperate terrain outside where the fabled desert father, Ol' Pap, lived.

The bridge loomed nearby. Augustus knew better than to come this way, but his heart pulled him here. He had to experience the reality of it in person, much the way one couldn't help but pick at a nearly healed scab.

Drinking from his canteen, Augustus stalked the perimeter of the clearing, allowing his horse, Chango, to rest. Careful not to push her the way he drove himself—he was fueled by rage and hellbent on revenge, so he could go all night. And often did.

With the lightening skies, the shadows among the trees played with his imagination. Though far off a ways, an ominous shape hovered. Augustus ducked under the protruding brush—each branch determined to stop his approach—slowly making his way toward the object. A body slowly swung in an unfelt breeze. Augustus withdrew his ax, and he cut the rope suspending the body. It tumbled to the ground and, despite already knowing he was too late, Augustus rushed to the corpse's side. He rolled the body over.

A young woman in a matronly frock. Her round, brown face retained a cherubic innocence. Checking for her pulse, any life signs, he pulled his hands back after touching something wet and sticky. Leaning closer, he made out the word written across the woman's forehead in blood.

"Sassy."

Augustus glanced around, his ears alert for anyone nearby. He wondered what kind of abomination wrote its quarry's crime in blood like this, but he knew that monsters who lynched took a variety of forms. Still, it wouldn't look good for him to be caught in the woods at such a scene. The law was a fickle thing when it came to protecting folks like him.

Rubbing his hands clean with some water from the nearby creek, he crept back to Chango. As he approached the clearing, he noticed three men huddled about his horse in slow inspection. No, four. That last one remained cloaked in shadows, determined not to be noticed.

The men locked onto him. Releasing Chango's bridle, their leader stepped forward. Even in the dim light, Augustus recognized the man. George Littrell.

The postcard nearly scalded his lurching heart.

George Littrell was a landowner, Freemason, and Democrat politician on the rise. He was well known in these parts. Dressed more for a stage show than any frontier work, his vest bore a chain looped from a button to the watch in his pocket.

One of the men wore fringed buckskin with a kerchief

wrapped around his neck, his Winchester leaning against him. The other man wore a brown canvas duster with matching trousers. With a scarf about his neck, he came off as some playtime cowboy. Augustus figured them to be hired hands with no particular military training.

The menacing figure clung to the shadows, obscured by a cowl draped over his head. Augustus shifted to make sure that one stayed fully in his view.

"Look here, boss, she belongs to me." Augustus drew his hat low across his head but kept his hands in plain sight as to not overly rattle them.

"Who are you?" Littrell asked without a trace of recognition in his eyes.

Why would he recognize me? I was just another darky to him. "I'm a man. A free man. Free to go off to take a piss without having his horse messed with."

"You didn't answer my question." Littrell attempted to add steel to his tone, but it was a brittle, insecure thing.

"I don't answer to you. I know my rights." Though born into slavery, Augustus had joined the 28th Regiment in Indiana and served in the war. He knew he was outnumbered, but these men didn't come close to cowing him. And they knew it. His instincts told him the fourth member of their crew would be the problem.

"You don't know much. Not enough to not be around here," Littrell said.

"Especially after dark," Buckskins said.

"With so many trees," the pretend cowboy tittered into the wind.

"What are you doing here?" Littrell straightened and strutted toward Augustus.

"Me? I'm just searching for some of that neighborly Christian spirit I've been hearing so much about," Augustus replied.

"You sure have a recalcitrant tongue for someone who doesn't fully appreciate his circumstance." Littrell liked to flaunt his fancy East Coast education, wanting everyone to know he was the smartest man in the room. He grew especially eloquent when he believed he had the only ace to play. "It's not safe for you around these parts."

"Around any parts, far as I can tell."

"That's the beginning of wisdom right there." Littrell had a long family history of sympathy to the Confederacy. Augustus ventured that any time spent in an outhouse lasted longer than the Confederacy had. But here stood Littrell. "There seems to be an antagonism of interest between the races. The Oklahoma Territory is eighty five percent white, ten percent colored, and five percent Indian. Which is about fifteen percent off from where I'd like the situation to be."

"There's a rumor that some folks have taken fixing that situation into their own hands," Augustus said. "Lynching folks. Intimidating folks to steer clear of the Territory."

"Those are stories spread by mendacious press, mendacious politicians, and mendacious persons propagating their agenda."

"Anyways, hangin' is too good for most of them, if you ask me," Playtime Cowboy said.

"I'll admit, on occasion, law abiding men might get caught up in an...uncontrollable passion. For justice. All to protect their community. Defend what's theirs," Littrell said. "We're here as a...safety posse. There are rumors that some coloreds might be planning an uprising."

Buckskin took a few steps away, giving himself distance. "Boss, we better take care o' this one before he makes trouble."

If lynchings were the opening of Littrell's terror campaign, the rumors were the second act. Get folks riled up enough they were liable to do anything, like create an armed perimeter around Langston. They weren't a posse; they'd be an occupying force. Littrell and his boys feared Augustus's people, even though the Exodusters meant them no harm. But they were a threat because if the situation were reversed, Littrell could not conceive of a world where they wouldn't want retribution.

Littrell and his boys didn't have the decency to know that they were going to hell.

"Ain't no insurrection on our part being planned. If anyone was going to get up to something, it'd be you." Augustus let his coat jacket fall a little further open, his hand drifting toward his waist.

"You better watch your mouth, boy."

"Or what? You can't take anything else from me."

"There's one last thing. Starting with that smart mouth of yours." Littrell shifted, the man's attentions deferring to the cowled figure.

"Uppity." The cowled figure stirred, its voice like jagged glass across Augustus' soul.

Littrell stepped nearer, his head tilted to one side as he scrutinized Augustus' face. "Do I know you? Your bearing strikes me as…familiar."

"Don't know why you would. I'm just passing through."

Littrell snapped his fingers. "I do recollect why you seem so familiar to me. You're the husband of—what was that gal's name? Bridget Villard."

My Biddy. Augustus pressed his vest closer to his chest, until the postcard poked him with its edge. "You'd best keep my wife's name out of your mouth."

"Uppity." The cowled figure took another step closer, without so much as crunching a leaf beneath his feet, as if he floated on air.

"From what I hear, your wife had an indissoluble femininity." Littrell withdrew his pocket watch and turned his back to Augustus. "Shame what happened to the boy."

Augustus couldn't talk to a man who didn't have no soul, and he had better things to do than waste his breath. He pivoted, throwing a punch, but the cowled figure glided between him and Littrell. It took the blow without so much as a flinch. Augustus whirled, his ax brought to bear with a motion so smooth, like a thing he'd practiced many times. He buried the blade deep within the figure.

The cowled man turned his gaze to Augustus, face lost in the swirl of shadows, revealing only twin red orbs glaring with disdain at him.

"Uppity," the figure said again. A glint of metal being drawn and targeting him was all Augustus' mind registered.

The dawn's sunlight pierced the horizon and with it. The cowl figure turned toward it. All the men froze, anxious for the next moment. Augustus regripped his weapon, not knowing what to expect next. The figure blurred, like his very essence began to break down, becoming unreal in the light of day until he burned away like morning mist. Suddenly it was just Augustus, Littrell, and his two henchmen.

"I don't want no trouble, but I'll gladly finish anything started," Augustus said.

Littrell's grin faltered as he realized even though they had superior numbers, he and his men were outmatched. He held up a hand to stop his boys from further instigating something. "We've had a full night. The desert judge is bound to our family. I'm the only thing keeping it in check. Besides, next full moon's only a couple days away. The demon'll finish what it started and come for you."

With that, Littrell's people mounted their horses and left Augustus in the clearing. Stroking Chango's nose, Augustus knew he couldn't defeat Littrell on his own. Not with that thing backing him up. Another reason he had to find Ol' Pap.

"I'm not done with you Littrell. Everything in its appointed time."

Several hours later, Augustus paused at a sandy ridgeline, scrambling down from his horse to get a better view of the sunbaked terrain. The floodplain below stretched into a sea of rock-strewn sands. Somewhere along the mountain's edge, somewhere among the hidden caves, was his quarry. He spat dryly off to the side.

Emptying his canteen into a bowl to leave for Chango, he tottered down the mountain. When he reached the sleeping mass of rock fragments that tapered from the cliff, he knew he was in the final leg of his journey. He trudged across the butte, following the crest of the ridge the way the instructions had been passed to him.

A series of boulders hid the entrance to the cave, but Augustus knew he was in the right place. He staggered toward the shadowed opening. With his destination so close, his sleep-deprived body began to give out. Strength ebbed from his muscles with each step, until the cloying darkness threatened to completely engulf him. As he collapsed, waiting arms reached out to catch him.

"I got you," the elder's voice said.

Augustus' eyelids fluttered against the dark until he was sure he was awake. A wizened figure hunched over a wan fire whose light barely illumined him.

"I see you're back with us," the old man said.

"Ol' Pap?" Augustus sat up. There was a great migration of black people from the south out West after the Civil War. They called the people the Exoduster Movement. Its leader went by many names. Augustus wasn't sure who he dealt with. His hand drifted to his revolver, reassured that it was still there.

"If I am, there's no need for me to disarm you or for you to even need arms. You're safe here. In fact, this land has been sanctified. This is consecrated ground. Also, I found your horse, so I brought her 'round. Fed and watered her."

"Ever the caretaker, Reverend?"

"Don't call me that," Ol' Pap snapped. The words must have come out harsher than he intended, because he recovered his gentle demeanor quickly. "It's been a long time since those days. Plus, it seemes mite inhospitable to do otherwise when company comes all this way to be with you."

"Especially when you go so far out of your way to not be found."

Ol' Pap didn't respond. The desert fathers were early Christian hermits who withdrew to the desert of Roman-controlled Egypt. Many of their elders moved away to pursue a monastic life to hone their faith, focus on wisdom and matters of the spirit. They took themselves out of the fight.

The elder Exoduster tended the flames of the campfire. The smoke spiraled up a chute hidden by the malformations of the cave wall. Behind him was an old trunk, the closest thing to furnishing in the cavern. "What brings you out here?"

"The same spirit that brought all of us out here. We are free to move. We have the right to…be." Augustus nearly choked on the last word, his cool facade showing its cracks.

"Take your time." Ol' Pap came around to rest a weary hand on his shoulder. "I led over a hundred folks out here to help settle these lands. Saw more than I was meant to in my travels. Thought I could retreat to these desert caves to live out the rest of my days in peace. Don't mean I don't remember, though. How it was. Why we left. I'm sorry I got you into this."

"No, be sorry we had to flee the dust of our home soil to chase a living. Debt could drive even a God-fearing man mad." Augustus tamped down the swell of keening anger. "Back then, after the Army, I worked hard as a farmer, raised big crops. Turned it over to the man I rented from. He'd sell it, keep the money, and all I got was more debt. I needed to strike out on my own, make my own headway."

"To be like a white working man."

"Exactly."

"A black man attempting to live free like a white man sounds like a recipe to get his head shot clean off."

"It cost me." Augustus turned his head, careful to avoid the old man's steady gaze. His heart tightened with a familiar heavy pang, one he'd learned to live with as his constant companion. He squeezed his thumb along his fingers, stopping just short of balling into a fist. "Cost me dear. Worse than any bullet to the head. Farming one's own land meant being one's own master. Instead, I made our homestead their coffin."

The Homestead Act of 1862 offered land at low cost to any who dared to brave the harsh conditions of travel. Yet in the late 1870s to 1880s—1879 being the official Exodus Year—over 20,000 black folks left their respective homes for the Great Plains. Exodusters seeking a chance to start a new life, free, and away from the hate that dogged them wherever they lived in the South. Even the North.

"The first time we got to our 'stead, I dropped to my knees and ran the soil through my fingers. 'This here's free ground.' I declared. Then I turned to the heavens with the sky stretching out in all directions. 'Here, we're free.' Biddy's joy hit her all o' a-sudden and she cried like a child." Without realizing it, his hand had slipped into his vest, touching the postcard as if checking to make sure it was still real.

"I heard what the townsmen did. We all heard."

"That's what they wanted." Augustus reached for the postcard and sat it between him and Ol' Pap.

"I'm so—"

Augustus waved him off. "Don't. It's not on you. I should have been there to protect them."

Augustus remembered sitting alone in his cell, having been jailed on suspicion of trespassing. Trespassing. On his own property. He allowed the men to take him without protest, thinking that it would make things easier on his family. Even such a blatantly trumped-up charge could be sorted within days. But this left Biddy and his son, Jeremiah, alone at the house. His son's only mistake was sneaking out at night to hunt lizards with a sharpened stick. He accidentally came across Littrell's men. Rustling. They spied him and chased him back to the house. Augustus could only imagine how scared they were—Biddy holding Jeremiah—as Littrell's men held a rally, accusing *them* of the cow theft. Completely fabricating a tale wholesale out of air, he spread the news of Biddy having shot at the sheriff. With a large enough lie, it wasn't hard to form a white mob to seek justice.

Whenever he closed his eyes, Augustus pictured his wife and child yanked from his home—their home—and imagined their last moments. Dragged through the streets, gagged with tow sacks, taken out of town. For the rest, he had the postcard.

His finger traced the half inch hemp rope which had been tied into a hangman's knot. Their bodies dangled twenty feet below the middle span of the river's bridge. Biddy's arms swinging by her side, unrestrained. His son swinging nearby, his clothes partly torn off, hands bound with saddle string. Done in broad daylight with hundreds of witnesses, just to show how powerless Augustus and his people were. Littrell and his fellow townsmen even posed for a photograph, like they were taking a Sunday School portrait. Then everyone just walked off and left his family there like discarded trash. The photographer made a postcard with their image, which Littrell sent around to discourage further black migration to the Territory.

"I need to know what I'm up against. Littrell's power seems to have only grown. I got close to him, but there's this creature that seems to be in his employ. Or, rather, control."

"Describe it."

"I couldn't get a good look, like my eyes refused to fully focus on it. He called it a desert judge. Wears a cowl. Glowing red eyes."

"Damnation. A desert judge?" With his hands clasped behind him, Ol' Pap paced back and forth between Augustus and the small fire. "The Confederacy only lasted a few years, but its taint has been with us from the birth of this nation. Its spirit continues to leave an indelible mark, like a cancer in the soul of the country which spread even out here. Dogging us everywhere we go on the off chance that we might carve out a life, any taste of happiness, for ourselves. They set up the law against us. Their sheriffs. Their judges. The juries. Turning a blind eye to citizens taking the law into their own hands, deciding we were often guilty of 'hangin' offenses.' Their victims, mostly our people, hauled to the nearest tree and strung up."

This was a story Augustus had become all too familiar with. The atrocities of these good, God-fearing men hoping to usher in an age of fear. If they produced sufficient levels of terror, his people would learn and stay in their place.

"A desert judge is a demonic embodiment of their hateful Black Codes. They are relentless hunters," Ol' Pap continued. "Stalking trails, murdering folks, carrying out the will of those who summoned it. It's the unholy muscle that Littrell hid behind. Or at least leave his hands free for him to better enjoy the show created by his terror campaign. This one has been bound to Littrell. I'm guessing that it still first appears at the old oak tree where it was originally summoned. That's Littrell's place of power."

"I buried my ax in it. It shrugged it off like I barely scratched its itch."

"Let me see your ax." Ol' Pap held out his hands with grave expectation.

Augustus reached to his side. Without the adrenaline of a fight, the movement was slow and considered. He nestled the ax in his hand for an extra heartbeat, appreciating its weight. It was the one he'd used to shape the wood out of which he built his house. His family's house. Reverend or reverend-no-more, Ol' Pap rocked back and forth once it was in his hands. Eyes shut, he whispered a prayer of blessing. Rolling his palm across it one last time, he handed the ax back to Augustus.

Examining it, not knowing what he expected to see, Augustus thought it still looked like just an ax. "I get the feeling it'll take more than a sanctified blade to stop this thing."

"You're right. Hold your right hand up." Ol' Pap ransacked his trunk of belongings, piling its contents to the side until he retrieved a thick family Bible. "Place your left hand here."

"What are you doing?" Augustus asked, though he found himself complying.

"Augustus Villard, do you solemnly swear to uphold the laws and values of our cities? From Nicodemus to Langston to Boley, patrolling them, looking out for your people, so help you God?"

"I so swear."

Ol' Pap placed his hands on Augustus's head and prayed, his hushed tones steeped in the reverence of an incantation. "Then I hereby deputize you as a sovereign lawman, able to carry out justice, even to a desert judge."

"I'm supposed to impress them with the power of my good looks and strong personality?"

Ol' Pap fished through his belongings again until he found a handkerchief that protected something. He unwrapped it to reveal a tarnished tin star. Ol' Pap pinned the badge onto his vest. "To end the threat of a desert judge for good, you need to hang 'em high."

"The word has been spoken, and the message sent."

Augustus straddled Chango and trotted along the ridge overlooking the gnarled oak tree. Its branches twisted with rot, more dead than alive, held upright by eldritch energy. As the sun set, shadows began to coalesce beneath it. It gained substance, its physicality slowly swirled—a coalescing trail of fog—as it corporealized into this this plane of existence, as if absorbing the night. A frail, gaunt form staggered about like a newborn colt gathering its legs under it. Its hood draped over the tattered remains of a Confederate soldier's uniform. A small sack dangled from its neck. A gun belt slung low about its waist. Each hand clutched an Army revolver.

Its gaze immediately snapped toward Augustus, red glowing eyes fixed on him. Its hollowed eyes had studied the abyss too long, learned the ways of men's souls. Its broken yellow teeth drew up in the approximation of a smile before it raised its cowl, shadowing its face.

"*Uppity.*" Augustus knew the creature whispered.

He spurred Chango, allowing the demon to trail him to old Farnum Road at Loney Crossing, near the river. Augustus stopped at the clearing that led to the bridge. Hopping down from Chango, he strode to the clearing's center. Opening his jacket allowed easy access to his revolver's holster. Moonlight glinted from his deputy's badge.

The desert judge slowly emerged from the tree line. It paused to allow its presence to be felt, wanting fear to settle in and do most of the work for it. It moved with a depraved fluidity, the tuneless hum on its unseen lips.

Augustus' heart thudded in his chest, threatening to burst through his ribcage. His military training swept over him, tamping down the fear so he could move in the moment. He crept forward with a boxer's grace.

"Uppity," it repeated, moving toward him with deliberate speed. Its hip motion mimicked a step, yet its gait produced the effect of a hovering glide. Its broken-nailed hand raised a revolver, training it on Augustus.

With barely a flinch to signal his response, Augustus drew and unloaded his revolver dead center into the creature's chest. Each bullet caused the demon's form to jerk. Billowing clouds of spirit essence spewed from each wound. It canted its head, protesting in wordless surprise before tumbling forward.

It was over.

Augustus exhaled a long, lingering breath, hoping to rein in his runaway heart although the body remained still. Ol' Pap's deputizing of him made all the difference, as even in its undeath, the desert judge was vulnerable to an actual lawman. Still, being so near to the creature left him on edge—its preternatural stillness unsettled him. But he had one job left to do.

He retrieved the length of rope from the saddle pack on Chango.

His revolver empty, Augustus reached for his ax and tentatively approached the creature, nudging the body with one foot. Nothing. Not so much as a final spasm. Its lower half appeared as some sort of spirit trail, but its torso was solid enough. Augustus shoved it over with his foot. The cowl covered its face like a shroud. Studying it for a moment, he regripped his ax and bent low to secure the monster. Red eyes glowed to life, searing the shadows of its face. The creature fired as it moved, the bullet missing him as Augustus rolled for cover. A bullet from the second volley of shots managed to graze his side.

The desert judge fired repeatedly; Augustus counted off

the shots, but when the cylinder should have been empty, the weapons continued firing. Augustus wove through the copse of trees, but the demon continued to track him. He wasn't going to elude it this way.

Augustus doubled back along his trail and hid behind a thick hickory tree. Clutching his ax to him, he held his breath as the desert judge approached. It hesitated, not fooled by the tracks before it. Augustus leapt out, cleaving the ax into the creature's wrist. Without any howl of pain, it dropped the revolver. With its other hand, it batted the ax away and fired again. Augustus tumbled toward the dropped revolver. If his bullets weren't enough, perhaps the judge's own in his hands would be. Augustus scooped up the gun and in a single fluid movement, took aim and fired.

The revolver clicked, its barrel empty.

Whatever energy that allowed it to fire in the demon's undead hands, Augustus didn't possess. The desert judge reared up, unfazed. Scooping up his ax, Augustus charged as the demon drew down on him again. But he knocked the gun arm to the side and slammed into it with his full weight, plunging the blade into the creature's chest. His momentum carried them to the ground. When he found himself atop the creature, its red eyes faded to darkness again.

Not knowing how long he had before the creature regained enough of its dark energy to resume its pursuit, Augustus dragged the still form back to the bridge. On instinct, he snatched the bag from around its neck. Pouring it out, his inspection only found bits of burnt bones and dirt. A necromancer's pouch. His mind shuddered at whatever grim ritual Littrell had used.

Hooking one end of the rope to the bridge, Augustus formed a noose with the rope and wrapped it around the desert judge's neck. There was no mob contagion to blame for his actions, only the memory of what happened to his family. He kicked the desert judge free from the platform. The rope pulled taut; its sudden weight tugged at the bridge. The creature dangled in mid-air, swaying in an unfelt breeze. After a few, terribly long minutes, its body crumbled into dust.

Augustus rode out to Littrell's ranch. Night still covered him as he snuck up to the front of the main house. He left his wife's postcard nailed to the door. Littrell's time was drawing short, and Augustus wanted the man to realize no matter what eldritch creature he enslaved, no matter how many men he hired, Littrell was powerless to stop him.

"The word has been spoken, and the message sent."

IN THE END, THE BEGINNING

LAURA ANNE GILMAN

The east wind came calling at dawn, dropping down from the mountains with the chill of snow, spreading itself over Older Brother's valley, sneaking its way under the heavy wooden door and through the plank walls, finding its target seated on a chair before the fire, a fur thrown over bare legs and a clay mug in clawed hands.

The figure ignored the intruder.

Older Brother. Then again, louder. *Older Brother.*

Older Brother opened eyes the banked fire of earth's blood, a grumble rising in his throat that it would have been wise to heed. The wind, rather than fleeing, settled on his shoulders like a cape, and tugged with cold fingers at his ear.

Older Brother grumbled louder. "Whatever it is, no."

The wind tugged harder, thinner strands of it swirling around the figure, bringing with it the distant smell of beasts and men, foreign smells, foreign sounds. Blood, shit, and sweat, and the screams of the dishonored and the dead.

It was nothing Older Brother had not heard before in his

very long life. He cupped the mug more carefully in his hands, keeping it away from the wind's chill, and shook his head.

"If you're looking for someone to fight, go bother Cousin Bear, maybe he will oblige you."

The wind pushed against his back, sneaking sharp fingers under the robe, scratching at the hair on his face, pushing and nudging like a grandmother. It didn't want Bear, it wanted him.

"And what do you expect me to do?"

Older Brother had chosen to be a teacher, not a warrior; he had no desire to fight, particularly not with those who had picked no battle with him. Although, if the wind poked him one more time…

You fought once.

Only the wind remembered that, the wind and the stone, and the stone knew better than to speak. It had ended badly, and he fought no more. Those who came to this valley sought to learn, not fight.

"There will always be squabbles," he told the wind. "That is what men do."

"Who do you speak with?"

Older Brother glanced at the mortal woman stretched out under the furs piled on the bed, watching as she turned on her side, propping herself up on one elbow. The woman, who well-named herself Trouble, had come to him the month before to learn what she could from him, the magic of her spirit drawn to his. But she was only human and could not hear the wind, no matter how much or how well she might learn.

"Who do you speak with?" she asked again.

He sighed. "The wind. It wants me to do something."

"Must you go?" She stretched, one arm stretching over her head, turning her body so the furs slipped just enough, long black hair failing to preserve even false modesty. He grinned, running fingers through his hair to shake the ice loose.

"No," he said, putting down his mug and dropping to the bed beside her. The wind huffed around them. He cast out a hand, pushing the wind back out the door and barring it from within.

The wind, frustrated, swirled in a huff, and disappeared.

Had it been anyone else, that would have been the end of it. But the wind was persistent and it did not know tiredness. Three times more the wind came to the small house tucked into the curve of a slow-moving creek, and three times it would not leave him alone, swirling first from the east, then the south and north, crying of danger, of risk and change. Each time Older Brother told them to leave him be, that the matters of men were for men to worry over, not the likes of him.

Four times should have been the end of it.

And then the west wind came.

West wind did not whine, it did not cajole. It spoke for a night and a day of treachery and malice, of towns burnt to ash, entire peoples enslaved. It spoke of the end-of-all, the time when all the Ways disappeared, and silence fell upon the world. And then it asked Older Brother to come with it, to see what it saw.

Older Brother was no longer a warrior. But he had been named true, when all things had been named; the magic he carried would not allow him to refuse one who needed help. And so, as the sunlight faded and night rose, he stood and stretched, shifting shape to a four-footed form, the better for covering distances. And in that form, he followed the wind across the plains, east to the river called Grandmother.

And there, as they came over a ridge and stood silhouetted against the sky, he saw what the winds had spoken of.

Men. Too many to count. On the other side of the river they had erected tents and strung banners, smoke rising from too many campfires. Figures massed along the edge of the river, their horses restless under the unease of their riders. Distantly, pigs squealed as one was butchered for dinner, and vultures circled overhead, biding their time.

Nothing else moved near them. Even the smallest of things had fled.

His nose twitched—he could smell, even from there, that hunger and illness stalked their camp, a threat they could raise neither sword nor hoof against. It made them twitchy, it made them whisper of evil creatures and malign spirits, shifty eyes and pursed mouths studying every possible omen, seeking the source of whatever had cursed them.

He could feel their spirits, shivering within their bodies. They had not been cursed; they *were* a curse, one that could never be appeased. Greed was too tame a word for it. They consumed all they encountered, the way locusts consumed grass, until only dust and mourning were left behind.

West wind had been correct. The end-of-all had come, on horseback and wagon, speaking a foreign tongue.

The wind curled around his back and draped over his neck, sliding under his feet and ruffling his fur. He batted at it, frightened by what he saw, and angry at his own fear. "You wanted me here, I'm here. I see them. I don't know what you expect of me now."

Stop them.

"Can't be done." Despite his own emotion, he said it gently. For all its strength and determination, the wind was much as a child, with little understanding of anything other than itself. It saw danger but could not comprehend its consequences.

Make them go away.

"It's not that simple."

Older Brother had breathed in magic in the First Days, had learned for the love of learning, had shared what he knew. And what he knew was that humans were driven by emotion: by love, by greed, by pride, by all the fleeting passions that made even the wisest of them fools. In that foolishness, a single human he might manipulate, a band of them he might bend to a new direction, confusing or confounding them. But the sheer number of men told Older Brother that whoever led them had money and power, and the scent of illness could not conceal the equal stench of greed.

He exhaled and breathed in, tasting the emotions that flooded them. Hunger. Anger. Fear. Lust. They wanted the Territory, as they had wanted the lands south, as they—or men like them—wanted the lands east and north and west. An arrow or cudgel would not stop them. Illness might pause them, but it would not stop them. It would take a greater magic than his to keep them from sweeping over the waters and into the plains.

"You should have asked for stronger help than mine." Someone less tired of fighting. Old Bear, or the Storm Sisters, or—

No. The wind sulked behind his shoulder. *You.*

Older Brother sighed, wishing to be back under warm furs and a soft companion, far from here. He wished that he had hidden his valley from even the winds, that he had never allowed even a single student to find him. But it was not his nature to refuse.

Closing his eyes, he let the paths unfurl in the darkness, watching every possibility roll forward. In every path, it was the same.

"They will finish building their rafts, and swarm across the river. And when they do, it will be impossible to contain them. They will spread and multiply, until this becomes their land."

The wind poked him and he growled, opening his eyes. "Nothing I do will change the end."

"Everything we do changes the end," a voice said from just behind him, light and familiar as a reed flute. "That's the fun of doing things."

"Why am I not surprised that you are here?" Older Brother said, not bothering to turn around. Wherever there was trouble, White Foot was sure to appear.

The grasses rustled, and a slight form emerged, elongated ears barely reaching Older Brother's haunch. "I saw you go by and wanted to know what had you running at such a pace. I'd hoped for some entertainment to brighten the day."

Older Brother shook his head. White Foot was a mild trickster, as such things were measured, but he had a fondness for chaos that led him into trouble more often than not—and boded ill for those around him.

"There is no entertainment here," Older Brother said. "Only death."

"There's always entertainment. You're just looking at it all wrong."

He had looked at it every way he knew. "Death is death."

The trickster made a rude noise, reaching one soft-clawed paw up to tap his nose. "Death is just another change, Older Brother. Look again."

He frowned. White Foot often played the fool, but he was not always foolish, and his words often had many meanings. Had he missed something?

Older Brother stared across the waters, then closed his eyes again and tried to look differently. Look for the change. Possibilities branched like lightning, stretching out as far as he could see, but nothing changed. White men came, and came, and came, until they filled the territory, and the territory shifted.

It...shifted.

The end-of-all would come. The ending does not change. But everything we do changes the end.

Many meanings to a word.

Older Brother reached out, stilling that single branch, turning it over, examining it from every side. Change the meaning. A push here, a pull there. A trickster and a teacher.

And the wind, the wind promised.

It was a terrible idea. A dangerous idea. But it might work.

"What changes," he asked, "to remain the same?"

"A riddle," White Foot said in delight. "I'm good at those!"

As dawn light reached into the sky, Older Brother stretched, reshaping into a man, clothed as a man in buckskin pants and a woven shirt, his feet bare and mud-stained, skin shimmering sun to shadow, as though it could not decide upon a color.

The Spaniards had chosen a decent place to camp, where the river narrowed and the waters slowed, the banks sloped enough that they could get water, but the water would not reach them. On the Territory's side, the bank was gentler; if—when—they crossed, they would have an easy time gaining ground.

They had hewn the logs within reach, leaving the ground stubbled with the remains, branches stripped and tossed aside. Men hauled the logs to the river's edge, ragged-clothed shoulders curved in the broken slump of the enslaved.

As he drew closer to the water's edge, White Foot half-hidden behind him, some of the men broke from their group and stood on the shore opposite him, staring as they approached. Five men, four ruddy-pale, one darker of skin, dressed as the others, with his hair cut short, but lacking the beard.

Older Brother had not spoken Spanish since before the fathers of these men were born, but he spoke slowly and clearly, trusting the wind to carry over the waters between them, speaking as clearly as he could. "Go no further. These lands are not yours to take."

There was a spate of too-rapid Spanish, then the darker-skinned speaker threw up his arms as though exasperated. Older Brother felt a moment's kinship with the unknown man, who now turned to face Older Brother, clearly under orders to speak for the group.

"Who are you to give us orders?"

Older Brother wove his magic into his mouth, pushing it out with his tongue. "It is not an order, but a warning. As you are, these lands are not for you."

The man flinched, feeling the power carried in Older Brother's words, but the white men laughed as though he had said something amusing.

Older Brother and White Foot waited, even as one of the white men lifted a long metal weapon to his shoulder, pointing it across the slow, flat waters. One of the older men knocked the tube aside, snapping something Older Brother could not understand, then turned and, in the same language, clearly issued orders to the darker-skinned man, who looked as though he wanted to argue. Instead, he made a gesture of resignation, and turned back to Older Brother.

"You are one, and we are many. But if you agree to guide us across the river and into your lands, you will be well-rewarded."

He had not expected they would heed his warning, but felt a surge of exasperation nonetheless. Crossing his arms across his chest, Older Brother repeated his words. "As you are, these lands are not for you."

If it was a riddle, that was the key. He gave it freely, as it would be given to all.

Change the meaning. Change the ending.

He had not expected them to heed him, had seen no branching where they listened, and they did not. The white men returned to their camp, turning their backs to him. The man who had spoken, who had felt the magic stirring, lingered a moment as though he would say something, but when a shout summoned him, hurried to join the others.

Older Brother watched them go, then found a comfortable rock and settled in to wait, the wind curled like a dog at his side. White Foot, not surprisingly, moved higher on the banks where he could see, but not be seen. His voice, when it floated down, carried hot mischief, ready to play. "What do you need from me?"

Older Brother reached up a hand, palm toward the voice, fingers stretched to the sky. "As much of your clever as you can spare."

All through the remaining day, the men worked, lashing the logs together to create rafts, unloading their wagons and leading their livestock closer to the water. Older Brother did not watch them with open eyes, but rather breathed deeply, sinking into himself. The power, the magic that had been born in him and the magic he had earned, he scraped it from him, thread by thread, weaving it into the clever magic White Foot shared until it was a braid as long as the river, as wide as the land, as high as the moon.

Every end he had seen, white men came and claimed. The wind, who sees further than any living creature, had spoken of the end-of-all. There was no escaping.

But everything we do changes the end, White Foot had said, and there was truth in that as well.

He could not change the end. Not forever. But he could change those who *brought* the end. If they listened.

"Take it," he said, and the wind dropped to his feet, brushing the tips of his toes as it lifted an edge of the braid, and took it away.

"These lands are not for you," he said to the figures, still working in the dusk. "Not as you are now. But someday. Maybe. If you live that long."

There was a soft thump, and White Foot landed by his side, a comforting warmth as the night's chill settled around them.

"You think they'll ever learn?"

No. He was unsure any of them ever would. But at least now, there would be time to see.

He could not change the end. But they could change what it meant.

Older Brother and White Foot sat by the waters as the men finished their rafts and readied themselves to cross, thinking to use the cover of night to escape eyes that could see as clearly under moonlight as the sun. Waited and watched as men splashed into the waters, pushed their rafts into the current...

and found themselves back on the shore.

Beside him, he heard White Foot snicker, pleased with his contribution. "The angrier they are, the harder they'll get tossed back."

Over and over again the men attempted to cross, until the unease and whispers grew into shouts and cries, pointing fingers and accusations of *el mal! el diablo!* thrown across the darkened waters.

Older Brother and White Foot waited, watching, until the men pulled their rafts and their horses from the river, retreating as though they feared the water itself would attack them. One of the white men lingered, an older man, standing in the water up to his knees as far out as the magic allowed him, one hand clasping an object around his neck as he stared at Older Brother, his lips moving around words they could not hear.

And then he too retreated, sloshing wetly through the mud and grasses to where they rebuilt their camp.

"And now we wait," Older Brother murmured. For a day and a month, and as many years as the magic would hold, filtering those who would do harm, the wave to a trickle, the flood to a gentle soaking the land could absorb. He could not change the end. But he could slow it. Give them time.

The magic would find those who came. With each step deeper into the territory they took, it would seep into them, until the magic was part of them. Until the land itself was part of them.

Until they too understood and would do no more harm.

Older Brother stood, then dropped to his knees, feeling the weakness of his body in every inch of bone. The wind might not feel tiredness, but flesh did. Seeking the comfort of a four-legged form, he tried to shift…and failed.

The wind swooped back, pulling him to his feet, even as White Foot poked a paw at his leg. "What's wrong?"

"Nothing." He pushed down the panic; his magic wasn't gone, it was just…elsewhere. Sinewy-thin now, stretching him out as well, but still his. He could feel it, pulsing through the land where the wind had dropped it, north and south, stretching far to the west, and east, to the waters at his feet. It touched the bones of the land and…

Older Brother exhaled. The bones had taken the magic—and Older Brother with it. He, too, was bound.

He glanced down at White Foot, who did not seem to notice any difference. It had wanted the teacher, not the trickster.

The magic wouldn't last forever. It didn't need to. Just long enough to change those who brought the ending.

And, the magic had decided, he would be there for them when it did.

NIGHTFALL ON THE BLACK DRAGON LINE

JAMES A. MOORE

"That wasn't a snake." Doc Sweets shook his head, pulled the cigarette from between his lips and spat. "A snake did that, I'll eat my duster."

Bill Parker looked at the hole descending into the ground that had destroyed the train tracks ahead of their ride and shook his head. He'd had his doubts. The hole looked like someone had dug it right there—not like something had burrowed out, but like something had dug down to get out of the heat, maybe. Or just to try fooling folks into thinking it was a rattler. In any event, the hole tore railroad ties and warped metal rails into so much twisted wreckage, bringing the train to a dead halt. Couldn't very well ride the rails if the rails were gone.

"Then what was it, Doc?" Parker took off his top hat to scratch his head and then readjusted it. The day was too hot to go without his hat for long.

Sweets looked his way and spat again. "Someone trying to slow down a train ride might use a tactic like this."

Parker's hand slid to the Peacemaker in its holster. "Last thing we need is a damned train robbery."

Doc chuckled and wiped a kerchief over his brow. The man was from Louisiana and didn't seem to mind the heat. His eyes squinted up at the setting sun glaring down from the west and he frowned. They were several hours away from San Francisco, another territory best avoided as far as Parker was concerned. There was maybe an hour before the sun set and darkness claimed the land. It would be a long night if they couldn't get the train moving. Harder to make repairs by torchlight, and there were any number of possible threats in the disputed areas.

"Wouldn't be a first and I daresay it won't be the last. And believe me, there's worse things to face." Sweets was a strange man, with his dark skin, and scars covering both arms, running across the backs of his hands and along his neck to just above his collar. It was impossible to deny that he'd had a hard life, but he had long since shoved all of that aside, and seemed perfectly content moving his charges from one location to another, no questions asked.

Bill Parker was not a kind man. He was efficient. He kept his brown hair short and favored a mustache without the matching beard, unless he was on the trail for too long. He almost never shaved when he was out on a job. He'd been working with Sweets for the last two years and found their arrangement to his liking. Sweets didn't ask questions, didn't try to have conversations, just played with his cards, delivered his goods, and occasionally brought Parker along on his deliveries. Mostly there wasn't too much trouble, but the four they had with them? They were trouble. Parker felt it in his guts, and so far his guts didn't lie to him.

Currently there were four prisoners on the train that Sweets and a few others were moving to a prison affectionately called Haven for reasons no one seemed to understand, located at Fort 17, an area best not talked about in polite society.

Sweets didn't ask questions about the men he was moving, and he discouraged others. That suited Parker just fine. Sweets paid him and he helped with deliveries. It was enough for him.

Doc Sweets rolled a cigarette with practiced hands, his broad face working into a half smile. The cigarette wound up in his mouth in the same move that had him lighting a match with his thumbnail and bringing the flame to the tip of the cigarette with the sort of speed one expected from a gambler. Doc leaned back and drew in smoke, closed his eyes and exhaled slowly. Allegedly the man was an actual doctor, but all Parker knew for certain was that he worked with the Bureau and seldom lost at cards. Two others, Victoria Hawks and Walter Dover, were currently guarding their charges. They were good men, not trigger happy, but they'd shoot to kill if they had to.

Cook, Blake, Howell and Carson were all locked in boxes. Something was very wrong with them, and they were going to be thoroughly studied. That was all he knew and all he needed to know. They weren't to be touched if it could be avoided. The ride by horse or wagon was too long and too risky, so they were taking their charges by rail along the Black Dragon line. Of course, all of the rails were effectively disputed territory as the different companies fought to claim the rights to run their railroads. Turned out the rails weren't working out to be much faster; the giant snakes they'd discovered in the area were a problem, and one best avoided as far as Sweets was concerned.

Someone told him the damned things were a type of land-born sea serpent. All he knew was they were bigger than horses, ate meat, and tore hell out of the ground when they went through an area. His Uncle Cecil had lost ten head of cattle to one a few years back before the thing went on its way elsewhere.

"Where is this Haven, anyways? Are we gonna be in California?"

"No. we'll be getting off the rails before then." Sweets was back to examining the snake hole. Well, what looked like a snake hole to Parker. He wasn't a greenhorn, but he'd probably never be as good a tracker as Doc was. The man could spot danger like a hawk spots fresh meat. "Keep your eyes open. I think it's gonna be a hit of some kind. Could be someone wants our cargo."

Far as Parker was concerned, they could have them – except, of course, that would mean not getting paid. He had every intention of earning his money. He just didn't have to like it.

Four men from the Black Dragon were looking at the damage done, too, and speaking to each other in Chinese. They weren't particularly large men, but the way they carried themselves marked them as dangerous. They were the sort that he kept his eyes on automatically. They walked like predators.

Whatever they were saying, they seemed to agree with Sweets. They were agitated and looking around the area, checking to see if there were any new threats.

That was when the horsemen rode up. There were a lot of them, and they came in hard and fast, at least half of them with guns drawn.

They didn't speak much. Men and women, looked like a few Native folks, a mix of races. Quite a few too many working together to be anything but hired muscle in Parker's estimation.

One man, tall and lean with a long black goatee and a strange looking pistol in his hand—strange in that it had four barrels and seemed too large—nodded amiably enough and said, "There's something on this train that we need. Stay out of the way and no one gets hurt." He was speaking to the men from the Black Dragon when he talked.

The four of them looked at each other and then back to him. One man, apparently the leader, said in flawless English, "You will leave this place now, and if you do, you will ride away alive."

Parker figured there wasn't much chance of getting out of this mess without weapons being fired.

He was not wrong.

The goateed spokesman took aim and fired at the man who'd responded. Parker had no idea what sort of bullets the man

NIGHTFALL ON THE BLACK DRAGON LINE

used, but the missile screamed as it was fired, a sound like a damned soul falling all the way to Hell, and when it hit the spokesman, he caught fire. Not a little flicker of flame. No, he was engulfed in a ball of fire that knocked him back several feet and seared everything around him, including two of his companions. One man got scorched a bit. The other burned almost as fast as the first man had.

The four barrels rotated, giving the smoking tube just employed a chance to cool down, he supposed. The metal looked nearly red hot.

Doc Sweets cursed under his breath and slid to the side as he reached under his duster and drew a pistol from its holster in one move. By that point Parker was pulling, too, and both men were moving away from each other without saying a word. It wasn't the first time they'd been in trouble and they were smart enough not to remain together. Better to make the enemy have to look for multiple targets.

Sweets said, "What are you after?"

Goatee looked his way and said, "There's an iron lock box, big enough it'll take two men to carry it." He didn't sound particularly worried. Even as he spoke the uninjured man was retreating toward the train engine. Another of the raiders, a heavyset woman with bright red hair and more freckles than a clear night has stars, aimed a rifle at him and barked at him in another language, maybe Chinese. Whatever it was, the retreating Black Dragon worker shook his head and stepped back even further.

The rifle hiccupped, and an instant later the man fell back with a hole in his chest big enough for Parker to slide a fist through.

Doc Sweets held up both of his hands, his pistol aimed for the sky. "We have no quarrel with you."

"You sure about that?" The goateed man eyed him carefully. That Doc was a dangerous sort was obvious to anyone who paid attention, in Parker's eyes. He was as much a predator as anyone else in plain sight, but he wasn't a rabid dog. If they left his charges alone, there was every reason to believe Sweets would leave them be. He had his job. He wasn't a lawman, per se. He was a man with a mission.

"I've got four men I'm in charge of seeing safely to their destination. I ain't paid to care about a lock box."

"Then we can get along just fine."

Sweets nodded and stepped back. He gestured for the large band of men to help themselves. Parker knew he meant it, too. Sweets had a job. He would see it through.

Parker said, "Would have been easier for us if you hadn't wrecked the rails." He was talking to himself, but his voice carried. He expected he'd made a mistake. The men might take offense, and he didn't really want to have an argument with anyone.

Goatee scowled. "Wasn't us. We figured to have to climb on a moving train. Just thought we were getting lucky on this one."

Parker shook his head. "Well, shit."

Sweets looked his way, and shook his head. "Couldn't have said it better."

Goatee looked from Sweets to Parker and then back to Sweets. "Did we miss something?"

Sweets pointed to the hole in the tracks up ahead, the twisted metal of the rails pointing off in different directions around it. "Snake hole. Only it isn't. It's fake."

Goatee frowned and spit. "Well, shit."

Parker nodded. "My point exactly. If it wasn't you, who was it?"

Goatee shook his head and started looking around the area

with a sharp eye. The ground was flat, but there were hills nearby and enough obstructions between the saguaro cacti and the low hills and scrub to leave plenty of hiding places for an ambush.

Goatee pointed to the train and looked to a few of his men, who immediately rode in closer, dismounted, and climbed aboard the first of the cars.

Sweets looked at Parker and silently suggested that he follow. There were still a couple of others watching over their charges, Dover and Hawks, two very competent guns, but there were a lot more raiders than two could easily handle. Parker said nothing, but followed just the same.

It wasn't that anyone would want the boxes holding their prisoners, but if they didn't know any better and tried to open the boxes, the mayhem would be immediate and probably bloody.

By the time he entered the train, six men were ahead of him and doing their best to upset the calm of the day without actually firing their weapons. They stomped and warned people to stay in their seats, and one of them toward the center made sure everyone saw the rifle he was carrying at port arms.

The first car was strictly for passengers, and though there were a few silent prayers and loud exclamations, no one got stupid. The raiders left them alone and so did Parker. If the six men gave any notice to Parker, they didn't seem bothered by him and that suited him just fine. He preferred to stay as unnoticed as he could.

The fourth car had his charges on it, each of them in a long wooden crate. Hawks and Dover never said a word, but the six gunmen got tense as they entered the car. Hawks was a tall, lean woman with dark eyes and thick dark hair. Like as not the only thing the six men noticed about her was the double barrel of her shotgun. That would be because Hawks was aiming said shotgun at them.

Walter Dover was short, lean and mutton-chopped, sported a

bowler hat at a jaunty angle. Dover had a repeating rifle pointed at the back of the lead man's skull and said, "Keep on walking. Don't stop, don't look around." He'd been hiding alongside the entryway and had the man dead to rights.

Hawks looked at the man who'd been waving his rifle around and shook her head in warning. The man shrank down a bit as the barrel of the shotgun swiveled toward his face. It was harder to look tough when 16-gauge barrels were staring you down.

The raiders were not amused about being caught off-guard, but there wasn't a damned thing they could do about it that wouldn't result in fatalities. They had been on the opposite end of the equation outside. They understood how it worked.

"We're just passing through." The man speaking lifted his hands above his head, complete with the pistol he was sporting. He was smart enough to keep his head forward and his eyes on the door at the far end of the car.

Hawks said, "That's for the best. Let's all stay friendly." Her voice dripped venom as she spoke, making it clear that finding another way off the train would be in the best interest of everyone. A few of the people walking through noticed the four long boxes occupying most of the available space in the car, but they said nothing and weren't foolish enough to dawdle.

The last of the boxes rocked violently as Parker walked past, and he looked, just to make sure that what was inside stayed where it belonged. So far, so good, but he didn't like the way the heavy wooden box shuddered, or the sounds coming from inside of it. Whoever was inside let out a loud hiss and then groaned.

He cast an eye back toward Dover, who looked his way and shook his head.

This wasn't going at all to plan. Parker didn't like it. Not in the least.

Several workers were moving out of the next car, carrying heavy supplies with them. It looked like they were preparing to fix the broken tracks up ahead, and that at least would be a benefit. Still, he and the six men in front of him had to wait while they carried out lumber and a few devices that made no sense to Parker. All he knew for certain was that there was a small furnace in the heavy equipment, and he only knew that because the container was clearly marked with the word "furnace" on the side.

He watched the men with their heavy payload heading to the rails up ahead and then concentrated for a moment on the men in front of him. They did not turn back toward his charges, and that was good enough for Parker. Instead of following them further, he headed back outside and toward the hole in the tracks.

Sweets was alone with over a dozen raiders. Parker intended to back up his employer in any way he could.

Doc and the raiders were watching the Black Dragon workers as they set about repairing the rail line. The box marked "furnace" had been opened and was smoking quite a bit as whatever was inside heated up. He guessed they'd be trying to repair the railroad track rather than replace it and had his doubts about what they could do with the torn and twisted metal.

If it hadn't been one of the giant snakes that tore the tracks up, he wasn't sure he wanted to know what was strong enough to rip the metal aside so easily.

Several of the raiders were still on their horses, looking around the area. Like as not they were wondering the very same thing. If the hole was meant to stop the train and wasn't caused by one of the oversized venomous serpents, something would be coming along to cause trouble soon. That was enough to worry anyone.

Sweets spoke up as Parker approached. "Everything okay in there?"

"So far. Went through the car and left everything alone, but one of our prisoners is getting awfully restless."

"I can't think of anything good coming from that."

"I don't want to shoot 'em. I know it ain't their fault, but I will if I have to."

"You won't be alone. Whatever's wrong with those fellas, I want no part of it, and we can see it spreads. Went from Cook to the other three."

"Gotta wonder what the man was doing to get that sick."

"Something dark is all I know. Ungodly rituals, is what I hear." Sweets spit out his latest cigarette and crushed the cherry under his heel until there was nothing left to see but a trail of ashes in the sandy dirt.

Parker scratched at the stubble on his face and shook his head. "I don't know as I believe in any of that folderol. Sounds like rumors from the *Epitaph* to me." He had never seen a giant snake but knew men that had. Other things he heard about, like witches and shamans and black magic? He didn't believe they were real. How could anyone hide that sort of thing?

"I never did see the ocean before I was a freed man." Sweets shook his head and shrugged. "Still knew it existed. That's the way the world is. Ocean don't care if I believe and hoodoo don't care if you believe. They're both still real." Doc Sweets chuckled and wiped at his brow again. The man had a perfectly good hat sitting back in the train, but hadn't brought it with him, and the heat was enough to stagger almost anyone, to say nothing of the glare from the sun as it descended. "Repair crew thinks they'll have us on our way in a couple of hours."

The man with the goatee rode in closer to them and dismounted from his horse. The pistol he carried was too bulky for a regular holster, so he carried it in one hand. Up close Parker could see the odd assortment of small tubes running along the sides of the thing and guessed it might well be powered by sorcery as anything else he could imagine. Judging by the sounds coming from the portable furnace the railmen were using, he half expected demons were heating their device. For now, the sounds were faint, but most times which magic was employed, the cacophony of infernal screams wasn't far away.

Three men were placing heavy wooden ties over the deep hole in the ground. They settled twice as many of the slats as were used elsewhere, as if to completely hide the damage done. Parker frowned. Seemed foolish not to at least make sure there was nothing down there first, even if Sweets was sure it wasn't the entrance to a snake's nest.

When everything went wrong, it seemed to happen at once.

The riders on their horses all had to fight at the same time as their rides got suddenly skittish. Several horses got wide-eyed and looked ready to head for the hills. At the same time, the world went a touch blurry and Parker felt his teeth clack against each other unexpectedly.

Sweets shook his head, cursed under his breath, and said, "I maybe was wrong."

"The hell is that?" Goatee asked the question out loud, frowning as he looked around.

One of the horses got fidgety enough to buck its rider and the man in the saddle sailed sideways through the air, cursing before he smashed into the hard ground.

Several heavy wooden ties erupted from their new resting places as the biggest creature Parker had ever seen in his life came out of the hole under them, several tentacles at the head of the thing whipping around its open maw.

It sure as hell wasn't a snake.

It had too many heads. No. Too many tentacles. They didn't have heads, they whipped around and hissed, but he saw no features other than what looked like open mouths at their ends. No eyes, no noses, just mouths with teeth.

The thing came out of the ground in a giant column, rising higher and higher into the air before crashing down like an axed tree. It was black and glossy enough to look wet, and when it landed the ground shook. The horses bolted. One horse, the horse's rider, and the man who'd been thrown off his mount were all in the wrong place and got themselves crushed under the massive weight of the beast. Parker felt himself lifted from the ground by the impact and barely kept his feet as he landed.

Doc was already moving, heading away from the writhing nightmare even as it lurched across the sand and swatted the railroad workers aside with its bulk. Their equipment soared sideways, the furnace tumbling end over end and spilling burning rock as it rolled past. The stones glowed like the sun, and whatever they touched burned, including the titanic serpent-thing, which roared in pain and flinched away from the incredible heat.

Parker moved toward the train's engine, paused long enough to fire a round at the nightmare thrashing across the landscape. He damned near whimpered when the bullet bounced off the armored hide of the tentacled thing.

Goatee had better luck. He braced himself carefully and aimed his odd pistol, which screamed, belched a tongue of flame out its odd muzzle, and ignited a section of the creature near its thrashing head.

Madness.

People and horses scattered in every direction, and the serpent rolled and twisted, shaking the earth as it turned halfway on its side, extinguished the flames burning near its mouth. Two of the long, whipping tentacles along its head were severely burned and blistered and it seemed like the hellish thing had enough sense to get away from any more flames.

Or maybe it just wanted something bigger to eat. It aimed

itself right at the train engine and lurched hard in that direction, a ten-yard long stretch of body heaving out of the hole it came from in the process.

That meant it was heading right for Parker, who ran for all he was worth. He was a brave enough man, but the mouth of the snake monster was big enough to swallow him in one bite and he had no intention of becoming anything's meal. The earth rumbled under his feet and the massive thing lunged forward again as he veered hard to the right, praying it didn't follow him.

His prayers were answered, and instead the desert serpent charged right at the steam engine of the train, twisting to the side at the last moment and tearing up part of the track as it writhed past the locomotive.

Parker had never felt so small in his entire life, so insignificant. The body kept pushing past him, past the train's engine, across the hot desert floor. He moved out of the way, heart hammering in his ribs.

He wasn't sure if the snake-thing was big enough to smash the engine aside but was glad it chose not to. There weren't enough horses for him, his companions, and their charges, even if he could manage to steal that many animals without the raiders taking it personally.

The beast changed course and ran next to the far side of the train until it decided the locomotive was in its way and slammed half of its body into the first few cars. The entire length of the train rocked and shuddered and four of the cars slid sideways, breaking loose of the tracks as Parker watched on, horrified.

"Well, shit." He headed back toward the train, dreading what might have happened to Dover, Hawks, and their four charges.

Doc Sweets caught up to him long before he got there. "This can't be happening."

"Better get your cutlery ready."

"Cutlery?" Sweets frowned and shook his head, un-comprehending.

"Gonna be eating your duster. That was a damned snake."

"We got bigger problems than right or wrong just now."

"Yeah. Just a bad joke. I could use a reason to laugh if those things get knocked out of their boxes." He had only fired one bullet, but he took the time to reload anyway, eyeing the train to see if it had any more surprises in store. Happily, it remained where it was.

"That train ain't going nowhere." Sweets looked angry enough to spit; he also looked scared witless at the same time. It was a combination of expressions Parker was not used to seeing on his employer.

Several shots were fired from one of the cars. He had no idea which one, but felt his stomach drop a few inches at the notion. Doc ran hard and fast, leaving his gun holstered and reaching for his cards, of all things.

Parker doubted it was time to play poker.

The closer they got to the train the easier it was to see how much damage the snake-monster had done. The wheels had been broken from the train itself in a few cases, effectively disabling the cars. Even if they were put back on the rails, they were going nowhere. Doc cursed as they got closer and Parker clenched his jaw as they climbed into the second car, dreading the sound of additional gunfire. The silence was almost worse. The fourth car had been slammed off the tracks and tilted threateningly to one side. Too much movement might well knock it on its side, and he didn't like that notion at all.

When the gunfire started again, it was several cars back. That was a positive sign as far as Parker was concerned. Somebody else could dodge bullets and pray to get lucky. The snake-thing was enough of a close call for him. As it was, he was trying to figure out how they were going to deliver their prisoners without a train to ride in. Not that it was his concern so much as it was Doc's, but he had to consider options.

The people in the second car were shaken but were unhurt. The third car seemed a little worse for wear and a few of the passengers were still climbing back into their seats as the conductor helped them and assessed the situation. Through the closest window Parker could see the path the snake had made alongside the train and the direction it had headed off in. He could not see the enormous creature itself and considered that a good sign.

The door on the far end of the car opened up and Dover stepped through, his face pale, eyes wide with fear.

Dover saw Sweets and shook his head. "Cook's broken free."

"Where did he go?"

"Whatever hit us broke a hole in the side of the car. That thing got out through the hole."

That thing. Not Cook. What was left of him.

Sweets asked, "Where's Hawks?"

"Watching the rest of them. They're…restless."

Sweets nodded and said, "You two with me. Let's fix this."

Parker wanted to hide. Whatever had happened to Michael Cook, whatever he'd become, all Parker knew was that it was dangerous, and maybe even contagious. He didn't want to become something else.

He'd been trying to ignore the rumors, but now that the thing was out of its containment, all of the whispers haunted him. Cook was a sorcerer. Cook's whole bloodline was tainted by some insidious disease that made leprosy sound pleasant. Cook was cursed by witches, or in cahoots with them, or both. All he knew for sure was that the bastard was dangerous. He didn't believe in magic, but it was harder to trust that notion in the darker places and the areas where monsters like the tentacle snake could knock a train around like a kid with a toy.

He looked down at his revolver and nodded. That was all he needed to know. He'd blow the man to pieces before he'd let himself get infected by whatever it was that had twisted Cook into something else.

He hadn't seen the man before he was boxed up. Hadn't seen him before he was changed. All he knew was that whatever had happened left Cook and the rest nearly mindless, and strong enough to need manacles and additional restraints.

Doc Sweets ushered Dover back through the door between cars, and the men climbed the short ladder down to the ground beside the train. Parker followed after them, adjusted his hat and uttered a prayer to a god he really wasn't sure he believed in.

They could see the hole in the side of the car where the serpent had swiped the train, and through that hole Parker saw Hawks looking at the tracks Cook had left as he exited.

Those footprints looked wrong. The bastard wasn't even wearing boots, or shoes. His bare feet left long tracks, and at the front of those prints were deep trenches where claws had dug into the earth.

"What the hell is he?" Parker looked toward Sweets.

"Dangerous. Shoot to kill. Don't matter if he's alive when we take him in, long as we take him."

The sun set on the other side of the train, and twilight embers lit the sky, but the land was rapidly growing dark. The world around them filled with shadows big enough to easily hide a man, or what had once been a man.

Parker looked everywhere around them and tried to stay calm.

Cook was out there, somewhere, and like as not he was hungry.

"I'd about kill for a good lantern right now." He thought it was Dover talking, but he wasn't sure. The words were half whispers and a distraction he didn't want. Somewhere out in the darkness, what had been human once was lurking, and maybe even hunting.

Sweets said, "Shut up now. I need to listen."

Off to the left something moved, and Parker took aim and fired. The flash of the muzzle lit up the area directly ahead of him and showed him a glimpse of the thing Cook had become. It looked dead. Lips had pulled back from impossibly long teeth, and the sockets around those glittering eyes were dark hollows. Cook's face was marked by a long scraggly beard and mustache, and his hair was an unkempt tangle of thinning strands. His skin looked gray and withered in the faint light, his limbs too long, too thin, and his fingers were spidery, ending in blackened nails, long and unnaturally sharp.

Cook's hands lashed out and ripped into Dover, tearing open bloody trails running down the man's chest and side. He hit Dover hard and knocked the man off his feet. The two of them rolled away, Cook hissing and Dover screaming in pain and surprise. Gaunt arms reached out, slashing down across Walter Dover's body several times, ripping flesh, drawing blood, rattling the ruined chains still trapping the thing's thin wrists. Dover fought back as best he could, but his rifle was knocked away from his hands. He never had a chance to reach the knife sheathed on his hip.

Doc cursed and kicked his boot heel into Cook's side hard enough to dislodge him, but it was too late to do any good. Dover was bleeding from a dozen wounds and didn't look like he would make it.

Parker stepped closer to Cook and fired four rounds from his Peacemaker into the man. The bullets hit true, and parts of him were blown away, but still Cook moved and hissed and, before Parker knew for certain what was happening, Cook was on him in the darkness.

The man's mouth opened impossibly wide and he lurched forward, gnashing his teeth, snarling and trying to bite chunks from Parker.

One of Parker's hands was busy holding his revolver. The other pushed back against that lunging face, fingers hooking to get a better purchase as he defended himself. The flesh he caught was feverishly hot to the touch and felt greasy enough to make his fingers slide.

Cook's hands tore at him, claws hooked at his clothing and tearing roughly, shredding his jacket's sleeve and the shirt beneath. The man's breath smelled of rotting flesh and worse.

The darkness closed in. Cook lurched and bit and drew blood.

Parker shoved the Peacemaker against Cook's neck and fired. A hot spray painted his face in the semidarkness. The report was deafening so close to his own head, but his attacker stopped biting down and then stopped moving at all, except to shiver and thrash as he died.

Parker kicked with his legs and pushed with his free hand and Cook's feverish corpse fell away from him.

"Damn it. Damn it, damn it all to Hell. I'm bit!" Parker tried to see the wound clearly in the growing darkness, but couldn't get a good glimpse. All he knew for certain was that his left palm was bleeding freely.

Doc Sweets eyed him carefully and nodded. "You're covered in mess. Let's get you cleaned up."

"Are you really a doctor, Doc? Or is that a nickname."

"I'm a doctor, you damned fool." Sweets rolled his eyes toward the heavens as if asking the Lord for patience. "Come on now."

Each of them grabbed an arm and started hauling Cook's remains back toward the train.

"What if what he got spreads to me?" Parker closed his eyes for a moment; he could feel something crawling into his body like ants from that bite mark. He prayed it was his imagination.

"We'll deal with what comes next, but let's clean you up first and hope for the best."

"What was he?"

"He got an infection. Not a sickness. Not like a pox, but something different, Bill. I know you don't like to believe in hoodoo and the like, but what happened to Cook happened because he was working with dark magics. Him and the people with him."

"So maybe I won't get infected from a bite?"

"Can't say as I know." Doc shook his head and frowned. "Mostly we're gonna have to watch and see what happens."

It was easy enough to put what was left of Cook back in his long box. Easy to see where he'd snapped the links on his manacles and how he'd clawed his way through the wood to break the locks.

Outside the darkness grew, and inside the train car lanterns were lit and candles ignited, and they waited for repair on the tracks, while Doc cleaned Parker's wounds and Hawks kept guard over everything.

Time would tell if he was in the clear.

"We'll be on the way in the morning," Sweets said, and Hawks made an agreeable noise as she walked the car's length. They'd have to switch cars come daybreak, but for now the world grew silent enough.

Time would tell. It was all Parker could think about. Time would tell.

$\mathscr{S}$IMPLE SILAS

SCOTT SIGLER

"I get his toes."

Silas could only take so much. He knew he wasn't the smartest man in town. Maybe someone else could understand this better than he, but he'd summoned the thing, and there was no one there to help.

"His…toes? What do you mean?"

The giant wolf let out a snort. Thin black smoke curled up from its oversized nostrils. The smoke drifted up into the branches of the ironwood grove, filtered higher into the night sky. The light of the moon gleamed off black fur.

"Those little piggies on the end of your feet," the giant wolf said. "Those are *toes*. Do you understand what toes are, Silas?"

Those words coming out of the mouth of a man or woman might sound insulting. Demeaning. People making fun of Silas, as people often did. But the wolf sounded… *patient*, like it had had many conversations like this, and knew sometimes people like Silas needed a little help.

"I understand what toes are."

"Good. I get them."

Silas scratched his nose. It was still broken, still sore, still scabbed over. It hurt to scratch it, but it itched. What was he supposed to do if it itched? Not scratch it?

"I know what toes are. I guess I don't understand what you mean by *you get* them."

The wolf's name was Malsum. It backed away. Gosh darn but it was big. Bigger than a horse. Nineteen hands high, maybe twenty. Thick in the chest, like a bull. Fur as black as tar. Claws the size of Silas's whole chest. If the thing wanted to, it could eat Silas in three bites. Maybe two.

The wolf turned in a circle, its wide butt bumping against the grove's ironwood trees, making the branches vibrate and the leaves rattle. Silas thought the ground should shake with each step, but it did not— the big black wolf was light on its feet. A terrifying thought all by itself, that the biggest animal Silas had ever seen could probably sneak up on you in the night.

The wolf's gut contracted; the beast grunted a sick grunt, the same kind Silas had heard his dogs make when they'd eaten something bad. The wolf kept turning in place, kept knocking against the trees, kept heaving, kept making that pre-retch retching noise dogs made.

When the big head came around again to face Silas, the wolf lowered its open mouth to the ground. It threw up a glob of something thick and yellow and stinky and nasty. The glob hit the ground. Something in that wet mess. Hard to see in the moonlight. Strands of vomit hung from the beast's jaw.

"Pick those up," the wolf said.

Silas looked at the mess. Something in there. Something metal.

"Don't want to," he said.

"Do you want revenge, Silas? Isn't that why you summoned me? Do you want to pay them back for what they did to you?"

Silas did want that. He wanted that very much.

"I thought you'd kill them," he said. "You being all giant-size and all. With those teeth."

The wolf smiled. Its black tongue twitched.

"I'm not a killer, Silas. I'm merely a facilitator."

"*Facilitator*? What's that word mean?"

"It means I help people get what they want. You want revenge." A giant, clawed paw tapped the ground at the edge of the vomit puddle. "These items will provide it."

The wolf talked all fancy. Who would have thought the conjured spirit would talk fancy? Silas wasn't surprised the big-ass wolf talked—that's what the legends said it did—he'd just assumed it would talk like an Indian. He hadn't expected it to sound like a schoolteacher or one of them shifty bankers.

Holding his breath, Silas reached down into the muck. It was still warm. Warm like sand at midday, but wetter. And sand didn't have chunks of things in it. Meaty chunks that maybe had once been alive.

Silas lifted the objects.

In his right hand, a pistol. Heavy. Long. Slick with stinky vomit. Maybe the handle was pearl, maybe not—hard to tell at night, in the darkness of the old ironwood grove.

In his left hand, a bone-handled knife. Looked a bit jagged and crude. It wasn't steel. It was stone. Obsidian, maybe?

"How'd you barf this up without cutting yourself? Did it hurt to have it in your belly?"

"My belly is fine," the wolf said. "You will use that gun to shoot your enemy. You will use the knife to cut off his toes. You will bring me his toes. Do you understand, Silas?"

Silas didn't understand. Not really. But he was used to that.

"I suppose so," he said.

"Listen carefully now, Silas. This part is important. Are you listening?"

Silas might be dumb, sure, but he didn't know how anyone could be face to face with a giant wolf that had just puked up a gun and a knife and *not* listen when the wolf talked. Also, since most wolves did not talk, at least as far as Silas knew, it was a thing to pay attention to, to be reckoned with.

"I'm listening."

"Good," the wolf said. "It is important that you cut the toes off *before* your enemy dies. I don't want them if you cut them off after. Repeat that back to me so I know you understand."

Silas was beginning to think maybe this hadn't been a good idea.

"I understand. Cut off his toes before he dies."

"Good," the wolf said. "Because if you bring me toes that are cut off *after* he dies, or you don't bring me his toes at all, I get *your* toes."

Not a good idea. Maybe even a really bad idea.

"I think I changed my mind." Silas offered up the knife and the gun. "You can take these back."

The wolf snorted. Black smoke. It lifted its big head to its full height, looked down at him with eyes that weren't just black, they weren't really there at all. Starless midnight sky for eyes.

"It's too late for that, Silas. You picked up the gun and the knife. The deal is final."

"You didn't tell me that part."

The wolf sighed. It sounded like a human sigh. Like a banker trying to explain why he wouldn't give Silas money for the farm.

"Silas, I'd hoped you thought this through before you summoned me. The bargain is struck. I help you kill your enemy, you give me his toes. It's his toes or yours, Silas. Which do you choose?"

Well, a fella didn't have to be all that smart to figure that one out.

"His toes," Silas said.

The giant wolf's not-there eyes narrowed.

"That is wise, Silas. Do you know where your enemy lives?"

"I do. He's a hand at the Cooper Ranch. Maybe a mile from here."

"Which direction?"

Silas looked to the stars. He oriented himself. He had always been good at looking to the stars, at understanding the pattern of glistening lights, of knowing where he was. He liked the stars. The stars were how he'd summoned Malsum.

Silas pointed northwest.

"Do not let go of the objects," the wolf said.

The dark creature that looked like a living shadow *became* a living shadow, darkness flowing in all directions like a river going everywhere at once. The rivers flowed onto Silas, swept around him, drowning out the ironwood grove, the sky, the puddle of vomit, and even the stars that got him into this mess in the first place.

He felt himself rising up into the air.

He made sure to hold on to the knife and the gun.

Ground beneath his feet again. The blackness faded away, the rivers flowing in reverse, back into the shape of the huge wolf.

"I believe we are here," Malsum said

Silas blinked, unsure of where he was. The stars were back.

He turned, saw Abel Cooper's house, the barn, and the log cabin where Tripp slept when he wasn't managing Cooper's cattle, drinking at the saloon, or punching Silas in the face.

Punching him in the face.

Knocking him into a pile of horse shit.

Then pissing on him.

Pissing on him.

In front of the whole town.

"You shouldn't wait long," the wolf said. "If the sun rises and you haven't brought me his toes, then I get yours."

"There's a time limit?"

"Of course there's a time limit, Silas. Is life anything but a series of time limits?"

"You didn't tell me about no time limit."

"You did not ask," the wolf said. "There are many things you did not ask, Silas."

Yeah, that was probably right.

"There's three other men in there with him, most likely," Silas said. "Three other hands. Kevin Murph, Daniel Dozier, and Tom Randklev."

Murph and Dozier had been there, watching Tripp piss on

Silas. Tom hadn't been. Tom didn't leave the ranch all that much, as far as Silas knew. When they'd been kids, Tom and Silas had been friends. After Tom came back from the Army, they were friends no more

Murph and Dozier had stood on Silas's hands while Tripp pissed on him. Pinned them down so he couldn't even cover his face.

"Then you should aim carefully," the wolf said. "You can only miss twice. If you miss three times, you'll have to use the object for more than toes."

Something about the wolf's words didn't sit right. Silas looked at the pistol. The vomit strands had dried flat to the metal.

"You gave me a six-shooter," he said.

"Look closer."

Silas did. He turned it this way and that. The cylinder had five rounds, not six.

"Oh," he said.

Then he understood.

"You mean you want me to shoot Kevin Murph and Tom Randklev, too?"

"I don't want you to do anything," the wolf said. "You, on the other hand, want your revenge. If those men get in the way, how do you think it will turn out?"

Not good, most likely. Not good at all.

If Silas didn't go in there, he'd lose his toes. He liked his toes.

He'd never fired a gun, but he'd seen others do it. He thumbed the hammer back until it clicked in place.

He took one step toward the log cabin.

"Yes," the wolf said. "Vengeance is yours. I'll even help you."

Black shadow-rivers flowed from the wolf, coursed along the ground, rose up the walls of the log cabin, oozed in through the edges of the doors.

The door opened inward.

Silas didn't want to do this anymore. But he liked his toes. And Tripp deserved it. Tripp deserved it.

Another step toward the log cabin.

Then, another.

Then, Tripp stepped into the door's blackness, his big body ghostly in the starlight. He wore long johns that looked dirty even in the night's dark.

Silas froze.

Tripp tried to shut the door. It wouldn't budge. He looked at it, sleepy and not understanding, tried to shut it again. Still it would not move, held open by the wolf's dark magic.

The man paused. His head turned. He looked out at Silas.

"What the hell?" Tripp's eyes narrowed. "Peeler?"

Tripp was like a log himself, hardened from decades spent in the sun and wind, as much a thing of the land as the sand and trees and stones.

Fists like mallets.

Mallets that had hit Silas so many times.

"You little limp-dick idiot," Tripp said. "You're here with a gun? How'd you fix this door open?"

He again looked at the door, gave it a test rattle—it did not move.

Silas heard a voice calling from inside the cabin.

"Tripp! What the hell you on about? I'm trying to sleep."

It was Dozier. Now there were two of them awake.

"It's Simple Silas," Tripp said. "He brought a pistol. Looks like maybe a knife, too."

When Malsum spoke, Silas realized, for the first time, that he didn't hear the creature with his ears, he heard the voice inside his head.

"It seems strategy is not your strong suit, Silas," the wolf said. "Perhaps you should kill him now before the other two awaken."

The wolf was right. But to actually shoot a man? To *kill* him? Silas hadn't given any thought to what that might be like. It just hadn't crossed his mind.

Tripp stepped out of the cabin. Dozier came out behind him—Dozier held a pair of gun belts. He handed one to Tripp.

"Sumbitch," Dozier said. "Simple Simon's got a gun, all right. Hey, Simpleton—you come here to shoot us?"

Silas shook his head, even though that was exactly what he'd come to do.

Another voice from inside the cabin—Kevin Murph.

"Would you two caterwauling cocksuckers shut the hell up? Don't wake me up again!"

Tripp was a big man. Kevin Murph was bigger. The words frightened Silas, but not Tripp or Dozier.

Tripp held up the gun belt. He was trying to look casual, look relaxed, but Silas saw something in the way he stood. Feet spread wide but not too wide. His weight on the balls of his feet. He held the belt in his left hand—the finger of his right curled and relaxed, curled and relaxed.

"You want me to put this belt on, boy?" Tripp smiled, but Silas could tell, somehow, that smile was fake. Even from this distance, even in this dim light. Fake.

Silas remembered he held his pistol. At his side, but in his hand, not in a holster.

"You want a shootout," Tripp said. "That it? Tell you what, Simple Silas. Put your pistol behind your back, let me put this belt on, and we'll draw. That what you want?"

Tripp snickered. Dozier snickered.

The same way they snickered when they pissed on him.

The same way they'd snickered when they forced him to eat pig shit a few years back.

The same way they'd snickered when they hit him with rocks, when they shoved him out of the saloon, when they slapped him in public and dared him to take a swing.

Silas felt the wolf's blackness now, felt it in his flesh, in his bones. It calmed him.

"Yeah." Silas put the gun behind his back. "That's exactly what I want, Tripp Alcott. I'm calling you out. Put that belt on. And Dozier? You're next."

To his own ears, Silas's voice sounded different. Maybe Tripp and Dozier thought it was different, too. Their snickers faded. Maybe they didn't look scared, but they looked real concerned.

Tom stepped out of the door. He wore long johns like Dozier and Tripp did, only his were red where theirs were white.

Tripp and Dozier looked concerned — Tom looked horrified.

"Jesus my lord and savior," he said. "Boys, *run*."

Tom spread his hands out from his sides.

His hands blazed with white flame, as the outline of a crucifix formed on his chest beneath his red long johns.

Tripp and Dozier moved away from him. *Now* they were afraid.

"He sees me," the wolf said in Silas's head. "The one in red is mine."

The wolf bounded forward, each stride covering ten yards. Only then did Silas realize that Tripp and Dozier didn't see the wolf — only Silas and Tom did.

Running sideways, the belt still in his left hand, Dozier reached for the pistol.

Silas knew there wasn't much he understood. Things were always mystifying to him. Numbers. Money. Women. Men. How things worked in the town. The government. The law. He understood the stars. He didn't know why. He always had. And now, there was one more thing he understood, understood it as sure as he knew how to breathe and how to take a shit — he knew who to kill first.

Tripp was also pulling his gun, but he was running full-tilt and his back was mostly to Silas. Dozier still faced forward, and his gun was clearing leather.

Silas raised his pistol and pulled the trigger.

Dozier's neck blew apart in a puff of flesh and blood. He fell like a dropped rope, his head flopping from the thin shred of muscle still connecting it to his body. Daniel Dozier hit the dirt and did not move.

The wolf's darkness smashed into Tom's brightness, popped like a giant campfire coal exploding and showering away sparks and cinders. Light flashed from the two, a stuttering illumination, and in that mad, magical, sputtering torch flare, Silas saw Tripp turn, gun in hand.

Silas didn't feel anything at all. He just acted. He stepped wide to his right as he thumbed the hammer back. Tripp fired. Silas heard the bullet whiz by. Tripp adjusted his aim, but before he could fire Silas pulled the trigger. Trips right shoulder popped in a flower of white fabric and red blood that looked black in the moonlight. He spun. He fell.

Silas pulled back the hammer again. Three shots left.

"Silas, he tricked you!"

It was Tom, shouting. He was up in the air above the cabin. He was… he was *hovering* there, his body aglow with angelic luminance. And all around him, curving shadow fingers reaching for him, trying to wrap around him.

"Save yourself, Silas," Tom screamed. "Fight against his control! Run!"

Hovering. Silas's old childhood friend was *hovering*.

As wild as that was, Tom was wrong. The wolf didn't control Silas. Silas had made this choice.

Through the crackling, sizzling sounds of a giant black shadow wolf fighting a glowing, underwear-clad childhood friend, Silas heard an angry, pain-filled grunt from Tripp. On his knees, he held his revolver in his shaking left hand.

As calm as taking a drink of water from a mountain brook, Silas aimed and fired—Tripp's left hand blew apart, two fingers pinwheeling away, his pistol sliding across the dirt.

Silas would never be sure what happened next, not until many years later, when he was used to such things. He ducked because he knew he should duck, and for no other reason, cocking his pistol again as he did. Where his head had been an instant before, a double-barreled shotgun opened up with the roar of a landslide.

Still crouched, he turned his head, slightly, found himself staring at the bare, burgeoning belly of Kevin Murph. Kevin wasn't wearing long johns. He wasn't wearing anything save for his boots.

The big fat man raised his shotgun to bring the butt down on Silas's head, but that was a lot of motion compared to the two effortless movements Silas made: turning his right arm to touch the man's hairy belly, then pulling the trigger.

The bullet punched through Murph's fat, blasted out the back with a chunk of meat so big Silas heard it thud wetly against the dirt.

Murph stepped back once, twice. He stared. He blinked. With a bloody hole in his belly, he tried to aim the shotgun, forgetting it was no longer loaded.

Silas cocked the pistol and shot Kevin Murph in the face.

The big man dropped.

A scream that sounded like a dozen wild dogs lit on fire.

Up above the log cabin, Tom shone like the sun. White light ran from his fingers and his chest, pouring into the giant wolf, who howled in agony. Shreds of shadow rained down like a light snow, and where they touched the cabin's roof, flames sprang up.

Tom was killing Malsum. Or maybe sending Malsum back to the stars. Silas didn't really know how any of that worked.

What he did know, though? He knew that Tom had been Tripp's friend. Murph's friend. Dozier's friend. He'd once been Silas's friend, but that had been long ago. Tom could have found work somewhere besides this ranch. Tom knew those three men made Silas's life a living hell. He knew how they humiliated Silas, made Silas a pariah in the town where he'd been born and raised.

Tom had done nothing for Silas.

The wolf, though? The wolf had given Silas gifts.

Silas cocked the hammer on his pistol, aimed up, and fired.

Silas didn't see the bullet hit, didn't see any blood on the red long johns, but he heard Tom cry out, saw him grab at his thigh, saw him fall to the burning roof.

The wolf pounced.

They would have to fight their battle. Silas still had a job to do.

He walked to Tripp, who lay on his back in a wet spot-spattered patch. When Tripp moved this way or that, his right arm remained still. His left arm had only two fingers and the thumb remaining. His eyes were open, blinking madly, clouded with pain, and yet he saw Silas.

"I'm sorry," Tripp said. "I'm sorry."

"I'm not," Silas said, and he pistol whipped Tripp across the face, once, twice, three times. Broken teeth scattered across the ground. Blood sheeted the man's face, shimmering in the moonlight.

Tripp coughed, a bubble of blood billowing up from his lips.

He was barefoot.

Silas still had the knife in his left hand. He'd never let go of it. He'd forgotten all about it, as all that had mattered was his right hand and the gun it held.

He knelt, even as the sound of the battle between wolf and

Tom echoed across the plain. Silas heard another sound—the clattering of horse hooves, fading away—and knew that the Cooper family had fled. They would ride for town. They would bring the sheriff. They would bring that old witch Harriet, probably. They would bring many men with guns.

That was a problem for another time.

Silas pinched the empty gun in his armpit, grabbed Tripp's big left toe, and slid the obsidian knife across it, just above where it met the foot. The knife's sharpness surprised Silas, slicing through with such ease that the toe came free and Silas fell back to his butt.

Tripp screamed. He sat up like a shot, his face contorted with rage and fury. With his mangled hand, he reached for Silas.

Silas sliced as casually as he might shoo away a black fly. The uneven black blade cut Tripp's forearm to the bone. Blood sprayed on the dirt, on Tripp's legs, on Silas's face and chest.

Trip rolled to his side, crying, choking.

Silas had seen cuts like that before. Tripp would be dead soon. In seconds, maybe. He had to hurry.

Gun still pinched in his armpit, Silas sliced off the toes of his tormenter, who twitched and groaned and grunted but fought back no more.

The pinkie toes were the hardest. Silas moved awkwardly to keep the gun from falling to the dirt, and his fingers were slick with blood. Tripp's pinkie toes were little stubs, kind of too small for man his size, and it was hard to get a grip. Still, Silas managed well enough, and the two little toes joined the pile sitting in the dirt.

Tripp stopped moving. He wasn't dead yet, Silas knew, but it wouldn't be long now.

"That's for making me eat shit, Tripp."

Clumsy from too many things to hold at once, Silas held the pistol butt against his belly, used his knife hand to pick up the bloody toes one at a time and awkwardly placed them in the crook of his gun arm.

By the time he stood—stood *carefully* so as not to spill—he saw Tom crawling across the ground. He wasn't glowing anymore. His crucifix had come out from under his red long johns. The cross dragged across the ground.

The giant wolf dropped down from the sky, giant paws bracketing Tom like shadow-furred boulders.

Tom rolled to his back. He gripped the cross, held it up before him, held it up toward the smiling wolf's head just a yard away.

"Begone, demon!" Tom's voice trembled, sounded scratchy, like he'd yelled too much. "Begone, foul being, or—"

The huge teeth snapped down and bit Tom Randklev's head clean off.

As Tom's arms twitched and his feet gave little kicks, blood poured out of his neck to make yet another gleaming puddle in the dirt.

The wolf spat the severed head. It hit the dirt once, tumbled through the air, hit the dirt again, then vanished through the still-open door of the smoldering log cabin. Small flames reached up from the roof. In minutes, the whole thing would be ablaze.

"I got his toes," Silas said.

The wolf's head turned. The nose wrinkled. Silas heard deep sniffs.

"So you did, Silas. Well done. You may drop my offering now."

Offering? Oh… the toes? The toes were an *offering*. Silas didn't get it, but he parsed enough to know he could be done with the bloody little stubs. He let them go. They plopped against the ground like dropped fruit.

The wolf made a strange noise, a *deep* noise, one Silas couldn't possibly describe. Ten shadow tendrils stretched out to the pile, lifted the ten toes one by one. As Silas watched, the shadows retreated into the black absence that was the wolf's eyes. Retreated, and vanished.

Out of all the strange things Silas had just seen, had just done, and hell's bells had there been some strange things, that was the strangest.

"Ranch owner rode away," Silas said. "He'll bring the townsfolk if he makes it."

The giant wolf sighed a very human-sounding sigh. In that sigh Silas heard a rattle, deep within, the kind of rattle a sick man makes when he's near the end.

"I'm afraid the holy one pushed me to my limit, Silas. I neither have the energy nor the interest in chasing down a rancher."

Well, that was that. Silas certainly wasn't going after them. There were probably horses still in the barn, but he'd never been much of a rider, and horses always bit him. If a giant supernatural wolf from the stars couldn't catch Abel Cooper and his family, Silas couldn't catch them, either.

Silas looked at the dead men: Dozier, chest-down in the dirt although his almost-decapitated head looked up at an angle; Murph, on his back, his long johns blood-soaked at the belly, his head misshapen, his right eye and most of his nose all kinds of messed up; Tom, also on his back, the skin of his face and forehead probably starting to bubble and blister and cook in the log cabin; and Tripp, his shoulder a ruin, his hand mangled, his face a mask of blood, his mouth full of broken teeth…

…and his toes cut off with what might be some kind of magic stone knife.

Three of those four men had badgered Silas all his adult days. The fourth had stood by and let it happen.

"I can't believe I beat them," Silas said. "They always got the better of me. They were bigger. Stronger. Smarter."

The wolf grinned, so wide this time Silas could see his black tongue in his black mouth.

"When you have a gun, Silas, you don't need to be big. Or strong. Or smart. Or even brave. You just point it, and you pull the trigger. A gun is the great leveler of mankind."

Silas didn't understand what that meant. Or maybe he did. He was a small man. Four big men were on the ground, four big holes in their four big bodies. All the times they'd beaten him up, whooped him, humiliated him, he hadn't stood a chance.

A *great leveler* had changed that.

Yeah… maybe he did understand after all.

"You did well," the wolf said. "You seem to be proficient at shooting. Have you trained in some way?"

Silas looked at the now-empty pistol. The puke strands weren't just *on* the weapon, they were *part* of it, a pattern of yellowish streaks and smears in the metal.

"Ain't never shot one before in my life," he said. "It just… well… it seemed easier than I thought it would be."

The wolf smiled.

"You have a gift, Silas. A gift."

Maybe. Or maybe he'd just got lucky. For once in his

miserable life, he'd got lucky, and that "luck" left three men dead. Four, if he counted Tom. Which he didn't. The big wolf killed Tom.

He had to run. The sheriff and men from the town would come after him.

This wasn't what he'd wanted. He'd thought it was, but... Tom... cutting off those toes... all the blood... the way Tripp had screamed.

The way Tripp had begged.

Silas held the gun and the knife out to the wolf.

"Here's your stuff back."

The eyes that weren't really eyes didn't look at the gun and the knife. They stared at Silas. Maybe *aimed* at Silas was a better way to describe it.

"You will keep them," the wolf said.

"I... I will?"

The great black head nodded.

"You will. When others summon me for revenge, Silas, I will not come to them directly. Instead, I will send you."

In a night of horrors and a monster wolf and flying lead, Silas realized he hadn't been scared. Not that much, anyway. Not until now. An oily sensation in his stomach and chest and neck, a sense of dread that he'd made a mistake. A mistake even greater than killing three men.

"So, you want me to work for you now?"

"In a manner of speaking," the wolf said.

"But you didn't tell me I'd have to work for you."

"You did not ask," the wolf said. "There are many things you did not ask, Silas. So many things."

Black shadow rivers flowed from the wolf, crawled across the ground like carpets of jumping spiders. Silas wanted to run, but he knew there was no point. This being from the stars wanted him. This being from the stars had him.

"You will come with me now," the wolf said. "You will sleep, Silas. When I need you, you will wake."

The blackness swept around Silas, once again blocking out the stars. As all light faded away, he made a vow to himself.

A vow to ask more questions.

Hell and Destruction Are Never Full

MARGUERITE REED

Banjo was in no mood to be saddled, but Rio walked the dun mare in a circle before tightening the girth again. Even at this precious hour Rio felt the time slipping away. She glanced over her shoulder at Larkin on the ground, huddled in his blanket. She had miles to ride, but if he didn't behave, he'd be walking.

The cigarillo clenched between her teeth was about to die. She took a long drag then a series of quick little puffs until the tip glowed once more, the dawn sun in miniature.

She nudged the man with her foot. "Get up," she said.

For answer he groaned and burrowed into the blanket.

"Everything's packed. Get on your horse; I don't have time for this."

Muffled: "Go *away*."

Rio sighed. "I won't get as much with your corpse. But I will get something."

She drew her revolver. The hammer's click pierced the dawn

silence. "I already wasted one bullet on you." She paused. "I could just leave you be in that blanket—"

"*That* would be nice—"

"And ride the horses over you a few times."

The blanket flailed about until he managed to shed it. He had not slept well, Rio thought—his eyes glittered, cauldrons of blue. "This is a terrible mistake," Larkin said. "Lady, how many times I have to tell you—"

"I gotta gag you again?" Rio said.

He heaved himself up with more of a growl than a sigh, all six feet and some change. It took him a moment, since his hands were tied behind his back. "No. No, you don't 'gotta gag' me. But I have to—" He ducked his head toward the little cluster of cedar trees.

Rio untied one hand and held the other, the gun to his head all the while he clumsily unbuttoned his trousers. "Do what you need to do," she said. "I don't want nothin' to do with your prick. Seen enough of 'em."

"Jezebel," Larkin muttered, but managed to piss and put it away. Rio did notice that he needed to do up quite a few buttons. She reminded him nicely that if he had any unwise thoughts, she would not kill him right away, only disable him, so it was best that he let her bind his wrists to his saddle horn while she led his horse, a thick-boned chestnut gelding.

Rio knew some man-hunters used shackles. Too fancy for her; she didn't want the bother of a key, and she could always find rope or even buckskin fringe to truss up her quarry. As big as this fellow was, she found herself regretting the lack of anything weightier. She figured he'd go maybe two hundred; and, shoeless, would still tower over her by a head.

The only thing she had going for her against this bounty's size and strength was her speed and attitude. She'd been kicked out of the Sugar Grove for her attitude. Two years ago, and it still rankled. But at least she didn't have to whore around anymore. And she wasn't going to lose her livelihood if she gouged some bitch's eye out in a fight.

Rio made Larkin ride a little ahead of her. All along the trail she kept her pistol on him, his horse's reins in her left hand as they meandered along the dry creek. If anyone saw them, they would see nothing that looked like a Sioux or a Mexican. Only a couple of tired white men; hunters, maybe.

The white man in front of her was not too tired to try to make conversation. Others had tried it before. Trying to draw her out, get on her good side.

"What kind of man would let you do this kind of work? Don't tell me you don't have some sweetheart somewhere, face like yours."

She gestured with her gun, just to remind him it was still there. "Ain't my face you should be thinking about."

His gaze flicked back toward the revolver. Good. He kept talking. Bad. "How'd you find me, anyway?"

"I looked."

A specimen like him? Stood out like a marble in a goat's ass. *Big and blonde*, Dr. Fisher had said, that nasty little man in a green rumpled suit that looked as if he'd stolen it from an undertaker. Constantly looking down at his shoes. What did he expect to find in a livery stable?

He likes the faro tables. Fisher had patted his vest, where a pocket bulged like a tumor. *There's forty dollars in silver for your trouble.*

At her exclamation he shushed her, his hands fluttering like bats. *Please! Calm yourself. That is all I have been authorized to give you at this point.*

At this point? she'd hissed. Fisher flinched and tried to pull his coat into more respectable lines.

My master — that is, my employer — can promise you a larger sum upon delivery of this rogue.

Rio had wanted to laugh, but kept her scowl straight. Fisher thought forty dollars wasn't enough for her. Hell, forty dollars was more than most people saw for a month's worth of honest work. As for dishonest work —

How much larger?

My employer is prepared to pay another five hundred dollars on delivery of Mr. John Larkin.

Rio had felt her face go hard as stone. Inside her brain was yipping like a pack of coyotes. She had tried not to let Fisher see the long steadying breath she took before asking the second most important question: *Dead or alive?*

Girl, you just have bad luck thinking.

Rio had heard that, or similar, all her life. God didn't make her clever, he made her thorough. She stuck her head in every two-bit gaming house between Abilene and Ellsworth and back to Wichita. Every tent that boasted a door on a couple of sawhorses and a deck of cards. Like a feral dog she kept to the thresholds, on the edge of the light. She wore her clothes disheveled, her face dirty, her hair short; and over the course of two weeks she saw a lot of saps bucking the tiger and a lot of people happy about it. Sharpsters and calico queens leeched onto the old men, young men, on each other, just as the beasts of prairie and plains, outside those lamplit haunts, fed on each other. Many faces she recognized from her Sugar Grove days.

Everyone this side of dirt was a sucker.

The last night, the night when Rio had decided she'd pull up stakes and try her luck in the hide towns, she'd found Larkin. Just like Fisher told her, at the faro table in the Capitol Saloon. She had slouched into the saloon just as he was laughing at something the dealer had said, and the light from the oil lamp above pointed him out just as surely as if he'd worn a sandwich board. Big frame, big voice, making everyone around him seem like canvas cut-outs that had been too long in the sun.

Balls to that. Just as easy to turn in a handsome man as an ugly one.

Rio drifted with the patrons, never pushing or elbowing her way, adjusting herself to the current, easing herself step by patient step to the faro game. She stood behind Larkin for a while, a little to his left, as if interested. Cards bored her to tears. What she focused on was the smell of liquor on his breath; how many whores were circling around the group, picking off men; who was squinting at the cards and who was clear-eyed.

Fortune favored her. The sound of breaking glass by the piano turned heads and then she was right up by Larkin with her Colt snug in his armpit. Her lips brushed his ear. "That's a gun. You're coming with me. Twitch wrong and you're dead."

Rio felt almost cheerful as she and her captive rode: early in cattle season, with only a few hundred head on the outskirts of town, the stench and kicked-up dust was still tolerable. She hoped that later in the summer the man-hunting business would take her to parts in the cooler north and west. Unlikely, though. Most wanted men couldn't stay away from the gauds of civilization and returned, like dogs to burned-out houses, to the places and people that felt familiar.

Leaves of the cottonwoods along the river flashed and shivered in the sunlight, brilliant as what she imagined emeralds must look like. The call of red-winged blackbirds clashed from the foliage growing closer to the river's edge. The river itself smelled like an old cold iron knife.

Larkin, of course, spoiled it by trying again. Lord God, dead men were so much easier to deal with.

"Who're you taking me to?" Fifth time he'd asked that. She hadn't answered him the first four times; did he think she was going to change at five? "I haven't done anything wrong. I'm not a criminal. There's no warrant out for me. I'm not a wanted man."

"Someone wants you, that's for sure." Rio kicked her horse to a trot and broke into song. "*Ho for Lousiana! I'm bound to leave this town—*" Larkin's horse put its ears back and shuffled into a trot as well. That shut Larkin's mouth as he had all he could do to keep in the saddle.

When they stopped on the lee side of a little bluff for a mid-morning rest, Larkin started in again. He must've taken her caution in helping him dismount for some variety of feeling, because as soon as she helped him piss and then sit down with his back against a scrubby tree—tied to it, of course—he could not keep from opening his trap.

"You must—" and she shoved a biscuit in his mouth. Because it was dry, the biscuit took all his attention not to choke, which gave her a few minutes to see to the horses and squat. When he had stopped coughing, he was blessedly quiet. Tired, maybe. She couldn't blame him, she thought. Imagine going about your day, like always, seeing people, doing business, all's right with the world, when a stranger walks up behind you and shoves a pistol in your side. And then said stranger threatens to shoot you in the foot when you won't get on your horse.

"Could I have a drink, please?"

Should she waste clean water on him? Easier than scooping it up from the next shallow stream, Rio guessed, and it might be the last taste of clean water he ever had. Flat and metallic, she knew, coming from her canteen, but better than something with fish eggs in it.

"Thank you," he said when she took the canteen away.

"You're welcome," she said without thinking, then swore. *Now he's gonna think we're having a conversation.* She whipped her neckerchief out of her pocket and had it tied across his mouth before he could jerk away. "No you don't," she said.

His gaze as he glowered up at her was hot as the center of a match flame.

"All right," she said. "I'll tell you." She expected him to start squawking behind the gag, but he remained silent and still.

"The fellow who's paying me is meeting us up by the big hill north of that Swedish place."

Larkin muffled two syllables.

"Yeah, Lindholm. Lindsburg. Whichever. He's already paid me forty dollars in silver. And he says when I deliver you, I'm getting five hundred dollars. Feature that!" Rio shook her head. "Five hundred dollars! That's the biggest payday I've ever had in this line of work."

She squinted at him, puzzled. "Is it who you are? Or what you have?" She drew her gun and used it to push back his coat, to poke at his vest. There it was—a chain around his neck. A cross, and if it wasn't silver, she'd eat her gunbelt. A nice, weighty piece, worth some coin. With a twinge she remembered her old life: if a customer had come in with that around his neck, she'd helped herself to it after getting him glassy-eyed drunk, fucked senseless, or both. She peered at it, and saw it was not just a cross, but an actual crucifix, what the Catholics her daddy had called mackerel-snappers wore. Little skinny Jesus, looking both serene and uncomfortable. A little shiver ran through her. Someone had walked over her grave.

No, she didn't need his trinket. He needed it more than she

did if he was going to die soon. Maybe after that, though, she might be able to get her hands on the thing. A girl always needed to keep an eye out.

———————————————

Rio felt generous and undid the gag before she got Larkin mounted up. Wonder of wonders, he even waited maybe half an hour before he started talking again.

"All right," she said. "I'm in a good mood, so I'll tell you. Fellow by the name of Fisher was the one who paid me."

"Fisher?" Larkin's voice sounded a little strained, but he was facing away from her, so she couldn't see the expression on his face.

"Doctor Fisher. My height, maybe. Greasy hair, pop eyes. Looks like he couldn't get hired by an undertaker."

"He go work for an undertaker, he'd get fired out the next day," Larkin said.

"You know him?"

"Yeah. I know him."

They rode on in silence for a while. Rio found herself opening her mouth to ask a question, and had to laugh. Larkin glanced back at her.

"Just laughing at myself," she said. "Been telling you to keep your mouth shut all this time, and I about asked you a question." She chuckled again.

"Ask away."

"So—who is he?"

"Doctor Fisher is a lying murderous snake who works for an even bigger lying murderous snake."

"They're government?"

"I wouldn't be surprised if his boss has some government influence. His boss is very rich. And...not right in the head."

"What did you do to piss him off?"

Larkin remained silent for a long while. Clouds sailed overhead, fat confections of blinding white, silver beneath.

"He's a monster."

Rio chuckled.

Larkin looked back at her. "Is that funny?"

"Someone's paying a lot of money to bring you in, I don't reckon you'd have a high opinion of him. I haven't heard 'monster' before, though."

"He is." Then his mouth shut like the trap Rio had compared it to, and they rode on.

To Rio's frustration, Larkin said not another word. Not while the eternal Kansas wind nearly whipped off both their hats; not while the sun bore down upon them; not while they forded the Little Arkansas and Turkey Creek. Fording a watercourse at the best of times gave Rio the fantods: all manner of creatures lay in wait in the shade and mud of the banks. Snakes. Snapping turtles. Big damn birds who would boom up right under a horse's hooves and spook them forty ways from Sunday. To cross a creek while managing Banjo, Larkin's horse, and Larkin himself wound her tighter than a fiddle string.

After crossing a deep draw that took a good deal of profanity and boot work on her part, Rio was mad enough to chew her hat. Damn if this vagrant was going to keep his lip buttoned when before he'd been trying to talk her ear off. She hated anyone to get the best of her, but at the end of all this, she'd be the one out ahead, loaded down with coin.

"All right," she said, once she'd made sure Banjo was going to mind her manners and Larkin was still secure. "What kind of monster is he?"

"The blood-drinking kind."

"He's a lunger? That don't mean he's a monster; I've got a cousin up Chicago way who goes to the slaughterhouse twice a month and drinks a cup of blood. She wrote me that it helps her consumption something wonderful."

Larkin gave her a sour look. "I wish he was just a lunger. That servant of his, Fisher, gets blood from animals. But Elazar Bronze gets his blood from human beings."

Rio stared at him. With her rider's weight shifted in the saddle, Banjo stopped, and Larkin's horse stopped as well. "I never heard of such a thing."

"It's true. He's an honest to God vampire."

"A what?" In disgust Rio clucked to her mare and dragged Larkin's horse along. "No sir, that's just some booger made up to scare soft-headed fools and babies who won't do what they're told." Hunkered down by the fireplace, she and her sisters, the orangey light playing over their faces, on Ma's kettle, and on her knitting needles. Ma told them stories about the Boo-Hag, about the Leeds Devil, about hair balls and what would happen if you left a rocking chair rocking. Her sisters always got galloping nightmares after such a story night. She never did. Not those kinds of nightmares, anyway.

If this wasn't the most outlandish way of trying to escape a bounty—his handsome face all sober as Sunday morning. "You look all right," she said after another assessing gaze. "Why in the nation do you think he's an actual vampire?"

"You think I'm crazy?" He shrugged, as well as he could with his wrists bound to the saddle horn. "You think whatever you like. Maybe I am a little crazy, after what I seen."

Banjo was beginning to get a little snorty, a little bouncy and short in her stride. "Gonna run a bit," Rio warned Larkin, and legged the mare into a canter. Larkin's long-suffering gelding loped alongside, his ears back.

To the west a few turkey vultures climbed a spiral of air. Maybe five miles away. Distance was tricky on the plains, where the horizon was a ruler stroke and the sky taller than the moon. If there wasn't a river in sight, there weren't any trees, either; and nothing to tell a body where *there* was without studying the lights of Heaven above. Even the Kansas wind wasn't to be trusted, a wind that blew from all directions, wailing and slamming through everything in its path like a demented crone. Wind like that drove folks mad.

Those vultures could be studying anything, Rio thought. Dying antelope. Steer with its leg broke.

Born on a farm, gone for a sporting woman by her fifteenth birthday, killing men six years later, Rio thought she had seen all kinds of death. A corpse never troubled her at all. But Larkin's insistence that the fellow who'd hired her was a vampire—and the dim memories of her mother's stories—the prairie wind that drove the madness right into folks—anything could happen out here in God's great loneliness.

Rio had heard tell of a homesteading man and wife out near Dodge City that met with a grisly end that had stuck with her. The man left for a week at a time to work carpentry jobs in the growing town. Someone had to make money and someone had to stay on the land so they could prove up their claim. It was the wife who stayed out there, miles from town, with the silence of the plains muffling everything like the satin lining of a casket. One week the husband didn't show up for his work. After a few days the foreman drove out to the farm to see whether his employee was ailing or whether he'd run back east. He said afterwards that the sound of the flies could be heard half a mile away from the house. Despite the smell, he opened the door and was greeted by the sight of his employee at the table staring into the infinite, face stretched in a sound-less scream. Little more than a skull was left—eyeless, lipless, tongueless. Only the eye sockets and tortured rictus exposing brown chipped teeth remained.

To one side of the table slumped his wife. She had no face, the shotgun blast had destroyed it and splattered the back of her head all over the stove behind her. Before she had shot herself though, she'd set a place on the table in front of her husband. And on the plate, black and droning with insects, rested three strips of flesh, which were not bacon; and two spheres that were not eggs.

This part of the world made people do horrible things. Was it possible that this Elazar Bronze had committed a deed so bloody that Larkin had to use a word bigger than monster? And that he knew that Larkin knew?

Rio brought the horses down to a trot, then a walk. "What was it Bronze did that has you calling him a vampire?"

Larkin twisted his hands and wrists uselessly against the rope. "I'll tell you if you untie me."

Rio sighted down the barrel of her revolver at his right cheek-bone. "Nope."

"Suit yourself. When we meet up with Fisher, before handing me over, just you ask to meet his boss. And God help you."

By the time they got to the big bluff north of Lindsborg, the battering wind had dropped to a caress, the land had soft-ened to the color of doves, and Rio was mad enough to chase snakes.

Not so much of a true bluff as a rocky shoulder humped up out of the prairie at the southern end of the Smoky Hills, the summit offered a view of McPherson and Saline counties. Rio had ridden up there once or twice during her ranging about; it was an excellent place to spot game, whether buffalo or men. Fisher hadn't specified where at the base of the hill they should meet. The horses needed rest, so Rio pulled up at a likely outcrop of limestone and dismounted.

"Hey," Larkin said.

Well, Fisher could find her. She poured a little water into the crown of her battered hat and let the horses drink from it, staying out of range of Larkin's feet.

"I'm talking to you," Larkin said.

Would Fisher and Bronze let her keep Larkin's gelding on top of the bounty? She'd been needing a second-string horse, and since Banjo hadn't killed him yet, he might do very well.

"He killed my father," Larkin said.

"Jesus Bluebonnet Christ." Rio clapped her hat back on. "You just swing any old way, don't you, like a scarecrow in a cyclone. Why didn't you say that? No, you just say, 'God help you,' and leave me hanging."

"Because I wanted to tell the truth, but you're the biggest bitch I've ever met, and I want to see your face when you catch sight of his."

"I'm surprised a mouth that pretty can say such things."

He wouldn't meet her gaze. "My mouth said too much and that's why I'm here, I reckon."

"Bronze killed your father and he's afraid you'll get some lawman on his tail?" Rio shrugged. "So whyn't you just kill him?"

Now he did look at her, with an expression that shook her to her bootheels: he grinned like a dog rolling in carrion. "I got you to do it, don't I?"

She took a breath, to wither him with a brothel insult, when he looked past her and tipped his chin. "Yonder he's comin'."

She made herself turn slowly, hand on the butt of her gun.

Pulled by a pair of grays, a rockaway carriage pitched side to side over the uneven ground towards them. Fisher huddled in the driver's seat, hands full of reins, bowler hat shading a sour grimace. Maroon curtains were drawn shut behind the glass panels that guarded the occupant.

"That's a damn fancy buggy," Rio said. "I should've asked for more money."

"Oh, he's got money like a hound's got ticks."

She called out to Fisher. "You can see I found him! Now I want to see something!"

The little man reined in the team. "Terrible woman," Rio heard him mutter. He climbed down from the seat and flapped a gloved hand in Rio's direction. "Yes, all right! I have the five hundred here in diverse coin! One moment—" He unlatched the side door of the carriage and reached in.

"My god, I'm going to New Orleans." Rio sighed. "I'll get a little house with a wrought iron fence and roses all year round. What's Bronze gonna do to you, do you think?"

"Kill me," Larkin said. "Like he did my father. But first he's going to have Fisher drain all the blood from my body. He said dead blood is no good."

"Damn him for a preposterous heathen," Rio said cheerfully. The smile stayed on her face she watched Fisher walk toward them carrying a small canvas bag. When he was about two yards away, she drew her gun. "Close enough."

"I don't understand," Fisher said. "Excuse me, I—" Free hand to his mouth, he coughed, a horrible hacking spasm.

When he took his hand away, Rio was unsurprised to see blood on his palm and glittering in his moustache. "Never mind," she said. "I don't want you touching any more of my money than you have to. Just pour it out on the ground. With the hand that's not bloody."

She and Larkin watched while Fisher fumbled with the drawstring and then tipped the entire amount out onto the ground. Brown, red, silver, gold in the sun's fading rays. Such a sight, indeed. Out of the corner of her eye, though, she caught the twitch of the carriage curtains. Someone else was taking in the sight.

"One more thing, Doc."

The lenses of his spectacles shone red in the sunset. "I think this is what we agreed on, Miss."

"Is there a rifle aimed at me right now?"

Fisher laughed. "A rifle? You're afraid of getting shot? By the person in the carriage?" He laughed again, coughed, bled. "My master—*employer*—would never stoop so low."

"Then I'd like to meet him. Elazar Bronze, ain't that right?"

"How do you know his—"

"I've had to listen to your boy here jawin' non-stop about him, and Should be I must confess to a mighty curiosity about him. Giddy up, Doc, I want to see this specimen of evil." She cocked the hammer. "I have no problems with a little low-stooping now and then."

Before Fisher could turn, the curtains twitched again, more convulsively this time. "Oh dear," Fisher murmured. To Rio's fascination, a person—a personage—emerged from the carriage. Among the hues of dust and ochre, fawn and fallow and puce, a scarlet-clothed leg appeared, followed by an equally scarlet sleeve. The resulting frock coat, trousers, and vest seemed to float out. Only in the next blink did all this painful color resolve into a man. A man thin to the point of emaciation, tall almost as the roof of the carriage. White hair straggled from his scalp to his shoulders. And then he donned a top hat black as a bat's wing.

The man drifted up to Fisher, head bent a little so that Rio could not make out his features. Abruptly she decided she did not want to.

The pair of grays rolled their eyes as Elazar Bronze passed them, but otherwise stood in the scrubby grass as if nailed. Rio found herself taking a step backwards, and another, until she was level with Larkin.

"I see he's granted your wish," Fisher said, smiling. "Are you satisfied, Miss Rio? I trust you'll wait until we leave to pick up your money."

"I am indeed granting Rio Rivière that wish." Elazar Bronze finally lifted his head and met Rio's gaze.

Her breath came out in a whine. "Oh Larkin, you were right. You were right; I'm sorry…." She raised her gun, but the barrel shook as if she had the ague. The more she tried to aim the more her hand shook.

Elazar Bronze laughed. He laughed, and the grass wilted; he laughed, and the horses moaned in a terrible echo of that laughter.

Beneath the brim of his hat, parched skin stretched over his skull. His lips were thread thin and could not close to hide his canine teeth. Canines like a fox's, curved and sharp and gleaming whiter than any natural teeth. Were they worse than his eyes? Each socket was a bone cup holding not an eyeball but only flattened eyelids. Black stitches fixed the lids in place.

Rio's ears buzzed. How loud those flies must have been at the dead couple's homestead. Her vision darkened and she realized she was on the verge of a faint.

"My dear Doctor Fisher. How embarrassing." Bronze reached out and with one withered finger swabbed away the bloody expectoration clinging to Fisher's beard and moustache. He brought the finger to his nose to sniff, then ran out a narrow tongue to lick it clean. "Yes, still slowly dying, I'm afraid. After

I'm done with the boy, you can have him and his horse, how does that sound? You'll feel right as a trivet is no time."

Fisher's complexion had gone pearly as he watched Bronze, but his gaze remained soft and adoring. "Thank you, Master."

"You mean you'd let me go?" Rio croaked. As much as she wanted to brace her right hand, she needed her left hand to unsheathe her knife and bring it up to Larkin's saddle horn. "Here!" she hissed.

"Whattaya think I'm going to do with my hands tied?"

"Just—fucking—I don't know!" She moved the knife until it touched something, and made a slicing motion, hoping some part of the blade was reaching the rope.

"Ow, you bitch!"

Fisher giggled. Elazar Bronze did not laugh, but Rio thought she saw a tinge of pleasure on his face. "What you're doing is most amusing, Miss Rivière. Are you purposefully whetting my appetite by trying to decant a little of Mr. Larkin's ever so fine claret? He hints at an even more bountiful pressing than his father's."

"If you go," said Fisher, "you have the assurance of even more money in the future if you bring us another specimen."

Now it was Bronze's turn to giggle. "On the hoof, as they say. Such fine cattle you colonials breed. Put away your weapons, girl; I won't hurt you."

"Be damned to you if I do," Rio said, and pulled the trigger.

The shot blew away most of Fisher's throat. His head flopped to one side, nearly decapitated and he crumpled in a blood-sodden heap.

In the next heartbeat Banjo charged. She knocked Rio aside and went for Bronze with her ears clamped back against her head and her neck stretched parallel to the ground. With her teeth she seized the monster by the face and shook him like a terrier with a rat. He had time to scream once. Then she dropped him and trampled him. Nine hundred pounds of enraged animal plunged again and again with iron edged hooves, and to Rio it sounded like kindling breaking.

When Banjo finally fell still, she stood over what was left of Elazar Bronze in a cloud of pink-tinted dust. Then she turned her hindquarters about and shat a load of horse apples onto the remains.

Rio holstered her gun. She leaned against Larkin's gelding, trying to stay upright on wobbly legs, and painstakingly cut Larkin loose. The last strand snapped apart, and she let herself fall down.

Leather creaked as Larkin dismounted, accompanied by a few mild oaths. Rio stared at the ground past her boots. Little yellow flowers. A clump of prickly pear. Ants, busy with ant business.

The pile of coins.

"Are you all right?" Larkin said.

"I'm sorry I cut you." Soft hoof falls and a nuzzle of her hair. Banjo, curious as to why Rio was sitting down with no food or fire.

"Nothing a little goose grease won't mend."

"Take the money," she said.

Larkin hunkered down on the other side of her. "I know that's not the first time you've shot a man."

"No—no." She nodded and sucked her teeth thoughtfully. "First time I ever seen my horse go for a murderer, though."

He thumped her shoulder. "Come on. Get on your horse, we don't have time for this."

"The hell you say?"

To her amazement, Larkin laughed. "Or I could just ride the horses over you a few times."

She climbed to her feet, using Banjo to steady herself. "You turning *me* in?"

"Like I said, you're the biggest bitch I ever met." He nodded in Banjo's direction. "Maybe. But didn't you say you wanted to go to New Orleans?"

Slowly: "Yes?"

Larkin shrugged and rubbed his wrists where the rope had chafed. "All this rig would fetch a penny, don'tcha think?"

Rio looked at the elegant carriage, the matched grays, who were now cropping the grass. "That's a thousand dollars easy," she said without thinking.

"That's what I thought," he said. Wind-burned, sunburned, three days of stubble on his face, Larkin looked as miserable and merry as any man she'd ever seen. What a goddamn country this was. "We don't have any shovels, though."

"Aw hell, we don't need shovels. We'll just burn Fisher's clothes and drag him a ways—why are you laughing at me?"

"You're a horrible woman. And I'm coming to New Orleans with you."

Rio squinted at him warily. He was looking at her now the same way many a man had looked at her back in the Sugar Grove days. "You think you are, huh?"

"Oh, yes. My father'd still be hunting vampires today if he'd had you and this mare with him." He gave Banjo's neck an approving slap. "Lots of vampires in New Orleans."

THE LEGEND OF LONG-EARS

KEITH R.A. DeCANDIDO

1912: A bar in Chicago

"That ain't the craziest story I heard about Long-Ears," said the short man sitting at the long bar. "Fella I knew down in Florida saw him in the Everglades. Seminole folks down there warned him to watch out for the smell."

"Which smell?" another man asked through his unkempt beard. "It's the damn Everglades, whole place stinks like a swamp."

"'Cause it *is* a swamp," said a man in a bowler hat.

The short man said, "The point is, fella I knew didn't listen, and he smelled the smell, but he didn't turn back. Then he saw it: big as a mule, head like a wolf, tail like a horse, and furry like a bear. Long-Ears gave him diphtheria."

A tall man who'd been very quiet suddenly spoke. "I got a story about Long-Ears. And it ain't about no diseases—that's just a story the Seminoles came up with to explain how they get sick. But I can tell you it also involves Calamity Jane and Bass Reeves, and the one time they met."

Laughing, the short man said, "You expect me to believe that

Wild Bill's girlfriend and that colored marshal met? I never heard'a that."

"Calamity Jane wasn't Wild Bill Hickok's girlfriend," the thick-bearded man said. "She was a scout. Saved Captain Egan's life, back in the day."

The tall man took a sip of his bourbon. "That's one story, but I ain't here to tell that one. I'm here to tell about how Long-Ears brought two heroes of the West together."

1877: A saloon in Deadwood

"Hey Jane, you heard the news?"

The voice penetrated through the whiskey-induced stupor that was wrapped around her mind like a blanket. The woman who was born Mary Jane Cannary, but whom everyone referred to as "Calamity Jane," summoned what care she could manage and contrived to open her eyes. She saw a man with no left leg, supported by a wooden crutch. It was Martin Callister, who'd been a soldier under General Crook when he came to Deadwood on the Horsemeat March.

"Why ain't you in Rapid City, Martin? And why you got a crutch?"

"'Scuse me?" Martin frowned.

Then she remembered that was one of her visions of Martin, still serving in the Army and stationed in Rapid, not the reality of Martin, who'd lost his leg to gangrene, was discharged, and now lived in Deadwood permanent.

It was so damned hard to keep it all straight.

She put the bottle to her mouth and upended it, but nothing came out. "Need 'nother bottle."

"'Need' is prob'ly too strong a word, Jane," Martin said. "Just came from the telegraph office. Got a wire from Yankton. They hanged Jack McCall today."

Jane stumbled to her feet, only then realizing that she had been sitting on the saloon floor, which explained why her back hurt so much. She staggered to the bar and placed the bottle down on top of it with a distressingly loud thunk.

Tina, the barkeep, stared at her for a second, sighed, and then retrieved another bottle of whiskey from the shelf.

"I thought," Martin said slowly, "that you'd wanna know that Wild Bill's killer finally got what's comin' to him."

"He shoulda listened to me," Jane said.

"Who?"

"Bill! I told him, no matter what, do *not* sit with your back to the door! I *saw* it! Long's he sat facin' the door, he was safe! They never listen!"

Wordlessly, Tina placed a freshly opened bottle of whiskey in front of her.

Jane saw Tina lying dead from childbirth complications the night her daughter was born, and also saw her dancing at her daughter's wedding. At the present time, Tina was unmarried, and Jane had no idea which would come true.

She rarely did.

"Never listen," she muttered as she raised the bottle to her lips.

1867: A house in Salt Lake City

Fifteen-year-old Mary Jane Cannary woke up from the

nightmare with a start, and then ran downstairs to the sitting room, where Daddy was reading a newspaper by the fire.

"I had the dream again, Daddy!"

Bob Cannary lowered the paper and looked at his daughter with disdain. "Now Mary Jane, I won't be hearin' of this nonsense. Dreams is dreams, and that's all they is."

"I saw you get took by the stinky wolf, Daddy! You gotta believe me!"

"I don't gotta do nothin', Mary Jane, you hear me?" He rose and loomed over her, fists clenched.

But Mary Jane didn't let Daddy scare her no more. She'd seen far too much for something as simple as a man to frighten her. So instead of cowering at his approach she leaned toward him. She was tall enough now that her face was almost as high as his.

"Momma died because she didn't listen! I ain't gonna let you go too!"

"Mary Jane, you will go back to bed, and you will cease this foolishness, do I make myself clear?"

She went back to bed, tears streaming down her cheeks. Last year, she warned them not to go to Montana, because Momma would die in Montana. They didn't listen, and Momma caught pneumonia and died. If they'd stayed in Missouri, Momma'd still be alive, she was sure of it!

The next day, Daddy went out to meet with some men who'd loaned him some money. That night, while on his way home, he was menaced by a strange creature that some described as a wolf, others as a hairy horse. But everyone remarked on the smell.

Mary Jane Cannary never saw her Daddy again.

1877: The sheriff's office in Deadwood

"So you're the famous Deputy Marshal Bass Reeves," Sheriff Seth Bullock said to the mustachioed man sitting across from him.

Nodding slowly, Reeves said, "Can't speak to bein' famous, but I am Deputy Marshal Reeves, yes, sir."

"Thought you worked for Judge Parker down in Arkansas."

"I do, sir, but my pursuit of this one fugitive brought me up here." Reeves reached into the pocket of his overcoat and pulled out a ratty piece of paper.

Bullock took the paper and unfolded it to reveal a wanted notice for Oscar Olson. The drawing at the notice's center portrayed a broad-shouldered man with a round face and a dark beard. The notice promised two hundred dollars for whoever brought him in, dead or alive.

Handing the notice back to Reeves, Bullock asked, "And what'd this Olson fella do to earn himself so great a reward that it brought you all the way up to Deadwood?"

"Kill his wife and children."

"A horrible crime, but not one that usually has so much of a bounty attached to it."

Reeves allowed himself a tiny smirk. "It does when the wife's the daughter of a county sheriff, the niece of a state judge, and the granddaughter of a congressman."

"I see." Bullock nodded and folded his hands together on his desk. "I've not heard of any such man coming into Deadwood, but this town has as pliable a relationship with the law as your territory down south. It tends to draw in malefactors of all kinds."

Getting to his feet, Reeves said, "It's my job to draw one of them out, sir."

Also rising, Bullock put out a hand.

Reeves looked at it with suspicion, as white men rarely offered to shake the hand of a man with skin as dark as his. But after a moment, he returned the handshake.

"Good luck, Deputy Marshal."

"Thank you, Sheriff Bullock."

Reeves and Bullock exited the sheriff's office. The marshal's big white horse was tethered to a nearby pole set up for the purpose, and Reeves walked over to the mount and patted him on the side of the head.

"Y'r gonna die f'm th'stinky wolf," said a voice from behind him.

Whirling around, he saw a young woman who was wearing a battered overcoat and a brimmed hat askew on her head. She was clutching a whiskey bottle for dear life. "Excuse me, ma'am?" he prompted.

Bullock shook his head and chuckled. "The famous Deputy Marshal Reeves, may I introduce you to the infamous Calamity Jane."

Putting his hand to the brim of his own hat, Reeves said, "Ma'am."

"I ain't no 'ma'am,' an' you an' that Swede y'r pursuin're gonna die f'm th'stinky wolf."

That brought Reeves up short. "How do you know who I'm pursuin', ma—er, Miss Jane?"

"Y'think y'r th'first?" She moved closer to him, and he could smell the whiskey on her breath. Indeed, he could smell it in her sweat. "Stinky wolf killed m'father and woulda killed Cap'n Egan if'n I had gone t'Goose Creek. Gonna get you an' that Swede too!"

Jane was now practically on top of Reeves, which meant that when she passed out, she fell against him.

Instinctively he reached out to catch her, but the woman weighed far more than she seemed, and Reeves stumbled back, nearly colliding with his horse. He recovered quickly and gently set her down on the ground.

"And that," Bullock said ruefully, "was one'a her more lucid conversations."

1873: A house in Piedmont

Since her father's death at the hands of the stinky wolf, Jane had been caring for her siblings, having moved them to Wyoming. She'd been thinking of going to Fort Russell over in Cheyenne and trying to find work there, maybe as a scout. She'd successfully tracked some Arapaho who'd ambushed the oxcart she drove last month, and maybe she could parlay that into working for the Army.

But then the vision came right after she tucked the last of the children in.

…you're riding back to the fort when you're ambushed…

…you're part of a convoy that's heading north, away from Wyoming…

…the report of rifle-shot is heard all around you as you kick your horse into action to get away…

…the convoy continues north, as far away from Fort Russell as you can get…

…Captain Egan falls from his horse, and you turn around, hoping to rescue him…

…little Delilah, the daughter of a textile merchant who's also in the convoy, takes ill, and you care for her…

...the stinky wolf comes back, having already claimed your father, and now comes for Captain Egan...

...after a week, Delilah's fever finally goes down, after you've sat with her the whole time...

Jane reached for another bottle of whiskey, but there was only a tiny sip left. She gulped it down, making a note to go to Grania's Store tomorrow to buy more.

She'd had her heart set on becoming a scout, but now it seemed that if she did that, Captain Egan would die—and so would this Delilah girl, whoever she was.

Of course, maybe Egan would die anyhow. She couldn't be sure. The vision stopped before she saw Egan completely taken by the stinky wolf. Maybe she was going to save him, and not becoming a scout meant that he definitely *would* die.

Maybe she could save him.

But then what about Delilah?

It was a fever, sure, but the girl could easily survive without her.

Jane dry-sipped the bottle, then angrily threw it across the room, hearing it shatter against the wall.

She'd have to clean that up, lest she or her siblings get broken glass in their feet.

But she just stood there, wracked with the horrible indecision of not knowing which action would lead to more death and another victim for the stinky wolf.

What she needed, truly, was more whiskey, to modify the hurt enough to be bearable. But that wouldn't be available until morning, which meant another sleepless night...

1877: A house in Deadwood

Jane awakened to see Bass Reeves standing over her, concern on his face.

She tried to sit up, but the room commenced to acting rather ridiculous when she attempted that, and so she lay back down.

"Where am I?"

"Your bed, I'm guessin', Miss Jane. Sheriff Bullock told me this was your house, and it's the only bed in the place."

"Yeah. Why you still here?" Her tone was unnecessarily harsh toward the man who had taken care of her after she passed out from drink, but that was mainly because she didn't *have* a drink in hand, and she rather desperately wanted one.

"Wanted to finish our talk. You said me and my bounty were bound for bein' killed by Hatcko-tcapko."

"What-co, who-ko?" Jane had never heard that name before.

"I'm guessin' that's the 'stinky wolf' you were talkin' 'bout. Seminoles got a legend 'bout a monster that's part wolf and smells awful. They call it Hatcko-tcapko. Most white folks call it 'Long-Ears.'"

"I guess." As far as Jane was concerned, the tribes were for fighting against and not getting killed by. She couldn't give a damn about their stories.

"What I gotta ask you, Miss Jane, is when this vision-sight'a yours is to come to pass."

"Whatcha mean?"

"This happen after I already captured Oscar Olson?"

Again Jane sat up, but this time she did it more slowly to give her head a chance to stay on straight. She struggled to recollect the vision. "It's on the road back to Arkansas. The Swede's tied t'that big white horse'a yours. An' the stinky wolf shows up. It goes after the Swede, and you shoot it, but it don't do no good, and then the stinky wolf takes you both. Already took my Daddy and woulda took Captain Egan. Don't wanna see it take nobody else."

"*After* I shoot at it, Hatcko-tcapko comes for me?" Reeves was very insistent on that point for some reason.

"Look, Mr. Reeves, I seen one hero die 'cause he was too dumb t'listen t'me. Wild Bill got hisself shot 'cause he wouldn't pay me no heed. So pay attention! Get outta Deadwood an' forget about that Swede. He gonna be the death'a you."

Reeves got to his feet and reached for his hat, which he had set down on a sideboard. "Afraid I can't do that, Miss Jane. I come too far to give up two hundred dollars. But don't you worry none. Hatcko-tcapko ain't gonna be takin' me no-where."

With that, and with a tip of his hat and a short bow of his head, the deputy marshal left Jane's house.

She debated what she wanted more: whiskey, or to sleep off more of this drunk.

Clambering out of bed, she searched for more whiskey. There had to be some in the house—even she couldn't have imbibed all of it. And it was the only thing to dull the pain of knowing that Bass Reeves was also going to die.

Bass Reeves found Oscar Olson in a cave in the Black Hills outside Deadwood.

Olson had hired a Sioux orphan boy to fetch food and coffee and various sundries for him once a week. Reeves followed the boy to the cave and then walked in and aimed his revolver right at Olson.

The Swede barely had time to realize that Reeves was in the cave with him when the marshal shot him between the eyes.

Reeves had purchased a small cart on two wheels that his stallion would drag behind him, carrying the corpse of his bounty.

As he came through town on his way out of it to head back home, Sheriff Bullock stopped him.

"You couldn't take him alive?" Bullock asked.

"No, sir, I couldn't." That was true, as far as it went.

"Pity. Man should face justice proper."

"Not sure there's any such thing as proper justice on this Earth, sir," Reeves said. "I'm just doin' my bit to enforce the law."

"Ain't we all," Bullock said ruefully. "Well, be on your way then, Marshal. It was a pleasure makin' your acquaintance."

"Likewise, Sheriff."

Calamity Jane then approached his horse. Well, in truth, she stood in front of his mount, almost daring the giant stallion to trample her. But his horse had more sense than she did and stopped in front of her.

"You killed 'im," she said.

"I did."

"The whole point'a tellin' you was so that *nobody*'d die!"

"Mr. Olson was gonna pass from this Earth one way or the other, Miss Jane. If not from my bullet, or from Hatcko-tcapko, then from the hangman's noose."

"Not if you'd *left*! If you'd just gone, you'd be alive, and so'd he be!"

Reeves snorted. "Miss Jane, you know what this man done? He killed his wife, his four-year-old boy, and his seven-month-old girl. His wife's family is some powerful men, Miss Jane—a sheriff, a judge, and a congressman. You do *not* kill the kin of men like that without consequence. If I came back to Fort Smith empty-handed, they'd send someone else, and Oscar Olson would still end up dead."

"He's still tied to your horse! What about the stinky wolf?"

Shaking his head, Reeves said, "Hatcko-tcapko only punishes the wicked and them that keep it from its task. You said yourself, Miss Jane, it was after I shot at the creature that it came for me. I'm not one to give up a bounty without a fight, so I made myself into them that kept it from its task. But now?" He indicated the corpse in the cart behind him. "There's nothing for Hatcko-tcapko to take. The Lord's already sent his soul to hell."

Calamity Jane just stared at him for several seconds.

Then she looked away. "I need a drink."

She wandered toward the nearest saloon. Reeves's horse, no longer impeded, started to trot down the road once more.

Reeves called out to her. "Miss Jane!"

Turning, she regarded him with an expression that was half confusion, half fury. "What?"

Tipping his hat, he said, "I thank you very kindly for saving my life."

And then he continued to ride out of town. It was a long way back to Fort Smith…

1912: A bar in Chicago

The tall man finished his story. "Calamity Jane commenced to drinkin' some more, as she often did to keep the visions at bay. But it never worked."

"Wait," the short man said, "you tellin' me that Calamity Jane *wasn't* no scout?"

"That's nonsense," the man in the bowler hat said. "I read Calamity Jane's biography. She went on at some length about her time helpin' the Army."

Finishing off his bourbon, the tall man said, "As she grew older, Jane had trouble keepin' straight what was a vision and what was the real world. Lotta what she put in that book was either tall tales or visions that didn't happen. But the important thing to her was tryin' to save people from dyin'. Everyone knew she had a generous spirit, especially when the chips were down. When a smallpox outbreak hit Deadwood, she was right there carin' for everyone—folks woulda died, but for her. And Marshal Bass Reeves woulda died, too."

The man with the beard asked, "So wait—why did she keep seein' visions'a Long-Ears over and over?"

"Good question." The tall man got up from his bar stool and headed for the exit.

As he walked down the Chicago thoroughfares, he contemplated where he might go next to tell tales of Calamity Jane. Her visions had done much to ruin her own life, which had finally ended eight years previous. But so many other lives were saved because she knew the possible futures and worked to prevent the worst of them. She was not often successful—indeed, there were times when she made things worse—but she did her best, and he respected that.

He decided to head to another city and tell tales of Calamity Jane to a new audience. Perhaps he would go to Indianapolis next.

Once he was beyond the Chicago city limits, he reverted

to his true form of a four-legged being with a wolf's head, a horse's tail, and a bear's fur.

Hatcko-tcapko continued onward to tell more tales of his greatest foe, of the woman who denied him more souls than any other.

THE NIGHT CARAVAN

JENNIFER BRODY

"The desert comes for you—no matter who you are. There's always a price to pay."

That's the last thing my lil' sister said before they gagged her and dragged her away to collect the bounty on her head. That was six *long* months ago. Now, I'm back in Gulch Hallow. The last place I want to be…but she's my blood. And that runs thicker than water in these parts. If you can find water. I'd reckon blood is more plentiful.

I speed my Zebyr down the main drag that makes up this scraggly desert outpost that they call a township. But really, that's an insult to townships. I glide up to a spare hitching post and slide into the charger. I admire the brown stripes painted across the body to help my bike blend into the landscape, like those extinct animals that used to roam another desert on another continent. I've got the Ragnarok model with lightning bolts etched into the sleek engine. Solar-powered and built for speed. I've got Sissy's older model towed behind me. They both levitate above the sand.

I shut off the engine and make sure the panels are tilted toward the sun-side and the bike has the proper connection to the charger. Then I dismount. I catch sight of my reflection in the warped standing mirror on display in the general store's dusty windows. I quirk my lips.

My mouth is still my best feature. Still smooth and rosebud pink, despite all that time baking in the sun. I have curly auburn hair, but that's tied back under my stiff-brimmed hat. Leather chaps and a denim, button-down shirt conceal my curves—or at least, they *try* to—along with a thick, sheep-skin jacket. It might be hotter than heck during the day, but the temperature drops precipitously at night. And that's not even close to the worst thing about the high desert.

Strange things come alive in the dark of night. Deadly things. Blood-spillin', rip your throat open things. Or worse yet... burrow into your flesh and latch onto your spine things.

That makes me shudder, but I push it from my head and focus on my mission.

Sissy.

My boots crunch the sand, sending the granules skittering away. Eyes find me from under stiff hats, tracking my progress. The town itself looks like all the rest in these parts. Flat, rickety buildings that once had paint, but that's now been sand-blasted off. Hitching posts galore packed with Zebyrs charging, mostly older models lucky to still run, all soaking up the vital sun with their solar panels and feeding off the batteries. My eyes track down the street. A post office, a bustling saloon, and a brothel keep one another company, while my destination sticks out alone.

The jail.

I tilt my gaze. It stands at the dead end of the street. That's where the town abruptly stops. Everything beyond that is open desert. Next to it, I spot the gallows. Freshly built. The wood still drips sap. A thick noose dangles, begging for company. Blood for blood, or so it goes.

There's always a price to pay.

Sissy is darned lucky it ain't for her, I think as I near the hanging platform. I spot the trap door built into the floor, ready to drop your body and snap your neck. Fresh sap and pine scent the air. I taste it on my tongue. Guess the girl pleaded with her fiancé for leniency. *She must've been pretty damn persuasive*, I think with a frown. But her old man built the gallows anyway, like a warning flag pitched dead in the center of town. *Stay away—she's mine.*

I hope Sissy got the message loud and clear. But there's no telling with her stubborn, impetuous streak. Chances are fifty-fifty on that one. But six months in a cell—not to mention almost hanging—can change a person. It can make them think about...well...everything. I've been out on my own this whole time, and I've sure done a lot of thinking.

Too much. Even now...

I continue toward the jail, passing a caravan loading up on the outskirts of town. It's a wagon train of settlers likely bound for Oasis. Some folks say Oasis is a rumor, others a fairytale. Some say it lies at the edge of the world, where the sea meets the sand. I try to picture such a thing, but come up short. All I know is sand, sand, and more sand. But they all agree on one thing: it's the only place where seeds can still grow like in the old days before the Blight.

As for me? I don't know what to think.

I do know this, however: these settlers look pale as the sand. Not a good sign. They aren't used to hard living. Two of them look like the leaders. Their wagon's got the largest solar sails in the caravan. That's a dead giveaway. It sits on twin skies and glides over the sand, driven by the wind. And if the winds decide to die out? I see the backup solar generator attached to twin-fan jets off the backside.

And something else. Something that stands out and sucks all my attention. *Their seed bank.* It's a solid wood and iron box with a huge padlock chained to the lead wagon. Despite those protections, I could make off with it. Hell, I've done it before. But a voice interrupts me.

"Hey, you Buster?" the woman calls to me. She's standing

by the lead wagon. She's dressed in an ankle-length skirt, the kind that drags in the dust. The lacy hem is dusty and fraying. She's trying to maintain some fashion sense, despite the hardship of settler life.

"Sorry to disappoint you," I say with a teasing wink. She's a dainty, pretty thing. I can't help flirting a little. Sissy shares my taste in women. That's something we have in common. But then her husband thrusts his arm around her protectively.

"You're Missy, then?" he asks in a gruff voice. While she's pretty and slight, he's blocky and clumsy. "You're later than the dickens. And where's Buster at? How're we gonna get this caravan up and sailing 'fore nightfall?"

"Look, mister," I say, frowning at him. I save my smiles for her. "I ain't Missy, and I sure don't know any Busters. You've got it all wrong. I'm here to collect my sister."

"Sister?" the woman says.

"Yes, ma'am," I reply with a flirtatious smirk. "From your town's lovely accommodations in the jailhouse."

Now she's smiling back with a knowing glint in her eyes. She *knows* about Sissy. Hell, the whole population of Gulch Hallow must know the story by now. It's a bit of a scandal. Plus, she's been locked up in their midst for the better part of half a year.

"So, you're not our guide?" her husband says, tilting his hat and scratching his head. He's blockheaded as well as block-shouldered. How'd he land that pretty lass?

"Afraid not," I say. "Name's Mabel."

"Oh, I thought you were our guide," he goes on in plodding voice. "We've got a whole bunch of Oasis Chasers chomping at the bit and rarin' to go," he says, gesturing to the restless caravan. About fifteen covered wagons in all. I spot young women and children among them.

Poor fools. But that's how I finally put it together. He landed that pretty lass cuz he fed her those damn fairytales about Oasis. A place where the land meets the sea, where everything grows like weeds and water is as plentiful as sky, and rain actually comes on a semi-regular schedule. Not this all-or-nothing, drought or deluge that's sure to kill you either way.

"Well, I've been known to guide some here and there…for the right price," I admit, patting my seed pouch. His wife has got me in a generous mood. "But not through the high desert. And especially not for more than one night. That's a sure way to chase death."

She flinches when I say that while he remains stoic, foolishly so. But I don't tell them everything. The first rule of survival out here. Always keep a few cards close to your chest. I don't mention that Oasis is exactly where I'm headed once I get Sissy back. It's been our dream since…well…since we woke up to two dead parents and not one shriveled seed to our name.

In an automatic gesture, almost as natural as breathing, I pat my pouch again and feel the hard nubs tucked inside. I've finally banked enough seeds over these last few months while Sissy withered away in that cell, doing odd jobs and fetching a few quick bounties, scrimping and saving, and drinking more gulch water than whiskey, not my preference.

Maybe we're crazy Oasis Chasers, too. But we're not as crazy as this caravan of settlers. For starters, there's just two of us. We can ride fast on our twin Zebyrs. We travel light too. We're used to hardship and Blight life. Not like these pale, scrawny fools saddled with runts.

Don't settle down. And sure as heck don't get knocked up.

That's been our mantra since we started on this journey together. Though, perhaps Sissy took the notion a bit too far this time. She didn't get knocked up, thank the desert stars. Our lifestyle pretty much guarantees that outcome, unless it's the immaculate conception. But she did get herself *settled down* here for six long months on account of that harlot.

I think all of this. But I keep my mouth shut.

"Go fetch your sister," the woman says finally with a proper curtsy. But the glint in her eyes remains and gives her away. She likes me—and not in a *friend* way. "We'd best find Buster and Missy, else your prediction might prove true."

"Good luck to you," I reply, tipping my hat—to her, not him. "And cover up that seed box 'fore you get heisted. Sticks out around here like a sore thumb…and makes you a target."

It's solid advice. I've been scoping it as an easy mark myself soon as I rode into town. But this lass is too sweet to bring that kind of pain. That seed bank is everything they have, lumped together. It's how they'll pay their guides and also how they'll farm once they arrive.

If they arrive…if Oasis is real.

Suddenly, a sharp voice echoes down the street. I drag my gaze away from the woman and her crew's seed bank—though both still tempt me—and focus on the source of the commotion.

"Prisoner, don't lollygag," the sheriff mutters, shoving open the door to the jail. "Get your ass out here. Else you wanna stay longer?"

A tall, thin silhouette staggers forward and darkens the doorway. She squints at the midday sunlight. Well now, she's gone and acquired more lines around her bright sapphire eyes, but otherwise she looks the same. Long, straight black hair, dark as the night.

I spit in the sand—hardpan and merciless—and tip my hat at my sister. She wobbles out of the rickety lean-to jail with shackles on her wrists and ankles, altering her smooth gait. Or, it used to be smooth before they crammed her into that 6x6 cell. Who knows how bad her muscles have atrophied, especially since we've spent our whole lives free-ranging. That's the only word for it. Traveling where we want and doing what we want and screwing who we want, sometimes dipping our toes on the outside of the laws. I'll cop to it. We're bounty hunters, but that's not the *outside* the law part. Not only is our profession legal, it's state-sanctioned and highly rewarded.

Seeds.

I tap the leather pouch cinched to my waist, next to my revolver resting in the engraved leather holster, both equally necessary. This store has to last us through the long nights of the high desert. You can trade for food and water, or better yet, whiskey. It's safer and doesn't run the risk of making you sick. I tap the other side of my belt, where there's always a flask at least half-full.

Or half-empty.

Guess it depends on your point of view. I'm the half-full type. Least I was 'til they nabbed Sissy like that. Charged her with kidnapping. Total bullshit. Look, she did get romantic with that young lady from Gulch Hallow. But she didn't know the girl was engaged to the crusty old sheriff. The one shoving her from jail. But justice is fickle these days, just like fiancés.

"Stop manhandlin' me, you old coot," Sissy snaps at the sheriff, yanking her shackles out of his hands. Just as feisty as ever. Yeah, I don't reckon she learned anything in there.

The sheriff looks downright perturbed, but then gives in, unshackles her, and mutters, "Good riddance." He gives her one last shove, making her pitch and stumble forward into the street, for spite. Guess he reconsidered lengthening her stay. She tends to have that effect.

"Hey..." she says to me. What else is there left to say?

Her voice sounds rough, though. She waddles over, rubbing her sore wrists. I thrust a bundle of clothing into her arms, along with a pair of worn snakeskin boots and a revolver.

She cocks it and tests the trigger. "You miss me? Took you long enough."

"Quit your griping," I shoot back, though I can't help smiling, making it clear that I missed her and that sassy attitude. "You're lucky you're not dangling from that noose."

There's movement by the caravan. The infamous Buster and Missy have finally showed up. They're riding older model Zebyrs. But that's not what concerns me. Something about the hunch of their shoulders. The shifty nature to their eyes. Are they married? Coupled? Related? Maybe all of the above? Either way, they give me a bad feeling. I gaze at the woman on the lead wagon—for a bit too long—as she unlocks the seed bank. I almost gasp at how many seeds they've got squirreled away. She reaches in and hands the guides a fat satchel, which they count.

It's a fortune.

But I remind myself, she ain't my kith or kin. It's none of my business. I got enough on my mind with my sister and our damned foolish Oasis Chasing dreams. Sissy follows my gaze and notices that the woman, the one with the blockheaded husband, smirks at me.

"So, what do you wanna do now?" I say, dragging my gaze away and hiding the blush creeping up my neck. "Hot shower and a shot of whiskey? Maybe that brothel down the way?"

But Sissy shakes her head and sets her lips. I've never known her to turn down those three things, in any particular order. So, maybe she has changed since I last saw her.

"Sure you're in shape for hard travel?" I say, studying the crimps cut into her wrists from the shackles. "We've gotta travel fast and light. Not much sleep. Only midday naps. We can't risk being caught unawares in the long night."

I'm hemming and hawing now, giving into fear over facing the danger that lies ahead. But once the heart wants something— especially Sissy's heart—there's no delaying the inevitable. It's coming for you, no matter what.

"Nah, let's blow this shit town," she says, pulling on the chaps and holstering her rifle. "I already overstayed my welcome. Plus, we've put this off long enough."

"Still wanna chase this thing?" I ask, though I already know the answer, like I know my own heartbeat.

"Oasis or nothin'," she says. "Get busy living…"

"Or get busy dyin'," I finish for her. She's right. We've both chickened out on more than one occasion and wasted too much precious time. That kind of life ain't no life at all.

This is our chance to live—really live.

With that, we mount our Zebyrs and power up the engines. They ripple softly and levitate off the hardpan, rumbling with full charges. We blast way, leaving the caravan and coming sunset in our dust.

Day breaks hard and bright. I don't want to talk about what we saw in the night, but I got us turned around and off-course. Rookie mistake. I can't explain it, except to say that I spooked when their high-pitched shrieks erupted in the darkness. I lost my wits and got us lost.

Claw marks are sunken into the back of my ride from the parasitic swarm. Their claws cut metal like butter. They've earned many colorful nicknames. Bloodsuckers, Night Leeches, or simply the Desert Plague.

It's bad luck, I think, *right from the start*. We rode over a nest. We escaped, just barely. Sissy blasted the translucent parasite off the back of my bike. They snuck up in the darkness. Their bodies are completely clear, so they're invisible at night. But it was close…too close.

I picture the creature's undulating jaws that crack open, hoping to latch onto your back and burrow into your spine, attaching to you and sucking the melatonin from your skin and hair until both turn shock white, then feasting on your veins that stain their bodies blood red.

And that's only the beginning of the nightmare.

I shudder at that thought, glad that daylight finally broke and saved us from that winged, blood-sucking Desert Plague. They can't go out in the sunlight unless they snare a host.

And now by getting us lost, I've cost us a day. And a day in the high desert might as well be a lifetime. We finally fixed our rides and got back on course again around midday. We crest the next dune when I spot something shimmering in the desert heat like a mirage.

I blink, but it's no mirage.

It's the caravan.

Only they're not moving. That's strange. We lost a day, but even though they move slower, they should be ahead of us. But then I see it, as we ride closer. No guides. The blockheaded husband blasted dead, slumped over the lead wagon. The seed box heisted.

"Buster and Missy…" the woman starts when she sees my familiar face.

"They took the seed bank?" I say, while Sissy patrols the caravan and spots the guides' tracks leading away. The woman nods and tells me her name is Rayan. I'd tell her it's a pretty name, but now ain't the time. I tell her we only have one choice: we've got to get the seeds back.

Sissy resists at first, but then I persuade her. She owes me.

I figure Sissy and I will handle it. It's not our first such adventure. We're bounty hunters. Perhaps they'll reward us for our trouble. But Rayan insists on coming along. She doesn't trust us…or maybe it's something else. I spot that mischievous glint in her brown eyes.

"You sure?" Sissy says. "It's your funeral."

"My funeral it is," Rayan says. She ties off her skirts and grabs her husband's—or rather, *former* husband's—revolver, strapping it to her waist.

We ride through the scrub and sand, dotted with yucca plants, prickly trees, and cacti, all ready to deploy their defenses and prick you. This is hostile country. Even the plants are weaponized. Rayan rides behind me. Her surprisingly strong arms straddle my waist. The wind whips her hair all about, bouncy, dark brown curls only slightly lighter than her skin. Sissy tracks the guides for us. Finally, we come across their hideout in a twisted canyon.

We cut the engines and creep to the edge of the ravine, cut out of rock by flood water, and peer down. There's twenty, maybe a few more. I spot Buster and Missy among them. I point to the seed bank, still strapped to the back of a Zebyr. They haven't cracked the lock...yet.

Rayan scowls. "Sand *bastards*."

"Shit...they've got attachments," Sissy says, her voice turning ominous.

I flash back to the swarm that attacked us. This is infected country. About half the outlaws have them, attached to their backs and burrowed deep into their spines.

What's the word? Symbiotic.

They help you survive, keeping other predators away, while they feed on you. They also make you stronger and faster. That's the trade-off. The parasites gain immunity to sunlight. Without a host, they can only go out at night. But there are downsides. Their thoughts bleed into and influence you, though you can still fight back at first and remember who you are. Only eventually, the parasite renders you completely braindead and becomes your puppet master.

You're alive, yet not alive. That's the kind of thing gives me nightmares. *I'd rather kill myself,* I think, *than succumb to that.* But outlaws like these surrender to the parasites on purpose; they think the trade-off is worth it. They survive by raiding caravans.

Like this one, that brought us here.

"There's too many of them," I say with a frown. "Plus, those bloodsuckers feeding on them. How're we going to get the bank?"

Sissy lets out a sigh. "I've got an idea—and you're not gonna like it."

"What is it?" I ask, bracing myself.

"They killed my sister…" she says.

"Ugh, that's dangerous. What if they don't buy it?"

She shrugs. "Then, we'll have to blast our way out. And hope for the best."

Rayan looks at us both. "You weren't kidding 'bout the funeral part. Were you?"

"It's not too late to back out," Sissy says in hard voice, but then she softens slightly. "Though actually, we need your help for this plan. This only works with three of us."

It's decided.

Rayan and Sissy mount up and take off, heading for the canyon below, while I pull out my rifle. I take up my perch and aim carefully. A few minutes later, the commotion breaks out. My heart stutters in my chest as I watch it unfold. Sissy speeds into the outlaw hideout with Rayan strapped behind her, motionless with her skirts hitched up and covering her face.

"Help…they killed my sister!" Sissy yells and leaps off her

bike, dashing into their midst, waving her blaster and screaming for help. "And they're coming…this way…"

"Who the hell are you?" snarls one of them. Their unofficial leader, I'm guessing. His eyes are black. His large attachment breathes under his shirt. "And who the hell's coming?"

"Bounty hunters," Sissy hisses, ducking down and aiming her revolver at the canyon entrance. "But I have seeds…I can pay…for safety. That's why they're after us."

He looks irate. His black eyes, stained from the parasitic infection, bug out. But she said the magic word—*seeds*. His brain can't understand much anymore, but it understands that.

"Well, where are they?" he demands.

"We stole a bank and hid it," Sissy says, looking around. "Think I'd be stupid enough to bring them into this hideout? But I can lead you to it. If we die, then the location dies with me."

She remains hunkered down, but the outlaw hesitates. "Sure they're coming?" he says, growing suspicious. "You ask me, I think this is a hoax. And you're about to die…"

He cocks his pistol to shoot her.

That's my signal. I blast the rocks by their heads. Then, rapid-fire, I hit several closer targets. That gets 'em running and stampeding around. I'm fast, so fast, that it offers the illusion of more than one sniper. A whole posse even, if you're spooked enough. Sissy and the outlaws take cover behind the rocks and return fire. I hit one with a flesh wound, for good measure.

He screams and collapses in the sand.

Meanwhile, Rayan is playing dead. But she peeks her eyes open. She sidles over to the seed bank, tied to the back of the bike. She climbs into the saddle while I keep them distracted by showering them with blasts. I hit another outlaw. He shrieks and goes down hard. His parasite immediately shoots a tentacle out to leech blood, but it also seals the wound.

Rayan revs the bike, making it purr to life.

That's my signal. I take aim and ready to clear a path for their escape. Sissy immediately breaks for it. I cover her retreat, picking off anyone who gets close. Then I pivot and blast the rest of their bikes, rendering them useless for giving chase. And so, with my help, Rayan and Sissy escape.

Whooping and cheering—and still flush with adrenaline—we reunite on the bluff. Rayan got her wagon train's seed bank back. It's strapped to the stolen Zebyr. Better yet, we still have plenty of daylight left to reach the caravan before nightfall. We race off through the scrub, still joking about taking those outlaws down…but then…something darkens the sun. It's subtle at first.

But it grows dimmer.

"What's happening—" I start.

But then it darkens even more. Like something took a bite out of the sun.

That's when it hits me—*it's an eclipse.*

Suddenly, the Night Leeches flood the skies in thick swarms, erupting out of burrows and cracks in the hardpan. They're ravenous. This is dangerous, infected country.

"Oh no…watch out!" Sissy screams.

We speed away, hoping to outrun them until the sun reappears.

But seconds pass in slow motion. And they're winged and fast. It all happens so quickly in the darkening. One whips down toward my face, but I duck and blast it. The parasite shrieks, then shrivels and falls dead. But more keep coming, an endless swarm. We blast and ride hard.

They fly into the gears and clog up our bikes, stalling the engines when they kamikaze into them. My bike slams to a halt, pitching me into the sand. I land in a gulch and climb out.

Sissy isn't so lucky.

She lands exposed on the hardpan with nothing protecting her from the bloodthirsty swarm. Worse, her pistol comes loose and skitters away. She's completely vulnerable. The swarm immediately pivots, moving like one organism, like one consciousness, and flies at her.

"Sissy, watch out!" I scream, drawing my gun.

Rayan tries to pull me back into the safety of the ditch. I fight her off, struggling toward Sissy. I blast several right out of the sky. But one *gets* her. The parasite clings to her back, wriggles under her shirt, and sinks its tentacles into her flesh, welding to her spine. It's a small one, but now that it has a host, it will engorge and grow to several times its current size.

Bone to bone.

Blood flows to blood.

"Don't let it take me...please...kill me ..."

That's what the *real* Sissy gets out before it latches onto her. Her eyes darken, and her irises bleed from bright blue to pitch black. But so do the whites, turning into black holes.

Her consciousness flickers in and out as the creature bonds to her.

But then she loses the battle.

"You killed...my friends..." she shrieks in a possessed voice.

I gape in confusion for a moment, then it hits me. She means the other leeches I blasted. Those are the *friends*.

That's when she turns on me. She moves faster than should be possible, spidering across the sand and scrambling for her blaster. She pivots on all fours and cocks it, aiming right at me. Her lips stretch into an inhumanely wide, grotesque smile, while black eyes lock onto me.

I stare at her. Everything happens in slow motion. I'm holding my gun, but I can't do it. I can't blast my sister. She's all I have left. Suddenly, she fights the parasite off and comes back—

"Kill me...hurry...can't hold it off...forever..." she begs me. She lowers her gun.

I need to kill her...it's the only way now.

But I can't.

For once, I can't shoot.

Sissy spiders over to me—faster than should be possible—and presses my cocked gun to her forehead. Her black eyes bore into me, pleading with me. She presses it harder to her head.

"Please, I can't live like this..." she whispers, urging me to squeeze the trigger.

But I shut my eyes and cringe back, pulling my gun away from her head. I can't kill my sister. I know eventually Sissy will lose control again and shoot me. It's only a matter of time.

I hear a *blast*.

I wait for an explosion of pain to blossom and then to quickly fade into death.

But I don't feel anything. I crack my eyes open.

Relief animates Sissy's face. The parasite on her back howls in pain. They're melded together, symbiotic, making their fate the same. Death comes for them both now.

My sister pitches forward into the sand. *Thud.* Rayan stands behind her. She's clutching a pistol. The barrel is still smoking. "I had to do it," she whispers. "I'm sorry…"

The sunlight returns, slowly at first, then all at once. The swarm shrieks and flies away, some burning to ash in the skies, caught unaware by the sun's fierce return. I want to stay and bury my sister. I want to pay my respects. I want to pry that leech off her back.

But I turn away from my sister. We need to get moving. The sun is back, but it won't last. Night will fall again, and there's still the matter of the outlaw gang, not to mention the parasites.

They're angry now. They're coming for us. But there's more. There's Rayan now.

She needs me. And maybe, just maybe, for the first time in my life…I need someone other than my sister. The caravan is all she has left. Now, it's all I have left too. As we speed away on our twin mounts, I make this solemn promise. "Let's chase Oasis…together."

"*Together*," she repeats. And I know she means it.

I can see it in her eyes. She reaches for my hand and clasps it. We ride together like a symbiotic pair, not the deceptive kind that demands flesh and blood payment. The kind that makes your heart leap and mouth go dry, and makes you want to chase Oasis dreams.

Together.

Whatever comes for us next, I think as we ride into the sun, *it comes for both of us now.*

DREADFUL

JOHN G. HARTNESS

Cherijo Starnes thought she'd seen it all in her fifty-four years. She'd watched Sherman burn Atlanta to a smoking rubble, lost a husband to cholera, loaded up everything she owned onto a wagon and driven it out past any place hospitable to set up a new life for herself, met a gentle farmer she thought to share the rest of her life with, and buried him after he met the business end of a rattlesnake. But she'd never seen anything like the mess laying on her front porch staring up at her through a mask of blood.

"H-help me," the man said. He was lean, with decent clothes and a fine pistol on his hip. His face, what she could see of it through the crimson coat splattered across it from a jagged cut on his forehead, was covered in salt-and-pepper stubble, but looked like one that was usually clean-shaven. She appreciated that. She didn't like beards. Honest men should show their faces.

The man's horse lay on its side just inside her fence, its sides heaving. The horse and man both looked like twenty miles of rough terrain, but they also weren't alone. She couldn't see anyone else, the feeble light from her lantern barely reaching far enough to illuminate the dying horse, but she could hear the hooves pounding as they approached.

"You running?" she asked the man.

He nodded. "Help me. I'll explain inside. Please…" His eyes

rolled back, the whites showing, and his head thumped to the rough planks. Cherijo muttered a few choice words, leaned her shotgun just inside the door, and stooped down beside the unconscious man. She got a good handful of his tattered chambray shirt and dragged the man into her small cabin, all the way across the main room, leaning him near the crackling fireplace.

Stomping back over to close the door, she thought about those hoofbeats and drew a chair over to press against it.

Cherijo's life had been a mostly solitary one since her Robert had died three years back. She had Dino, the man who worked for her running the small farm and tending the twenty cattle she kept on sixty acres out here in the wilds of the Montana Territory. She had her church, not that she saw those people more than once a week. But at night, when Dino went home to tend to his aging mother and there was no work to keep her mind occupied, well, she had to admit, it did get lonely sometimes.

All that seemed to be over, at least for tonight, she thought as she bustled around the small cabin looking for bandages, her smallest sewing needles, and something she could use to mop up the worst of the blood.

When she returned to the main room of the small house several minutes later, the stranger was sitting up, his back pressed up against the hearth and that fancy pistol in his hand. "Is there another door?" he asked.

"No," she said, kneeling by his side and laying out her supplies. "Never saw the need for one, since it's just me here." Part of her wondered if it was a good idea to tell this stranger that there was no man living there, but if he wasn't completely deaf, blind, and stupid, he'd probably figure that out without her telling.

"Good," he said, then sucked in a sharp breath as Cherijo pressed a cloth to his forehead.

"Hold that there," she said. "I need to get the bleeding

stopped so I can see what we're working with." She walked over to the stove and ladled out a cup of hot water. She knelt by the man's side again and dipped another rag in the water, then began to dab and wipe at his face and neck, scrubbing away dirt and blood in a thick, ruddy paste.

"Thank you," he said. "They would have killed me for sure if I couldn't get inside."

"Still might, if those hoofbeats I hear are any indication," Cherijo said. "Sounds like four horses out there, maybe more. You think they'll try to come in?"

"They can't," he said. "Not unless you invite them." He gave her a thready laugh and a weak grin. "And I sure do hope you won't do that. For your sake, as well as my own."

Cherijo smiled at the man. "Well, contrary to what you might be seeing tonight, it's not my custom to just invite strange men into my home in the middle of the night. Now, Mr....what should I call you?"

The man chuckled, then winced as the effort strained something in his middle. "Morris. Quincy Morris, ma'am, and it's a pleasure to make your acquaintance, despite the circumstances."

Cherijo let out a long laugh at that. "Yes, Mr. Morris, I believe it's safe to say that I would have rather met you in the noonday sun strolling down the streets of High Rock. But who are the men chasing you, and why are you so sure they won't come charging in here and drag you off to find a tree tall enough to stretch your neck?"

Morris reached into his jacket pocket and withdrew a small silver flask, uncorked it, and took a long drink before speaking. "Well, ma'am—"

"Cherijo," she said. "If I'm going to be scrubbing your blood out of my floorboards, we might as well be on a first name basis."

"Well, Cherijo, please call me Quincy," he said. He took a moment before speaking again, in a more serious tone. "The men out there aren't men at all. They're demons in the shape of men. Bloodsucking fiends that will drain the very essence out of you and leave your lifeless corpse behind dry as the dust it lays in."

Cherijo's brow knit in confusion. "I don't think I understand. What are you trying to say?"

Morris let out another long breath, took another drink from his flask, then said, "They're vampires."

Cherijo laughed, a harsh, braying sound that filled the small house. "You're pulling my leg!"

"Why would I do that?" Morris asked, his simple question cutting off her laughter quick as blowing out a candle. She gaped at him, realization dawning that the man stretched out by her fire was serious. "I show up at your farm bleeding like a stuck pig, riding my horse to death, without even the strength to get myself all the way through your door. For a joke? No, ma'am. I have a sense of humor, but that's a bit much for me. The things out there aren't men. They once were. But now they're parasites, no better than ticks on a dog's behind. But far more dangerous."

Cherijo sat staring at the man for long seconds as she tried to reconcile the calm sentences coming out of Morris' mouth with the insanity of *what* he was saying. It sounded so reasonable, like it was the most normal thing in the world, except for the part where he was talking like they lived in a cheap dime novel. "You mean…vampires? Like Varney?"

He chuckled. "Yes, like Varney. There's more truth to that penny dreadful than one would imagine. Have you read the stories?"

Cherijo blushed. "Yes," she admitted. "My first husband enjoyed them, and I read them after he was done."

"Then you know a lot of what we're up against. It's not all true, though, and that's how I know I'm safe in here. A vampire can't cross the threshold of a home unless invited, and even if you invited the person into your home when they were alive, or if they lived there in life, they must be invited again once they have become a fiend."

"Do they really drink blood?" she asked, her hand drifting unconsciously to her neck.

Morris nodded. "They do. And they are powerful hard to kill. Regular bullets won't do it, unless you shoot them in the head. You have to use silver, or fire. Or you can decapitate them. I've heard a stake through the heart will do it, too, but I've never tried it. They are powerful fast, and strong. They move so quick it seems like they just turn into smoke and reappear somewhere else, and they can leap so high it seems almost like they're flying. But they can't go about in the daylight; that's one thing *Varney* got wrong. Sunlight burns them as sure as a torch, so they hunt at night."

"Like now," Cherijo said, lowering her voice as the sound of boots on her porch echoed through the house.

"Hello?" came a booming voice from outside. "Anybody in there? This is Sheriff Daltrey from Timmons' Landing. We've been chasing a fugitive that we think might be holed up in there."

She looked at Morris, suddenly suspicious. He shook his head. "I promise you, that's a lie. Those things out there are no more lawmen than I'm a saloon girl in Tombstone."

Cherijo walked to the door, her hands shaking as she reached up and pressed one palm against the wood. "I don't know any Sheriff Daltrey, and Timmons' Landing is a far piece to come chasing one man. What did he do?"

"He raped and murdered a woman who lived alone on a farm outside of town. We thought he might come this way and caught sight of him about ten miles from here. That's his horse in your yard, so he's either in there with you, or he's hiding out in one of your buildings."

She shook her head at the audacity of the man. She was no silly child to be fooled with the tale of a horrible killer who just happened to slaughter a woman living in the exact same circumstances as her, only three towns over. That was too much to believe, and she was a bit insulted. This man, or vampire, or whatever he was, thought she was *stupid*?

"Well, there ain't nobody in here but me, and I intend to keep it that way, least until sunup. If y'all want to go hunting through the barn and the shed out back, help yourselves, but if you want to come in here, you'll need to come back in the daytime with either Sheriff Avery from High Rock, or Major Connely from over at Fort Ellis. Either way, I don't know you, and it's late, so you should ride on." Cherijo tensed, hoping Morris was right and the creatures couldn't come in without an invitation, if they really were what he said they were.

The man on the other side of the door went silent for a long time, then she heard a new voice, this one familiar. "Miss Cherijo, it's Dino. I know these men, and they really are hunting a dangerous outlaw. He's a stone killer, Miss Cherijo, and you need to let them come in and look for him."

She looked back at Morris, who was waving frantically at her and shaking his head. "They can mimic the sound of any voice they've ever heard. If they've seen this fellow Dino before, they can sound just like him," he said in a whisper.

"How would they have seen Dino if they just rode in from Timmons' Landing? That's a three-day ride from here."

"They didn't come from Timmons' Landing," Morris said. "I came upon the pack of them in High Rock just after sunset. They were in the Gold Coast; hunting I reckon, because they weren't playing faro and they weren't drinking, and they didn't show any interest in the girls, neither."

Something in the man's story bothered Cherijo. "High Rock

ain't but a couple miles from here. If they didn't chase you no further than that, how come your horse keeled over?"

"I wasn't running east at first," Morris replied. "I have friends in Mason City who could help, so I tried to go south, but got cut off. Then I turned back north, but there was a pack of them right outside town, so I headed this way."

She ran over the distances in her head and figured he must have covered close to fifteen miles. That much at a gallop would be enough to ride a horse into the ground, and with Morris on its back, it was a miracle the poor beast got him this far.

"Miss Cherijo, please," came Dino's voice. "You just need to let these men go about their business and we can all get some sleep."

Cherijo's mind raced. She knew somebody was lying to her, but she wasn't sure who. Suddenly, inspiration struck. "Dino, what did they do to haul you out of bed at this late hour? Did you leave Annemarie back with all five boys by herself? I know little Terrence has been colicky, and Annemarie'll have a time getting him back to sleep."

"No," the voice said. "He didn't wake up. I reckon Annemarie probably went right back to bed after I left to come over here. I just couldn't live with myself if anything happened to you all alone out here."

Well, that answered that, Cherijo thought, picking up her shotgun and taking a few steps back from the door. She leveled the weapon right at the center of the door and pulled both hammers back. "Dino ain't married. He lives with his mother Elizabeth. And he doesn't have any children, much less a passel of sons. Now y'all said you wanted to come in, and the door ain't locked. But I'm standing here with two barrels full of lead aimed right where your unmentionables lie, and if you want to leave with all the parts you brought, you better get back on them horses and ride on out of here."

The voice didn't sound anything like Dino's anymore. It was

a low, angry thing, terrifying and inhuman. "Open this door, you stupid cow! Give us Morris and we'll kill you quick. Make us work for it, and I swear by all you hold holy that you will beg for death before we grant it."

She looked back at Morris. "Mr. Morris, I sincerely hope you are correct about those people, or *things*, not being able to come in here uninvited. Because I think I might have made them mad."

The morning dawned bright and crisp, the bright Montana sky stretching all the way to heaven as they rode into town, Cherijo on her old mare Daisy, with Morris sitting uncomfortably astride her plowhorse Herman. When they'd come outside, they were greeted by a horrific scene—Morris's horse had been cruelly butchered and strewn about the yard in a bloody temper tantrum, its head mounted on one of Cherijo's gate posts.

"Sorry I didn't have another riding horse," Cherijo said as they neared High Rock. They had ridden mostly in silence, but with the town in sight, she had some questions she wanted… no, *needed* answered.

"Don't worry about it, ma'am," Morris replied with an easy cowboy's grin. "I've got by with worse." Now that he wasn't coughing up blood and rasping like a man dying from consumption, his broad Texas accent was more apparent. This Quincy Morris was a strange man, swinging between deathly serious and rakish humor at the drop of a hat. She wasn't quite sure how to take him all the time, but she liked the man. She might even, if circumstances were different, or if they both lived through the next few days, be disposed to *really* like him. But that was a thought for tomorrow, if she was still alive tomorrow to think.

"Mr. Morris—"

"Please, call me Quincy."

"Quincy, then. How do you know so much about vampires? Don't most folk think they're just stories?"

He sighed. "Yeah, I reckon they do. I did. I…travel a lot. My family has money, and Father expects me to sow my wild oats before I come home and settle down. I don't think he expected me to sow them for quite as long as I have, or to roam quite as widely as I've roamed. But I've been all over the world and seen things that before I left Texas I would have chalked up to myth or legend. Vampires are one of those. I first met up with bloodsuckers when a flock of vampire bats killed my horse down in South America. Drained every drop of blood from the poor animal, and probably would have come after me next, if I hadn't blown half a dozen of them to pieces with my shotgun.

"Since then, I've been hunting these creatures all over the world, following every rumor of strange deaths, odd puncture wounds on the corpse's necks, or just pale, drained bodies being found under strange circumstances. I met a master vampire in Texas a year or two ago, but he got away from me. Then I was in Colorado a few weeks back and heard about a pack that was moving north, heading to Canada where the winter pickings are easy, and the description of their leader matched the one I'd been hunting in Texas, so I started tracking them. I found him last night and killed three of his pack before the numbers got too much for me. I ran, they gave chase, and that's where we met."

"And now we're riding into High Rock so we can…what, exactly? Do you think the vampires are holed up in town?"

"Most likely. They couldn't have chased me half the night, made such a mess in your yard, and covered much ground before sunrise. So they're either here, or close by. If I'm lucky we catch them unawares and kill them all before anyone in High Rock has to know that vampires are more than some storybook monster."

"And if you're not lucky?" She asked.

"Pardon?"

"You said that's what happens if you're lucky. What if you're not?"

"Well, judging by the state of your town's main street, looks like we're going to find out sooner rather than later."

Cherijo turned her attention away from the man beside her and back toward town as they rode past the shiny new train depot, with its bright white paint and gleaming steel rails. The station, completed just a few months ago when the railroad came through town, usually bustled with activity even when a train wasn't due, what with people waiting for stagecoaches, mail riders, or even telegraphs. But there was no one visible around the big building, not even Benjamin, the ticket seller, telegraph operator, porter, and maintenance man.

As she looked past the depot, Cherijo saw that the streets were deserted. No one was shopping at the dry goods store, no one sat in Reggie's chair on the porch of the barber shop getting a shave or a tooth pulled. Even Mr. Jones the hostler was nowhere to be seen, despite the restless sounds of hungry horses coming from the stables.

"It seems deserted," she said. "Do you think…?" She let her question trail off, not wanting to put her fear into words.

"Yes, ma'am," said Quincy. "I do think indeed. Let's see if we can find anyone who can tell us why it's so quiet. Hopefully I'm wrong." His tone said he was certain he wasn't going to be proven wrong.

It took less than an hour to confirm Morris's fears. There was no one alive in High Rock. Not even the children were spared, which seemed somehow more horrific. What was even more terrifying was the lack of bodies, or even graves. There was nothing but the odd drop of blood here and there to indicate that anyone had ever walked the streets. Otherwise, the whole town looked like it had been built empty and never occupied. There were no signs of struggle, no broken doors or windows, and nothing damaged in any of the homes. It was as if someone had just snapped their fingers and made all the people of High Rock vanish in the middle of the night.

"But where are they?" Cherijo asked as they left the small teacher's apartment built onto the back of the schoolhouse.

"They must be close by," Morris said. "Even with their speed and strength, it would have taken some time to clear out a whole town, and it was well past midnight when I made it to your homestead."

"Are the townsfolk likely to be with them?"

"Mrs. Starnes, let me be very clear. The townsfolk are dead. Everyone who they have touched is dead. All the people we didn't find just now, they're dead. There might be something walking around wearing their skin, looking like that person, sounding like them, perhaps even still in possession of their memories. But it is not the person it seems to be. All that is left is a demon wearing a person suit, and it has but one driving force—hunger. These things exist only to feed, and if given half a chance, they will destroy you as completely as they tore my horse to bits."

Cherijo didn't speak for a long moment as she tried to make sense out of all this. Everyone in High Rock, dead? It made no sense, and yet the evidence was right there in front of her face. The town was deserted, as dry as the winter air.

"So what do we do now?" she finally asked, squaring her shoulders. Nothing for it but to do it, as she always said.

"Now we find them. And we kill them. Every last bloodsucking one of them. They'll be weaker in the daytime, and like I said, even the touch of sunlight is enough to cause great pain, and with enough exposure, to destroy them. But first we have to find them. Is there any place in town big enough to hold everyone? Someplace we haven't been yet."

They'd already explored the church, the school, all the shops, the Gold Coast, and the new depot. And that's when it hit her. "I know where they are."

Morris turned to her, and she continued. "The old stagecoach office, over on the west side of town. It was abandoned when the railroad came in on the south end instead of where they expected, and the town built the new one."

"This old station, it's big enough for everyone in town to fit inside?"

"Most likely," she said, musing over the building in her head. "It's got room to work on coaches, load two or three at one time out of the snow in winter, and hold baggage and passengers if need be. Yeah, everybody could fit, if they weren't real interested in privacy."

"That's not something that vampires worry about," Morris said. "But let's make a detour by that dry goods store before we go knocking on the door. I expect I'm going to need more bullets, and we need to get you something a little better than that scattergun."

"I feel stupid," Cherijo said as they left Harrison's store. She was loaded down with a shotgun slung over each shoulder, and one in her hands, plus a pistol on a gun belt hanging low over her hips. She had the belt cinched tight over a heavy brown duster, and a pair of wide leather belts cinched around her throat, not tight enough to constrict her breathing, but providing a modicum of protection against a bite.

"Well, I'd say you look fierce, but you're wobbling around like a bear cub trying to walk on its back feet, if I'm being honest," Morris said, grinning. "Besides," he continued. "You said you can't hit the broad side of a barn with a rifle, so that leaves us with only one option better than a shotgun—a bunch of shotguns."

"All this hullabaloo is heavy," Cherijo complained.

"And every pound will be worth it if we walk out of this abandoned station into the sunlight again," Morris raid.

They walked down the street side by side, making no effort to hide their approach. It wouldn't have been possible, regardless. They were the only things moving in town.

The abandoned station was situated at the end of town nearest the church and the school, as far from the saloon and the jail as you could get and still be in High Rock proper. Now that it had fallen out of use with the coach lines and post office in the new depot, it stood alone and abandoned, slowly falling into disrepair.

"It looks like one good sneeze could blow this whole mess down," Morris said, pointing at the boarded-up windows, high roofline, and sagging walls. He stepped up to the front door. "Let's see what lies within. I reckon the door is probably locked?"

"I wouldn't know, Mr. Morris," Cherijo replied. "I am not in the habit of going into closed down businesses snooping around."

"You ought try it, Mrs. Starnes," the lanky cowboy said. "It's a lot of fun. Now let's just give this a tug, knowing full well that it won't...oh." Morris's words trailed off as he put a hand on the knob and pulled.

The door swung outward, opening a dark mouth into the belly of the station. Cherijo could only see clearly a few feet in past the entrance, and she had a hazy view of the rest of the interior, which seemed empty from where they stood. Morris looked at the door, perplexed.

"Well, that's ominous," he said, drawing his pistol.

Cherijo cocked both hammers on the shotgun in her hands, keeping the barrel pointed at the floor as Morris slipped inside the building and almost immediately vanished in the darkness. She followed him inside, stopping just inside the door to let her eyes adjust to the near-blackness. She felt a tug on her sleeve and stepped to the right, then pulled the door closed behind her.

"Good," Morris said. "No point standing right there in the doorway so everything knows exactly where you are."

"We already know," came a hissing voice that seemed to originate from all around them, curling around them like a venomous snake.

Cherijo whirled around, bringing her shotgun up to her shoulder, but there was nothing to shoot. Nothing but Morris, who put a hand on the barrel of her gun and gently pointed it up toward the rafters. Her gaze followed, and as her eyes adjusted to the darkness, she began to make out shapes in the gloom.

As her vision cleared, Cherijo was able to pick out more and more details and she gasped as she realized they were *all there.* Everyone from High Rock dangled from the rafters upside down, their feet hooked over the thick wooden beams, eyes closed as if they were in the deepest of sleeps. Which, after a fashion, they were. The very deepest sleep imaginable.

Except for one. One pair of eyes was wide open and staring straight at her. She recognized the look in those eyes. Hunger. Then every set of eyes above her opened in unison, and the world erupted into noise and movement and terror.

A clap of thunder from her left, a flash of red lightning, and when she saw Miss Gina Bredlove's head explode, she realized that Morris had started shooting. Then she saw Peter Montague, the ruddy-faced piano player and part-time faro dealer at the Gold Coast, running at her with fangs bared, and she pulled the trigger on one barrel of her twelve-gauge without even realizing she'd done it. Peter Montague realized it, though, because the buckshot caught him right in the throat at close range, decapitating him.

Cherijo screamed as the blood and bone shards sprayed her, but she had no time to consider what she'd done. There were too many of the monsters, too many of the people she once thought of as neighbors, to allow for thought of any kind. Thinking was something to be done when the shooting was over.

And there was a lot of shooting. Cherijo blew the head off a young man she recognized as one of the porters from the train station. Then she smashed her empty shotgun upside the head of Sally Deacon, a beautiful olive-skinned girl from the Gold Coast with a dazzling smile but cold eyes. She pulled another gun off her shoulder and put one shell through the eyes of Reggie Beckdoll, former mayor of High Rock and town barber. Right behind him came his wife Anna Marie, and she got the other shell in her face.

"I'm down to one scattergun," she called to Morris.

The lean man didn't reply, just stood in one place calmly putting bullets through the gleaming eyes of hungry monsters. She saw him click empty on a gun in his left hand, and without hesitation, drop that pistol, draw another, cock it, and fire without missing a beat in the symphony of death he was conducting. She pulled her last shotgun off her shoulder, fired twice at the nearest vampires, then threw the empty gun at another as she drew her pistol.

With a shotgun, she felt confident that she could mostly hit what she was aiming at. But a six-shooter? Between the darkness and the gun smoke, she couldn't see more than a few feet in any direction. But she didn't have to, because vampires swarmed all around them both. She stretched out her right arm, and the gun pressed up against the forehead of a big Black man she knew as Newt, who worked for Lucas Bander, the blacksmith. Even she couldn't miss from half an inch away, and when she pulled the trigger, the back of Newt's head turned into red mist.

She spun, fired, ducked under grabbing hands, popped back up, jammed her gun under the chin of a white-haired woman she vaguely recognized as someone who sang in the church choir, and blew the top of her skull off. But all too soon there was no more thunder, no more lightning belching from the barrel of her purloined Colt, only the *click-click-click* of a pistol hitting on spent bullets as she cocked and squeezed, cocked and squeezed, until a hand reached over and pushed the pistol down.

"It's over," Morris said. "Look."

She did look then, and as her eyes washed over the bodies of people she'd known, people she'd done business with, the gorge rose in her throat and the contents of her stomach joined the mess on the floor. Morris held her hair back until she was finished, then patted her on the back.

"All done?" he asked.

She nodded, her stomach still threatening, but empty.

"Good, because that was the appetizer. He's the main course." She followed Morris's outstretched arm to see a skeletally thin man leaning up against a beam, watching them.

"Hello, Quincy Morris," said the vampire. "Been a while." The man's voice was familiar, but Cherijo was certain she'd never seen him before.

"Hello, Charles," Morris replied. "It has indeed. You've been busy."

"Didn't have to be like this," the vampire named Charles said. "You could have joined me. Then all these people would still be alive."

"You're a liar," Morris said. "You've done nothing but sow death and destruction everywhere you've gone since you were turned."

The vampire nodded. "That's true, but the only reason I sowed it here was because I was chasing you. If you'd let me catch you down in Colorado, this could have been over months ago."

"If you'd let me put a bullet in your face in Texas, we could have been finished months before that," Morris replied. The lanky man never took his eyes off the vampire, but he emptied the cylinder of his pistol and slid six fresh bullets into the gun. Cherijo tried to do the same, but she found she couldn't watch the drama before her and load her gun at the same time, so she holstered her pistol and picked up one of the discarded shotguns. Not only was she more effective with the broader spread, but she could reload a double-barreled shotgun with her eyes closed and one hand tied behind her back.

The vampire's eyes flicked over to her, and he smiled. This time when he spoke, it was in Dino's voice, a voice that chilled her to the bone. "I'm sorry, Mrs. Starnes, I tried to fight them bad men off, but I wasn't strong enough. They ripped me and Mama to pieces. Didn't even turn us. Said we wasn't good enough to run with them. But that bossman, he sure did like the way I screamed."

The vampire's cold smile stopped well short of its eyes as he said, "I did, too. Love the way your hired man screamed. Too bad his mother died so quick."

"You son of a mangy dog!" Cherijo yelled, swinging her gun up. Both barrels barked, but the vampire moved faster than she could see.

"I'm not a fledgling," came a voice from right beside her ear. "You won't catch me that easily."

Then came an immense pressure on the side of her neck as the vampire tried to sink its teeth deep into the artery there. The pain was incredible as the monster bore down on her throat, but Cherijo had been expecting pain. She'd known pain was in the offing from the moment she dragged a bloody stranger into her house the night before, and if there was anything her life had prepared her for, it was coping with pain. So her neck hurt, but she knew the leather belts wrapped around her throat were keeping the monster at bay, for a few seconds at least.

And a few seconds was all she needed. The vampire drew back in confusion at his blunted attack, and Cherijo whirled around, drawing a derringer from a sash around her waist. She pressed the little pistol to the creature's left eye and pulled the trigger, cocked, and fired again. Two small bullets smashed into the monster's brain, and without enough power to blow through the back of its skull, the bullets just rattled around inside the vampire's head, turning its brain to pudding. The monster dropped straight down to its knees, then toppled over, truly dead.

"Well, I'll be darned," Morris said from beside her. "I almost can't believe that worked."

"You said he was a prideful creature," Cherijo reminded him. "That he would want nothing more than to destroy me to hurt you, to prove to you not only that you couldn't beat him, but that you couldn't protect anyone, either. So using me as bait made perfect sense."

"There's a lot of things in this world that make sense, Mrs. Starnes, but they seldom work out how we intend."

"Well, that's as may be, Mr. Morris," Cherijo replied. "But this time it worked out. For us, at least." She let her gaze drift across the dozens of townsfolk that lay dead on the floor, their brains blown out by her or Quincy. *Here lies High Rock*, she thought. *It was a good town, once.*

"What now?" she asked.

"What do you mean, what now?"

"I mean, where are you going now? And where am I going? There's nothing for me here. There's pretty much not even a 'here' anymore. So what's next?"

"Are you asking to join up with a vampire-hunting cowboy, Mrs. Starnes?" Quincy asked.

She thought for a brief second about her farm, her little house, her old life. Then she nodded. She could take her memories with her, but her life in High Rock was as dead as the bodies piled at her feet. "Yes, Mr. Morris, I reckon I am."

THICKER THAN WATER

CARRIE HARRIS

The mugs at Barley's Waterin' Hole looked like they'd been cleaned with old tobacco spit, but when you're the youngest of five brothers, and the older four tell you to fetch a round or take a beating, you do as you're told. I bellied up to the bar and placed my order. Used my manners and everything. Didn't impress Old Barley, though. He probably couldn't hear me through all the hair sticking out his ears.

"You're a pretty one, ain't you?" croaked the woman to my left.

I might have said the same to her, but hard living and even harder drinking had made their mark. When she smiled at me, there were more gaps than teeth. But my mam had raised me to be a gentleman, and I held onto those lessons with every bit of gumption I could scrape up. They were all I had left of her.

I touched my fingers to the tip of my hat.

"Ma'am," I said.

"Yer one of those McDonald boys, ain't you?" she asked.

Our reputation had preceded us. I didn't like that one bit. These days, I did a lot of lookin' over my shoulder, if you know what I mean.

"Spencer McDonald, at your service. Folks call me Specs, on account of the glasses," I replied.

"I heard you McDonalds were all giants, but yer a cute little thing."

The words took me back. On her deathbed, Mam had called me in special. She was the giant of my childhood, a sturdy woman who could whip up a mean cornbread, then turn around and scare off a wannabe poacher with a well-placed shot from Old Glory, her prized rifle. Many a man had ran off with a hole in his trousers, close enough to his privates to give a fellow a chill just thinking about it. But the illness had robbed her of her sharpshooting abilities and her round toughness. That day, she'd barely tented the sheets.

"Spencer, Lord knows I love your brothers, but they're idjits. When I'm gone, it'll be up to you to keep their heads out the noose," she'd said.

It was an impossible task. I had book learnin' aplenty, but the only use they had for books was to wipe after sitting a spell in the privy. They wouldn't listen to the likes of me. But I agreed anyway, because that was what you did when your Mam was dying, and I been trying to keep my word ever since. It had been six months. Longer than I expected to last, but my luck was slipping.

"Specs! You coming with those beers or what?" snapped Big Man, my oldest brother.

"Hold yer horses. Old Barley is drawin' 'em up now," I said, hoping to avoid a scene.

"If I have to get up, somebody's gonna be takin' a dip in the horse trough," said Loco. We called him that because he hit as hard as a locomotive, and also, he was crazy. He thought trying to drown me was good entertainment.

The rest of the boys laughed, all mean like. Ever since they killed the stationmaster and robbed the train coming into Shelter

City, they'd been on edge. I'd hoped the money would slake their thirst, but it only made 'em meaner.

"Barley, can you shake a tail feather?" I said. "My brothers get a little hot under the collar when they're thirsty."

"Barley!" shouted the gap-toothed woman, rapping on the counter to get his attention. He looked over, and she held five fingers up. At that, the man quit puttering around and began to draw them. "He's stone deaf, the old coot."

"Thank you, ma'am," I said, and I meant it. She'd probably saved me a swim. "Can I offer you a drink?"

She beamed. "Why, that's mighty kind of you. I'll take you up on it."

Another rap. Another flash of the fingers. Old Barley moved fast once he'd gotten the message, and I began to deliver the grimy mugs over to the table. When the final pair arrived, I slid one over to my savior and tilted my hat at her again.

"You have a good night now, ma'am," I said.

"Wait." She grabbed my arm and pulled me close. For a horrified moment, I thought she'd taken my kindness the wrong way and intended to plant a kiss on me, but instead, she whispered in my ear. "You didn't hear this from me, but that train in Shelter City? It belonged to the likes of Chester Grantholm, and he's got his ladies lookin' for you and your brothers. Somethin' tells me that ain't gonna end well. Those scoundrels aren't worth their weight in piss, but yer a good boy. I'd hate to see you come to a bad end."

The news made my throat so dry that I took a big swig of my beer without gagging. I knew it! I'd told them! But they didn't listen to the likes of me.

"Maybe it's time for us to get out of Memphis. See the sights a bit," I said.

She nodded in approval. "The sooner, the better."

———————————————————

There was just one problem with this plan: my brothers were idjits. They ignored my attempts to coax them out of their stools, and when I flat out told them that Grantholm's posse was probably on their way this very minute to shoot us full of holes, they laughed. Then Romeo made a lewd gesture with his hand over his crotch.

I couldn't force the issue, so I did the next best thing. I started pouring beer down their throats as fast as they could drink. It would take a lot to knock them out, but then I could pile them into a wagon and skedaddle. Some folks would call me a coward for that, but it's only common sense. My mam used to work for Chester Grantholm, and he only hired the best. Once she'd realized I wasn't an idjit, she taught me a thing or two. So I knew what we were facing, and I also knew that my brothers didn't stand a chance. By the time they took the threat seriously, they'd already be dead.

The drink took Romeo down first. One minute, he was laughing at some stupid joke, and the next, he slid onto the floor. Slick put his feet right on Romeo's ribs before draining another mug.

"Tell you what," I said. "I'll go find a wagon. We'll dump Romeo in it."

"And then drive it out of town and leave him there for the coyotes. He'll piss himself when he wakes up!" crowed Loco. "Maybe you aren't such a stiff after all, Specs."

I forced a chuckle and made my escape before Loco could "improve" upon my plan. Bright sunlight stabbed at my eyes as I pushed through the doors, and the dust hanging in the air made me cough something wicked. A horse trotted on by, kicking up more of the stuff. Annoying, but I said nothin'. Last thing I needed was more trouble to heap on top of the mess we was already in. I needed a wagon yesterday.

A man rolled by in an empty cart with open-slatted sides, but that wouldn't do. Carting around a quartet of unconscious murderers in plain sight would attract the kind of attention I was desperate to avoid. I needed something that would hide them. Heck, even the stinking corpse cart across the street would be a better choice. As I watched, the driver tugged his kerchief off his face before heading inside the general store across the way. It was a prime opportunity, but my brothers would kill me for piling them in with all them bodies.

As I hesitated, a trio of women turned the corner at the end of the street. They were the kind of dames a man dreamed about, except in my case, those dreams were nightmares. They all had curves in the right places, and you could see 'em real good too, because not a one wore a skirt. No, they were all in black, light-gulping leather trousers and vests over bright silk blouses. Red, blue, and green. Twin holsters sat on rounded hips as they strolled toward Barley's with the confident slink of predators on the track of wounded prey.

I hadn't been personally introduced, but it didn't take much in the way of brains to put two and two together. Grantholm's posse was all female, all pretty, and more lethal than a nest of angry rattlers. I didn't need no introduction to know these gals were his, and in all likelihood, they were lookin' for us.

Although my brothers thought me a coward, I could shoot better than all of them put together thanks to Mam's lessons. But the odds didn't please me none. My brothers were stubborn and none too smart to boot, so negotiating was right off the table. If I was gonna keep them alive, we needed to go. Now.

The posse hadn't clocked me yet. So I strolled across the street as casual as you please, pulling my kerchief out of my pocket and tying it over my face just like the gent with the corpse cart. As I got closer, I had a nice whiff of the bodies in the back. At least one of them had gone to rot, a sad scrap of flesh on the top that had been picked apart something awful by scavengers. Other than a few bits of fur, there wasn't much clue as to what it had been.

Most of the small, sad pile was animals too far decayed to be eaten or skinned, but sticking out the bottom was a human hand, all waxy and fake looking. But I knew it was real. I seen enough death in my time.

I climbed up onto the seat and took the reins, noting with relief that Grantholm's posse had gone into some establishment down the street. They'd be thorough until someone told them about the idjits currently drinking themselves into a stupor at Barley's. Then they'd be at the door lickety-split. I intended to be gone by then.

With a cluck of my tongue and a flick of the reins, I directed the cart around back. Nobody stopped me, but I knew that luck wouldn't hold. As quick as I could, I tied the reins down outside Barley's back door and hurried inside. Loco and Slick had joined Romeo on the floor, leaving the Big Man to soldier on. He was methodically working his way through the dregs left on the table and rubbing his slobber all over a drab in a flouncy dress.

"Help me get them out to the cart," I said, not really holding out much hope that he'd listen.

He grunted and went back to his kisses. I had no time to argue. I hoisted Romeo over my shoulder and lugged him out the back door. When I threw him on top of the bodies, I didn't feel a lick of guilt, neither.

I got Slick out the door and onto the cart without much problem. But as I was struggling with Loco, the door swung open, and in came the posse. I dragged Loco out of sight none too gently, hoping they wouldn't recognize Big Man. But the lady on his lap must not have been as pleased with his attentions as she'd seemed. She caught the eye of the gal in blue, who seemed to be the leader of the group, and nodded all significant-like.

"Benedict McDonald," said the blue-shirted woman, her left hand resting idly on her holster while the right sat on the curve of her waist. "My employer wants to talk to you."

"Wait 'til I'm done with thissun," slurred my brother. "There's enough of the Big Man to go 'round."

"I'm not askin'," she responded.

I hesitated. Showing myself now would only get us all captured. If I was smart, I'd cut and run, but the thought of leaving Big Man behind rankled something awful. After all, I'd promised. I thumbed the grip of the Peacemaker Mam gave me and thought like blazes, but I couldn't come up with a devious plan right on the spot. There wasn't a handy chandelier to drop on them or nothing.

The girl quick-drew her pistol in a blur, pointing it at him, and my brother grinned like she was flirtin'. Idjit. I stepped out into the main room, noting the stillness. Everyone who could flee already had. A few folks huddled behind the bar with Old Barley, who clutched an ancient rifle in his hands. I gave him what I hoped was a reassuring look. Last thing I needed was to take a bullet to the back from a panicking deaf man. But the woman who had warned me crouched next to him, and I trusted her to keep him off my back.

"Did you know Caroline McDonald?" I blurted, turning my attention back to the posse.

The lady frowned at me, her gun unwavering.

"She worked for Chester Grantholm about seven years back," I prompted.

"That was about when I joined up. She taught me to shoot. What about her?"

"That's my mam. And his." I nodded to Big Man, who mercifully kept his trap shut. "She taught me too. I could have put one between your eyes before you even realized I was here."

She paused thoughtfully, then nodded.

"I suppose. If you are who you say you are," she allowed. "Prove it."

"When a man got fresh with her, Mam would shoot a hole right in his trousers. As far as I know, she never took a man's ballocks, but she'd come close enough that they'd leave her alone."

A ghost of a smile flitted over the girl's face.

"She did once. He deserved it too." A flicker of uncertainty crossed her eyes. "I don't like the thought of shooting her brats dead, but Mr. Grantholm won't just let this go. Even if you walk out of here, he'll hound you to your grave. It's nothing personal. The minute he lets you go, he'll have everyone thinking they can walk all over him."

"I don't want Mr. Grantholm as an enemy. If we'd known we was robbing him, we would have steered clear. We already spent some of the money, but here's what I got left."

I set a jingling pouch on the table between us, and she gave it a considerin' look. Maybe we could have come to some arrangement if not for my brother.

"You ain't giving away my money!" he thundered, flinging the girl from his lap and grabbing at the pouch.

The lady's gun went off, deafening in the small room. Warm liquid splattered me. My brother's blood tasted coppery in my mouth. I drew without even realizing it and fired. A perfect round hole appeared right between her pretty eyes. Her finger spasmed convulsively, squeezing off another shot as she toppled backwards.

I could hear Mam in my ears, as clear as if she'd been standing next to me.

"Don't stand still. Make them try and figure out where you'll be. It's harder to blow you to bits that way," she said.

I threw myself to the side just in time. The table exploded into a shower of splinters. I came up shooting, blowing the shooter in green to kingdom come. Then I whipped my gun around, ready to face the third one, but there was only a blank space next to the door. She'd buggered out. Probably intended to circle around back.

She'd find my brothers. I leaned down to check on Big Man, but I didn't need to look twice to know he was dead. Most folks don't go on livin' without half their head. If I'd had the time, I coulda decided how I felt about that, but I could only manage a murmured prayer as I grabbed up the cash and rushed out.

The final lady stood next to the corpse wagon, her hand hovering over her sidearm. Only cowards shoot folks in the back, but I couldn't afford to get into a lengthy battle. It only took a single bullet to take her out, and she never even saw me coming.

I tore the reins free, leaped into the wagon, and left like the hounds of hell themselves were on my tail. It weren't too far from the truth.

It was only a matter of time before Grantholm's people mounted a full-on search, and they'd be inclined to shoot first and ask questions later. I took the side roads, trusting that the wagon's stench would keep most folks at bay. It worked better than I expected. At one point, a sweating craftsman flagged me down to drop the corpse of his dog on top of Loco. I should have felt guiltier about that than I did, but I didn't even move the body off him.

My plan was going so swell that I started to relax. But of course, that's when disaster struck. One of the axles on the wagon let go with a loud snap that startled the horse. He reared back, front hooves pawing the air in fear and anger, and it took a minute for me to settle him. When I slid from the cockeyed seat to survey the damage, I near on panicked too. This wasn't the kind of break that could be jury-rigged long enough to get us out of town.

I looked around hopefully for another wagon, but no dice. The cramped back alley I'd been driving down was cluttered with boxes and barrels, acting as storage for the storefronts beyond. Nobody drove back here if they could help it.

The door to my right opened, startling me so bad I nearly drew. But the woman who entered the alley wasn't one of Grantholm's. She was dressed in a right funny manner, though. Her skirts glittered with all kinds of trinkets sewn right to them, and matching gold hoops hung from her ears. The sleeves of her blouse showed off impressive muscles. Reminded me of Mam. She had something of Mam's confidence, too. She eyed my floating gun hand with amusement, as if to tell me to shit or get off the pot already. I dropped it, tipping my hat to her.

"Ma'am," I said.

"If you're looking to loot, I wouldn't bother. Most 'o the stuff back here is empty," she said.

"Not at all. I was taking a shortcut, and my wagon here broke down. You wouldn't know where I could hire another one, wouldya? My brothers need a ride. They're alive and breathin', just in their cups."

I lifted Romeo up to illustrate. As if on cue, he let out a prodigious snort. The lady looked equal parts amused and horrified.

"You put them in with the corpses?" she exclaimed.

"I'm the youngest of five," I said with a shrug. It was the truth, even if it weren't all of it. "They've done put me through a lot over the years. Let's call it payback."

Her mouth twitched.

"Fair enough. Where y'all going?"

"Anywhere but here. I'm willing to pay."

"Willing to travel by steamboat?"

"I'd be interested," I said cautiously. "You know somebody with a craft for hire?"

"Me." She bowed with a flourish. "Captain Scarlett Leroux, at your service. My boat is the *River Lady*, and if your coin is right, I'll take you anywhere with a port."

"Specs McDonald. Let's get down to hagglin', then," I said.

I talked her down just a bit, because I didn't want to rouse her suspicions. My poker face must have needed some work, though, because once we'd settled on a price, she said, "You know, we could put you all into some of these here empty barrels if you need to get out of town without being seen." When I turned to stare her down, she didn't so much as flinch. Instead, she laughed. "Come on. We both know you don't pile your relatives up with a bunch of corpses unless you're desperate. I don't care how mean they are."

"No, I suppose not." I sighed. "If you get us to the steamboat safe, I'll toss in a little extra."

"Aye aye, Specs," she said.

Trusting Scarlett was a risk, but it paid off. Maybe I had a knack at reading folks too. She opened my barrel somewhere in the depths of the *River Lady*. Crates and barrels were stacked all round, lashed to the walls with sturdy rope. I could hear the great steam engine clinking and clanking, and the creak of the wood as the craft rocked to and fro. It took me a minute to find my sea legs, but I adjusted. I hadn't been on many boats and didn't know much about 'em, but I'd always enjoyed the experience.

"Thanks much, ma'am," I said, dipping into my money pouch and handing over a little extra like I'd promised.

"I'll help you uncork the rest of them. I bet they could use a little airing out," she offered.

We made quick work of opening the other barrels but left my brothers to sleep it off. It wouldn't be too long before they were awake and ornery, and I figured I'd better warn her.

"Can we have this compartment to ourselves?" I asked. "Or will you have other passengers?"

"At the price you're paying, it's all yours," she said. "As long as you're happy with it?"

"Oh, it's fine. It's just...well, my brothers are idjits."

"I remember you saying as much."

"I'll try to keep them under control, but I want to be clear that I'll cover any damage or insult. I just want to get out of town."

"With the likes of Chester Grantholm on your tail, I don't blame you," she said.

I froze, my heart sinking. I shoulda known it wouldn't be that easy.

"How'd you know about that?" I demanded.

"His ladies put your description around. Didn't take much to put two and two together."

"But you offered us a ride. Either you've got it out for Mr. Grantholm or you're planning to sell us out. Which is it?" I sighed. "Not like I'm in much of a position to do something about it anyhow."

"I believe in second chances." She echoed my sigh. "And I know what it's like to have stupid siblings."

I snorted. "Yours can't be half as bad as mine."

"You wouldn't believe me if I told you. Look, I won't stick my neck out for you, but I won't go out of my way to hand you over, neither."

It was the best I was gonna get, and honestly more than I'd hoped for.

"I 'preciate it. I know that don't matter half as much as the money, but I mean it."

She offered me a ghost of a smile.

"And that, Specs, is the only reason you're on this boat."

Romeo came to first. I didn't have to explain nothing to him 'cause he was too busy vomiting. Slick and Loco woke at approximately the same time and shook me around a bit, demanding to know what had happened. My summary of the past few hours only served to piss them off. Loco kept insisting that I'd lied and left Big Man behind on purpose. No amount of evidence would sway them. I pointed out the spray of blood on my shirt and the stench on their clothes from the corpse wagon, but they refused to listen.

"We're gettin' outta here," proclaimed Loco. "Let's force that captain to turn around so we can pick Big Man up."

"I'll sweet talk her," offered Romeo. Then he bent over his bucket and puked again.

"Big Man is dead," I said flatly, for what felt like the hundredth time.

"Shut yer mouth!" said Loco, his voice all high.

That wasn't a good sign. Loco usually only talked like that before one of his episodes. You never knew what he was gonna do when he snapped, but it weren't good. Trying to talk him down only made things worse, but sometimes you could distract him. I looked around the cabin. Dried jerky and beans weren't gonna cut it, but I tried anyway.

"Anybody want some grub?" I asked. "There's plenty to eat down here."

"There ain't even nothin' worth stealing," grumbled Slick.

"No? Have you looked?" I prompted.

"Yeah, I looked. It's junk. Unless you think yer gonna make a killing in the dried meat business," he said, snickering.

Loco just shifted from foot to foot, clenching and unclenching his hands. He was close to snapping alright.

"What about that door at the back?" I said, somewhat desperately.

It had a padlock on it the size of both my fists put together, so I figured it was safe to point them at it. Loco could hit it a few times. It would hold.

But I'd underestimated the size of his anger.

"Big Man's fine. We're gonna get him, and yer gonna apologize right to his face. Then I'm gonna string you up and drag you clear to California, you traitor," he said, real quiet like.

Then he launched himself furiously at the door, hitting it like a cannonball. The door gave way with a crackle of wood. My stomach sank. Scarlett had locked that room up for a reason. I just hoped I had enough cash left to cover whatever my brothers were about to steal or destroy. I couldn't see through the opening from this angle.

"Well, well, what do we have here?" cooed Loco.

I tried for the doorway, but Romeo shoved me so hard on his way past that I went sprawling on the floor. Then Slick kicked me in the ribs and followed Romeo. I grunted, trying to marshal my anger. Some days, I just wanted to put a bullet in them. But I'd promised.

It took me a few moments to get to my feet. It had been a long and miserable day, after all. But when I finally peered round the door frame, the sight that greeted me made no sense. Each of my brothers was cozied up…to a pretty lady? What were pretty ladies doing locked in the belly of a steamship?

Loco let out a choked noise, and I looked a little closer. He was kissing his girl already, even without exchanging names or nothin'. But his hands was balled up into fists, and they beat weakly at her sides. Her hair covered his face, wet and dripping. At first, that made me worried that there was a leak, and maybe that was why the room had been locked, but the rest of the place was dry.

"What the…?" I said.

The noise caught her attention. She looked at me, and I swear on my mam's memory, her eyes glowed like dim lights in swampy water. Rivulets ran down her face, like they come straight out of her skin. Her hair moved all on its own. Blood ran from her pointy-toothed maw. She'd chewed Loco's mouth clean off, and now her hair was chokin' him to death.

My gun was in my hand before I even realized I drew it. I emptied the barrel at her, faster than I ever shot in my life. It weren't my best aiming, but I hit her. I know I did; I saw the spray. But she just hissed at me and turned back to her meal. In the room beyond, two more like her fed on Romeo and Slick. The slurping, wet noises echoed in the small chamber, making me shudder.

"What in Sam Hill is going on down here?" yelled Scarlett from somewhere behind me. "Don't you know not to fire a gun on a steamboat? You'll kill us all!"

"They're killing my brothers!" I shrieked, overcome by panic.

With an unladylike oath, she grabbed me by the collar and

yanked me across the floor, pulling me out of the room. I struggled some, but she weren't a weak woman, and I really didn't want to go back in there again anyhow. What I'd seen was already branded onto my brain.

"We gotta get out of here!" I exclaimed.

"No use," said Scarlett. She stopped at the foot of the stairs and hung her head. "I barely got them in there in the first place. Now that they're out, they'll run through the boat until nobody's left. They're slow right now, on account of they haven't eaten in a while. But once they get their strength up, they're mighty fast."

"What are they?!"

"My sisters." I recoiled, and she clucked her tongue at me. "I thought you of all people would understand. From what I heard, your brothers are monsters too. Mine are just...more literal, I guess."

I couldn't say anything to that. I knew my brothers were awful people, and I didn't feel the kind of grief you'd expect, knowing that they was dying right now. They'd killed all the love I ever had for them, but I'd still stayed loyal. As much as I wanted to blame that on my promise, it was at least partly me. After all, blood is thicker than water.

I nodded, the panic draining from me under the comfort of familiar familial obligation.

"Yeah," I said. "I guess I do understand. Can't you...talk 'em down?"

"They don't seem to care. I just wanted to keep 'em from killing innocent folks, but it's been harder than I expected."

The wet, drinking sounds from inside the chamber had begun to ebb. I knew what that meant. They'd be coming for us soon. We had to do something. Maybe Scarlett was ready to give up, but I wasn't.

"You got chains?" I asked. "We could hook 'em up to those rings on the wall there."

"You've got to get close for that. They'll eat you."

"We'll need to work together then. You hide. They come out to feed on me, and you sneak up behind them."

My voice shook when I said it, but I couldn't think of no other way. It was either that, or we all died. After a moment, Scarlett took a deep breath.

"Okay," she said. "We should at least try."

She fetched the chains. We set them out, laying them in the shadows that clustered around the edges of the room. Hopefully Scarlett's sisters would be so intent on their next meal that they wouldn't notice.

We got set up just in the nick of time. Scarlett backed into a corner just as the first of her sisters appeared in the doorway, a pool of bloody water gathering at her feet.

She smiled at me. Despite her wet and bedraggled condition, she'd been a pretty girl once. I could see how my brothers would have waltzed right in, thinking they'd won the pot when they seen her. I smiled back, trying to resist the urge to run screaming for the stairs.

"Listen," I said, "we can be friends. You ate my brothers, but I don't hold it against you none."

She laughed at me, a wet gurgle rising from her throat.

"Bargain as much as you want, boy," she said. "The fear makes the flesh sweeter."

That made my heart stop for just a minute, and then it began racing so hard it was a wonder it didn't hop right out of my chest. But I kept on talking, hoping that Scarlett would make a move soon, before her sister showed her teeth.

"What do you want?" I asked, gulping against the lump in my throat. "I got money. Just let me go, and I'll pay you."

A soft clank from the corner suggested that Scarlet had made her first move. The sister hadn't noticed yet, but those chains weren't going to be quiet. I had to cover up the noise, so I threw myself on the ground, begging like I used to do when I was just a boy and my brothers used to bury me in the back field for fun.

"Please!" I demanded, with as much wailing and hollering as I could manage. "I'll do anything. I don't want to die! Have mercy!"

The sister leaned down toward me, cruel delight on her pretty, sodden face. But the emotion vanished in a flash when the manacle closed around her wrist, the bolt snapping shut. I scrambled backward just in time. She lunged at me, the restraint pulling her back seconds before her teeth closed on my arm.

One down, two to go.

They came out hissing like angry tomcats. Scarlett snagged the first one, clamping a manacle on her forearm. But the sister turned on her, driving her down to the floor. I would have gone to help, but the third sister was on me already, her hair winding round my neck. I whipped out my knife and began to saw at it, making her bare those pointy teeth in a screech of fury. She darted down at me like she wanted to bite my face off. I barely got my arm up in time to hold her at bay. Her teeth snapped shut just shy of my nose. Brackish water pattered down into my face.

She didn't like me playing with her hair, so I grabbed on with my free hand and yanked as hard as I could. The hair ensnared my hand, but she shrieked again like a hot teakettle, so I pulled again. A few strands ripped free and went limp in my palm, all their eldritch energy fading away. I grabbed and pulled again, my confidence growing.

But the sister lunged at me again, taking me by surprise and grazing my cheek with those razor-sharp teeth. I grunted with pain and effort, trying to drive her back, but there was no use. She was inhumanly strong, and she had the upper hand. Grinning, her face dipped down, closer and closer.

"Say goodnight, little morsel," she said.

I didn't say nothin'. I wouldn't give her the satisfaction.

She darted down toward me. Just before her teeth closed on my flesh, a manacle clanked closed around her neck, and Scarlett pulled her off me with a yank of the chain.

I scrambled backward, a wild and panicked retreat. But after a while, my heart slowed, and I could think again. My sense returned, I surveyed the situation: three very angry river creatures, chained to a panel on the wall used to bolt down heavy cargo. Scarlett, bleeding from a long scratch along one arm, but otherwise intact.

We'd triumphed.

But my brothers had paid the price.

I made my shaky way to my feet. My gorge tried to rise, but I pushed it down. I had a responsibility now. Maybe I hadn't loved my brothers, but I couldn't just waltz away like nothin' happened.

"Here's what we're gonna do," I said slowly, thinkin' with all my might. "I'm sailing with you now. We're gonna find out what happened to your sisters and cure them if we can. If they need feeding, no innocents. Murderers and brigands only. At least we can live with ourselves that way. But we keep them hungry so they're a little easier to deal with."

Scarlett stared at me for a moment, shocked. Then she said, "Steamboats don't sail, Specs."

"You know what I meant," I grumbled.

"Why are you helping me?" she blurted.

"Just like you said," I responded. "Blood is thicker than water. Mebbe it's too late for my siblings, but it's not too late for yours. You could have them back."

She stared at me a while longer, like she couldn't believe what she was seeing. Honest, I couldn't believe it myself. But something told me my mam would be proud of me. She'd never backed down from a challenge, and I wouldn't neither.

"And if not, at least we'll know we tried?" She nodded, answering her own question. "You're a good man, Specs McDonald."

"I keep my promises. I promise we'll try everything."

And I meant it.

BARNFEATHER'S MAGICAL MEDICINE SHOW AND TENT EXTRAVAGANZA

JEFFREY J. MARIOTTE

"Step right up, boys and girls, ladies and gents! Don't be shy! Gather 'round! Come on in where you can see the entertainment we have devised for you tonight!"

Young Samuel Beaton's eyes were the size of the saucers in his mother's china hutch, his father thought.

"My name is Eustace T. Barnfeather," the hawker continued, "but some folks simply refer to me as the Dancin' Fool, because that's what I like to do. Some prestidigitation, some music and dance, and before you leave our tent tonight, you will have the opportunity of a lifetime—the opportunity to acquire for yourself some of Barnfeather's Miracle Elixir! Come in, come in, the extravaganza will begin momentarily!"

James Beaton had brought his family to the tent show under protest—he thought such things were foolish, the elixirs one could purchase nonsensical wastes of good money, and the entire event unsuitable for children. But Samuel and his older brother Thomas, who played at being unimpressed by anything and everything, had made such a fuss as soon as the circulars had been posted in town, and finally Maggie had persuaded

James that it couldn't hurt. She had, since the moment they met, been able to convince James of just about anything, including moving halfway across the country to Pine Glen, Arizona Territory and opening a boot and shoe store there.

Most of Pine Glen had made the same decision, James saw. The tent quickly filled with familiar faces. Samuel and Thomas darted toward the front, close to the stage. When Maggie started after them, James took her arm and restrained her. "Not too close," he whispered. "The boys are likely safe, but I wouldn't want to be splashed with whatever potion Barnswallow might produce. It's probably half acid and half lye."

"Barn*feather*," she corrected with a smile. She pushed a stray lock of copper hair back behind one ear and captured his gaze with her emerald eyes. "And I'm certain that you're wrong, but we can keep our distance if you prefer."

"Thank you, darling," he said.

The tent was enormous, its interior far larger than that of Pine Glen's biggest saloon. Brilliant lanterns hung from rafters over the stage and around the interior, burning with a steady, even brilliance. The interior of the tent seemed strangely shadowed or textured, but James was hemmed in and couldn't get close enough for a better look.

Barnfeather cleared his throat loudly several times, and the audience quieted. "What you're about to see is nothing less than a miracle, ladies and gentlemen. A true, honest-to-goodness miracle. I mentioned, I believe, that people far and near call me the Dancin' Fool, and it's the gospel truth. I dance. I love to dance. And the reason I love to dance, ladies and gents, is because I *can*. I couldn't always—oh, no. My legs were little old things when I was a boy, yellow and thin...like I had chicken blood in my veins! If the wind blew too hard I would topple right over like a stack of snap pea shells. But now I can dance, and so I will. Music, please!"

Musicians somewhere out of sight behind the stage began to play. After a few moments, James realized that to call them musicians was to pervert the meaning of the word beyond all reason, because what they performed sounded more like the noises that might result from a catfight in a henhouse. But a blissful smile settled on Barnfeather's face, and his feet began to move. They shifted side to side, at first, then one lifted off the wooden stage, came back down with a thump, and the other went up. Within moments he was prancing across the stage, feet tapping and sliding and then pushing him high into the air. He clicked his heels together three times before beginning to descend, and when his black shoes again touched down, he spun around several times.

Watching the performance, James was impressed in spite of himself. Barnfeather looked to be at least fifty years old, his long hair and beard the white of fluffy clouds on a sunny day. An enormous man with a belly so prominent as to be nearly spherical, he had to weigh three hundred pounds or more, but he spun and whirled and flipped like someone half his age and half his weight. And he did it all in perfect time to the music provided by those thankfully off-stage butchers.

When Barnfeather finished, he mopped sweat from his forehead with the back of one pudgy hand, grinned, and gave a deep bow. The audience applauded and cheered, the whistles and shouts so loud that they hurt James's ears. Unable to resist the enthusiasm, he joined in.

Barnfeather stood there, accepting it for a while, then motioned for quiet. As the audience stilled, Barnfeather seemed to notice something in the air. Then James saw it, and others did as well: a bee, buzzing around the performer. Barnfeather watched it silently for several moments, then reached out toward it, fingers spread as if to pluck it from the air. Finally, his hand darted toward it, fingers closing around it.

But instead of capturing a bee, that hand suddenly held a deck of cards, slightly larger than one would find in a saloon or gambling house. Whoops and cheers and whistles erupted again as Barnfeather fanned the deck out toward the audience members, so they could see the colors, suits, and numbers on the card faces.

"That's amazing!" Maggie said. "How does he do it?"

"Mirrors," James said with confidence he didn't really feel. He had been fully prepared to dislike the man and his show, but he had been won over.

On stage, Barnfeather seemingly made the cards dance in his hands, individual ones leaping into the air, flipping around, then landing back in the deck. At the applause, he took another bow, then said, "For my next trick, I'll need a helper." He scanned the crowd before him for a moment, then pointed at someone near the front. "You, young man. Step up here, please."

Maggie gripped James's arm as Samuel climbed awkwardly onto the wooden stage. "It's Sam!" she whispered.

"I know!"

Samuel appeared to be entranced by the man. Hampered only a little by his clubfoot, he walked toward Barnfeather, beaming. Barnfeather bent toward him and said, "What's your name, my friend?"

"Samuel," the boy said.

"Samuel. A fine name. Biblical. It is a pleasure to make your acquaintance, Samuel. Please, select any card from this deck."

He held the cards out toward the boy and Samuel closed his fingers around one. Barnfeather pulled the rest away, leaving the boy holding it. "Show your card to the audience, if you please," Barnfeather said.

Samuel turned it around so the crowd could see. As he did, Barnfeather said, "Ah, the ace of hearts! A fine card, fine. That one means you'll marry well, young Samuel. You'll find a wife as lovely and clever as your mother there." Saying that, he turned his gaze toward the crowd, fixed on Maggie.

Her grip on James's arm tightened. "How does he know?"

James could only shake his head. The boys had entered the tent ahead of them and dashed toward the front. At no point, he believed, had Barnfeather seen Maggie and him together with the boys. But there could be no confusion as to whom he fixed with his gaze. Others in the crowd had turned to look at her, too.

Barnfeather returned his attention to Samuel. "Now then, young man, please put the card into a pocket, if you have one. If not, tuck it under your shirt."

Samuel, slightly flustered, checked his trousers, then put the card under his shirt and held it there. Barnfeather nodded his approval. Then he faced the audience and started to shuffle the cards, but he seemed to lose his grip. The cards sprayed onto the stage, a few even flying into the crowd. "Oh, dear," Barnfeather said. "Clumsy of me."

He stooped, picked up one card, and glanced at it. Then, with an expression of shock, he turned the card toward the crowd.

It was the ace of hearts.

He picked up more cards, showed each to the audience. Each one was an ace of hearts. Sporadic applause and cheers grew into a cacophony as he showed more and more of them, every card in the deck now an ace of hearts, even the ones handed back by audience members. When he had every card back in the deck, he turned back to Samuel. "Your card, please."

Samuel fished the card from under his shirt and handed it over. Again, Barnfeather looked surprised. "Oh, my gracious," he said, flipping the card over for the crowd to see.

Now, Samuel's card was the queen of diamonds. "Astonishing, young Samuel!" Barnfeather did. "Look what you've done!"

Samuel's mouth dropped open when he saw his card, and his eyes grew wider than ever. When Barnfeather slipped the card back into his deck and fanned it for the audience once more—and every card had become a queen of diamonds—those eyes went wider still.

Barnfeather pocketed the cards, bent toward Samuel, and said, "I had no idea you were such a skilled magician, young sir. It's truly an honor to share a stage with you. In return for the favor of your presence, I'd like to give you something. There's absolutely no obligation on your part, naturally, except to give it a taste. Does that sound fair?"

Words wouldn't come to Samuel's mouth, but he nodded his agreement.

Barnfeather reached into the air again, and instead of cards, this time his right hand suddenly held a bottle of his elixir, and his left hand a spoon. "If you would be so kind, Master Samuel, as to tell our friends in the audience what you think of the flavor of Barnfeather's Miracle Elixir."

Samuel nodded again. Barnfeather poured a little into a spoon and held it to Samuel's lips. James clasped a hand over the one that Maggie still held his arm with. "Heaven knows what's in that," he whispered.

"I'm sure it can't hurt him," she said. "Likely it will have no effect at all."

Samuel sipped from the spoon. His face went through about a dozen different expressions in a matter of seconds, from disgust and revulsion to pleasure and finally something like love. He took the spoon in his hand and hungrily finished off what remained there, licking it when he was done.

"It's good?" Barnfeather asked.

"It's very good," Samuel said. "Very very very good. I ain't never tasted nothin' better."

Barnfeather again turned to face the audience. "There you have it, ladies and gentlemen, from the lips of one of your very own. There's nothing better than Barnfeather's."

As he spoke, a shocked murmur began to spread through the crowd. James, watching Samuel's face, didn't know what it was about at first. But then he heard the words "His foot!" James's gaze traveled down Samuel's body, down his legs, and finally to his feet, where he saw that the clubfoot the boy had suffered with his whole life was slowly correcting itself. By the time it stopped, he stood on the soles of two feet, his ankles straight for the first time.

The crowd went wild, and James went right along with them.

Once again, United States Marshal Charley Porter had arrived too late. Pine Glen was the closest Barnfeather's show had come to his office in Papingo—where he typically dealt with lawbreakers in and around Camp Huachuca—since he had heard of the goings-on. He had raced north through the Arizona Territory as quickly as he could, but even so, Barnfeather was gone before he arrived. Worse, a man and a boy of thirteen were dead, found on the site where Barnfeather's tent had stood only the night before. According to locals, the flesh on their bodies was singed, blackened in some spots, their eyeballs melted out of their heads, their hair reduced to crisp stubble. They had been buried immediately in the cemetery behind Pine Glen's only church, but enough people had seen them and talked about the sight that Porter had no trouble finding out about them.

After what he had heard, he desperately wanted a drink. But he knew where that led—one drink to another and then to a third, and then everything he had built these last few years would come crashing down around him. If he could resist the temptation to take the first, he would be fine. If he couldn't, however…well, he had to. No other choice.

He was sitting on a bench outside the small town's barber shop when he saw a woman start toward him from the other side of the street, holding up her black dress with both hands to keep it from scraping the dust. She was slender and handsome, her red, curly hair worn up, though a few coiled locks had escaped the pins she wore. Her face might have been beautiful if not for eyes puffy from tears and a nose red from blowing. Her lips were straight, her jaw set. She was determined to do something, and Porter guessed it involved him. From her apparel, he guessed she was the widow.

When she got nearer, he stood up and waited for her on the boardwalk. She stepped up, but it was high here, with no stairs, so Porter extended a hand. She took it, her grasp firm, and hoisted herself the rest of the way.

"Good afternoon, ma'am," he said.

She skipped the pleasantries. "Folks tell me you're a lawman."

"That's right. United States Marshal Charley Porter. Please call me Charley."

"Marshal," she said pointedly, "my name is Maggie Beaton. You may have heard that my husband and my older son were buried today."

"You have my deepest regrets, ma'am."

"Yes, well, nothing I can do about that. But my other son, the younger one—his name is Samuel. He's missing."

"Missing?" he repeated.

"That's right. He slipped out of the house three nights ago. We had come home late from a traveling show—"

"Barnfeather's?" Porter interrupted.

"Yes, his. It was…something of an experience. You see, Samuel was born with a clubfoot. At the show, Mr. Barnfeather chose him to assist in a card trick. More than one, really. It was quite spectacular. Then he gave Sam a sip of his elixir." She stopped, swallowed, dabbed at her eyes with a lace handkerchief. "I could not believe what I was seeing, but it was *real*. Before our eyes, his foot shifted forward. He was so excited. All the way home, he ran and skipped and jumped, things that had always been a challenge before. It was truly a miracle."

"I've heard about Barnfeather's miracles," Porter said. "They're why I'm here."

"I see," she said brusquely. She wasn't interested in his story, and he understood. He closed his mouth and let her continue. "In the morning, he was not in his bed. My husband assumed that he was playing outside. He and our other son, Thomas, went out to look for him. They found his tracks, heading toward where Barnfeather's tent had been." She dabbed at her eyes once more, then found the strength to continue. "And that is the last anyone saw of them. They never came home. The next day, I went into town and demanded that the marshal send some deputies to find them. They came out to the house, followed the tracks, and...and when they reached the clearing where the tent had been, they found my husband and Thomas. Dead."

"And no sign of Barnfeather," Porter offered.

"Yes, that's right. No sign, in fact that he had ever been there."

"Sounds like him."

Mrs. Beaton shook her head as if to toss away his words. Tears brimmed at her eyes again. "He cured Samuel's clubfoot, Mr. Porter. I can't believe he would harm the boy, after that. There's nothing I can do to bring back Thomas and James. But Samuel is still out there somewhere. Please, find him. He's all I have left. Please, I beg of you, find Sam and bring him home."

"Mrs. Beaton," he said. "I've been after Barnfeather for some time. He is not just another showman, I assure you. He is a malevolent force, and yours is far from the first child who's gone missing. Sooner or later, I will find him. If your boy is with him, I'll return him to you. I promise."

"He will be," she said. "He *must* be!"

I hope he is, Porter thought. He didn't speak the words, though. Because he knew that hope was slim indeed, and she was already in mourning. She could mourn her other son later, after he knew for sure. Until then, he would let her hope.

He assured her that he would do everything in his power to find her son, and he would let her know whatever he found out when he finally caught up with Barnfeather. He walked with her to the town's only hotel—she said she couldn't bear to go home to an empty house—where she gave him a tintype of Samuel so he would recognize the boy. Porter offered empty promises, then stepped back out onto the boardwalk.

He was only there for a couple of minutes when another boy found him.

"You Marshal Charley?" the boy asked.

"Close enough," Porter said.

"Telegram for you, down at the depot."

Porter handed the boy a nickel and he ran off. Pine Glen was a small town, but just big enough, he supposed, for one of the various rail companies to add a spur. He found the telegraph operator—also the depot manager, ticket salesman, and janitor—and got the telegram from him. It was brief and to the point.

BF IN DEMING NMT 2 NIGHTS.

"That's it?" Porter asked. BF had to be Barnfeather, and he knew what Deming, New Mexico Territory was—a bit closer to home than he was now, which he liked. But he still had questions.

"Every word of it," the operator said.

"I can't tell if this means that he'll be in Deming *in* two nights or *for* two nights."

The operator shrugged. "Life's tough."

"Thanks for understanding," Porter said. "How soon can I get to Deming?"

It turned out Porter could get to Deming in two days, though it meant hopping a train south, and then riding some distance to a connection with another one headed east. But whether Barnfeather would be there in two nights or for two nights, he should be there tonight. A few discreet questions pointed him in the direction of town constable Pete Bergin, who appeared to have hung a shingle at a table in a saloon called Montalvo's. The name turned out to be fancier than the interior, but the smell of liquor that reached Porter's nose as soon as he passed through the batwing doors was strong, enveloping him like the arms of a lover hungry for more.

He tried to ignore it and made his way to the table. The man slouching in a chair there was tall and blond, with hooded eyes, a thick neck, and sloping shoulders. Big hands cupped a glass of beer. "Constable Bergin?" he asked as he approached, hoping the aroma of the beer wouldn't prove irresistible.

"That's right," the man said. He had a bit of a Southern accent, but Porter couldn't place it exactly.

"I'm Marshal Charley Porter, out of the Arizona Territory. I believe you sent me a telegram."

"Oh, right." Bergin sat up straighter, interested now. "Thanks for comin'. Heard you was lookin' for that feller."

"I have been. Mind if I sit?"

Bergin shoved a chair out with his foot. Long legs, Porter figured. He sat.

"Beer?" Bergin asked.

"They have coffee here?"

"They call it coffee. Tastes more like mud."

"I'll try some of that in a little while," Porter said. "Tell me about Barnfeather. Is he here yet?"

"Shows up tonight, according to the notices posted all over town. Why you lookin' for him, anyhow?"

The saloon wasn't too crowded at this hour, and Porter didn't want anyone to hear. He leaned closer to the constable and lowered his voice. "He's a huckster," he said. "Gets the townsfolk into his tent, sells them on his fake potion, and leaves town in a hurry. Thing is, in every town I've been able to find out about, at least one child is missing when Barnfeather's gone. One in this last town disappeared, but his father and brother went looking for him. When they got to where his tent had been the night before, they both got fried."

"Fried?" Bergin asked. His interest was piqued even more, his sleepy eyes alive now.

"Burned to death somehow. Didn't catch their clothes on fire, but their skin and hair were burned, their eyeballs cooked clear out of their heads."

"Nasty bidness," the constable said.

"It is that. I went out to the spot before the train came and backtracked to the house of the kid who disappeared. His mother and everybody else in town swears that Barnfeather cured the kid's clubfoot during his show the night before. They figure that's why he snuck out of the house to go back to the tent during the night. But I saw his tracks. One shoe print was clear, and the other was just a scrape on the ground. His foot wasn't cured at all."

"An illusion, then."

"But a good one. Barnfeather convinced people that they saw it, and the illusion lasted until the next day and even made them think his tracks looked like those of two normal feet. That's some serious sorcery."

The constable's eyes widened. "I think you mean that literally."

"Unless I see a better explanation for it," Porter said.

Bergin nodded. "I don't like the idea of it, but I don't see no room to argue the point. How's about this? Tonight, I reckon we go out to where the show's s'posed to take place. We don't watch nor listen, so's we don't get magicked. Then when the people leave, we move in."

"Or," Porter suggested, "we wait long enough to see if he means to take another kid. This last time, the boy went home with his family, then came back by himself. If some child or children show up, then we'll have him dead to rights. Barn-feather and his people will most likely be focused on the kid, and we'll take them by surprise."

Bergin grinned. "I like that. Tonight, then."

"Tonight," Porter said. "I expect I'll try some of that coffee now."

Barnfeather's gigantic tent was erected on a stretch of desert scrub west of town. The random chollas, barrels, and other small cacti would inconvenience some audience members, but Barnfeather didn't seem too concerned. When Porter and Bergin got close enough to watch through field glasses, Barnfeather and his crew were busy setting up the stage inside the tent.

As the sun set behind the distant Chiricahua Mountains, a member of Barnfeather's outfit hung lanterns that were already glowing on poles and from rafters inside the tent. "Those aren't oil lamps," Porter observed. "Burning too bright. And he wouldn't want them going out during the show."

"More sorcery," said Bergin. A look of understanding passed between them. Porter wasn't used to working with a lawman who knew as much as he did about the eldritch horrors the world was largely ignorant of, and he was glad he wouldn't have to waste breath convincing Bergin. Porter wished he didn't know as much as he did, but his work had a tendency to veer into uncomfortable arenas.

The moon that night was only a sliver in the sky, but the tent glowed like a fallen star. Flying insects, always numerous in the desert, were drawn to it and probably incinerated when they neared the lanterns. Crawling insects, also many in number, were another matter altogether. The two men had to endure ants and beetles of various sorts, shoed away a few tarantulas, and changed positions to avoid scorpions and biting centipedes.

But they kept watch as people streamed into the tent from nearby Deming. Bergin kept up a quiet commentary, identifying those he recognized and speculating about those he didn't. The tent filled quickly, and when the people stopped coming, the show began. At that time, Porter and Bergin turned away and stuffed cotton wads into their ears. Porter could hear Barnfeather's muffled voice, even at this distance, but he couldn't make out a single word, and he guessed that was good enough.

He hoped so, anyway.

An hour passed, then two. The crescent moon etched its track across the sky. A ferocious roar of cheers and applause signaled the end of the show. Bergin risked pulling the cotton from one ear, then signaled to Porter that it was safe.

Staying low, using creosote bushes and the occasional mesquite or cactus for cover, the men moved closer. After a bit, all the townspeople had left, out of sight and presumably back home in Deming. Now it was just a matter of waiting to see if any children showed up. Porter was certain Barnfeather was behind the disappearances, but he hadn't actually seen any evidence of it. So far it was just a supposition, and he didn't want to confront the man over that. A slim possibility existed that he wasn't a practitioner of evil magics at all, and that some other threat explained the missing kids.

Slowly, the constable and the marshal closed in on the tent. If any children did show up, they would have to be within range to step in and stop whatever Barnfeather's plan was. The tent remained erected, the lanterns within still burning bright.

"Hey, Pete," Porter said. "I don't know why it took me so long to notice, but I just did."

"What's that?" Bergin asked.

"You see any wagons?"

"Now you mention it, I ain't."

"Me neither. How's he get from place to place so quick? Nobody ever seems to see him in transit. He's just here and then he's there. But he doesn't even have wagons to carry that great big tent and the stage, much less his potions."

"That's powerful strange," Bergin agreed.

Porter looked out from behind a clump of mesquite. The stage was no longer visible. Barnfeather stood by himself in the empty tent, speaking almost silently and moving his hands in awkward gestures. Every few seconds, he turned, toward another wall of the tent and repeated the same motions. "Something else," Porter said. "Remember those people helped him set up things? And the musicians? They're not there."

Bergin looked, too. "Sure enough," he said.

"You think they went into town with the crowd?"

"Might could be," Bergin said. "But then, who took down the stage? I ain't seen Barnfeather do it."

"I haven't either."

"Might be he just magicks himself from place to place," Bergin suggested.

"That's possible. And those other men might have been illusions, in case any townspeople come early to watch him set up."

"I don't like this," Bergin said. "I don't like none of it."

"Shh!" Porter grabbed the lawman's arm and pointed. "Look there."

Two boys and a girl hurried toward the tent from the direction of Deming. They didn't look related—different facial features, different hair colors, even their clothing hinted at varying levels of prosperity. But they walked together, heading straight toward the tent. Barnfeather saw them coming and offered a wide smile.

"I've seen enough," Porter said. "Let's go."

Both men were well armed, Porter with a Winchester lever-action shotgun, a Colt's revolver, a Bowie knife, and a couple of sticks of dynamite in a pouch that dangled from his cartridge belt. Bergin had two single-action Remington pistols and a wicked-looking knife of his own, and possibly other things tucked away in pockets.

They gave up their cover and darted toward the tent. Barnfeather saw them coming and turned toward the children. "Come, my young ones, hurry! Those men mean us no good!"

The kids started to run toward him. Porter increased his speed, ignoring small obstacles and vaulting larger ones. Bergin's long legs put him slightly ahead.

"You don't touch them kids!" Bergin shouted.

Barnfeather was beckoning the children with both hands, urging them to go faster. When the first one, a taller boy, reached the tent, Barnfeather stood up straight, a welcoming smile on his face.

"Stop, boy!" Porter cried.

The boy slowed once he was inside the tent, but he kept walking toward Barnfeather. Then, about eight feet from the showman, he stopped altogether. Something about Barnfeather held him back.

Barnfeather threw back his head. As he did, he opencd up at the waist, as if it were a cavernous maw. Porter saw teeth the size of beer bottles on the upper and lower sections. The boy tried to back away, but as Barnfeather's upper half tilted backward, some force—like a powerful suction—grabbed the boy. Against his will, fighting all the way and screaming in pure terror, he was drawn toward Barnfeather. As he got closer, his feet left the ground, and the suction drew him *inside* the big man. As soon as he had disappeared, Barnfeather's upper part snapped back into place and the ghastly mouth was gone.

Porter and Bergin had both frozen in place, the sight so horrifying that they were transfixed. But one boy was gone, and two children remained. They had not come as close to Barnfeather as the first one, but they kept walking, as if they had no choice in the matter.

"Let's finish this," Porter said. He shouldered the Winchester and opened fire. Shot flew toward the showman—and stopped short, dropping harmlessly to the ground about a foot away from him. Beside him, Bergin's pistols barked, but his rounds did the same. Barnfeather just shuffled his cards and bade the children to come toward him.

And they did.

"We can't let him have those kids," Porter said.

"We ain't."

"You think his magic's in the motions he's making?"

Reloading, Bergin studied for a moment. "I think they're a distraction."

"Then what?"

"Only thing he ain't took down is the tent. The rest mighta been illusion, but the tent's real."

"Right," Porter said. "The lanterns."

He shifted his aim. Bergin raised his pistol and did likewise.

Both fired at the lamps hanging from rafters and poles, trying to knock them free.

Finally, one fell from its perch and broke open near a tent wall. Whatever preternatural substance kept them so brightly illuminated spilled out and spread to the fabric of the tent, which caught like it had been dunked in oil. Porter heard a strange sound over the roar of the fire, but he couldn't place it.

Horror showed on Barnfeather's face. He ran to the blazing tent wall and tried to beat the flames, but they raced up too fast for him, igniting the roof and spreading from there.

And as they did, the strange sound grew louder and more distinct.

It was the sound of voices, dozens of them—no, hundreds— screaming in agony.

Young voices.

With Barnfeather distracted, Bergin dashed into the tent to block the unwitting progress of the other children. Porter followed, but something else caught his eye when he got inside.

On the inner walls of the tent were the images of young faces. They were little more than shadows, but so realistic, so lifelike, he didn't think they were painted.

As the flames consumed more of the tent's surface, the cries grew louder. And the faces changed, each one taking on an expression of absolute terror. Spittle ran from open mouths, snot from small noses, tears from ten thousand eyes.

But as he watched, the tenor of the cries changed from horror to what seemed to be elation. And the faces took on a look of joy, as if the flames were not engulfing them but instead releasing them from their terrible bondage.

Porter was again frozen in place by what he saw. Wind from the flames batted at the other tent walls and the fire's heat shimmered the air. Then he saw a face he knew.

He had a tintype of the boy in one pocket.

Samuel Beaton.

"Sam!" he called.

The boy's face pushed toward him, as if he were trying to climb out of the tent wall. But then fire consumed him, and with a cry of the purest relief, Samuel Beaton vanished.

Barnfeather waved his hands ever faster. He had given up on the other two children; he was trying to escape while he still had some of the tent's magic working for him. As he gestured, he chanted something—a spell, Porter guessed, that would spirit him away from this place. While Bergin held back the kids, Porter ran to Barnfeather and jammed the barrel of his shotgun against the man's middle. Almost involuntarily, Barnfeather's upper half swung back again, and that gigantic mouth started to open.

Porter felt the pull of it as it did, like a magnet drawing iron filings. He remembered the dynamite in his leather pouch and took out a stick. As he fought the urge to let go and fly into Barnfeather's insane gullet, the dynamite slipped from his fingers and was whisked inside the showman. Porter had one more, but he couldn't strike a lucifer in time to light it. A rank odor, like rancid meat and offal, grew more intense as he was drawn inexorably nearer.

He had one idea, which he feared would be his last. Almost inside the vast opening, he let the last dynamite stick go. It flew into Barnfeather's maw. Then Porter stuck his shotgun in and fired straight down, over and over. As the gun emptied, and he thought all was lost, one of the dynamite sticks must have caught. The explosion sounded far away, but a fireball welled up from what seemed like miles below, coming higher and higher and higher.

Barnfeather started to scream, a sound that first echoed and then drowned out the cries of the hundreds or thousands of tent-children he had swallowed through the ages. The rising fireball seemed to dull the magnetic pull, and Porter discovered that he could move again. In desperation, he used the empty shotgun to sweep Barnfeather's legs out from under him. The man went down on his back, and as he did, his middle snapped shut.

Just as the fireball reached it.

The explosion blew Barnfeather to shreds, which soared around what little remained of the tent like wisps of paper burned in open flame. It knocked Porter off his feet. Across the tent, Bergin threw himself on the children and covered them with his body. The last of the tent went up in flames, and the screams of the swallowed finally ended. Then the wooden rafters themselves caught fire and caved in. Porter found his feet, helped Bergin and the children up, and they all moved away from the last bits of flaming wreckage littering the desert floor.

The children blinked and rubbed their eyes, as if just waking up from a sound sleep. "What's going on?" the girl asked.

"Where are we?" asked the boy.

"It's nothing," Porter said. "It's all over. Let's get you home. Your folks'll be worried. You two might remember some of this when you wake up tomorrow. But it's all just been a nightmare, you understand? You're still sound asleep in your own homes."

"But I ain't—" the boy began.

Porter cut him off. "You're dreaming, and that's all there is to it."

Porter wished he were dreaming. Come morning, he would have to go back to Pine Glen and tell Mrs. Beaton that her other son had died, too. It was the part of the job he hated most.

But he would never have to worry about Eustace Barnfeather again, and that was something. Plenty of horrors remained—that was a fact about the world that would like as not never change—but each one down was one less to worry about. A man could hang his hat on that.

And he would.

AUTHOR BIOS

JONATHAN MABERRY is a New York Times bestselling author, 5-time Bram Stoker Award-winner, 3-time Scribe Award winner, Inkpot Award winner, anthology editor, writing teacher, and comic book writer. His vampire apocalypse book series, *V-WARS*, was a Netflix original series starring Ian Somerhalder. He writes in multiple genres including suspense, thriller, horror, science fiction, epic fantasy, and action; and he writes for adults, teens and middle grade. His works include the *Joe Ledger* thrillers, *Kagen the Damned, Ink, Glimpse*, the *Rot & Ruin* series, the *Dead of Night* series, *The Wolfman*, *X-Files Origins: Devil's Advocate*, *The Sleepers War* (with Weston Ochse), *NectroTek, Mars One*, and many others. Several of his works are in development for film and TV. He is the editor of high-profile anthologies including *The X-Files, Aliens: Bug Hunt, Out of Tune, Don't Turn out the Lights: A Tribute to Scary Stories to Tell in the Dark, Baker Street Irregulars, Nights of the Living Dead*, and others. His comics include *Black Panther: DoomWar, The Punisher: Naked Kills* and *Bad Blood*. His *Rot & Ruin* young adult novel was adapted into the #1 horror comic on Webtoon and is being developed for film by Alcon Entertainment. He the president of the International Association of Media Tie-in Writers, and the editor of *Weird Tales Magazine*. He lives in San Diego, California. Find him online at www.jonathanmaberry. com.

CULLEN BUNN writes graphic novels such as *The Sixth Gun, Harrow County, Basilisk, The Ghoul Next Doors, Deadpool Kills the Marvel Universe*, and *Uncanny X-Men*.

KEITH R.A. DeCANDIDO (www.DeCandido.net) has written sixty novels, a hundred short stories, and a mess of comic books and nonfiction. Recent and upcoming work includes the fantasy novels *Phoenix Precinct* and *Feat of Clay*, the *Resident Evil* comic book *Infinite Darkness: The Beginning*, the urban fantasy short story collection *Ragnarok and a Hard Place: More Tales of Cassie Zukav, Weirdness Magnet*, the *Star Trek Adventures* role-playing game module *Incident at Kraav III* (with Fred Love), and stories in the magazines *Star Trek Explorer* and *Weird Tales* and the anthologies *Joe Ledger: Unbreakable; Sherlock Holmes: Cases by Candlelight Vol. 2; Phenomenons: Season of Darkness; Thrilling Adventure Yarns 2022*; and two anthologies he also co-edited, *Double Trouble* (with Jonathan Maberry) and *The Four ???? of the Apocalypse* (with Wrenn Simms). He also writes about pop culture for the award-winning webzine Tor. com, is a fourth-degree black belt in karate, and a professional percussionist.

JENNIFER BRODY (a/k/a Vera Strange) is the award-winning author of the Disney Chills series, The 13th Continuum trilogy (Moonbeam Children's Awards Gold Medal winner), and the Stoker Finalist *Spectre Deep 6*, prompting Forbes to call her "a star in the graphic novel world." She is the co-author of *Star Wars: Stories of Jedi & Sith*, where she penned the Darth Vader cover story. She's a graduate of Harvard University, a film/TV producer and writer, and a creative writing instructor. She began her career in Hollywood working for A-List directors and movie studios. More on her: **www.jenniferbrody.com**.

CARRIE HARRIS is a full-time writer in New York, and has done a variety of cool things like organizing WriteOnCon (an online writers conference) and serving as the president of the Class of 2k11 (an author marketing group), and her book *Bad Taste in Boys* was named a Quick Pick for Reluctant Readers.

JOHN G. HARTNESS is the author of over thirty books, including the Quincy Harker Demon Hunter novels, The Black Knight Chronicles urban fantasy series, and the Bubba the Monster Hunter comedy horror stories. He has had stories featured in *Lawless Lands*, *Tales of the Weird Wild West*, *Fantastic Hope*, and many other anthologies. He lives in Charlotte, NC with his wife and three furry overlords Daisy, Gandalf, and Stevie.

JAMES A. MOORE is the award-winning, bestselling author of over forty novel length works of fantasy, science fiction, and horror and over 100 short works of fiction.

AARON ROSENBERG is the best-selling, award-winning author of nearly 50 novels, including the DuckBob SF comedy series, the Relicant Chronicles epic fantasy series, and, with David Niall Wilson, the O.C.L.T. occult thriller series. Aaron's tie-in work contains novels for *Star Trek*, *Warhammer*, *World of WarCraft*, *Stargate: Atlantis*, *Shadowrun*, and *Eureka*. He has written children's books (including the award-winning *Bandslam: The Junior Novel* and the #1 best-selling *42: The Jackie Robinson Story*), educational books, short stories, and roleplaying games (including the Origins Award-winning *Gamemastering Secrets*). Aaron lives in New York.

MAURICE BROADDUS is a community organizer and teacher. His work has appeared in places like *Lightspeed Magazine*, *Black Panther: Tales from Wakanda*, *Weird Tales*, *Magazine of F&SF*, and *Uncanny Magazine*. His books include the sci-fi novel *Sweep of Stars*; the steampunk works, *Buffalo Soldier* and *Pimp My Airship*; and the middle grade detective novels, *The Usual Suspects* and *Unfadeable*. His project, *Sorcerers*, is being adapted as a television show for AMC. He's an editor at *Apex Magazine*. Website: www.MauriceBroaddus.com.

MARGUERITE REED is a speculative fiction author born and raised in the Great Plains whose work has appeared in *Strange Horizons*, *Lone Star Stories*, *Weird Tales*, and received the Philip K Dick Special Citation in 2016.

LAURA ANNE GILMAN is the author of more than twenty novels, including the award-winning Devil's West series from Saga Press/ Simon & Schuster. Her most recent book is the Gilded Age historical fantasy, *Uncanny Times* (October 2022). She currently lives in Seattle with a cat, a dog, and many deadlines. -- *Uncanny Times* has been called "evocative" (*Publishers Weekly*), "entertaining" (*Library Journal*) and "a real hit" (*Cosmic Circus*) that "packs a punch."(*Booklist*). Have you gotten your copy yet?

SCOTT SIGLER is a #1 *New York Times* best-selling author and the creator of eighteen novels, six novellas, and dozens of short stories. He is an inaugural inductee into the Podcasting Hall of Fame. Scott began his career by narrating his unabridged audiobooks and serializing them in weekly installments. He continues to release free episodes every Sunday. Launched in March of 2005, "Scott Sigler Audiobooks" is the world's longest-running fiction podcast. His rabid fans fervently anticipate their weekly story fix, so much so that they've dubbed themselves "Sigler Junkies" and have downloaded over fifty million episodes. Subscribe to the free podcast at scottsigler. com/subscribe. Scott is a cofounder of Empty Set Entertainment, which publishes his Galactic Football League series. A Michigan native, he lives in San Diego, CA with his wife and their wee little Døgs of Døøm. Visit him online at www.ScottSigler.com.

C. EDWARD SELLNER founder and owner of Visionary Creative Services, is a transmedia creator, a professional artist, and writer of prose fiction, comics, audio dramas, and screenplays.

JOSH MALERMAN is the *New York Times* best-selling author of *Bird Box*, *Unbury Carol*, and *Daphne*. He's also one of two singer/songwriters for the Michigan rock band The High Strung. He lives in Michigan with the artist/musician Allison Laakko.

GREG COX is the *New York Times* Bestselling author of numerous books and short stories based on such series as *Star Trek*, *CSI*, *Planet of the Apes* and numerous Marvel and DC comic-book characters.

JEFFREY J. MARIOTTE, an award-winning author and publishing industry veteran, has written more than 60 books, including thrillers, horror, mysteries, westerns, YA, and tie-ins, as well as comics and graphic novels. Jeffrey wrote the Deadlands novel, *Thunder Moon Rising*.

R.S. (ROD) BELCHER is an award-winning newspaper and magazine editor and journalist, as well as an author of short and long fiction in a number of genres. He is the author of *The Six-Gun Tarot*, *The Shotgun Arcana*, *The Queen of Swords*, *Nightwise*, *The Night Dahlia*, *The Brotherhood of the Wheel*, *King of the Road*, and *The Ghost Dance Judgement*.